To the Stars

Also by Molly McAdams

Trusting Liam
Changing Everything (novella)
Letting Go
Sharing You
Capturing Peace (novella)
Deceiving Lies
Needing Her (novella)
Forgiving Lies
Stealing Harper (novella)
From Ashes
Taking Chances

To the Stars

A Thatch Novel

MOLLY McADAMS

WM

WILLIAM MORROW
An Imprint of HarperCollins*Publishers*

TO THE STARS. Copyright © 2015 by Molly Jester. All rights reserved. Printed in the United States of America. No part of this book may be used or reproduced in any manner whatsoever without written permission except in the case of brief quotations embodied in critical articles and reviews. For information address HarperCollins Publishers, 195 Broadway, New York, NY 10007.

HarperCollins books may be purchased for educational, business, or sales promotional use. For information, please e-mail the Special Markets Department at SPsales@harpercollins.com.

FIRST EDITION

Designed by Diahann Sturge

Library of Congress Cataloging-in-Publication Data has been applied for.

ISBN 978-0-06-235845-5

16 17 18 19 20   OV/RRD   10 9 8 7 6 5 4 3 2

For Cory . . .
My life and my heart would be so empty without you

Note for the Readers

If you or someone you know is a victim of relationship abuse, you are not alone; there is help available. Go to stoprelationshipabuse .org for more information.

To the Stars

Prologue

Harlow
Fall 2010—Walla Walla

"Happy birthday, Low. I waited for you."

The instant his voice filtered through the phone, my body stilled and warmed at the same time. My breath came out in a soft, audible huff, and my eyes shut as hundreds of welcome memories flooded my mind.

I didn't have to look at the screen to know who was calling. I would know that voice anywhere, and I should have been expecting his call. Not just his call. *This* call. We'd been preparing for and talking about this call for two and a half years now.

My lips and fingers trembled, and I almost dropped the phone as I tried to make my throat work.

"*I waited for you,*" played over and over again like a broken record. A broken record with the most beautiful music still coming from it.

Turning my head just enough to look over my shoulder, I eyed the guy shrugging into his shirt, and my chest ached when I faced forward again.

No longer seeing the dorm room I was standing in, I let our memories consume me. "I—" I took in a shaky breath, and my voice came out as a strained whisper. "I didn't wait for you."

There was nothing. No sound, no response—only the most heartbreaking silence I've ever endured.

And it was a heartbreak I would carry with me forever.

Chapter 1

Harlow

Present Day—Richland, Washington

MY EYES SHOT open as the dream faded away, and my dark bedroom blurred for a few seconds as the tears fell steadily across my face, dripping onto the pillow. Locking my jaw against the trembling, I took deep breaths to keep myself calm—to keep myself from giving in to the sobs that were building in my chest.

The heartbreak that had settled over the silence during that phone call was still one I felt today—as if it had just happened rather than four and a half years ago.

I should have known in those seconds that I'd said the wrong words. I should have known I was choosing the wrong man. He would have understood my mistake. He would have still been waiting for me, like he had been for two and a half years.

My Knox.

But I'd ignored signs; I'd gone with what my then-eighteen-year-old heart had been screaming over—and I hadn't heard from Knox Alexander since.

I lay on my side long after the tears had run their course and my cheeks had dried, clinging to the memories I knew I should let go of, but couldn't. I should have noticed the sky lightening outside, I should have been checking the time to get up before the alarm went off; but I was still there daydreaming when the shrill sound filled the room, and my body locked up as I waited for what would meet me this morning.

My fingers curled around the edge of my pillow when the alarm was turned off, my stomach churned when I heard him roll over behind me, and my jaw trembled almost violently when his arm slowly wrapped around my waist, pulling me closer to him.

I closed my eyes tightly as my husband's lips pressed firmly to my shoulder, and refused to acknowledge him until it was necessary.

"You're still in bed," Collin observed.

I nodded my head sluggishly against the pillow.

"Which means I don't have breakfast waiting for me; am I right?"

Swallowing past the thickness in my throat, I nodded again—waiting, always waiting.

His fingers slowly traced up my arm resting on my side until they reached just above the inside of my elbow. My body jerked when he dug two fingers into the pressure point there.

"Then why the fuck are you still in bed?" he growled against my shoulder before releasing my arm roughly.

I moved quickly, not wanting to give him an opportunity to do anything else, and released a shaky sigh of relief when I hit the kitchen. If that was all I got for still being in bed, I would take it and be thankful.

After putting his bread in the toaster, I mixed up some eggs and milk, then poured them into a skillet and ran across the kitchen to get the Keurig ready. I'd just put everything on the table and had started washing the dishes when Collin walked into the kitchen and right up behind me instead of going to the table.

He only had a towel wrapped around his waist, and when his arm snaked around my body, I saw there were still drops of water racing down his skin.

My hands fisted around the handle of the skillet and the dish-scrubbing brush when I realized he was testing me, but I didn't say anything. Collin never came out here like this. He ate either as soon as he woke up, or right before he left for work . . . if he was still in his towel, he was just looking for more reasons to be upset with me.

"Good girl," he whispered against the back of my neck before placing a soft kiss there.

My nostrils flared from my rough, nervous breaths when he stepped away from me, and after a few seconds, I began slowly scrubbing the skillet to calm myself.

"Now make it again since you were late."

I watched as he dumped the food and coffee into the sink before roughly setting the plate and mug on the counter next to me. I wanted to cry, I wanted to yell at him for being an asshole, but I knew both those things would only end badly for me. So with a defeated sigh and hollow feeling in my chest, I quickly cleaned and dried the skillet before making his breakfast all over again.

The dishes were cleaned, his food and coffee were on the table, and I was sitting in one of the chairs at the kitchen table by the time he came back out—this time ready for work.

He held my hand on the tabletop the entire time he ate, and even cleaned and put his dishes in the dishwasher when he was done before walking back over to me. Bending at the waist so he was eye-level with me, he stared at me for an entire minute with an apologetic look.

"I love you, Harlow," he said, as if he was trying to determine whether I knew that or not.

"I know," I responded softly. "I love you too."

His lips fell gently upon mine for a few seconds before he straightened. Grabbing his wallet out of his back pocket, he pulled out a credit card and let it fall to the table. "Go pick up your sister, take her out to lunch, and get your nails done or something. If you have time, go shopping."

"Thank you, Collin."

"Anything for my girl. I'll see you when I get home."

I just nodded and watched as he left the kitchen. I waited for the front door to close and his car to start before I finally let my body relax.

There was no point in telling him I didn't want his money. He knew he'd upset me, and having me buy things for myself was his way of apologizing. *Money* was his way of apologizing, but no amount of money could keep me in this house and married to that man.

The threat of my family's lives could.

When times were better, like just then, he handed me his credit card and told me to do things for myself. That way, he could show me off to his family and mine with how well he took care of me. He would joke with them that I loved him for his money, but he and I knew differently. And I knew that if he handed me his credit card and I didn't have anything to show for it at the end of the day, I would pay for it in other ways.

When times were bad, the jokes about credit cards and buying me off were something I longed for, because it was then that I got my monster. It was then that my husband would tell me in detail the ways he would kill my family in front of me if I ever left him or told anyone what happened in our home. I hadn't believed him at first. I'd been terrified of him—no, beyond terrified. Terror couldn't begin to explain the feeling that coursed through my body when I first came face-to-face with my monster, but I had thought he would come after *me* if I left . . . never them.

I'd planned for two months over a way to leave him, leave everything. It wasn't until my little sister was still here when he got home one night—something I knew wasn't allowed—and he came back into the living room with a gun in his hand and his lifeless eyes fixed on her, that I understood his threats were very real.

My sister never saw the gun. I'd been able to come up with a reason for needing her to leave before she could understand the underlying panic in my words or see the detached look in Collin's eyes. But according to Collin, I still needed to pay. I'd waited in the bedroom for him all night, trembling, but he'd never come after me. It wasn't until the next morning that I received my punishment. I'd walked into the kitchen to find him sitting at the table in his clothes from the night before, eating breakfast and drinking coffee like any normal morning . . . except our dog was dead on top of the table.

He'd told everyone that she'd been hit by a car, and as an

apology a few days later, had *allowed* me to buy a new kitchen table. Thankfully he had never put me through the torture of making me buy another pet.

So I'd waited until that summer when my family was on vacation in California before finally attempting to leave. I had thought if they were out of state I could leave and give them enough warning, especially since I'd never let it slip to Collin where they were going, or that they were even going, period. I hadn't known my parents had disclosed everything to him, since they hoped Collin would be able to get time off from work to fly us down.

I'd barely even made it into Portland, Oregon, before I was pulled over and arrested for "driving while intoxicated." It didn't matter that it was late morning, that I wasn't given any form of field sobriety test, or that the officer didn't bother to put me in a holding cell once we arrived at the station. It didn't matter that I hadn't been given the privilege of using the phone—not that I would have called Collin anyway. He still showed up at the Portland police station less than three hours later to pick me up; all of the charges were miraculously dropped.

That night Collin made me sit on the couch with my phone in front of me, and told me I wasn't to move until I'd received "the call." I didn't understand what call he was talking about since he sat across the room from me the entire night.

Then my phone rang.

It was my younger sister crying and telling me that the beach house they'd been staying in had caught fire. They had all made it out fine, but half of the house had been destroyed, and the cause was later determined to be arson. They never found who did it, but I hadn't thought they would. Collin had been able to get an officer from Portland to fake my intoxication; why would he hire someone in California who was so careless as to get caught?

I hadn't tried to leave Collin again.

After getting up from the kitchen table, I moved slowly through the house, making sure everything was still clean from the day before. Once the clothes in the bedroom were picked up, and the bed was made, I texted my younger sister, Hadley, and headed into the bathroom to take a shower.

I hated our shower. It was big; too big. You could comfortably fit ten people in there. Collin had one of those rain shower systems put in so the entire thing was heated and could be put to use. All it did for me was make it harder to push memories of Knox aside, especially after dreaming about him—which was nearly every night.

Our first kiss had been in the rain. We'd danced in the rain. And it'd been raining the last time I'd spoken to him. Everything about rain reminded me of him, reminded me of what I'd lost.

Summer 2008—Seattle

"BUT DO I look okay *for the concert*?" I asked my older sister, Hayley. "You keep skipping that last part!"

She rolled her eyes after pulling into a parking spot. "I'm saying you look hot; that's all that should matter."

"I've never been to a concert; it could totally matter!"

"This can't even technically be considered a concert. I mean, it is, but it isn't. There will be people coming and going, and just hanging out . . . it's just chill. You're fine, I swear."

I flipped down the visor and checked my makeup in the

mirror one more time before stepping out of the car with her.

She sent me an approving smile as I rounded the front of her car to join her. "Ready?"

"Obviously," I said, holding my arms out.

"You're such a brat," she said with a laugh. "Come on."

Wrapping an arm around my neck, she pulled me across the parking lot and over a large lawn to a building I would've sworn was abandoned, by the looks of it. But it was a local hangout, as well as the place to go to indie concerts. Mom never wanted me coming out here, but somehow Hayley had managed to get her to agree tonight. Usually wherever Hayley was, I wasn't far behind.

She wasn't just my sister; she was my best friend. Her friends were mine, her curfew was also mine, and this was our last summer together before she moved across the country for school. I didn't know what I was going to do without her; our other sister was too young for me to hang out with yet—and I'd never even had friends my age. My parents always called me an "old soul," whatever that meant. All I knew was that I never fit in unless I was with Hayley, and she was leaving me.

"Look who decided to show!" Hayley's boyfriend, Neil, called out as we reached the building. "It's Little Little Low Low."

"Hilarious," I muttered before he picked me up in a big bear hug.

"You're not looking so little there, Little Low."

"And you're a creeper," I said at the same time Hayley made a face and smacked his stomach. "Ew, don't be gross!"

"I'm not!" He flung out his arms then wrapped one around Hayley. "I'm just saying we should probably keep a leash on her tonight, or something. Babe, you know your sister doesn't look fifteen, and then you dress her in that? No one here is going to think she's underage. I should put a sign on her that says 'young one: untouchable.' "

"She'll be fine." Hayley smiled and winked at me. "She looks great, and she's here to have fun. She's not going to do anything stupid."

Neil groaned. "I'm going to be punching people, aren't I?"

"Probably," Hayley responded, and leaned in to kiss him. They soon forgot we were in public.

"Did we come here for a concert, or for you to maul each other?"

Hayley turned to grin at me. "Both?" When I made a face, she laughed. "Come on, let's go inside."

I found out very quickly that concerts weren't my thing. If it hadn't been for the fact that most of our friends were there, the bad music and heavy smell of something that I wasn't entirely sure was legal would have been unbearable.

I drummed my fingers on the table and blew out a heavy breath as I looked around us. "I'm going to get some fresh air," I stated loudly for whoever was listening.

"Not alone you're not," Hayley yelled over the music.

"I'm fine," I said as I stood, and the unmistakable sound of a grunt came from behind me when I quickly took a step back from the short stool I'd been on.

My body locked up and face pinched as embarrassment flooded my veins.

A chorus of "Heys!" came from our table, and I turned to see which one of our friends I'd backed into.

"I'm so sorr—" My words cut off when I looked up at him.

Not a friend of mine. I would have remembered having a friend like him.

"I'm sorry," I whispered, my words drowning in the music.

His lips tilted up in a crooked smile that was too perfect to be real. "No harm done," he said in a deep, fluid voice.

I'm positive my mouth was open as I continued to stare at him, not moving. His eyes quickly ran over my body, and his smile turned into more of a smirk before one of our friends said something and his head shot up to look at them.

I blinked rapidly and took a step away from him. Keeping my eyes trained on the dark floor, I tried to remember what I'd been doing before he'd walked up. Outside. I wanted fresh air. I wanted to look at him again. *No, walk outside, Harlow. Walk outside.*

I'd only taken two steps when I heard my sister's voice above the music. "Somebody take Harlow outside."

I turned to glare at her. "I'm not a dog."

Walking away from the tables, I pushed through the mass of people standing near the front doors of the building, and breathed in a deep lungful of clean air.

"They're just looking out for you."

I turned and looked up at the same guy I'd just stepped on.

"A girl who looks like you shouldn't be out here alone."

"Because of guys like you?" I challenged, raising an eyebrow, but there was a teasing hint to my tone.

That crooked smile was back, and he laughed softly as he leaned up against the wall next to me, close enough that our arms were touching. "Considering they asked me to come out here with you, I sure as hell hope not."

My face fell. "I don't need you to be my keeper; I'm just getting some air."

He bent down so that his dark eyes were directly in front of mine, the intensity in them pinning me to the wall. "And I never said I didn't want to be the one to come out here with you."

My pulse thrummed quickly at his admission, and my body warmed under his stare. I felt myself inching toward him, and my breaths deepened from his nearness. My eyes bounced over his face and body, taking him in more clearly now that we were outside in the glow from the setting sun. The fitted gray Henley shirt that stopped just below where his low-slung jeans began showed a lean, muscular build to his tall frame. His flawless, tan skin drew me toward his dark eyes, which I somehow knew would tell me everything, without him ever saying a word.

My eyes fell to his lips, and I caught myself wanting to know how they would feel against my skin. *Let them come to you.* Hayley's words ghosted through my mind, and I cleared my throat and looked away before I could do something stupid, like ask if I *could* feel his lips on mine.

I needed to find a flaw, and I needed to focus on it so I wouldn't start thinking this guy had been created by the gods for no purpose other than to make girls like me drool and forget how to have normal conversations. Ridiculous hormones—1, Harlow—0.

"So, uh, you're obviously not from around here."

"Obviously?" he asked, humor lacing through the word.

Well, you're gorgeous and I've never seen you. So, yes, obviously. I held back an eye roll and internally groaned at how I was already messing this up. "Um, I just meant I've never seen you before, but then again, everyone else seemed to know you, so I could be wrong."

"Knox Alexander," he said, and stretched out his hand for me to take. "And you weren't wrong. I'm actually from Thatch, so a few hours from here."

"And somehow you're already friends with everyone even though I'm just meeting you?"

He nodded in the direction of the building. "Sara is my sister. She's been here in Seattle for about a year now, and knows some of them from school. I've hung out with everyone a few times this summer. Now tell me why I haven't met you before tonight . . . and why I still don't have your name."

I bit back a smile. "My name is Harlow. I'm Hayley's sister."

His brow pinched together. "Twins?" he asked, and I laughed at his honest question. It was one we got asked a lot.

"Uh, no. Not even close, but I'll take that as a compliment. Anyway, I've been grounded since school let out a month ago, but that finally let up."

Knox's face fell, and I could tell he was replaying my words in his head. "Wait, how old are you?"

"Fifteen."

He just stared at me, not saying anything while a conflicted look crossed his face.

"Why?" I asked, drawing the word out. "How old did you think I was?"

There was a pause before he mumbled, "Not fifteen."

"How old are you?"

"I'll be eighteen in a little over a week."

I didn't understand the problem with that. Everyone I hung out with was at least eighteen, but from the look on Knox's face, it was definitely a problem. "And?"

He forced a smile and cleared his throat. "And nothing. I guess I just hadn't expected that."

I didn't miss the way his eyes wouldn't meet mine after that, or how he moved his body away.

Wait, what just happened? Why did those intense eyes shut down,

and why is there a coldness settling between us? This is what I get for
listening to Hayley!

My shoulders sagged in defeat and I pushed away from the
wall to head in the direction of a lower wall that ran along the
lawn.

"Aren't you going back in?" Knox asked as he followed.

"No, but you're more than welcome to. I'll call my mom to
come get me."

"Why are you leaving?" he asked, and his hand gently grasped
my forearm to stop me from walking.

I looked down at where his long fingers wrapped around my
arm, the heat beneath his hand something so much more than
his body temperature. My breaths became audible when I looked
behind my shoulder to see him looking down at our arms.

When his eyes met mine again, the intensity was back. "Why
are you leaving?" he asked again; the huskiness of his deep voice
made me sway toward him—he didn't let me get close.

"Um, concerts aren't my thing apparently," I muttered as I
pulled my arm from his grasp. "I'd never been to one before, and
now I see I wasn't missing out on anything."

"Then I'll stay out here with you."

"I told you I don't need a keeper," I gritted out.

"Trust me, Harlow, that's the last thing I want to be."

My eyes widened at the suggestive tone, and I fumbled for
something to say that wouldn't have him shutting down on me
again. Nothing came to mind. "Really, don't stay out here for
me. I'll call someone."

"I didn't come here for the shows. I came to give Sara a ride
back to her place later." His eyes held that same conflict from

earlier as he stared at me for long moments. "Besides, if I had to choose between being in there, or out here with you, I would choose you."

"Because I need a protector." It hadn't been a question. I was frustrated that he felt like he had to baby me.

His head shook subtly and eyes darted away, and his voice dropped even lower. "I wish that were my reason."

Present Day—Richland

I KEPT THE smile on my face and pushed at my salad as I listened to Hadley rant about this guy she had been dating off and on. After shopping for a couple of hours and getting our nails done, we'd come to one of our favorite restaurants in Richland to talk in the remaining time I had left before I had to go home and make dinner.

Hadley was going to school at Washington State University Tri-Cities so she could be closer to me. I loved these times with her; they were something I craved on the days when I felt like I was drowning. But at the same time, they were a struggle to get through. Our sister, Hayley, had been too focused on her young kids the few times I'd seen her since Collin and I married— something that was a saving grace for me since she had always been the perceptive one. But now she lived in Connecticut with her husband, and we saw her once a year; twice, if we were lucky.

Hadley was different. Hadley didn't notice anything other than the perfect world around her. She saw life through rose-colored glasses, always had. So all I needed to do was keep a smile on my face when I was near her, and she'd never know anything was wrong. It wasn't hard keeping the smile. I was good at faking happiness for the sake of my family. The problem was that I could never offer anything about my life, and when I did, it was lies. It was exhausting. My body always stayed tense throughout our times together; I was afraid that somehow she would notice something was off—see something she wasn't meant to.

"Aren't you going to eat?" she asked suddenly.

Like that.

"I am eating," I said with a soft laugh, putting a forkful in my mouth to emphasize my statement.

She stole a bite of my salad, and waved her fork around as she chewed. "So, anyway, I just don't know what to do about him."

"Well, it's summer; it's the perfect time for you two to take a break since he's back home for a few months. Maybe date some other people. You're only nineteen, Hadley; don't just focus on this one guy. You have three more years of college; enjoy them, and enjoy all the different guys."

She looked at me skeptically. "You got married when you were nineteen."

"I turned twenty a month later."

"Like that makes a difference?" She smiled, because she knew she was right. "You can't preach to me about settling down young when you did it yourself." She sighed and pursed her lips. "I want to find a Collin."

My body tightened, and the smile froze on my face.

"I want to find someone who will take care of me the way he takes care of you. Admit it, sis, your life is pretty perfect. You don't have to work, your husband pays for us to have days like this; he's hot, he's rich . . . he's hot."

He's a monster.

"You know what I want for you?" I asked quickly as I leaned forward, my question coming across a little too urgent. "To find someone who will love you through anything. Years. Distance. Separation. Anything. That's what I want for you."

She smiled and rolled her eyes. "Okay, Mom."

I cleared my throat and attempted a smile, grateful that she hadn't noticed my tone. "Speaking of Mom . . . are you going home this summer?"

I sat back and resumed pushing my salad around when she launched into what her plans were for the summer. When I dropped her off an hour later at the apartment she was renting with some friends, I cried in relief as the tension drained from my muscles.

I hurried to get dinner ready when I got home, then walked through the house one more time, looking for anything I might have missed. I'd cleaned the bathroom from both our showers, the rest of the house still looked spotless, the new purse and shoes I'd bought this afternoon were sitting on display on the entryway table for Collin to see when he got home, and I'd just finished putting all the dishes away before I'd began my walk-through. My hands were shaking as I stared at the plates on the table. Something was missing. I just couldn't think of what it was.

Chicken, potatoes, green beans. Forks, knives, spoons, napkins. Salt. Pepper. I glanced at the time and swallowed thickly. *Oh God, oh God! What the hell is missing?*

I had two minutes before Collin drove up the driveway; he was never a minute late. I wasn't sure, but I'd started thinking he parked down the street waiting until the same time every day just so he could instill this fear in me for when he would show.

Drinks!

I rushed through the kitchen and pulled down four glasses. After filling two with ice and water and the others with wine, I set all the glasses on the table seconds before I heard the key in the lock, and my trembling increased.

The door opened and shut, and after a few seconds, Collin's footsteps echoed off the hardwood floors as he walked through the entryway and into the kitchen to look at me. There was a beautiful bouquet of pink roses in his hand—as there was every night he felt he needed to apologize—and I tried to keep my face neutral at the sight of them. I'd *always* hated roses, something Collin knew.

"Smells great." He smiled quickly, tossed the roses unceremoniously on the kitchen table, and then turned around to walk through the house. His eyes were going everywhere as he looked for something out of place. Anything. Two minutes later he walked back into the kitchen with a genuine smile on his face. He wrapped his arms around me where I was standing at the counter, clipping the end of each rose and placing it in a vase. "Do you like your gifts?"

"I do, thank you."

"And seeing your sister?" he asked as he turned me to face him. He captured my mouth to kiss me softly, his lips only moving far enough away to ask, "Did you two have a good time?"

"Yes," I whispered before he was kissing me again.

One arm moved slowly up my back as he deepened the kiss, and I tried to not let on to the fact that my stomach was churning from his touch.

A cry burst from my chest as pain spread across my scalp and down my neck when he fisted his hand in my long hair and yanked roughly to the side. With another hard tug, he turned—causing me to hit the counter and knock the vase onto the floor, where it shattered—and stalked into the entryway with me stumbling behind him, bent in half. Facing the entry table covered in the things I'd bought earlier, he pulled me up only to force my face down toward the table so fast that a scream tore through my throat. Everything halted when my nose was within an inch of the table, and my jaw shook as tears fell onto the dark-stained wood.

"Are you trying to get someone killed?" he roared.

"N-n-n-n," I stammered, then cut off on a sob.

"What is missing, Harlow? Tell me!" He jerked my head a fraction of an inch closer to the table.

I stared at the table, shaking, unable to figure out what he was talking about.

"Who do you want gone, huh?" he asked close to my ear. This time his voice was soft and dark. "Your sister? You want her gone, don't you?"

"No!" I choked out.

"Then where is it?" he yelled next to me.

Card. Credit card! "Wall—wallet! I'm s-s-sorry!"

Using a fistful of my hair as a handle, he threw me to the ground and stepped over me on his way to look for my purse. My hands immediately flew to my head to cover the tender parts as I listened to his footfalls fading away from me.

"Don't show your pain." The words trailed behind him. Another reminder. Another warning.

On shaky hands and legs, I rolled onto my knees and slowly stood. By the time I was upright again, he was walking back toward me with my purse in his hand. Pulling his keys out of his pants pocket, he walked out the front door only to come back a minute later.

"I'll give it all back in two days," he crooned, and kissed my cheek with deceptive softness. "Come on, let's eat. Dinner looks amazing."

Placing his hand on the small of my back, he walked us toward the kitchen. He pulled my chair out for me, and held my hand on top of the table as we ate. *He* ate—*I* sat there staring at the shards of glass and forgotten roses on the tile, wondering again how the boy I'd fallen in love with had turned into my monster.

Chapter 2

Harlow

Summer 2008—Seattle

I WAS ABOUT to see Knox for the first time since meeting him a week and a half ago, and I could barely sit still, I was so excited. We had ended up staying outside for the rest of the concert, sitting on the wall and talking about everything: Thatch, his move to Seattle, and his plans to go to the University of Washington here in the fall. I'd told him about my family and life as a high school student who didn't fit in—the story of most students' lives.

The more the night of the concert wore on, the more I'd felt myself slipping into a place where Knox was all that mattered, and I wanted to be that for him as well. When the shows were all over, I could've sworn he would kiss me good night.

But there'd been no kiss, and no words. His body had been pressed close to mine, and one of his large hands had come up to cradle my cheek. For minutes we stood there as I silently begged him to kiss me. As if a switch had been thrown, that conflict from earlier had come back into his eyes and he'd taken a step away from me.

The connection was broken, and I was sure I would never hear from him again even though I'd given him my number. But the next day he called, and the next, and it was just like being back up on that wall. Even over the phone I could feel the intensity that drew me to him, and that husky tone had me wanting to listen to him talk forever.

Yesterday was Knox's birthday, and tonight we were all hanging out at Neil's house to celebrate. And Hayley's car wasn't moving fast enough! I could have run faster. Okay, that was a lie, but couldn't she drive just a *little* faster?

I nearly sighed in relief when we pulled up to the house. Not waiting for Hayley, I threw open my door and took off for the guy standing on the other end of the lawn with a couple of guys I'd never seen before.

As soon as Knox saw me running toward them, a bright smile covered his gorgeous face, and he stepped away from the guys with his arms open just in time for me to launch myself at him. I'd planned to try to look cool walking up toward him—but there'd been no time for that once I'd seen him.

A soft grunt sounded before he laughed and tightened his arms around me. "Hey, Low."

I could hear the guys talking who had been standing with Knox. They were trying to figure out if I was "the girl," and something about that made my smile widen.

"Happy birthday," I mumbled against Knox's chest.

Pressing two fingers under my chin, he tilted my head back

so his dark eyes could meet mine. "Thank you." He studied my face for a while before asking, "Is it weird that I've missed you?"

Heat rushed to my cheeks. "You missed me?"

He gave me a look, like I should have known. "Yeah, Low."

"Good," I teased.

Knox laughed softly, and when I blinked against the drops that began falling from the sky, he quickly wrapped his arm around me and walked us toward the house without another look at his friends. And like we had every day on the phone, we picked right back up on our conversation from the day before. Only this time he was here again, in front of me. And this time my hand was in his, and every now and then he would cup my cheek and just stare at me—like my eyes held answers he was looking for.

"We've got some jailbait in here!" someone said loudly almost an hour later.

I wouldn't have paid them any attention if Knox's face hadn't suddenly hardened as he looked over to the guys he'd been with at the beginning of the night, and then over to whoever had yelled.

"Hope you look good in orange, Knox!"

This time my head whipped around. *What are they talking about?*

Out of the two dozen people all smashed together in the basement of Neil's house, almost everyone was cracking up as people started throwing around the word *jailbait* like it was a catcall or something.

Knox's hand tightened around mine, and I watched his face pale.

"What are they talking about?" I asked so only he could hear me. When he didn't answer, I looked around for Hayley and Neil—two of the other people not laughing besides us. She looked sad; he looked livid—I just wasn't sure who his anger was directed at.

"No pussy can be worth jail time, bro. Don't do it!"

That got everyone laughing so loud, the sudden roar made me jump, and Knox growled. His friends from outside were whispering urgently to him, but Knox didn't seem to be listening to them.

"The guy is about to start college, Harlow! You really gonna force him into jail before he gets that chance?"

My breaths were coming fast—too fast. Embarrassment flooded me, even though I had no idea what was going on. I looked back at Knox's blank face and pleaded with him to help me understand. "What are they talking about?"

He slowly turned his head to face me and offered me a weak smile. "It doesn't matter. Just ignore them."

Hayley was suddenly behind us on the couch, and her lips were at my ear. "Let's go."

"I don't underst—"

"Knox is eighteen," she said, cutting me off.

"And?"

"Which now makes you a minor for him. It's illegal for you two to have any kind of sexual relationship."

"We don't!" I hissed.

"I would never—" Knox began, and pushed his friends away when they urged him to leave, but Hayley's next words were all I heard.

"*I* know you wouldn't do anything with him yet, Harlow. But since he's not worried about hiding that he likes you, if anyone mentioned that the two of you *did* do something, he could go to jail. You two just being together the way you are right now puts him at risk."

All the blood drained from my face, and I could no longer hear the laughing, the jokes, or Hayley even though I knew she was still talking to me. I turned to face Knox again; the frustration and defeat were clear in his eyes.

I tried pulling my hand from his, and he squeezed tighter. "Harlow, I don't care."

"I do! I can't do this to you."

When I pulled again, he didn't try to stop me. Standing from the couch, I forced my way through everyone and to the stairs— ignoring their razzing and the tears that had started falling down my cheeks. I heard Hayley and Neil behind me as I climbed my way up, and soon there was only one set of footsteps following me. I was halfway across the lawn, my eyes blinking rapidly against the pouring rain when I was turned around.

I flinched away from Knox. "Don't!" I snapped. "Why didn't you tell me?"

"Because I decided it didn't matter."

"How could that not matter?"

"*I* know I wouldn't do anything illegal with you."

I flung my hands out toward the house, and my eyes caught Knox's two friends standing near the door with arms crossed over their chests as they watched us. Looking back at Knox, I hissed, "According to Hayley, it doesn't matter if we do or don't do anything illegal. If someone said something—God. I can't do this to you, Knox." He wrapped his arms around me, and held tight even when I tried to push away. "Don't do this; we can't risk anything."

"Then I'll wait for you, Harlow," he promised, and the sincerity in the words stunned me for long seconds. "I'll wait until you're eighteen."

Pushing against his chest, I shook my head. "For two and a half years, Knox? For a girl you barely know? Who can promise that after a week and a half?"

"I—"

"No, I can't do that to you or me. I get it now—what was so wrong the other night at the concert when you found out how old I was; I get it. You should have told me that *this* was what you were worried about."

"Yeah, I should have. I also shouldn't have stayed out there with you, or called you, but I couldn't help it. I told you; it doesn't matter to me. Do you think I usually go after girls your age?" His dark eyes searched mine, and he continued talking without giving me enough time to answer. "No, I don't, but there is something about you that calls to me. I knew that to continue even talking to you was dangerous because I would keep falling way too fast. But I did, knowing I would be eighteen soon, knowing something like this might happen."

"I didn't!" I said too loudly, my hand pressed firmly to my chest. "I cannot let you go into something that puts you at any kind of risk. Or that would be as uncomfortable as *that* was." I pointed to the house. "I won't do that to you." He started to speak, and I talked over him. "And I can't let you promise something to me that I can't even promise you. Two and a half years? You're eighteen and about to start college. You shouldn't have to promise me anything. I know I don't always act my age, but I *am* still fifteen. And as shitty as the truth sounds, I don't see boys in terms of years and futures together. I see them in the now, what they make me feel right this second. I can't even promise you the summer—let alone two and a half years."

"And yet, you're crying," he said gently.

"Because right now what I want is you, and I can't have you!"

One hand wrapped around my waist; the other moved to fist in my long, wet hair. Before I could think of what was happening, his lips fell onto mine, and a shocked whimper moved up my throat. I clung to his arms as our lips moved in sync for a few short, blissful seconds. When he pulled back, I pressed my forehead to his chest so I wouldn't have to look at his dark eyes. I would take back everything I'd just said if I looked at them now.

"One day, Harlow Evans, you will be mine. I *will* wait for you."

"You'll be wasting your time," I choked out. My hands tightened on his arms as I tried to hold back more tears.

A soft, amused laugh sounded close to my ear. "Never."

Present Day—Richland

TWO DAYS LATER my purse and keys were returned to me, as promised, along with one of Collin's credit cards. This time he wanted me to buy myself new earrings since I hadn't screwed anything up in the last couple of days.

I wanted to cut the card in half.

But I hadn't. I'd gone to a jewelry store downtown and picked a pair of diamond solitaire studs. I think the associate was confused by my lack of enthusiasm with the gift for myself, but it wasn't his job to know why I was buying them—only that he was getting paid for helping me.

That night I had my earrings on, Collin's credit card in hand, and dinner on the table when he got home. After inspecting the house as he did every night, he walked up to me with a smile on his face before pressing his lips to mine. Taking the card from my fingers, he glanced at my ears for less than a second before turning toward the table to throw another bouquet of pink roses on top. He'd never once *handed* me the flowers he brought home for me, always just tossed them somewhere for me to gather later.

"Do you like them?"

"I do," I answered automatically. "Thank you, Collin."

"Anything for my girl."

We ate dinner and he told me about work, spending only a few minutes to voice his annoyance that Alfred McKenzie—the Benton County treasurer, and the man Collin was waiting to replace—still didn't have plans to retire, then telling me the rest of the new government gossip. My mind drifted as he droned on; it was the same conversation as always. Everything from some of the men's sexual affairs, cases his dad had handled, to the new chief of police they were all in an uproar about. Collin's dad, Flynn Doherty, was the prosecuting attorney in our county, and a great man.

Unfortunately, he loved his son and was blind to any bad that could come from him, and had pulled some strings to get Collin a well-respected job in the treasury just after Collin had graduated from college. Alfred wasn't around much due to his old age, leaving Collin to deal with most of the duties, and I worried about how much worse everything could get once Collin *became* treasurer—because everyone knew that when Collin ran, it would be unopposed. Even though Collin had been a trust fund baby and had more money than he knew what to do with, I knew he was already using the county's money to keep police officers' mouths shut, and I had no doubt it had been used in the incident with the arson in California.

"Did you hear me?" he asked suddenly, and I glanced up.

I had my fork in the air, and wondered how long it had been there. I shook my head once to clear my mind, and cleared my throat. "Um, the new chief of police," I mumbled, and froze when Collin's eyebrows slammed down over his eyes. The only relief I felt was that his blue eyes were still his—they weren't lifeless, they weren't my monsters.

Collin's free hand clenched into a fist over and over as he watched me, and after a moment he started eating again. "As I was saying, we have a fund-raiser we're expected to be at in two weeks."

I swallowed thickly at the mention of it, and was only able to push around my food for the rest of dinner as I fought to keep down what I'd already eaten.

Fund-raisers and dinner parties meant we needed to impress people Collin or his dad worked with. They meant Collin expected me to be perfect, even though he had no problem showing me how *im*perfect I was while we were there, and again once we got home.

We'd been at a dinner party the first time I'd caught a glimpse of my monster—and it also should have been the last night I ever saw Collin. But I was in love, we'd just gotten engaged, and I kept making excuses for him in my head.

Spring 2012—Richland

"I DON'T KNOW if I should wear my ring tonight," I said, and bit down on my bottom lip as I tried to figure out what to do. I held my left hand in front of me, and my heart raced as my lips spread into a wide grin.

This is right. This is what I want, I thought to myself, and forced my smile to remain on my face as I wondered why I'd pictured Knox Alexander when I'd accepted Collin's marriage proposal three hours before.

Collin turned from where he was fixing his tie in the mirror and raised a dirty-blond brow. "You don't want to wear your ring?" he asked quietly; calmly.

My eyes widened, and I stumbled over my words as I tried to explain. "No, of course I do! I just didn't know if I should when we're going to your parents' dinner party. I mean, it's for the governor, and I didn't know when or how you wanted to announce to them that we were engaged. And now I'm worried that we'll steal the focus if someone sees the ring, because it's *really* hard to miss . . . so I just don't know what to do."

Collin smiled before pressing his lips to mine. "My parents already know. I promise it will be fine."

I blinked quickly in surprise. "They know?" It wasn't like I expected the screams of excitement that had poured through the phone from my family, but I would've thought the Dohertys would have said *something* when we'd shown up at their house earlier to get ready for the party.

"Of course they do; they're excited." Collin's eyes studied my face, then fell quickly over my ears, throat, and finally my left hand. Every place on my body that had jewelry from him. His eyes stayed on my hand when he asked, "Do you like it?"

"My ring?" I sputtered. *Is he serious?* I thought to myself. I glanced down to the five-carat, emerald-cut, Classic Winston, and giggled. "Collin, I *love* my ring. As always, it is way too much, but I love it."

"Then that's all I need to know—and no, you're not taking it off for the party." Glancing at his phone, he said, "We do need to go, though, or my parents will wonder why we aren't down there."

"Okay." I blew out a hard breath, and looked at myself in the mirror one last time before following Collin out of his bedroom at his parents' house, and down the stairs.

I was introduced to dozens of couples—some of them I would never remember; others left me forcing myself not to gawk, as celebrities were introduced like it was an everyday occurrence to see them.

"Do you know who that was?" I hissed in Collin's ear when we stepped away from the actor and his supermodel wife.

Collin's brow furrowed, like he didn't understand why I was about to hyperventilate. "Yes? Ah! There are my parents."

Nothing. No reaction. This is his life—my life now . . . and it is so amazing! How does he not find this amazing? I wondered, but put those thoughts to rest when I looked around his parents' house. I knew his family had money, but it was obvious some of their money came from something long before his father's job, because there was no way a prosecutor could have a house like this. Just like there was no way his son could buy me the things he did.

"Collin, Harlow, so glad you could join us." Mrs. Doherty said, and kissed my cheek. "These are some of Flynn's colleagues," she whispered, then straightened with a perfect smile on her face. "Gentlemen, you remember our son. This is his fiancée, Harlow."

A few nods and nice-to-meet-yous were thrown out, but other than that, it was if we hadn't just come into the conversation. As if Mrs. Doherty hadn't just announced so casually that we were engaged.

Just like that, I was brought into the family. I'd been worried it would be harder—like I would have to prove myself. Instead, it was anticlimactic—almost a letdown. The conversation that had been taking place continued, and Collin kept his arm around me as he threw himself into it. I tried to do the same.

Five minutes later I was still attempting to understand what was happening—or *happened*. All I understood so far was that the men were all talking about an old case.

"Still can't believe the bastard got away with first-degree murder," one of the men said, and the others all shook their heads and voiced their displeasure.

"Should've been capital murder," Flynn Doherty added.

"What's the difference?" I asked quietly, and regretted it when a few men laughed, and every pair of eyes in the small group focused on me.

Collin laughed softly and mumbled, "Excuse us for a few minutes. I haven't had much alone time with my new fiancée." His hand gripped mine as he practically tugged me across the floor to a corner that wasn't as busy.

"I can't walk that fast in these—"

He turned so his face was directly in front of mine, and though his mouth was curved up in a smile, there was something different about it. About him. "Are you fucking kidding me, Harlow?" he hissed.

My eyebrows rose in confusion. "Wait, wha—" My question was cut off when Collin released my hand, only for two of his fingers to dig into a spot on my wrist. The pain was instant and surprising. My mouth popped back open, whether to let out a cry of pain or demand why he was doing this, I didn't know—but it didn't matter, he spoke before I could.

"Do not show your pain, Harlow."

"What?" I asked breathlessly, and gave him a panicked look. "Co—"

"Do *not* show your pain," he repeated. His tone was soft, his face still carefully composed. If I weren't the one on the receiving end of the pain, I would've been so sure we were flirting instead, from the look he was giving me. "You know how stupid you are, don't you?"

Stupid? I thought lamely. The question would have frustrated me if I weren't trying to keep a straight face while simultaneously wondering how two fingers could cause so much pain. "Wh—"

"You will *never* embarrass me in front of anyone like that again, and especially not my father or his colleagues. Do you understand?" Collin leaned close and brushed his lips across my neck to whisper, "Do not say another word for the rest of the night." The words were emphasized by a relief so great it almost felt like the pain had worsened for a split second when he released my wrist. It was clear his words weren't just a demand— they were a warning.

I never once would have considered myself stupid before . . . but now I wasn't sure if I *was* for obeying his demand the way I did for the rest of the night.

I smiled pleasantly—well, I hoped it looked pleasant—stayed by Collin's side as we flitted from group to group, and never stopped studying him as he charmed everyone he spoke to.

I wanted to know what had happened. I wanted to know who the man was who had talked down to me and hurt me, because it wasn't the man I'd fallen in love with. And I wanted to know why each touch and caress throughout the rest of the night felt like something so similar—but somehow foreign now.

"Come here, Harlow," Collin murmured softly hours later when we finally made it back upstairs to his bedroom.

I stood a dozen feet away from him, staring at the floor as tears pooled in my eyes.

"You looked so incredible tonight," he said when he was behind me. His fingers trailed down my bare arms, and he wrapped one arm around my stomach to pull my body close to his.

"I don't understand," I choked out, and immediately wondered if I was allowed to speak now.

Collin turned me so I was facing him, and used his thumbs to gently brush away the few tears that had fallen. "All you need to understand is that I love you."

My head shook. "No, that's—you *hurt* me."

His blue eyes flashed with something I've never seen before, but it was gone just as quickly. He gently gripped my fingers to bring my hand close to his face and whispered, "I'm sorry," before he placed soft kisses along my palm and the now-sensitive spot on my wrist. "I lost control of myself for a second, Harlow, that's all," Collin said as he straightened my engagement ring.

"Collin," I began hesitantly, but didn't continue. I thought about what was going on in our lives right now, and knew he was under a lot of stress finishing his senior year and graduating from college in a month. I knew he was worried about getting a respectable job, and figured he might have been right. Maybe I had embarrassed him in front of those men—the same men he might or might not work with after graduation.

Because I'd been trying so hard to understand the conversation earlier, I *might* have said something I wasn't supposed to. Or maybe I wasn't supposed to say anything—I hadn't heard Collin's mom offer anything to the conversation other than introducing us. Could those conversations be only for the men? Something the women pretend not to hear? And now that hours had passed, I couldn't remember if I *had* said something I should've been embarrassed about.

With the way Collin's mouth was ghosting across my collarbone and playing with the zipper of my dress, I also wasn't sure if I'd over-dramatized the whole thing with him earlier. *Had it actually hurt? Had he meant it to hurt?* He'd never touched me in any way other than the way he was now. Like I was precious . . . like I was his everything.

"We'll go buy you something tomorrow," he promised just before his lips brushed my own. "Whatever you want."

I huffed and shook my head as I cradled his face in my hands. This was the Collin I knew and loved, the one who was absurd in his need to give me things. The one who knew how to make me forget the bad. "You're so ridiculous. You give me too much . . . I don't want anything."

"We're going," he assured me as he unzipped me, and my dress pooled to the floor.

"Just give me you."

With a look I knew well, he led me to his bed, and did just that.

Present Day—Richland

COLLIN HAD WORSHIPPED my body and made love to me for hours that night, and I'd pushed the bizarre encounter out of my mind. I'd slowly learned over the next six months that he knew about a dozen pressure points on each side of my body incredibly well, and every time we were in public and I did something he deemed stupid, he would be quick to show me, along with commanding me not to show my pain. If we were alone, he would dig his fingers into a pressure point until I ended up on the floor, begging him to stop. But it wasn't until just a few hours after we said "I do" that I understood I'd never known Collin at all, and that pressure points were the least of my worries with him. The guy I'd been making excuses for, the guy I'd loved, was no longer there.

He was still tall and handsome, with sandy blond hair and dark blue eyes. He still knew how to charm anyone into believing whatever fell from his lips, and he still held the hearts of my family. But everything I'd loved about him was now gone. My love for him died the moment he finally crushed my spirit, and I'd just been going through the motions, and praying for *better* days, every day for the last two and a half years.

My hands froze when Collin's arms slowly wrapped around my waist that night before I was able to calm myself enough to continue washing the dishes from dinner.

"Are you almost done?" he asked softly; his lips brushed the back of my neck as he spoke.

"Yeah."

His hands moved to slip under the bottom of my shirt, and I suddenly wanted to have more dishes that needed to be washed.

"Then hurry."

I didn't.

As soon as the last plate was in the dishwasher, Collin was pulling me back toward the bedroom. I don't remember him undressing me, and I wasn't sure when his clothes had joined mine on the floor. I just knew he was laying me back on the bed, and I was losing my grip on my safe place to block out what was happening. I needed to get back to my safe place in my head; I didn't want to be a part of this.

Gripping my chin in one of his hands, he forced me to look up at him as he moved inside me. Each thrust made my body jerk against the bed as I felt my hate for him grow. My arms lay unmoving at my sides, my body stiff as I fought with myself to push him away.

He could've been fucking a corpse and there would have been little difference.

Releasing my jaw, he sat back and moved his hand between us, and every nerve ending came alive when his fingers brushed against me. My head fell to the side and I stared at the window as my body started responding to him. I clenched my jaw shut against the shaking, and began hating myself for feeling any kind of pleasure from him. My throat tightened against the tears I was holding back, and my body jerked with silent sobs when he forced an orgasm from me.

Leaning back over me, he quickened his pace until he found his own release, and seconds later he was moving my head so I was facing him again. If he saw the wetness in my eyes, he didn't comment on it.

He pressed his lips to mine firmly. "I love you."

"I love you, too," I managed to say past the tightness in my throat.

"Go clean up."

As soon as he released my chin, I was moving out from underneath him and off the bed to walk into the bathroom. After cleaning myself, I stood in front of the mirror just staring at what I'd become.

My brown hair was dull and flat, and might have started thinning, but it was still too thick to be sure. My blue eyes had no life left in them, and I wondered what people saw in them even when I pretended everything was fine. I'd lost forty pounds when I'd only had about five I could lose when I'd met Collin. Bones stuck out that shouldn't, making the bruises on my stomach and tops of my thighs that much more apparent.

It wasn't that I didn't want to eat—I couldn't. I was always too afraid of what was about to happen, or was coming off whatever *had* just happened. If I did manage to eat, the stress from my life with Collin usually had it souring in my stomach soon after. And the bruises—there was never enough time for the old ones to disappear before there were new ones there. But Collin was smart: he never put them somewhere they could be seen. Which is why knowing pressure points and how to instill fear were his biggest allies.

I took in my whole reflection, and grimaced. Twenty-two, and I looked like I was days away from death's door. Maybe one day God would be kind enough to just take me, because Lord knew there was no other way to escape Collin.

Chapter 3

Knox
Present Day—Thatch, Washington

"OH WOW. HARDER. Harder. Oh my God, yes. Oh, it feels so good. Yes. Yes, I'm almost the—"

I crushed my mouth down onto the girl's to get her to shut up if even for a few seconds. She hadn't stopped talking once since I'd met her, and the talking only increased after the clothes came off. Depending on the girl and the talking she did, I loved it when they said exactly what they wanted in bed. But I was struggling to keep my erection with the way this girl sounded.

As soon as her high-pitched moan sounded against the kiss, I slowed my movements in a way that I hoped had her thinking I had gotten off, too.

Christ . . . I was turning into a girl. I was faking a goddamn orgasm just to be done with sex. Graham and Deacon were never

going to let me live this down. And then I realized I was thinking about my best friends during sex, and I wondered what in
the hell this girl had actually done to me. Worst mistake I'd ever
made. The way she tried to make her voice sound like she was a
child should have been a clue.

When I thought it was safe to move, I pulled out and immediately got off my bed and headed toward the bathroom.

"Oh my God, that was amazing. Really, so amazing. Thank
you so much. Oh, I just can't. I can't. Oh my God."

After disposing of the barely used condom, I gripped the sink
and bit back a groan as she continued talking.

"Come back to bed. I need to have snuggles after sex."

"Snuggles?" I whispered, and looked over my shoulder.

"If you take any longer in there, I'm going to be ready for another round by the time you get back here!"

I rolled my eyes and pushed away from the sink, but as soon as
I was in my room, I searched for clothes to put on.

She sat up and looked at me with wide eyes. "What are you
doing? Aren't we going to snuggle?"

"Uh, snuggle? No, not today. I have work in . . ." I glanced
down to my bare wrist and made a face. "Actually right now. So
you need to go."

"Oh really? Are you sure, I mean I can stay here. I can cook
for you when you get back and stuff. Or I can just be here in your
bed ready for another go; it will be great. I'll wait for you."

I paused from where I was grabbing a clean shirt—one that
she hadn't touched—and gave her a look like she'd lost her mind.
"I'm sorry, what was that last thing you said?"

She looked around like she had to think about it, then said in
an unsure voice, "I'll wait for you?"

I huffed and went back to getting dressed, but didn't look at her again. "Yeah, no, I don't need anyone waiting for me. But like I said, I'm late for work, so I need you to go."

I heard her scoff as she got off the bed, and in less than a minute she was storming out of my room. By the loud "Oh!" that came from my roommates not long after, I'd bet she left while carrying her clothes.

"Well, damn, what'd you do? She seemed like she was going to be easy to keep happy, Knox, and she was thinking of a hundred ways to kill you when she left."

I turned around to look at Deacon, one of my roommates as well as longtime best friend, and shrugged. "She was. It was just time for her to go." I walked past him into the living room, and a smile crossed my face when I saw my favorite girl walking toward our kitchen.

"Good God, Grey, pregnancy looks damn good on you!" Hooking an arm around her neck, I pulled her close to kiss the top of her head, then released her. Keeping my eyes trained on her brother, Graham—my other roommate and best friend—I said loudly, "When are you going to tell your husband that it's really my child, and you're madly in love with me?"

Graham turned to glare at me, but before he could say anything, Deacon cut in: "Dude, you know it's my baby. Stop trying to steal my girl."

"Both of you can fuck off," Graham grumbled. "It's bad enough knowing my sister had sex."

Jagger, Grey's husband, just laughed and nodded in my direction before starting up his conversation with Graham again. Deacon and I had been declaring our "love" for Graham's sister ever since we were sixteen just to piss him off. Neither of us saw her as anything other than family, but he was the only one who never understood that.

"You wanna tell me what happened?" Grey asked, and I looked down at her with my brow furrowed.

"What?"

She gestured toward the front door with her head. "My husband and I just had to see one of your nasty naked skanks walk through here, so you at least owe me an apology for that, Knox Alexander. But she looked pissed, and I know the only time you piss off women is when they realize you won't be calling them again, so what happened?"

The smile slipped from my face, and I shrugged as I looked up to focus on the wall behind Grey. "Nothing. Like I told Deacon, it was just time for her to go."

"And I think you're lying to me," she whispered.

My gaze darted back to Grey's gauging expression, and I dropped my voice to her same level. "Drop it, Grey."

She opened her mouth, but before she could say anything, Jagger came up behind her. "That girl looked pissed, Knox. I mean, not like the rest of them don't, but it's usually well after the fact."

Grey raised an eyebrow, and I shook my head. "You guys keep saying that like there's a lot of them or something."

Both of them laughed, and Grey said, "Are you kidding? Knox, I've never known you not to have at least four girls a week."

I swallowed thickly, and wondered how I had turned into this guy. But it didn't take long to remember that it didn't matter anymore anyway. It stopped mattering four and a half years ago, right about the time I turned into Deacon and Graham.

Grey abruptly stopped laughing. "Except . . ." She trailed off, and her eyes narrowed like she was trying to sort through the jumbled mess in my head. "Except when you were in college," she mumbled softly.

I shook my head slowly. "Don't," I warned, but judging from the way Grey's eyes widened, there hadn't been enough force behind the word.

She briefly glanced over to where Deacon and Graham were standing in the living room watching a baseball game, then whispered, "Is that what's wrong, Knox?"

"Grey," I began again, but her next word brought me up short. "Still?"

"*Still?*" I murmured, and huffed a laugh. "Wow. Who knew one word could make me feel so pathetic?"

Winter 2009—Seattle

I STOOD IN front of the door restlessly as I waited for it to open. I should've called. I should've asked her earlier in the week if she'd had plans today or tonight since she'd assumed I did—but I hadn't. Now I was standing there like a dumbass with two bouquets of flowers, hoping I wouldn't have to leave so Harlow could go on a date tonight.

The door finally opened, and Mrs. Evans's face brightened. "Knox Alexander, why doesn't it surprise me that you're knocking on my door this afternoon?"

I failed at hiding my grin, and handed her the first bouquet. "First, these are for you."

"Why, thank you!"

"Honestly, Mrs. Evans, I'm just worried that I'm not the only guy showing up today." I glanced inside the house, and asked, "Does my girl have a date tonight?"

She raised one eyebrow, the action making her look younger, and so much like Harlow. "I'm not sure," she said playfully. "Shouldn't I be asking you that?"

My face fell for a second before I was able to compose myself. All I wanted to be able to do was take Harlow out on a date—but I was afraid to risk even that. I cleared my throat and said, "Well, I'm hoping she'll let me spend the day with her. If it's okay with you," I added quickly.

Mrs. Evans rolled her eyes and stepped back to let me in the house. "I doubt my daughter would ever choose anything over a day with you, and you are always welcome in our home."

"Thank you, Mrs. Evans."

"Harlow's in her room. Remember: no closed doors," she said strictly, then turned to walk toward the kitchen with her flowers. Just as I started up the stairs, she called out, "I'll set an extra place for you at the table tonight, Knox."

I stopped to look at her, and said sincerely, "Thank you." She and her husband would never know how thankful I was that they didn't try to keep me from the girl upstairs.

I hurried up the stairs and barely slowed long enough to knock on Harlow's door. As soon as I heard her mumbled "Yeah?" I walked into her room, left the door as wide as it would go, and stopped trying to fight my smile when I took her in.

She was facing away from me, and lying on her stomach on the bed. Her feet were in the air, crossed at the ankles, and her eyes were glued to the book in front of her. Her hair was piled messily on her head, one side of her oversize shirt was falling off her shoulder, and the fitted black sleep pants she was wearing hugged every curve of her perfectly.

It wasn't morning, but looking at her then, I knew I wanted to wake up to *this* Harlow for the rest of my life.

She still hadn't looked up, so I took a few more steps into the room, then brought the bouquet of poppies in front of me. "For the girl who hates roses."

Harlow gasped and whirled around on her bed as soon as she heard my voice, and had launched herself at me by the time I finished talking.

I tossed the flowers on her bed in time to catch her, and tightened my arms around her when she did the same to me.

"Happy Valentine's Day, Low," I whispered against her shoulder, and gripped her tighter before setting her down on the floor. Something caught in my chest when her eyes met mine, and I wanted to live in that moment.

Have you ever looked at someone . . . just one look, and you knew that was it? There would never be anyone else who would compare? That was Harlow for me. Every time.

Her hands slid to my shoulders, then back to my face, like she was making sure I was real. "What are you doing here?"

I gave her an amused look, like the answer to her question was obvious. "Seeing you."

"But it's Valentine's Day. Shouldn't you be going somewhere with your girlfriend?"

Girlfriend was a very loose term, but every time I tried to explain that to Harlow, she thought I was only saying it for her benefit. "No, I'm where I'm supposed to be."

She tilted her head away, but not before I saw heat fill her cheeks and the corners of her mouth tilt up in a faint smile. When she looked back at me, her expression was stern. "That's not very nice to do to her," she informed me.

"Harlow, trust me. There's nowhere I need to be more than where I am right now."

She bit down on her bottom lip and looked like she might argue as her blue eyes searched mine. Just when I started to repeat myself, she huffed and her mouth quirked up in a lopsided smile. "If you were anyone else, I really would feel bad for your girlfriend . . . but you're not, and you know I'm selfish enough to want you here."

"Then it looks like I'm staying." Like I would've left. Leaning around her, I grabbed the poppies off the bed and held them up to her. "For you."

Harlow gave a giddy smile, then took the bouquet like it was something precious and breakable. Her eyes lifted to meet mine from where she'd been looking over her flowers, and she said, "Thank you, and perfect timing. My monthlies just met their unavoidable end with the trash."

I followed her stare, and let out a low laugh when I saw half a dozen little cards piled up on her dresser. I'd sent her poppies every month since I'd met her, and each one had come with a card letting her know I was still waiting for her.

My head whipped back around and my eyes widened when I felt Harlow's body press close to mine. Her head was tilted back as her vibrant eyes studied my face, and each breath made her chest brush against mine. My hand automatically went to her waist, and I tried to tell myself it was just to steady myself from being thrown off by her sudden closeness. I knew it was a lie even as I repeated it in my head over and over. My eyes fell to her lips. It would've been so easy to bend down and capture them with mine. So easy, and so wanted.

"Harlow," I warned, my voice hoarse.

"One of these days . . ." She trailed off, and brought the flowers up from where she'd been holding them down by her side. "One of these days I'll be able to kiss you to show you my thanks."

I nodded slowly, absentmindedly, and cradled her face in my hands. "One day," I promised, "and I'll be waiting every day until then." I gently pressed my mouth to the tip of her nose, then her forehead. "We need to get out of this bedroom."

A soft giggle bubbled up from her chest, and she reluctantly pulled away from me. After clearing her throat she looked around her room, then to the door. "Um, right. Movie downstairs?"

"Movie," I agreed.

"YOU HAVE GOT to be shitting me," Graham said as soon as I was back in my room at the frat house late that night. "You know what, no, I'm gonna give you a chance to give me a different story."

I eyed Graham and Deacon sitting in the room I shared with Deacon, and closed the door behind me to try to contain whatever was about to happen. Tension continued to fill the room as they glared at me, but I refused to say anything.

"Fine," Deacon said. "Do you want to know who showed up here tonight to see if you were going to take her out for Valentine's Day? Who was it, Graham?"

"Madison."

"Oh that's right!" Deacon said loudly. "Madison. Your girl-friend. Well, I'm just going to assume it's *ex* now. Anyway, she had a lot to say. A lot of *interesting* things to say. Like how you're waiting for someone else, so you don't want anything serious with anyone. Things that she thought were bullshit, still might, and things she doesn't have all the facts about, thank God."

"Are you gonna say anything?" Graham asked, but I just shrugged. There wasn't much to say. "Where were you tonight?"

"You know where I was."

"She's fucking fifteen, Knox!"

I ground my teeth and turned to look at the door, not that I could have seen if anyone was listening anyway. When I turned back around, I was glaring at Graham. "Sixteen," I corrected.

"Like that makes it better?" they yelled at the same time.

"And I didn't touch her. You know I won't touch her," I continued. "I just had to see her."

Both of them sat there staring at me like they didn't know what to do with me anymore. "Why?" Graham finally asked. "Why, Knox? This can only go bad for you. You have to be able to see that; you're not blind, man."

"I love—"

"Don't!" He cut me off. "Just stop. The way you talk to her, how often you talk to her, the fact that you went to see her to-night . . . all of those things are marks against you. Knox, you can go to jail. We can't let you do that over some girl."

Deacon didn't add anything, but he was nodding.

"Dude," Graham went on, "you need to stop talking to her, and you need to move on to someone who is at least eighteen."

I huffed. "To who? Someone like Madison? Someone I can't stand to be around, but *informed* me we were dating because she thinks we're perfect together? I only let it go on because it shut you two up about Harlow!" I ran my hands over my face and groaned. "Look, I know you two hate the thought of Harlow, but I love her. That's it; I love her."

"But you can't," Deacon reminded me.

I kept talking like he hadn't. "Throughout everything since middle school we have all been there for each other, and it is such bullshit that my best friends have turned on me now. Okay, yeah, I thought we were going to come to Seattle and party all the time and hook up with as many girls as possible. I *know* that was the plan. I *know* the plan wasn't to get serious until after college, but screw the fucking plans! I met Harlow and I knew immediately that she was it. It wasn't that I just wanted her; I *needed* her. I get that it isn't the best situation—trust me, no one gets that more than I do. But I don't need both of you making this that much harder for us! Harlow knows you both hate her. How do you think that makes her feel? How do you think that makes *me* feel? What would it be like for you, Graham, if Deacon and I hated the girl you were in love with?"

Graham looked like he was about to yell, but took a calming breath and said, "You aren't understanding that you can't be in love with her. Jesus Christ, Knox, Harlow is a child!"

My eyes narrowed. "That's disgusting, don't do that."

"She is! You think of Grey as a little kid, and they're the same age."

"Grey isn't as mature as Harlow. Harlow has spent her entire life with people our age; she doesn't fit in with people her age. She doesn't think or act like a sixteen-year-old. And no one has thought of Grey as a little kid since she got tits when she was twelve, Graham; get over it."

"That's true," Deacon murmured.

Graham's face pinched in disgust. "Okay, we're not talking about my sister's chest! Knox. You have to realize that this is probably just a game to Harlow. She likes that an older guy is interested in her, and she's going along with it. But she's not old enough to know what love is—shit, *we're* not even old enough to really know what love is—and by the time she's eighteen, she's not going to care that you wasted all this time waiting for her. And that's *if* she doesn't get you thrown in jail before that."

"Ditto," Deacon said. "We love you, man. Like you said, we've been there together through everything. And even though you think we've turned on you now, we're trying to protect you. We don't hate her, we hate that she has blinded you to all that can, and is going to, happen to you *because* of her."

I shook my head absentmindedly for a few seconds. "It's not going to change anything. I'm still going to wait for her."

Present Day—Thatch

"Knox, wait!" Grey called out from behind me.

I turned around and tried to seem unaffected from the short conversation in the kitchen as she stepped up to me. "Grey, you need to be on the couch resting or something."

"I'm not *that* pregnant." She waved off the suggestion. "Look, I'm sorry, I didn't mean to make you feel pathetic."

"You didn't," I said automatically, and turned back toward my truck.

"Why are you leaving?"

I knew I couldn't use the work excuse like I had with the nameless girl from earlier, and there weren't many places I could use as an excuse in Thatch. "I just need to go."

"So I was right."

I rubbed at my jaw and sighed, but didn't look at her yet. "About what?"

"That girl from college. That's what's bothering you still."

A smirk crossed my face as I turned to look at Grey. "Well, technically she wasn't in college."

Grey rolled her eyes. "When you were in college, you knew what I meant. It's been . . . it's been years, Knox. You haven't talked about her since, and there's been . . ." She trailed off, and thought for a second. "Countless girls. And you always seem happy. Why didn't you ever say anything?"

"I am happy, Grey," I told her honestly. "I have you and my best friends, I have my dream job, and I have more girls than I know what to do with. I *am* happy. This was the life I was always supposed to have. This was the plan with Deacon and Graham. Well, maybe not to go on this long, but this was it. It just took a long time to learn how to be happy without her, and sometimes it's still hard to remember how when something reminds me of her."

Grey nodded and pursed her lips. "The girl today, did she remind you of her?"

"No," I said with a laugh. "No, God, that girl was a nightmare. But she said something that I'd promised Harlow for a long time. And hearing someone say that to me . . . it just caught me off guard."

Grey wrapped her arms around me as much as her six-month-swollen stomach would allow. "I'm sorry. I know she meant a lot to you, Knox, but you'll find someone. Someday."

I gave Grey a tight-lipped smile when I pulled away, but didn't respond. I never did when a family member or friend said something similar, because all I could think about was a girl who stole my heart outside of a concert one summer night, only to shatter it years later.

Chapter 4

Harlow

Spring 2009—Seattle

"You can't keep doing this, Knox. If you're going to be in a relationship, then you actually need to *be* in the relationship. You can't let me get in the way of it," I scolded, but even as I said the words, I couldn't stop the smile from pulling at my lips.

Knox and I had agreed from the beginning that we wanted each other to still have our own separate lives. I think it had been my way of staying firm in my pseudo-argument that he was wasting his time waiting for me, and his way of making sure I didn't miss out on anything. We'd known it would be too hard to stay away from each other, and had decided that if school schedules allowed it, he would come see me once a month.

He doubled that, and I wasn't complaining.

If I had had my way he'd be with me every day, but I knew

I couldn't do that to him. I *wanted* him to have a life. As much as I wanted him with me, I was afraid that he would either resent me, or regret waiting for me if he missed out on college and all that it offered. So twice a month was our maximum. We hadn't said why, but I was sure his reasons were the same as mine.

That, however, didn't stop us from talking every other day. We always talked for hours, and it never felt long enough. Every time, I could still feel the connection I'd felt the first night I'd met him, and every time, I had to remember why we couldn't be together. It wasn't long before the word *jailbait* slipped back into my mind, and I would remember why we were staying apart even though neither of us wanted to, even though there was a tension that was tangible through the phone.

Unfortunately, the phone calls were something his girlfriend had just caught on to . . . just like Valentine's Day.

Who am I kidding? There was nothing *unfortunate* about it. I didn't care that she'd found out. It's something we'd done before her, and I was glad it hadn't changed during her. I also wasn't sad she was gone—I was actually surprised she'd waited another two months to dump Knox after he had ditched her for me on Valentine's Day.

As much as we had told each other that other relationships was part of us having our own lives, it still crushed me when I found out about her. Then again, I had dated a senior earlier in the school year. *Tried* to date him might be a better way of describing it. It took a couple of weeks to realize what I was doing, but whenever I saw him I compared him to Knox in every way. I finally decided a month in that it was pointless to pretend this guy could ever mean anything to me. I doubted anyone ever would, because meeting Knox Alexander had ruined me for any other boy.

Knox hadn't even tried to hide his happiness that night, and I knew I was failing at hiding mine now. Knox's girlfriend—I'd never wanted to know her name—had just broken up with him because of me.

"Relationship," Knox huffed. "Low, I've told you, you could hardly call it that. Besides, I told her about you before whatever she and I were, ever started," he said. "It's not my fault she thought I was joking."

"Well, it's kind of weird, don't you think? Telling her, 'hey, sure I'll be your date for this group thing, but there's this girl I'm waiting for, and she's my priority,' seems like a way to say you don't want to get too attached at the beginning."

"But I told her," he reasoned.

"You're horrible."

"Not horrible. I'm just in love with you, and I have a year and a half left until I can have you."

I gripped at my warming chest and tried to ignore it as I sighed. "I'm going to stop answering your calls whenever you get a new girlfriend."

"There won't be a new one, and I know you wouldn't."

My eyebrows rose even though he couldn't see me. "And how do you know that?"

"Because you love me, too. Through all this bullshit, you love me, and you need these calls as bad as I do."

"I do love you, Knox," I whispered into the phone. It wasn't the first time I'd told him, and I knew it wouldn't be the last. "I love you to the moon and back." My eyes fell to my dresser, where my monthly bouquet of red poppies sat. These had come just a few days ago. The card, as always, had read: *I'm still waiting for you*.

"To the moon?" A deep, husky laugh filled the other end of the phone. "The moon isn't that far, Harlow."

"Isn't it?"

"No. Not far enough." There were a few beats of silence before he confessed, "I want to love you to the stars."

My mouth parted and a soft huff slipped past my lips. I closed my eyes and let his words replay in my mind and move through my body as I agreed, "Then to the stars."

Neither of us said anything for minutes as we let that hang between us, and the familiar connection tugged at my chest even though he was miles away. I loved him. I loved him, and none of this was fair. But I still stuck to my word; we couldn't do this to each other. He needed to live, as did I.

"Harlow, sweetie, tell Knox good night," my mom said from the other side of my door.

"Okay," I called out. "You hear that?" I asked into the phone.

"Yeah. Sleep well."

"You, too."

He paused, and I knew it was coming—it always came. "I'm still waiting for you, Low." The words were just as sincere as the first time he'd said them.

I smiled sadly. "And you're still wasting your time."

"Never."

I ended the call and dropped my phone to the bed. Even though I never had asked him to keep waiting, and never would, I couldn't help but think about the fact that he'd already waited nearly a year. Another year and a half would come and go before we knew it . . . and, God, I wanted him to be there waiting when this was all over.

My phone chimed twice and I glanced at the screen to see messages from him. When I pulled them up, a laugh bubbled up from my chest as I tapped out my response.

> Knox Alexander: Moon = 238,900 miles away. Closest star (Sun) = 92,960,000 miles away.
> Knox Alexander: I love you to the stars.
> Harlow: To the stars. <3

Present Day—Richland

COLLIN'S HAND RUNNING over my stomach woke me a week after he'd given my keys and purse back, and my body instantly tightened as I prepared for one of two outcomes: him wanting to have sex, or him being pissed-off because I wasn't already awake and making his breakfast when his alarm went off.

"Good morning," he murmured against my shoulder.

"Morning," I said cautiously.

"Do you know what day it is?"

I thought for all of five seconds before it hit me, and dread filled me. It was Saturday. No wonder there had been no alarm; no wonder he wasn't mad that I wasn't awake. Weekends were the only days I didn't have to be up before him with breakfast already made. But I dreaded every other Saturday, only to restart the cycle all over again for two more weeks once the day had passed.

"It's test day, baby."

"It is," I squeaked out, trying to have something that resembled excitement in my voice rather than fear.

"You excited?"

I nodded my head and turned to look up at him. There was an expectant look in his eyes, and a thrill on his face that I knew wouldn't be there much longer. The anxious thrill never turned to joy, and despite my hate for these days, I prayed it never would.

"Well, let's go." He moved quickly off the bed and grabbed my hands, pulling me behind him.

A nervous energy flowed off him and through me, only causing my dread to deepen.

"You're shaking, baby," he said when we got into the bathroom. Collin turned to face me and pulled me into his arms. "What's going on?"

"I just want this," I choked out, trying to appease him in a vain attempt to have him go easy on me later. But it was a lie. I didn't want this. Not with him. And I knew that no matter what I said to him now, it wouldn't change his reaction—it was the same every other week.

"I do, too," he said softly. Kissing me gently, he released me and bent to pull a pregnancy test out of one of the drawers below our bathroom sinks.

After handing me the foil-wrapped stick, he faced me with his arms crossed over his chest and waited. He wouldn't leave, and he wouldn't take his eyes off me; he never did. I tore open the packet and walked to the toilet to pee on the stick. When I was done, he took it from me and set it on the countertop, and just stared.

I walked slowly over to him, my insides twisting and shaking as I briefly glanced at his hopeful expression. He pulled me into his arms so my back was against his chest, and his hands went to my stomach as we waited for three agonizing minutes.

"This is it, I know it is."

"I hope so, too," I responded, staring just past the stick to the counter.

The test would be negative, as every test had been, and hopefully would continue to be. Not long after we'd gotten married and I'd come to understand who Collin really was, I'd gotten a birth control implant in my arm. I knew Collin wanted to have kids early on, and he never wore condoms or let me buy birth control, but I couldn't bring a child into this life. So I'd gone with the only option I could think of that he wouldn't find out about.

I still had about six months left before I needed to get a new one, and I knew when that time came, I would do just that. I would take what was about to come for the rest of my life if it meant keeping an innocent child from my monster. I just had to keep praying that it continued to work.

I knew when the results showed by the pause in Collin's breathing, and the way his fingers went from making lazy circles against my stomach, to digging in. I closed my eyes, took a deep breath, and sent up a prayer that this would be over soon.

"What . . . the fuck . . . are you taking?"

"Nothing," I whispered.

"Do not lie to me, Harlow," he growled. Each word was emphasized as if it were its own sentence. "What are you taking?"

"Nothing. I promise I'm not taking anything."

"Don't lie to me!" he roared.

Before I could comprehend that his body was no longer behind mine, he grabbed my upper arms and threw me down onto the floor. A sharp cry left my chest when my head bounced off the tile, and my hands immediately went to cover my face—even though I knew he wouldn't do anything to mess with something that could be easily seen.

"Don't show your pain, Harlow!"

"Please! I'm not taking—" My words cut off on a wheeze as his foot slammed into my stomach three times in a row.

My hands left my face and went to cradle my stomach as I began curling into the fetal position. His foot stomped down onto my side, making me arch back as a scream tore through me. As soon as my stomach was exposed, the top of his foot connected with it over and over again.

I tried to beg him to stop, but all that left my lips were grunts and cries. My bloodied hands reached for him in a silent plea, and he smacked them away.

"What are you taking?" Collin shouted.

Hard sobs left me and I shook my head against the tile as I lay there, no longer able to curl in on myself. Blood smeared from the tile onto my cheek from where I'd hit my head, and each sob that shook my body felt like someone was stabbing my stomach with a white-hot poker. I couldn't take in anything more than shallow breaths, and breathing out felt impossible.

"I will find it," he assured me in a dark tone. "When I do, you will be begging me for this."

He kicked my stomach once more, and when I started to roll over to protect my stomach, his foot smashed down onto my back and pinned me to the floor. My tears and spit mixed with the blood on the floor, but I couldn't move my head no matter how hard I tried. The pain was unbearable, and the way he had me pinned was making it impossible to breathe. It was all I could do to keep from passing out—I'd found out in the beginning that passing out wasn't an option. He'd only start up again once I was conscious.

"Don't move until I'm back. If I find birth control, Harlow, I'll be sure to tell your mother that *you* are the reason she's about to die."

My face twisted in pain and fear as silent, agonizing sobs continued to torment me. I knew he wouldn't find anything, but that never made the time while he searched for something any easier. Every time I wondered if I was making the right choice. He threatened my family—but I was saving a child. I just had to keep reminding myself that in the two and a half years of going through this every other week, those threats had been just that. Threats.

Because once he came back from not finding anything, everything would change. It always did.

I don't know how long I'd been left there, but by the time I heard his bare feet on the tile as he entered the bathroom, my sobs and tears had stopped, and I was just lying there helplessly.

Collin rolled me over and hushed me when a cry bubbled up my throat. His dark blue eyes roamed over my face sadly for a few seconds before he said, "There was nothing, like you said." Brushing my hair back from where it clung to my face, he gently trailed his fingers along my cheek and down my neck. Just as the tips of his fingers touched my collarbone, they were digging in behind it, and he was whispering, "Don't show your pain, baby."

More tears welled up in my eyes before leaking out, and I smashed my mouth into a tight line to keep any noise from escaping.

"Don't show your pain," he repeated, but I couldn't stop crying. "Why aren't you getting pregnant?"

I shook my head back and forth, and he nodded a few times before breathing out heavily.

"What good are you if you can't do this for us? Don't you want a family? Don't you want to make me happy, Harlow?" he asked, his voice deceptively calm and soothing. When I didn't respond, he dug his fingers in harder. "Answer me."

"I do," I cried out before clenching my shaking jaw shut again.

He seemed to accept my answer, and the pressure left before he was wrapping his arms under my body and pulling me up to cradle me against his chest.

Another cry of pain filled the bathroom, and he kissed my forehead. "Don't show your pain," he said without moving his lips away.

Collin walked me into the large shower, sat me down on the built-in bench, and pulled the shirt off my body. He turned on the water as he walked away, and I watched vacantly as he cleaned the blood off the tile. Once he was done, he stripped down and stepped back in the shower. Sitting on the bench next to me, he pulled me into his arms and looked at the back of my head for a few minutes.

"Very small cut, I had trouble finding it. You'll be okay."

I nodded and bit back a groan when he stood us up. He washed my body and the blood out of my hair before toweling me off and dressing me in one of his shirts. Once he had me in bed with a few pillows propping me up, he disappeared into the kitchen for a while, and then came back with breakfast for both of us.

He slid in between my back and the pillows, and gently pulled me into his arms so he could feed me.

"Are you hurting?"

The pain had the edges of my vision darkening, and my body responding too slow, so much that it was taking me forever to eat what he was giving me. "I'm fine," I whispered when I swallowed a bite.

"Good girl. How's breakfast?"

I couldn't taste it. "It's great," I responded in a monotone voice. "Thank you, Collin."

He kissed my shoulder and fed me another bite. "Anything for my girl."

A lone tear slipped down my cheek as I tried to be thankful that I'd made it through, and started the countdown over again.

Fourteen more days.

Chapter 5

Harlow
Present Day—Richland

AFTER THANKING THE barista for my coffee, I began walking out of the coffee shop, only to stop. I didn't want to go home yet. I didn't need to start making Collin's dinner for four more hours at least, and sitting in that house would only have me anxious and paranoid for that time.

Turning back around, I walked to one of the large chairs and sat down, ignoring the dull ache in my torso as I did. It'd been three days since the not-so-surprise negative pregnancy test, and while the bruising just got worse, the pain was getting more tolerable all the time.

Setting my cup on the table in front of me, I pulled my mini iPad from my purse and smiled to myself when I found there was still a charge. I set an alarm on it to know when to leave in case I was able to escape my reality for a little while, grabbed my coffee, and gently sat back in the chair as I tried to get into the book I'd been reading last week on my Kindle app. I had more than enough time to read during the days; that wasn't the problem. It was whether I could push away my real life enough to let myself enjoy the fairy tale.

More often than not, I ended up staring blankly at my iPad long after it had shut itself off from lack of use as I thought about whatever was going on with Collin, or my own fairy tale that I'd given up.

Like now, I realized, when I noticed my screen was black again. I didn't even know how long I'd been sitting there just staring at it. I took a deep breath in, preparing for a silent sigh out.

My breath caught in my throat when a body next to me blocked the sun, and a deep, fluid voice asked, "Why would anyone waste their time only loving someone to the moon . . ."

. . . when they could love them to the stars?

He didn't finish, and I didn't say the words out loud. But everything stopped around me for several heavy seconds. The rise and fall of my chest halted; I no longer heard the background noise, music, and voices in the coffee shop . . . All time seemed to stand still as I sat there trying to assess whether I was dreaming or not.

"Harlow Evans," he said softly, and I let out a shuddering breath as everything came filtering back in. "The last person I thought I'd see when I woke up this morning was the girl I've been waiting seven years for."

My head snapped to the left, and my soul ached when I looked at Knox Alexander for the first time in four and a half years. Time had changed him in amazing ways—and at the same time, nothing about him was different at all. Those dark eyes began to lock on mine, and I quickly looked away from them. I didn't want to see what they would tell me; I didn't want to know what they would find.

I knew I still hadn't said anything, but at the moment I couldn't even force my mouth to open, and my vision was blurring as tears filled my eyes. I'd dreamed so many times of seeing Knox again, and every time I was much more composed than I was now. But to have him there—really there—in front of me had the last four and a half years of my life flashing through my mind and wishing I could have done it all differently.

"*Not* Harlow Evans . . ." he said quietly, the pain in his voice clear as his long fingers barely trailed over my wedding ring.

My head bowed and shook back and forth. I willed the tears to stay back but wasn't able to stop them.

"Hey," he said gently, and suddenly he was crouching down next to me. His fingers went under my chin to tilt my head back. "Why are you crying? What's going on?"

"I never thought I would see you again," I managed to choke out a minute later.

His full lips tilted up in the faintest of smiles, but his eyes showed he wasn't finding anything about this amusing. "*You* thought you'd never see me again? I thought you would go back to Seattle after you graduated from Whitman. And now *you* are sitting in a coffee shop in Richland, twenty minutes from where I live, and just a few from where I work. It's safe to say, Low, that *I* thought I would never see you again."

"I've been in Richland for years," I admitted.

Knox's eyebrows rose in shock, and a mix of frustration and pain showed on his face for a second before it fell. "Years," he stated dully. "You've been here for years? Why? And why didn't I know?"

My jaw trembled as I slowly held up my left hand. Knox didn't look at it, but his dark eyes hardened. "I never graduated."

"Years," he said again. His voice held no emotion, and though it hadn't come across as a question, I nodded my head anyway. "Then it's safe to assume *he* was . . ." he trailed off.

I didn't answer, I couldn't. Because if I did, I would say things I shouldn't. That I'd made a mistake, that I'd married a monster, that I dreamed of Knox almost nightly, that I'd dreamed of *this right here*. He must have seen the answer in my eyes—known Collin was the same guy I'd chosen over Knox—because he smiled sadly at me.

"I see." My tears fell harder at his acknowledgment, and Knox cupped my cheek with his hand. "Low . . . why are you crying?"

As much as I'd longed for this moment, I couldn't let it continue. As much as I wanted to fall into Knox's arms and never leave, I needed to get away from him. This was dangerous.

"I'm sorry, I have to go." I slipped out of the side of the large chair, and he rocked back from my sudden change in position.

"Harlow, wait!"

I'd barely gotten outside when he grabbed my arm; the action caused me to automatically jerk in preparation of what would come—but the shaking never came. Other than the involuntary reaction to being grabbed, my body knew he wouldn't hurt me; my heart knew the hand holding me.

When there was nothing but silence behind me, I slowly turned to face him. His wide eyes and slack jaw told me he hadn't missed how I'd responded to him, but thankfully he didn't comment on it.

"Please don't leave," he finally whispered. "Not after I've finally found you again."

"Found me?" I whispered in confusion. As much as those words warmed something inside me, I knew he couldn't have meant them. Not after what I'd done to him. "I'm married, Knox," I unnecessarily stated what he obviously knew.

"I know." The look on his face was something I wish I could erase. "Just talk to me. Tell me about all the years I missed. Let me feed you," he said with an uneasy laugh as his eyes quickly darted over my too-thin body.

"We can't."

"Low," he pleaded, and my eyes shut so I wouldn't have to see the look in his dark eyes. The one I knew I would give anything for. "I haven't seen you or heard from you in years," he said, his voice soft. "Please."

When I opened my eyes, I kept them trained on his chest, refusing to look up at his face. My mind was at war as everything in me screamed different things. Screamed what Collin would do if he found out, screamed to tell Knox everything, but most important, screamed at me to leave.

Fall 2009—Seattle

I JUMPED OUT of my car and ran through the parking lot toward the coffee shop as I tried to escape the rain. It was pointless, though; I was still soaked by the time I reached the door. I welcomed the heat and amazing smells that hit me as soon as I was inside, and tried to brush back my wild hair sticking to my face as I walked toward the front registers.

"Low?"

I paused midstep and brushed furiously at the wet strands of hair still stubbornly clinging to my cheeks before turning to find the man that voice belonged to. I'd know that voice anywhere. That voice that moved through my body like a welcome shiver.

Knox.

A wide smile spread across my face when I saw him standing up from one of the chairs in the corner of the shop. He quickly stepped around the other chairs filled with people he'd been sitting with and walked up to grab me in a hug that seemed to last forever—and not nearly long enough. It had been almost three weeks since I'd seen him, and while I noticed the feeling of rightness that only came with being near Knox, and how it felt like I was finally whole again, I loved that it still somehow felt like we'd never been apart.

He released me enough to cup one of my cheeks in his large hand, and just stared at me for a few seconds before saying anything. "God, look at you."

I was positive I looked like a drowned rat. But with the awe in his tone, and the way his dark eyes were moving over my face, I felt like I'd never looked more beautiful.

"Well, I guess this is one way to get around only seeing each other once or twice a month."

Knox smirked. "Less than a year, and then there's nothing keeping me from you."

"We'll see if you still feel that way when the time comes," I teased, and pressed my body closer to his.

He didn't find it funny. His smirk fell and his dark eyes held mine. "I'm still waiting for you; nothing's going to change that."

"And you're still wasting your time."

His eyes danced at my words. We both knew they held no weight anymore; they hadn't for a long time. "Never."

I smiled and glanced over to where he'd been sitting; my lips fell when I did. I faintly nodded in the direction of the girl glaring at us. "Are you sure about that?"

Knox's brow furrowed, and he turned his head enough to look at the group of people he'd been with. He was rolling his eyes when he turned back to me. "Not what you think, at least not for me. She's from our sister sorority."

I tried to move away from him, but he held me close. "You don't have to lie."

"I'm not. You know I would have told you. Are you busy?"

My head jerked back at the sudden change in conversation. "No . . . I was supposed to go study with a friend, but she got sick and left school early. I was just getting coffee on my way home."

"Can you be gone a little longer?" When I just narrowed my eyes in suspicion at him, he dipped his head lower so our faces were only inches apart. "If I'm already seeing you, I'm not willing to give you up yet. Let's go next door and grab some lunch."

"You want to have lunch with me?" I said each word slowly, like I was trying to make sure I'd heard him correctly. It was rare if we did something away from my house, and even then, it was never date-ish. This would feel date-ish.

He shrugged. "I ran into you here. No harm there, right?"

I fought back a smile. I wanted to jump into his arms and tell him of course there was no harm in just having lunch, but I could feel the glare from the table he'd been sitting at. I sucked a breath through my teeth and chanced another glance at the girl. "Are you sure?"

"Yes, I'm sure," he said with a soft laugh. "I told you, there's nothing there for me. And if choosing between people I see all the time, and the girl I love . . . Low, you know I'm going to choose you. Besides, I wasn't even paying attention to them; I was thinking about you."

"Sure you were, charmer," I said teasingly.

Knox looked surprised that I didn't believe him, but the look was quickly replaced by determination as he pulled out his phone. "Let me show you what I was doing just before you walked in." Angling the phone toward me so I could see what had been pulled up, he brought the phone back to life.

I tilted my head and waited for him to explain what I was looking at as I glanced over what looked like a confirmation to an order. My gasp came less than a second before his answer.

"Setting up a delivery."

I had no doubt my smile was embarrassingly big by the time we were facing each other again. "My flowers are coming soon?"

Knox shrugged. "I don't know, are they?"

I rolled my eyes, but my smile hadn't dimmed. "Okay, I'll stay if you answer something for me." One dark eyebrow rose as he waited. "How much do you love me?"

That perfect, crooked smile flashed at me before he dropped his forehead to mine and whispered, "To the stars, Harlow. Always to the stars."

Present Day—Richland

"OKAY," I FOUND myself saying. "But it can't be long."

"That's fine, I'll take whatever time you can give me." The

hand holding my arm slid to the small of my back, and Knox turned toward the little sandwich place near the coffee shop.

"I know you got married, but why didn't you finish school?" Knox asked after we'd gotten our food and were sitting at a table in the corner of the little bakery. "I was under the impression that graduating was important to your parents."

I wrapped my arms around my waist and stared at the table for a few minutes as I tried to figure out what I could say. I knew what he was hinting at with those words . . . I knew only because my dad had told me years ago. But to let on that I knew would lead this conversation in a place it couldn't go. So what could I say about why I didn't finish school? *Collin graduated when I finished my sophomore year and refused to let me continue going to school* wasn't exactly something I could just tell people.

"Did you have a baby?" Knox asked when I took too long responding.

"No!" My eyes widened, and I looked up at him in horror before I was able to conceal it. "I just—there wasn't a point. H-he was two years ahead of me, so when he graduated and had a job lined up back here, there was no reason for him to stay there, or for us to be separated since we were getting married a few months later."

Knox sat there studying me, his dark eyes narrowed with worry.

This was a bad idea; this was such a bad idea.

He finally smirked. "You always did like older guys." His dark eyes flickered down to the food for a second. "Why don't you eat." It didn't come across as a suggestion.

I picked off the edge of my sandwich and played with the

bread as I prompted him to talk. "Tell me about you. Not finishing school and getting married is really the only thing that's been going on with me since we last talked."

I didn't miss the way his eyes didn't leave where my fingers were playing with the bread, or the way his face hardened when I turned everything around onto him. "Uh, I finished school. Went through fire academy, work for the department in Richland now."

"Really?" I asked, a genuine smile crossing my face for the first time in years.

"Yeah. Was doing that the last year of school, so I've been there awhile now. I actually just finished a shift and was grabbing coffee before I headed back to Thatch."

"That's great, Knox!"

He flashed a smile at me, and nodded at my sandwich. "Actually eat it, Harlow."

I took a bite for his benefit, and chewed slowly. "What else?"

"Keep eating," he said softly. The words sounding like a cross between a plea and command. "I'll talk if you eat."

Panic gripped at my chest when I understood the worry in his eyes. He noticed the difference in my weight. It was different for my family, watching it gradually come off. Knox was seeing it all at once, and if the way his eyes kept anxiously darting over my body was anything to judge by, it was obvious that I looked drastically different. Trying to act like I didn't have a clue about what he was seeing, or that I knew what he was doing, I rolled my eyes and took another large bite.

"There isn't much else. I work a lot; that takes up the majority of my time. I live with Graham and Deacon. They haven't changed much, either."

I laughed uneasily at the reminder of his best friends. "Ah. I'm sure those two were happy to have me out of your life."

Knox's eyes darted quickly to mine, then down to the table. A few moments of uneasy silence passed between us before he said, "They know not to mention you."

I didn't know how to respond to that. I simply said, "Oh," and tried to change the subject. I figured he wasn't married if he was living with the guys, so I asked, "Girlfriend? Fiancée?"

He laughed softly. "No. I'm not the kind of guy to let things get serious now. I can hardly even stand to see a girl more than once. For years I didn't know why that was, until I just walked into the coffee shop and saw you sitting there—and all of it finally made sense."

I didn't want to think of the other women. Focusing on his last words, I said, "Knox . . . we haven't even talked in years."

"I know, Low, trust me; I know. But I had every intention of spending the rest of my life with you. Just because you weren't waiting for me in the end, doesn't mean everything I'd been waiting for and feeling for you could just stop."

My stomach and chest tightened, and I wanted to tell him that *everything* had changed for me. My feelings for Knox had multiplied over the years. I pressed my lips into a firm line to keep myself from saying things to him that would only cause Knox and me pain, and my family possibly their lives.

My head shook slowly back and forth. "This was a mistake," I said, and started to stand, but he caught my wrist.

"I'm sorry. I'm sorry; I'll stop. Please don't leave yet."

I pulled until he released my wrist. "I'm sorry, Knox. I can't stay—"

"Are you sick?" he asked suddenly, his tone grave.

My head jerked back to look at him and my mouth opened as I stood there in confusion. "Sick? No, I just have to go."

Knox's dark eyes moved around the bakery before pleading with me. "Sit."

I shakily sat back in the chair as I tried to figure out what this pained expression on his face, and his question, could mean.

"Are you sick?" he repeated, his voice barely above a whisper. "Don't look at me like you don't know why I'm asking."

"But I—"

"Your wedding ring is barely staying on your finger. You're drowning in a shirt that looks like it's meant to cling to your body."

My heart skipped a painful beat and I fell against the back of the chair, wincing when it hit a sore spot.

Knox's observations didn't stop. "I was afraid I would break your wrist just by touching it. Your collarbones and cheekbones are sticking out way too far. You're pale, Low, and the circles under your eyes are so dark." He leaned forward to rest his hand on top of mine. "Low, are you sick?"

"No," I answered honestly, but the word came out sounding like a horrified confession as I worried about what this would lead to.

The relief that filled his dark eyes was only there for a brief second before his entire frame tightened. "Are you—do you have an eating disorder?"

I needed to stop his questions before this could continue. Hardening my eyes at the man I'd missed, loved, craved, and ached for, I stood and gritted, "I don't, but after almost five years of not seeing you, Knox, I'm glad to know you now find me repulsive."

"Harlow!" he barked as I turned and walked quickly toward the door. "Harlow, stop!" he begged when we were outside.

I didn't stop until I got to my car, and then it was only to pause to open the door—but the pause was long enough. One of Knox's arms wrapped around my waist, and I bit back a cry of pain as he turned me, his other hand coming up to cup my cheek. A motion so familiar with him that tears began stinging my eyes again as I realized I felt whole for the first time in too long. But I couldn't stand here like this with him. Someone might see, and it could get back to Collin. I started moving away, but paused when he spoke again.

"If you think anything about you could ever repulse me, you're wrong," he growled. "I am *terrified* by what I see in front of me right now. When I look at you, I can't find the feisty girl whose blue eyes held so much fire for life. I want to know what's happened to make you look like this and I want to fix it—but not once has anything close to repulsion crossed my mind." His thumb brushed against my cheek when a lone tear fell out, and when he spoke again, his voice was soft. "You're still beautiful, Harlow. And seeing you today, right now, I know I'm still as in love with you as I was four and a half years ago."

"You can't say that to me, Knox," I whispered, and looked around the parking lot to make sure no one was around. "I'm married; you can't just say the things you've said to me today. And you can't touch me anymore."

Acceptance and hurt settled over his features, and he nodded once, but his hands never moved. "Why did you start crying when you saw me?"

"I told you, I never thought I would see you again."

"That—" He paused and blew out a harsh breath. "That was not a normal reaction to have only for you to be pushing me away the way you are now. My number never changed; you could have called if you missed me that bad."

I dropped my head and bit my tongue for the umpteenth time since seeing him in the coffee shop. It would be so easy. So easy to tell him everything—and it would be hazardous on levels I couldn't even begin to comprehend.

Dipping his head down low, he spoke directly into my ear. "I'm sorry, but you were always supposed to be mine. After all this time it was hard to keep my mouth shut." He released me and took a step back, and paused for only a second before he turned and walked away from me.

I didn't look up to watch him walk away. I couldn't. This was right, this was the way it had to be—but I knew if I watched him leave me now, I would break. And for the safety of my family, I couldn't afford to break right now.

Chapter 6

Knox
Present Day—Thatch

I QUICKLY PACED the length of our living room as I replayed my entire conversation with Harlow over and over again. Part of me thought I was so tired from this last shift that I'd made the entire thing up; the rest knew there was no way it wasn't real. She was there, in front of me . . . *my* girl, *my* world. She'd looked just as beautiful as I remembered, and at the same time, she'd looked too thin and sick. She was married, and to top it all off, she'd been living just twenty minutes from me for years, and I'd been fucking clueless.

Resting my fists on my hips, I turned in tight circles as my breathing got rougher, and finally let out a loud roar of frustration.

Of course I'd expected her to get married. It'd been more than four and a half years, and she'd made it clear that she didn't choose me. I just never expected to have to know about it, or to have to see another man's ring on her finger. That fucking ridiculous, massive ring.

I was still pacing and getting more frustrated by the minute when Deacon came home sometime later and immediately went into his room, and still later when Graham got home from work. It took me at least a minute to realize that he was standing there watching me, and I finally stopped pacing long enough to stare back at him.

"Yeah?" I asked when he didn't say anything.

His gaze dropped to the floor, then narrowed when it met mine again. "There a reason you're trying to murder the carpet?"

Yes. And the thought had me pacing again as I fought with myself to only force out a simple "Nope."

Another minute later, I heard Grey ask, "What happened? Why is he pacing?"

I started to dismiss her questions, but before I could even understand my movements, I was turning around to grab her arm. With barely a nod in Jagger's direction, I pulled Grey behind me toward my room.

"Hello to you, too," she mumbled.

"What the hell?" Graham barked from the entryway, then asked Jagger, "You're just going to let him take her to his room?"

I didn't hear Jagger's response, but I'd only had Grey seated on the edge of my bed and had been pacing again for about twenty seconds before Jagger slowly walked in.

"Graham wants me in here to make sure you don't try to steal my wife from me."

Grey rolled her eyes once I stopped pacing and was facing her again, and grabbed for Jagger's hand when he sat next to her.

"Are you going to tell me why you're so weird, or do I have to guess?" Grey asked me. "And by the way, that was super rude. You could have asked me to walk; you didn't have to drag me."

"I didn't drag you," I mumbled as I ran my hands over my face. I sighed heavily and tried to talk myself out of telling her, to play everything off as another way to piss Graham off, but I needed to tell someone. "She's in Richland, Grey. I saw her."

She blinked slowly, then asked, "Who?"

"Her!"

"Oh yes, of course, *her,*" Grey scoffed, and Jagger looked away to hide the smile slowly crossing his face. "And by 'her' I can only begin to guess you mean one of the many girls you've slept with since you all finally started sleeping with girls outside of Thatch," she said in a detached voice. "Come on, Knox, how on earth am I supposed to know who you mean? Is it one of the crazy ones? You know I can't keep up with all of them."

I glanced to my door then walked quickly over to shut it. When I was back in front of them, I spoke softly. "Harlow. *Harlow* is in Richland. She lives there—she has for years."

"No way," she whispered, and her eyes widened. "Whoa, wait. We *just* talked about her! Did you already know she was there and you didn't tell me?"

"No. Are you kidding? You think you would've just now found me like this if I'd known all along?"

Grey shook her head, then smiled widely as her eyes brightened with excitement. "Well, this is great, Knox! I mean, she's in Richland; that's not far—you work there! How did you even see her?"

"I saw her when I was grabbing coffee on my way home. We talked for a little while."

"She's married," Jagger said, speaking up. It hadn't been a question, and I could hear the sympathy in his tone.

"What? No, she's—wait, how do you know?" Grey asked, then looked back to me.

I ground my teeth and looked away from them for a second, and Jagger took the opportunity to continue talking.

"Knox looks how I felt every day of the seven years that you were with Ben."

At the mention of Grey's late fiancé, I automatically glanced in her direction to make sure she was okay. He had died suddenly just days before their wedding was supposed to happen three years ago. But instead of watching her break down, as I had so many times before, she just looked at me like she understood and felt sorry for me . . . and I knew her husband was to thank for that.

Jagger, Grey, and Ben had all been best friends growing up, and Jagger had been in love with Grey forever. When Ben had died, Jagger continued to be her best friend and help her through two years of grieving until Grey realized she was in love with him, too. It had been an easy transition for them, and it was obviously the best thing for Grey. I would always be thankful to Jagger for it—as I knew Graham and Deacon were.

If anyone knew how I felt, it was Jagger. He'd waited nine years for the girl he loved, and I'd been waiting seven. The only difference was Grey had never known that Jagger loved her, and Harlow had always known how I felt about her . . . and she'd chosen someone else.

"Is she, Knox?" Grey asked, her eyebrows pinched together like she was worried about what my answer would be. "Is she married?"

"Of course she is . . ."

"Knox," she whispered, and stood to take a step toward me, but I stepped back.

"*He* is why she didn't choose me." Grey tried to take another step toward me, this time with her arms outstretched, and again I took another step back. "Don't."

"Why?"

"If you do, then I know that it really is over."

Grey's face morphed from sympathy to worry. The room was silent for a minute before she said, "She's married. It is over."

I was shaking my head before she'd gotten it all out. "You didn't see her. You don't understand."

"Knox." Now her voice was stern. "You cannot try to break up her marriage."

"I'm not, but you don't understand. She started crying as soon as she saw me, Grey, I know she—"

"I always had your back when you were waiting for her to be old enough, but this is different. You can't do this. If she started crying when she saw you, then she has her own issues she needs to sort out, and you need to stay away from her while she does." I started to talk, but she cut me off. "What are you going to do? Have an affair with her and be happy with that?"

"Grey," I snapped, but to be honest, I didn't know what my answer would have been. All I knew was that I still wanted Harlow, and she was so close.

"If she's the kind of girl who would do that, then maybe Graham and Deacon were right about her all along. Maybe you *were* just a game to her, and maybe you still are."

"No—" I began.

"Yes."

"No, Grey, it can't be a game. *I* can't be."

Grey breathed out heavily through her nose, and her gold eyes narrowed at me for a few moments before she was able to calm herself. "You even agreed with them when she ended it," she reminded me with a whisper.

My stare dropped to the floor, and my head shook slowly, but not in denial. "Seeing her today . . . it brought back everything. I remember how it felt to be near her, to talk to her, just to *have* her—have her be mine. There's no way to think that I was a game after being reminded how all that felt."

None of us said anything for a few tense moments as Grey and I stared each other down. When Grey realized I wasn't going to say anything else, a hint of sadness fell on her face and she said, "This is dangerous, Knox. She's *married*." She emphasized the last word, as if trying to make me understand the fact. As if I hadn't already thought a hundred times today about what the rings on Harlow's finger meant.

"She's broken, Grey. I could see it, I could see how unhappy she is no matter how hard she tried to hide it." Grey opened her mouth, a mix of irritation and doubt on her face, but I kept talking. "No, before you say anything, that's not something I tricked myself into seeing. I saw her as soon as I walked into the coffee shop, and couldn't stop staring at the girl who looked equally beautiful and dead."

"Knox," Grey whispered.

"She's so broken I didn't even realize it was Harlow until I was about to walk past her."

"Knox," she said a little harder, and grabbed my arm. "Even

if she is, you have to understand that it is no longer your place to try to fix her."

I looked to where Jagger was still sitting on the bed, silent as ever as he observed and thought, and gestured toward him. "You guys have to understand. I know you understand."

"No, we don't. What you have to understand is that she's married and you need to step back," Grey bit out, and without another word, she walked out of the room

Jagger's head had turned in the direction Grey left, but he wasn't looking toward the door; his eyes were far away. I was about to beg him for a different response than what his wife had given me, just to feel like I wasn't the worst kind of bastard for again wanting someone I couldn't have, but the slow shake of his head had me biting back any plea. "It was different—Grey and me," he said. "We were both grieving a death, and I never once told Grey how I felt about her, or pushed any kind of relationship on her. So when I helped her, when I was there for her every day, it was only as her best friend—not as the guy who had loved her for years."

"You can't tell me there wasn't any part of you that was doing that because you were in love with her."

"I didn't say that. I love Grey, always have, and everything I've done has been because I love her. But, for the first nine years of loving her, she thought we were *only* best friends. What I'm saying is that she never saw that side of me until two years after Ben died, and as you know, she wasn't supposed to find out when she did. If she had known that I loved her before, I wouldn't have been able to help her the way I did; I wouldn't have been able to be there for her. Harlow knows how you feel, or felt; you can't just go in there wanting to help her for any reason other than that you love her. Everything you did for Harlow since you were eighteen was because you were in love with her, and she knew it. Do you see the difference?"

I ground my teeth and took a deep breath in, but didn't respond. I did see the difference, and I also knew that he and Grey were right. That didn't mean I wanted to agree with them.

"Besides, Harlow is unhappy in her marriage, according to you. Like Grey said, those are her own issues that she needs to deal with. And with your history, she can't do that with you interfering. I know what she meant to you—trust me, I do—and I know you just found her again, but Grey's right . . . you need to step back."

I nodded, but again didn't respond. There was no way for them to understand what I had seen in Harlow today. It was more than her being unhappy. I wanted to tell Jagger how Harlow had flinched when I'd tried to stop her from leaving, how when I said she looked dead, I *actually* meant she looked like she was dying, and seemed terrified that someone would see us talking. But I knew he would think I was reaching, and I knew in the disappointed way Grey had looked at me before she'd left that she had already made up her mind on this.

Fall 2009—Seattle

"Knock-knock," a familiar voice called out as the door to Deacon's and my room opened.

"Hey!" we shouted as Grey walked in, followed by Graham. "Happy Birthday," Deacon and I called out to Grey.

"One more year until you're legal," Deacon hinted, and she laughed. "Speaking of waiting until people are legal," he continued, and shot a look in my direction.

Grey gave Deacon a weird look as she hugged me, but didn't comment on what he'd said. "Can I just say that your frat house smells so weird?"

"Lies."

"She found the body."

"That's the smell of victory," we all spoke over each other.

Grey sighed and rolled her eyes. "Boys are gross. Anyway, what are we doing tonight?"

"What do you want to do?" Graham asked. "It's your birthday, and it took me almost an hour to get Mom and Dad to let you come back with me."

"Can we go to a club?" she asked with a hopeful expression.

"No," the three of us answered at the same time.

"There aren't enough of us to protect you," I said at the same time Deacon said, "Some guy is going to kidnap you."

"Or because she's only seventeen," Graham interjected. "Anything else?"

"Um . . ." She looked around at us like she was hoping for suggestions. It was obvious that she'd been banking on us sneaking her into a club.

My phone rang, and a smile tugged at my lips when I glanced down to see Harlow's name across my screen. It had only been a few days since I'd seen her at the coffee shop, but it was physically draining to keep myself from going to her now. We'd planned for me to somehow get away from Deacon tonight so I could go see her, but then I'd found out that Graham was bringing Grey back here. I'd called Harlow earlier to tell her, but she hadn't answered. I went to tap on the screen, but suddenly my phone was ripped from my hands.

"Let me guess . . ." Graham began. "Yup! Little Miss Illegal, herself."

"The fuck. Give me my phone." I lunged for it, but he tossed it over me.

I turned around in time to see Deacon put it up to his ear. "Hello, child . . . Nope, wrong friend . . . Yeah, he's gonna be a bit busy tonight, if you get where I'm going with that. I guess you'll just have to find something to do with people your age . . . Oooh, testy." He looked at the screen and shrugged. "She hung up."

I hadn't tried to stop him because I knew there was no point; I also knew Harlow wouldn't believe anything Deacon or Graham said. But with every word he said to her, my hands had curled tighter into fists, and my breathing had gotten rougher.

"Uh, what just happened?" Grey asked, but none of us said anything or looked at her.

"Give me my phone," I demanded softly, and Deacon handed it over with a shit-eating grin.

"Anyone?" Grey tried again.

"Do you want to tell her? It'd be great to get her thoughts since they're the same age," Deacon taunted.

Nodding slowly, I switched my phone over so my dominant hand was free, and without giving Deacon a second to see what was coming, punched him as hard as I could.

"Oh my God!" Grey yelled as Graham shoved me back, and shouted, "What the fuck, Knox?"

I didn't say anything to anyone. I just walked out into the hall to call Harlow back.

"It always warms my heart to talk to one of those two," she answered with a sigh.

I hung my head and rubbed the back of my neck. "Does it even make a difference when I say 'I'm sorry' anymore?"

Harlow laughed softly. "Of course it does, but you don't need to. I know they're just worried about you and being protective. After another year, they won't have a reason to be."

I held back a sigh. One more year—then all of this would be behind us.

"Hey, do you still think you'll be able to come over tonight?"

"No, I'm sorry." I rushed to tell her why when her disappointment drifted through the phone. "Graham called earlier to let us know he was bringing Grey back with him for her birthday. They just showed up before you called. I don't know what we're doing, but she's like my sister and I never get to see her."

"Well, good! I hope you have fun!"

I knew Harlow was genuinely happy for me. She was just that kind of person, and it was impossible to miss the smile in her voice. It didn't lessen the way I physically ached to see her, though. "If it weren't for her, I'd be with you tonight," I assured her.

"I know, Knox," she said. "I should let you get back to them. Tell Grey I said happy birthday."

"I have a few minutes; tell me about your day."

"You sure?"

Considering I'd just punched one of my best friends, and I was

missing a night I'd planned on spending with Harlow? Yeah . . .
I had a few minutes. "Of course, Low."

"There's not much to tell. Went to the movies with some
friends earlier—it was okay. That's where I was when you called,
by the way. And then I came home to a beautiful bouquet of
flowers."

"Oh yeah?" I asked, and my lips twitched into a smile.

"Mm-hm. Some random person sent me a bouquet of poppies."

"Some random person, huh? Should I be worried?"

I could hear the rustling of paper through the phone, and
she sighed teasingly. "I mean, I don't think so. The note only
said 'To the stars.' I don't know why you'd need to worry about
that."

"Yeah. Not threatened by that." My smile grew. Every month,
that note had reminded Harlow I was still waiting for her. Ever
since that night earlier this year when I'd tried to convey to
Harlow just how much I loved her, the notes on her monthly
bouquet had changed. Now I never wanted that note to change.

"Thank you for my beautiful flowers," she said so softly the
words were almost lost in the random noises of the house. "And
thank you for loving me the way you do."

"Always, Low." My voice deepened as I vowed each word to her.

"You have my heart, Knox Alexander," she promised. "You
have my heart, and in a year, I will finally have you."

"You already do."

There was a pause, then her next words rushed out. "I'm about
to beg you to come see me if you keep talking to me the way
you are, but I know you need tonight. So go hang out with them
before I change my mind."

I huffed, but nodded even though she couldn't see me. "All right. I'll call you tomorrow."

She waited—she always waited, and I loved her more for it—and I could practically see the expectant look on her face and hopefulness in her blue eyes.

"I'm still waiting for you, Low."

A soft laugh followed by a sigh filled the phone. "And you're wasting your time."

"Never." The smile on my face was massive when I hung up and turned to walk back to my room. I came to a stop, and my smile abruptly fell when I found Grey standing there watching me.

"She's seventeen?" she asked, but I didn't respond. Grey jerked her head in the direction of my room. "They gave me a quick rundown. I was also eavesdropping," she said shamelessly.

I nodded absentmindedly and gestured toward the room. "I'd rather not talk about this out here."

"I think what you're doing is the most romantic thing I've ever heard of."

Her admission stopped me again, and I looked at her like I'd heard her wrong. "Romantic," I stated dully. "I'm not romantic, Grey."

"Oh, I know. But what you're doing for her . . . it's romantic. It's also the most decent thing any of you guys have ever done for a girl."

I grunted and looked away.

"Really, though. Most guys wouldn't care to wait, or they'd make the girl feel bad because she was underage. Then here you are waiting for her until she is of age, not pressuring her into anything, just being there for her until then? That's amazing, Knox. I heard you tell her you loved her . . . but I could *hear* how much you loved her. Just because Graham and Deacon don't get it doesn't mean you're doing something wrong."

Grabbing Grey up in my arms, I hugged her tight. "Thank you."

Chapter 7

Harlow
Present Day—Richland

"LOOK AT ME, Harlow."

I distractedly turned my head to face Collin, and waited for whatever speech he had prepared for me.

His eyes roamed over my hair and body before shooting back up to my face, his eyebrows pinched in frustration as he studied it. "How are you feeling?"

"I feel fine."

"Then why do you look miserable?" he growled as he started driving again, the warning in his question clear. If I didn't fix whatever he was seeing soon, it wasn't going to be a good night for me.

But it had been four days since I'd seen Knox, and the memories and dreams of him were plaguing me more than usual. Even though I'd tried to run from him, I was left struggling more than I usually did. I no longer felt like I was drowning because of Collin and this life. I'd already drowned; I was just waiting for someone to find me and bring me back to life.

That, added to the fact Collin and I were on our way to the fund-raiser, was making it nearly impossible to remember how I normally forced my smiles. I sat there trying to smile, and tried not to feel the crushing pressure like I was surrounded by deep water.

"I need you to smile, mingle, and make us look good for my dad. The mayor will be there among other people we need to kiss ass with. I'm sure I don't need to remind you that saying or doing something stupid would be completely unacceptable?"

"Of course not, Collin."

He glanced at me and flashed a quick smile before resting his hand on my thigh and giving it a small, loving squeeze. "That's my girl."

We walked in with his arm wrapped around my waist as we tried to play the role of the perfect, happy couple. I was intro-duced to some new people, but mostly socialized with couples we already knew well from years of these things. It should have been so easy to play my part, but there was something nagging at me. My body came alive within minutes of walking in to the fund-raiser. There was a charge in the air, and my entire body tingled from it. I knew it, and I knew I'd felt it before, but I couldn't place when or where.

Then everything happened and went to hell at once.

I was so focused on trying to remember this indescribable feel-ing that I forgot the mayor's wife's first name and had just gotten two fingers into the inside of my elbow because of it. Collin's fingers dug in harder and he leaned in to whisper for me not to show my pain as his dad and the mayor continued talking, and an unwelcome hand came to rest on my other arm.

My lips parted slightly as I tried to breathe through the pain from Collin's fingers, and my eyes narrowed into slits the second I recognized that the meaty hand resting on my other arm belonged to my father-in-law's coworker Ren. All of it was too much, and my mind whirled with the sensations slamming into me over and over again.

Pain, pain, pain. Breathe, I silently commanded myself. *Don't show it. Stop messing up in front of Collin. Pain—get away from creepy Ren's wandering hands! Pain. How could I have messed up something so simple? So much pain! Both of you please stop touching me!* I internally screamed, all while the party and conversations went on around us, nobody having a clue that anything could be wrong.

"There're a lot of big pockets here tonight," Collin's dad was saying to the mayor. "This will be great for the firehouse and their charity."

My head snapped up and eyes widened at the word *firehouse,* and instantly I *knew* the familiar energy in the building—the one I'd thought was lost forever. I sucked in an audible gasp when my gaze locked on dark, murderous eyes. But Knox's eyes weren't fixed on mine; they were locked on Collin's hand still digging into my arm.

Collin moved fast. Suddenly I was in his arms with his mouth on mine. His blue eyes showed me everything his words couldn't, since we had an audience.

His mom and the mayor's wife made sounds of affection, and

his dad laughed loudly. "These two; you can't take them any-where. Two and a half years in, and they're still in the honey-moon phase."

Collin pulled away and glanced back at the group to shoot them a wink. "Can you blame me for not being able to keep my hands off her?"

The mayor, Ren, and Collin's dad all laughed this time, and the women whispered while sending me knowing smiles.

"Speaking of honeymoon," the mayor's wife said with bright eyes as she leaned in toward my in-laws. "A little birdie told me that the two of you will be sneaking away for another honey-moon soon after your anniversary party in a couple of weeks."

My mother-in-law blushed through her smile. "Can you be-lieve we will have been married thirty years?"

When Collin looked at me again, the other voices faded away as he held my gaze in warning for tense seconds. His handsome face was still in place for the public as he brushed some hair back from my face and nuzzled behind my ear. "Do not test me to-night, Harlow."

My eyes darted past his shoulder to where Knox was staring at us. Even from across the room I could tell his breathing was rough, and the murderous expression he'd had a minute ago had deepened. His hands were fisted at his sides, and he was walking toward us.

As Collin found the spot at my wrist and told me not to show any pain, I pled with Knox, using only my eyes, for him to stay away. For him not to interfere with this. But he didn't stop walk-ing, and I stopped breathing as he went right past us, his head turned enough for me to see him shoot one last look at Collin.

I blew out a relieved breath and my body sagged into Collin's.

Collin kissed my neck and mumbled, "Good girl." He released me only to pull me against his side as he tried to find his way back into the now semi-heated discussion about the new chief of police in Richland. I wasn't surprised to hear the mayor hadn't been happy about an outsider taking over, either—they liked keeping their people in all the places that had any kind of power.

"Don't you look rather beautiful tonight," Ren said quietly a couple of minutes later.

I murmured what I hoped was a polite "Thank you," but stilled when he touched my bare shoulder this time.

Ren's thumb made a lazy circle, but his eyes weren't on me; he was focused on the men talking. I'd met him countless times at these types of events, and knew his reputation for being too grabby with young women, but I normally wasn't in a position for him to be able to keep touching me. And now I didn't know how to get him to stop without embarrassing Collin or his dad in front of the mayor. I glanced behind me to see Knox watching me with a mix of disgust and anger, and started panicking as Ren's hand moved down and squeezed my bicep, then started making soft circles with his meaty fingers. I tried clearing my throat near Collin's ear and hitting my knuckles against his side, but I was only aggravating him, judging by the way his breathing was slowly getting more pronounced.

Collin finally turned his head to look at me, and I knew in his eyes that if he hadn't noticed Ren's hand, his fingers would have been digging into me within seconds. His eyes flashed over to Ren's face, then back to his hand, but his calm façade never wavered. With no more than a few words, Collin excused us from the group and spun me away from Ren's grasp.

As soon as we were walking away, he spoke against the side of my head. "*Nobody* touches what is mine," he sneered, but thankfully it was clear his anger wasn't directed at me anymore. "I don't care about Ren's work relationship with my dad or his position with the city—you do not have to put up with that; do you understand? If he touches you again, find a better way to get my attention." Another few feet passed before he growled, "Tell me you understand."

"Yes. Thank you," I said.

Despite the glimpse of the Collin I'd once loved, it only ended up being that—a glimpse. Over the next forty minutes I messed up too many times, and Collin's anger with me continued to grow. I knew I could have done a better job at being the wife Collin thought I should be; I just couldn't concentrate.

I could feel Knox's eyes on me, and it was too easy to turn and find him. But I was terrified that if I looked at him, Collin would notice. Forcing myself to look away from what my soul reached for was draining and taking every ounce of focus I had. I knew I needed to get it together, I needed to start impressing Collin even; but Knox was there. *There.* As was Collin. And both were incredibly pissed-off. The only good part of the night was that Ren had already left with a girl my age.

"You know what I'm finding hilarious?" Collin asked as he pulled me away from the latest couple we'd been speaking with, his lips brushing my ear. "It seems like for the past hour I've had to convince people you love me. You're holding yourself stiff and away from me, you seem distracted and your responses are delayed, and you've barely made eye contact with me. Now tell me, Harlow, why would I have to convince all these people that my wife loves me? Better yet, why would I have to try to convince *myself* that she still does?"

I froze. In the years of going through all this, in the years of him having sex with someone who couldn't bear to look at him or take part in it, Collin had never questioned my love for him. Dread filled me, making it feel like there were hands gripping and twisting my stomach. His questioning something like this would end horribly. "Collin, don't be ridi—"

"Do not speak." His fingers dug into the inside of my forearm, and my mouth immediately popped open, a harsh breath blowing past my lips. "Don't show your pain, Harlow," he warned.

I snapped my mouth shut and tried to control my expression, but I knew I wasn't succeeding when his fingers pressed in harder.

"Do not show your pain," he gritted out—his smile never wavered.

I clenched my jaw and somehow managed to plaster a tight-lipped smile on my face.

Collin's lips ghosted along my neck. "Do you love me, Harlow?" His grip loosened enough to allow me to answer.

I loathe you with every fiber of my being. I turned my face toward his so our cheeks were touching, knowing I had to play this the right way and answer correctly. Saying something as simple as "of course I do" would set him off.

Swallowing back my hate, I glanced over Collin's shoulder to the man who owned me and shut my eyes—keeping Knox's face in my mind as I said, "It hurts me that you would even ask that." I lifted the hand that wasn't being controlled by a pressure point to brush at Collin's blond hair, and let my eyes finally meet his as I made a decision that would spare me now, and cost me later. "I lied to you earlier, and I'm so sorry I did; I didn't want to ruin tonight for you," I said with a gentle smile on my face. "I don't feel well; the last few days have been iffy for me. I've been tired and nauseous. I really think when we take the test next week, this will be it for us."

Collin's face fell and his fingers instantly released me before his blue eyes brightened, and a smile I rarely saw lit up his face. "Harlow," he breathed.

"I just didn't want to get your hopes up since we've had such a hard time getting pregnant, and like I said, I didn't want to ruin tonight. But faking loving you? Collin . . ." I let the lingering pain in my arm lace through my voice for emphasis.

He wrapped his arms around me and pressed his lips to mine briefly before dropping his forehead onto my own. "I'm sorry, I didn't know. God, baby, I want this for us so bad."

I let my lips tilt up in a smile. "Me, too."

"You really think this is it?"

"I do," I said. The lie came easily. "At least, I'm hoping it is. I just—I'm trying not to let myself get too excited yet, you know?"

"Of course. Of course I do. God, Harlow, I love you."

My eyes flashed to the side and I kept my eyes on the man across the room as I said with more passion than I'd ever shown Collin, "I love you, too."

I tried to ignore the fact that the wrong lips were on mine when my husband kissed me. I knew what I'd just done. I also knew that if given a second chance, I would do it again.

For the first time in our marriage, I'd used the one thing Collin wanted against him. I'd just spared myself a week of any more pressure points and beatings. I'd spared myself a night of unknown torture. But I knew I wouldn't be able to use this again for years to come. And I knew that when it came time to take the test next week, it would be the biggest disappointment for him, and the worst Saturday since our wedding.

There was no way to win with him. And despite the upcoming dreaded day, I didn't let on to the fact that anything was less than perfect for us right now.

"Maybe I'll see if they have a bench I can sit on in the bathroom for a few minutes. I'm feeling kind of dizzy, and I don't want to keep embarrassing you in front of all these people."

"Never, Harlow. You're not embarrassing me. Do you need me to take you home?" Collin asked; worry coated his voice.

How he could contradict his words and change from my monster to the protective, loving husband in an instant was beyond me. But I didn't buy it. Just because I'd let him believe something didn't mean I could forget what had been happening just minutes before. I sent him a smile and ran my fingers over his arm. "No. I know how important it is for you and your dad to be here tonight."

"You're important."

"If it doesn't pass soon, I'll text you and you can come get me so we can leave. If you don't hear from me, I'll come find you as soon as I'm better."

He kissed my cheek and ran his knuckles over my flat stomach. "If it's longer than ten minutes, I'm coming to get you anyway. They'll understand."

I turned and kept my head down as I moved through the crowd

so they wouldn't see the tears welling up in my eyes. Tears that for once, at a party, had nothing to do with the pain and promises of more pain later from Collin. But tears that had everything to do with the fact that Knox had seen us kiss . . . had seen me in Collin's arms.

I walked into the women's sitting room and had made it as far as the first couch before a sharp sob burst from my chest. Pressing my fist to my mouth, I tried to take deep breaths in and out while willing the tears back before they could fall.

I straightened and swallowed roughly when the door opened behind me, and prayed it wasn't my mother-in-law, or one of the other women I knew.

"You didn't tell me your last name was Doherty."

I spun around as Knox locked the door behind him, and shook my head. "No, no! You can't be here, please," I begged.

"Is anyone in there?" he asked, and nodded toward the bathroom.

"I don't know, but, Knox—"

"Low, check."

I turned and walked quickly into the bathroom. All the stall doors were open, and no one was in front of the sinks. Walking back to the sitting room, I shook my head and moved closer to him. "No, but you don't understand. It's not just because this is the women's room. Knox, if someone sees us . . . you don't understand—"

"No. I'm pretty fucking sure I do," he growled, and my head jerked back. He started closing the distance between us, and I backed into the wall. "What the hell was I seeing in there, Harlow?"

"He's my husband, Knox!" I hissed. "You knew I was married, what do you expect?"

The murderous look on his face changed to something close to disgust for a brief second. "Watching another man kiss you destroyed me, but that's not what I'm talking about, and you know it." He pressed his hands to the wall on either side of my head, and leaned close. "Harlow, I will kill him for hurting you."

My mouth fell, and it was suddenly no longer a lie. I felt dizzy now. "Wh-what? I don't . . ."

"You think I don't know what's right here?" he asked as his fingers gently ran over the inside of my elbow, and then my forearm. "And here? You think I didn't see the pain on your face?"

"You need to leave, Knox," I pled. "If anyone sees you with me, it will get back to him."

"Low, he can't—"

"He's coming to look for me if I'm not back out there in ten minutes. You don't get it." I searched his face wildly and hoped he understood the urgency in my tone. "He can *not* find you with me. He can't find out about *you*. Please, Knox."

Knox didn't blink, and didn't move. "Why was he hurting you?"

"He wasn't," I insisted, and jumped when his voice boomed in the small space.

"Bullshit, Harlow!"

"Please!"

He gently grabbed the arm Collin had been torturing all night and held it out; a growl built up in his chest before he pointed at a small, two-circled bruise. "Look!" he seethed. "It's already bruising up here, and there's a red mark down here. Stop lying to me."

"You don't understand."

"You're right. I don't understand this. I don't understand why you would marry a man who would hurt you at all, let alone in public, when I would never lay a finger on you. What else does he do to you?" he demanded.

"Nothing."

"What else does he do to you?"

"Nothing!" I cried again.

"You're going to cover for him when I've already seen more than enough? You would've rather been with some bullshit excuse for a man who hurt you, than with me? Fuck, Harlow, all I ever wanted was to love you. To take care of you. To make you my goddamn world. Why would you choose *this* over me? Why would you *continue* to choose this over me?"

"Please leave," I sobbed. "He'll come after you if he finds you near me, Knox. If he suspects anything, I-I don't know what he'll do, but I know it won't—" I cut off on another sob. "It won't be good for you."

"You're out of your damn mind if you think I'm leaving you to deal with this by yourself."

"You're not; I'm fine. I promise I'm fine, but you *have* to leave. If he did something to you, I wouldn't be able to live with myself. I bought myself a week from anything else with him, so please go."

"A week?" he asked, his face twisted in disgust. "You *bought* yourself a fucking *week*? How often does this happen?"

I nodded and choked out more sobs. "He thinks I'm pregnant. He won't touch me as long as he thinks that."

Knox's face fell. "Are you?"

"No!"

Relief washed over his features for a moment, but his expression grew hard again. "What does he do to you?"

"Please stop."

"Tell me, Harlow. I can't help you if I don't know."

"He'll kill my family if you do!" I slapped a hand over my mouth to quiet the surprised cry that left me. My eyes widened along with Knox's.

"What?"

I shook my head slowly back and forth.

"What did you just say?"

"You need to go!" I whispered harshly, and fumbled with my clutch for my phone. Fear spread through me when I saw a text from Collin before I read it.

Collin: Stuck talking with a few people I know the mayor's counting on for donations. How are you feeling?

I sighed in relief and tapped out my response.

Harlow: It's starting to pass. I'll be fine. Be out there soon.

"Low!" Knox's exasperated tone filled the room. "You're just going to start texting someone after you drop that on me?"

"I'm making sure he doesn't come looking for me!"

Knox's large hand cradled my cheek, and when he spoke again, his voice was deep and soothing. "I'm taking you from him, Low. I'm not letting you live with him; we'll go to the police—"

I started shaking. "We can't! Knox, you can't! Do you know who his dad is?"

"Of course I do. How do you think I knew what your last name was?"

"His dad will somehow make sure nothing happens to Collin, but it will get back to Collin that you were the one who reported it. Please. Promise me you won't. I'm not being dramatic when I say Collin will come after you. I can't let anything happen to you," I sobbed.

"And I can't stand back and not do anything."

Tears fell harder down my cheeks, and I moved my hands to curl them around the sides of Knox's neck; my thumbs brushed his jaw. *I love you* flitted through my mind over and over. My entire body trembled now that I was touching him again, and it would've been so easy to say those words. They were on the tip of my tongue, begging to be spoken. Instead, I said, "Knox, I need you to leave. I need you to leave, and I need you to forget what you saw."

"How can you expect me to do that?" he asked, his voice rough with emotion.

I shook my head. I couldn't answer that, because I knew that *I* couldn't do that. "I can't let you get involved in this. Just *please* listen to me. Leave this room, forget about what you saw, and forget about me," I repeated, my voice shaking with urgency.

"I can't do that," he confessed, and for the very first time I watched as wetness gathered in Knox's dark eyes. "We'll run away, something . . . anything. I told you the other day; you were always supposed to be mine. I'll do anything to keep you safe."

My jaw trembled and my head dropped. "We can't. Didn't you

hear me? He'll kill my family. If I leave, if I tell anyone . . . they're dead."

"Then he deserves to be six feet in the ground or rotting the rest of his life away in a damn cell! He's fucking sick, Harlow."

"You think I don't know that? But this is what's happening, Knox. I'm dealing with it; you need to, too."

"I refuse to *deal* with this. I refuse to *deal* with the fact that you have a husband who not only hurts you, but lets older men touch you in front of him."

My head jerked back, and it took me a few seconds to remember that he'd seen me when Ren was still there. "No. No, Collin was furious when he saw that."

Someone pushed against the door, and my entire body went rigid. We both held our breath as we watched the person put pressure against the door a few more times before giving up, but that didn't ease my fear.

"I need to go back out there."

"Let me take you away from all this," he pleaded.

"You can't." My voice was hoarse as I pulled out of his arms. "I'm sorry, I know you don't understand, but you can't. I swear to you I'm much safer staying with him than if I were to leave."

"Harlow," he groaned. His shoulders sagged in defeat as he ran his hands over his head. "I can't make you leave your husband. If you think you and your family are in danger, I won't go to the police until you give me the okay. But I'm here. After all these years I'm still here. If it ever gets to be too much, if you ever can't handle it anymore, if you ever need someone to get you away from him, then call me and I'll be there."

I hesitated before nodding.

Knox's too-perceptive eyes narrowed. "What? Do you not have my number anymore?"

I shrugged and quickly shook my head; the action contradicted my next words. "I remember it."

There was a brief pause before he asked, "Then what, Low? Are you changing your mind? Do you want to get out n—"

"No!" I said quickly. "No, I just . . . I won't be able to call you. He looks for things that I don't even have, Knox. He searches the house and my car. He goes through my phone."

"What the hell?" Knox mumbled as I continued.

"I wouldn't put it past him to check the phone bills to see if I'm hiding something. I can't risk contacting you."

Knox looked lost, like he didn't know what to do with what he knew. His head shook absentmindedly, and he blinked slowly as he stumbled over his next words. "T-then you ne—we'll—I'll think of something," he promised. "I don't know what, but I'll think of something. Jesus . . ." he whispered, and I knew he was still trying to wrap his head around it all.

"It's not worth it." I appreciated what Knox wanted to do, but he still didn't understand what Collin was capable of.

"You, and knowing that you're ali—*okay* will always be worth it." He looked around the room, then nodded toward the bathroom. "I'll hide out in there for a few minutes just in case. If anyone sees me leave, I'll take care of it. But I don't want to risk it for you if he's standing out there right now."

"Thank you."

Grabbing my hand, he turned me around and cupped my cheek as he had so many times before. "Please keep yourself safe," he said through clenched teeth. Just when I thought he was about to release me, he dipped his head down and pressed his lips to mine.

The kiss started off innocent, but built slowly until he was pressing my back against the wall and I was gripping at his clothes and pulling his body closer to mine. There were three times in the years before I met Collin that Knox kissed me. The first was a promise; the last two—just weeks before I met Collin—were frenzied and unpreventable because of the chemistry that had been surging between us for years. While this one closely resembled the last two, it was so different than any of the ones before.

It was a claiming on both our parts. I was his and he was mine. The passion that rolled between us was something I'd only imagined sharing with someone. My head dropped back when his lips moved across my jaw and down my throat, and he moved his body between my legs. My body arched off the wall, a breathy moan escaped my lips when he moved his hand up my leg under my dress to hitch it around his hip, and I brought his head up to capture his mouth again.

Still fully clothed. Only kissing. Yet I was getting more of a rush from this than I'd ever gotten from sex with Collin.

"I love you," I breathed, unable to stop the words from leaving my lips this time.

He inhaled quickly at my confession, and his mouth curved up momentarily. "To the stars, Harlow," he whispered against my lips. "Always to the stars."

We froze with our arms still wrapped around each other when someone tried the door again. Our eyes stayed locked on one another . . . our lips brushed with each ragged breath.

"You're mine," he said softly.

I smiled weakly and brushed the tips of my fingers along his jaw. "I've al—" I cut myself off, but my mind screamed, *I've always belonged to you.*

His eyes pleaded with me to continue, but I couldn't—I'd already said too much.

Knowing I didn't have long before I gave in to everything I wanted from this man, I slowly untangled myself from him, and he looked like he was going to be sick.

"I won't pretend to understand why you chose him," Knox whispered. "But that choice . . . these years . . . all of it, Harlow, it doesn't matter. I said it and I mean it: I'm here. Say the word and I'll take you away."

If only he knew how much I wanted to scream for him to do exactly that—and how I would never get the chance.

He brushed his lips against mine one last time on his way into the bathroom, and I took a minute to collect myself and breathe before unlocking the door to go back to the fund-raiser.

Whoever had been trying the door thankfully hadn't waited around, and I quickly made my way through the room. My eyes darted around as I looked for Collin or his parents . . . or anyone who might have figured out what I'd just been doing.

I found Collin on the other side of the room talking with a few people, and as soon as he saw me, he quickly excused himself and walked over to me.

"You're red; you don't look like you feel good at all. Let me take you home."

It was selfish, but I wanted him to. I didn't want Knox to have to see us together anymore. I glanced around and tried to keep a straight face. "But all these people . . ."

"It's fine, Harlow, they'll understand. Come on, let's go."

He placed his hand on the small of my back to guide me out of the building. After a few steps, I turned my head to see Knox coming out of the hall where the bathrooms were. His eyes moved quickly around the room until they landed on me. A worried expression instantly covered his face, so I sent him a small smile, hoping he understood I was safe . . . for now. He nodded once, and I faced forward again as we left the fund-raiser, and I left my heart behind.

Chapter 8

Harlow
Summer 2010—Seattle

"ARE YOU SURE you want to go all the way to Walla Walla for college, Low? What's wrong with University of Washington?" my friend Zoe asked as she messed with her hair in her bathroom mirror. "I mean, you already live in Seattle, and I just got this amazing apartment and need a roommate, so it's perfect."

"And I've never left Seattle, which makes it not so perfect," I countered. "Besides, it's only four hours away. I could've been like Hayley and gone to the East Coast."

Zoe turned to give me a horrified stare. "And I would've hated you. Come on, I already have two years at UDub under me. I know everything so you don't have to learn it the hard way."

I laughed and looked back up at the ceiling from where I was lying on her bed. "I love you, and I'm going to miss you, but I

need some space from Seattle for a while. Besides, it's already of-
ficial. I got my packet today with my dorm and all that."

If I was being honest, it was the farthest my parents could get
me to go. I wanted to stay in Seattle, but my mom had seen right
through that. *Knox.* For how hard a time they'd had with letting
Hayley go away, they sure as hell wanted me to get away from
here because of him.

My parents didn't have a problem with Knox; they just
thought I was going to miss out on life because all I wanted was
to make it to my eighteenth birthday so I could be with him. And
since that birthday was a few short months away, they thought I
wouldn't be focused on academics and all that came with being
independent.

I wasn't about to say they were right.

"Hey, does this look okay?" Zoe asked, pulling me out of my
thoughts.

I turned my head and lifted an eyebrow. "Uh, yeah? You've
been wearing it for the past couple of hours."

"I know, but I want to look comfy without looking gross, because I don't want to look like a skank."

A short laugh burst past my lips. "Wow, I didn't know all this
thought went into what you wore around me for sleepovers, Zoe.
I'm touched. Really."

"Hush your face. Okay, so don't be mad . . ." She trailed off,
and my face fell.

"Zo!"

"He just texted me—it's not like I'm gonna say no to him!"

"Who is he? And what is it you're not saying no to?" I asked
as I sat up. "I thought we were gonna veg and watch movies."

She held up her hands to stop me. "We totally will . . . *after.*

And he is—" She cut herself off and her eyes widened when there was a knock on her door. "Here. He's here. But don't worry, he knows that I have a friend here, so he brought a friend."

"Oh nice, so now I won't be a third wheel. I'll just be the pity double date."

Zoe scoffed. "It's not like that; trust me. He's just a guy I hooked up with a week ago."

"Oh my God, wait! How do I look?" I hissed as we walked into her living room.

She stopped walking long enough to give me a once-over and a thumbs-up, and then continued to the door. I barely had time to glance in the mirror near the door before she was opening it, and my breath came out in a hard rush.

Knox.

I wasn't sure if time had stopped or if we were just experiencing the most awkward silence as we stared at each other. Because even though I'd talked to him the previous day and seen him the week before, and he was now standing feet from me . . . he was standing there because Zoe had a guy coming over that she'd hooked up with.

My stomach dropped and my chest felt hollow. I hated our situation now more than I ever had. I hated even more that Zoe, my slutty friend, had had a taste of the man I loved.

Graham stepped up behind Knox and, the second his eyes landed on me, breathed a low "Shit."

That one word fit this situation so well, and I suddenly wanted to laugh, and cry, and throw up. Hopefully not the latter in front of everyone.

"Low," Knox whispered. There was a hint of a smile on his lips, but I didn't understand what could be amusing about this.

All I could manage was a nod, which was probably a good thing since I wanted to yell at Zoe that he was mine.

Graham groaned then looked over to Zoe. "You didn't say your friend was a minor."

"Wait, you guys know her?" Zoe asked.

"Something like that," Graham said with a sigh at the same time Knox tilted his head to glare at Graham and accused, "You said we were going to a party."

"Because you needed to get over this," Graham said back, and gestured to me.

"Wow, thanks," I mumbled lamely.

"And look how well that worked out for you," Knox taunted.

"Someone tell me what is going on!" Zoe said louder, and Graham finally spoke up.

"Nothing. Let's go." With another worried look between Knox and me, he grabbed for Zoe's hand and towed her back to her room. As he did, he warned, "She's still a minor, Knox."

Zoe gasped, and yelled, "Oh my God! Like, *Knox* Knox? You're *the* Knox?" just before the bedroom door slammed shut. Her next words were muffled through the walls, but I could still hear the excitement in them. "Don't have too much fun, Low!"

"*Don't!*" Graham yelled. "*Don't* have fun."

Knox and I stood there staring at each other for long moments after Graham's clear warning faded, and the tension in the room slowly changed from anger to something that always accompanied us.

"I can't believe you're here," I finally whispered, breaking the silence, and within seconds I was in his arms.

"God I've missed you," he mumbled against the top of my head.

"It's been a week," I said laughing.

"Still missed you."

"When Zoe opened the door, I thought . . . I thought you were here for her," I admitted hesitantly.

"Are you serious?" Knox released me enough to look into my eyes, and his dark ones danced. "Low, I haven't *been* with anyone since I met you."

My eyes fell to his chest, and my cheeks heated in embarrassment. "Yeah, but—"

"No buts. Harlow Evans, I have waited for you for over two years, and I have loved you every day of that time. And in a few months, you are finally going to be mine."

I couldn't help but smile even as I said, "And you've wasted your—"

He cut me off with a searing kiss—one I hadn't been expecting for another few months, and one I'd been craving since our first. His mouth never left mine as he backed me up against the wall, and I pulled him as close as our bodies would allow.

My breathing was ragged as he made a trail of openmouthed kisses and teasing bites down my neck and across my collarbone, and I had to place a hand against the wall adjacent to us in order to steady myself when he pulled my knee up around his hip. It felt like I was going to fall—but it felt like I was going to fall into Knox in a way I'd only dreamed of.

I'd never dreamed kissing could be like this, but then again, I'd only had a glimpse of kissing Knox before.

Grabbing behind my other knee, he pulled that leg up so it was wrapped around his waist too, and soon we were walking toward the couch. I had no thoughts as he sat us down, other than how much I loved him and my need to have him. After years of keeping ourselves from each other, I didn't want to stop.

I pulled back enough to look into his dark eyes and whispered, "I want to finally be yours, Knox."

A deep groan sounded in his chest, and his fingers flexed against my hips. Indecision played out on his face for countless seconds as he tried to catch his breath; and when he didn't respond, I reached for the bottom of my shirt.

"You will," he vowed, and gripped my hands to stop me. "You will be mine. But I'm trying to do this the right way, Low, and I've already done more than I should have. So please help me out tonight. Just let me kiss you."

Heat flooded my cheeks, and I suddenly couldn't make myself move.

Knox tried to kiss me again, but when he realized I was just sitting there, he sat back and looked at me with worried eyes. "What? Harlow, what just happened?"

"I want you," I whispered timidly.

He laughed huskily. "And you think I don't want you?"

I shook my head. "No, I-I do. But what if things change? I want you now, I want to be with you in that way, and what if I finally turn eighteen and something happens so that we don't want to be together anymore? What if after all this, I still never get you?"

"Babe," he said, "after how long we've waited for each other, nothing is going to happen in three months."

"You promise?"

His lips twitched into a smile. "I promise. I love you."

"To the stars?"

"Always to the stars." Knox stared at me with his dark eyes as he absentmindedly pushed loose strands of hair behind my ears. After a handful of seconds passed, he asked, "Why would anyone waste their time only loving someone to the moon when they could love them to the stars?"

My heart pounded at his question. For someone who said he wasn't a romantic, he liked to say things that suggested otherwise. "Maybe some people aren't lucky enough to know our kind of love."

Cupping his hands around my cheeks, he pulled me in for a slow kiss, then turned me so I was sitting across his lap instead of straddling him. With his mouth still pressed to mine, he laid us down on the couch and pulled my body close to his.

"You are insane to think that there would ever be a time where I wouldn't want you," he whispered against my neck. His teeth grazed against the soft flesh there before he murmured, "I'm going to marry you, Harlow Evans."

I'm pretty sure my heart stopped for a few beats before it took off faster than I'd ever felt it.

"I'm going to give you my last name," he continued, then trailed his lips back up my throat.

My fingers fisted in his hair, and my eyelids slipped shut as I pictured it. The wedding, the dress . . . the way Knox would look as I walked toward him.

"I will spend whole days making up for time we missed." His meaning wasn't lost, and my blood heated with the promise. Knox spoke his next words against my lips, making each word feel like a teasing kiss. "You'll look so beautiful with a round stomach when we decide to have kids."

My mouth curved up against his next kiss. "How many?"

"Two?"

I thought for a second then nodded. "I'm okay with two." Opening my eyes, I found him watching me with intense eyes, and I wondered if he could see it all just as clearly as I had. Placing a hand against his cheek, I asked, "Then what?"

For the next half hour, we kissed and planned out our future. For that time, everything was perfect in my world.

"CHRIST, KNOX! SHE'S still a damn minor!" Graham yelled later, waking us up.

I tried jumping off the couch, but Knox just tightened his arms around me. Ignoring Graham, he cupped my cheek and stared into my eyes for long seconds before slowly crawling over me to get off the couch.

"Do you know what her parents can do to you if she ends up pregnant?"

"Fuck, Graham, I didn't touch her!" Knox yelled at the same time I said, "My parents love him."

"Oh, so that just makes all this fine then, doesn't it?" Graham mocked my same assured tone.

"Well, we didn't do anything!" I said defensively and crossed my arms over my chest.

Graham stepped close to me and clapped slowly as he sneered, "Good for you, do you want a gold star? Whether or not you *do* anything, it doesn't change the fact that you've been stringing him on long enough with this wait-for-you bullshit, and now with you going away, you're just guaranteeing another four years of the same. He deserves a life!"

"Enough," Knox growled, and pushed Graham back.

"That's what I want for him!" I yelled. "That's all I've wanted!"

"Bullshit!" Graham yelled back. "You're like a goddamn drug. He can't go three days without you, Harlow, and he can't even touch you without risking getting arrested! If you wanted him to have an actual life, you would've left in the beginning, and you would've stayed gone."

Present Day—Richland

"HARLOW," COLLIN SAID in a worried tone.

I jerked away from where I was washing dishes, and tore my eyes from the window just above the sink. "Hmm?" As soon as I made the noise I cringed. Collin hated it when I didn't actually answer him. Normally I wouldn't have made such a careless mistake, but I was having trouble leaving my daydream . . . something that happened more and more often since seeing Knox Alexander. Shaking my head to clear my mind, I asked, "Yes?"

He'd been walking toward me and now pulled me into his arms. "Are you feeling okay? I called your name four times before you responded to me."

My stomach twisted in fear, and I quickly tried to think of any reason why I would have made him call for me more than once. "I-I-I I'm so—"

"Baby, baby. Shh," he hushed me, and rubbed a hand gently up and down my arm. "You don't have to explain yourself; I know you haven't been feeling well." The hand that had been rubbing my arm moved down so his knuckles could brush against my stomach. The reminder of my lie made me breathe easier but I felt like I was choking at the same time.

I was still buying myself time, but that time was about to run out, and who knew what would happen then.

One more day.

"Still," I began, and cleared my throat, "I should have heard you, I'm sorry. Did you want more coffee to go this morning?"

"No. I was just letting you know I was leaving for work." Collin smiled and pressed his mouth softly to mine. "Are you sure you're feeling okay?"

"Of course."

With a careful look, he finally released me, then took a few steps away before turning and walking out of the kitchen. "Don't overwork yourself today, Harlow!" he called out just before I heard the door open and shut behind him.

Which, of course, meant do everything I normally do; just don't do anything that might be harmful to the "pregnancy."

I took a deep breath and slowly released it as I tried to calm my stomach. The more I thought about the impending test, the more nauseous I felt. I needed to try to keep my mind off it like I had been doing. But you can only deep-clean your house so many times in one week.

Seven hours later, the doorbell rang twice, followed quickly by a knock. My heart stopped and my head snapped up to look at the door from where I was on my hands and knees, looking for scuff marks that I could fix on the hardwood floor.

Our doorbell never rang.

I didn't have girlfriends that I spent time with. I knew the wives and girlfriends of Collin and his father's colleagues, but

Collin made sure I didn't get so close to them that we would ever do anything together, and he'd forced me to sever ties with every friend I'd had from growing up. Friends were too risky for him, and too dangerous for me to keep around. He was worried I would tell them about our life, and I was worried Collin would *think* I'd told them. The only reason he let me see my family was that he knew they would get suspicious otherwise. But Hadley would have called if she were coming.

That left Knox.

Well, it didn't leave only Knox, but he was all I thought about and I'd dreamed of him coming to take me away so many times that in my mind at that moment . . . that left only him.

I scrambled up from the floor and hurried to the door, not bothering to stop to see what I looked like. A dozen scenarios danced through my mind of what would happen when I opened the door, and every single one of them died when I finally did and found only a man in a uniform, holding a box.

"Package for Doherty?"

"Oh. Uh, yeah. Yes, that's us." I was so disappointed that I didn't remember until after I'd signed for the package and the man was walking back to his truck that we also never got packages.

My parents never sent anything. If they wanted me to have something, they used that as an excuse to come see their "favorite son-in-law." If Collin ever ordered anything, it was sent to his office. And I'd never been allowed to order things; Collin just had me go to the store to get it. I always figured it was because he didn't trust me with strange men showing up at our home to drop it off.

My eyebrows rose in surprise when I saw it was addressed to me, then pinched in confusion when I looked at the sender.

Sender: Tothe
92960 Stars Way
Thatch, WA

"Tothe?" I whispered the unfamiliar surname out loud, then slowly walked inside and shut the door as I looked at the address, and froze. Thatch . . . it was from Thatch. Where Knox lived.

The name and street, everything finally made sense, and I couldn't run to the kitchen fast enough to get a knife to open up the box in my hands.

To the stars. The closest star was the sun, and it was 92,960,000 miles away. Knox had told me that years ago, and it was a ridiculously large number I had never forgotten.

My hands shook as I sliced open the tape with a knife I'd grabbed from the block, and even though Collin had never once come home early from work in the years we'd been married, I kept looking over my shoulder in fear that he would barge through the door at any moment. Looking back at the box when I had it opened, my excitement turned to confusion, then dread when I pulled out a cell phone and charger covered in bubble wrap.

I powered the phone on once I had it uncovered, and after waiting for a minute, saw that the only things on the main screen were the texting and call apps. Despite the fear creeping through my body, my lips curved up when I saw that the sole contact on the phone was Knox. I don't know how long I stood there chewing on my bottom lip and staring at his name, but my shaking only increased by the time I finally tapped down on it.

It rang and rang, and finally on the fifth ring it cut off, but there was no answer and no voice mail.

"Knox?" I whispered.

"Jesus, Low," he breathed out in relief. "I kept wondering if he would get the phone before you, but I couldn't think of any other way to get it to you. I thought if I took it there someone would see me and say something to him, and then he would—"

"Knox, stop!" I said, cutting him off. "Why did you send me a phone, and how do you know where I live?"

"I told you I would think of something—this was it—and it's disturbing the things you can find on Google," he said, then blew out a heavy breath. "How are you?"

I covered my face with a shaking hand; he'd asked how I was doing as if he hadn't just put both of us in danger. "Knox, no, that's not—I *know* what this is. I meant *why* is it here? *Why* would you risk sending me this? Didn't you hear me when I told you that he searches *everywhere* for *anything*?"

"Because you need a way to be able to call for help—whether that's me or someone else. Put other numbers in there, I don't care. Just hide it somewhere he won't look for it, and use it if you need help. I need to know that you're not alone there with no way to let someone know that it's going too far when you're afraid to use your own phone or even call the cops."

"But this is dangerous, Knox! You just put your life in danger, too," I said through clenched teeth. Why couldn't he understand that?

"Letting you live with that man is dangerous, Harlow! If you can make me watch you walk away with that bastard, then you can let me do this. *I* need this, too." After a few seconds he said,

"It hasn't even been a week, but knowing what you live with, this week has felt longer and more exhausting than a year. And knowing you have this phone gives me the smallest peace of mind. Please, just . . . please."

I shook my head slowly, but whispered, "Okay."

He let out a sigh of relief. "Thank you. Now how are you?" he asked again. "Has anything happened this week?"

"No. I told you, he thinks I'm pregnant."

"And you bought yourself a week, which is bullshit and is also about to be over. What happens when he finds out you're not?"

My stomach churned. "It doesn't matter."

There was a pause, then in a low tone he demanded, "When is that week up?"

Tomorrow, I thought miserably. "It doesn't matter," I repeated.

"Harlow," he whispered. The raw pain and fear in his voice shattered me, but I couldn't do this.

"Thank you for this phone. This stupid, dangerous phone," I said, and laughed lamely. "I will find a place to hide it for when Collin is home, and when I can, I will let you know that I am okay. But, Knox . . ." I trailed off and worried my lip as I tried to figure out how to word what I needed to say. "Unless the day comes where I'm ready for you to take me away, I won't tell you what goes on in this house."

"Low—"

"Trust me, I am doing this for you!" I sobbed, cutting him off.

There was a long, heavy silence, interrupted only by my hushed cries. "Okay. Okay, then I'll wait for that day."

"Thank you."

The sound of a loud firehouse bell filled the phone, and Knox swore. "I need to go. I love you, Harlow. I always have."

The call ended before I could respond, but I wasn't sure what my response would have been anyway. The *I love you* that had slipped out the night of the fund-raiser came out so easily—as if my soul had said it for me. Now I was afraid to let my soul free. If I did, I wasn't sure I would be able to keep myself safe in this house anymore, because my heart, my soul . . . my *everything* was reaching for the man I could never have again.

I slid down to the floor with the secret phone still in my hand, and cried for the love I'd thrown away, as I had every day for the last two and a half years.

When my tears had run dry, I slowly looked over to the clock on the stove, and scrambled to get up. Collin was going to be home in an hour, and I still needed to shower, figure out dinner, and get rid of everything that was currently sitting on the kitchen island.

I made a quick call to a restaurant to place an order, then took off through the house, glad that I'd cleaned everything obsessively all week, since I didn't have time for it now, and ran to take a shower. Once I was clean and dried, I threw my hair up, put on a little bit of makeup and clean clothes so Collin wouldn't think I'd been in the same thing all day, then ran back to the kitchen to grab up everything on the counter before leaving the house.

I drove to the restaurant to pick up the food, ditched the box that the secret phone had been delivered in in the dumpsters behind the building, and headed back home with just minutes to spare. Once there, I grabbed a couple of Ziploc bags and went into the backyard—the only place I thought Collin wouldn't think of—and looked around for a spot to hide what now suddenly seemed like my most valuable possession.

I hated gardening, probably because I was horrible at it, and Collin laughed if anyone ever mentioned plants and flowers around me. I killed everything I tried to grow here because I'd grown up with so much rain and wasn't used to all the sunshine, so we had a landscaping crew to make it look as amazing as it did. And as far as I knew, whenever Collin went tearing through the house and cars looking for birth control, "hidden" credit cards, or whatever else he thought I was hiding from him, he'd never once looked in the garden.

Choosing one of the large, potted plants up on the porch, I pushed aside the annoying amount of greenery coming out of it and played with the soil inside, judging where and how deep I needed the phone to go. After making a little hole, I sent Knox a message, powered down the phone, double-bagged and buried it, then went inside to get any remaining soil off my hands.

I looked over at the clock as I finished drying my hands, and exhaled in relief. Collin would be home in two minutes . . . I'd done it. I had all the food set out and had just finished putting drinks on the table when I heard the key in the lock and Collin walked in.

"Harlow?" he called out in excitement.

"In here," I answered, and held back an eye roll. Of course I was in the kitchen. I was always in the kitchen when he came home from work. I was just caught off guard by his tone.

Collin rounded the corner and stopped short when he saw the takeout on the table. "Chinese?"

"Um, I fell asleep. I just . . . I got tired, and I crashed. The next thing I knew it was too late to make dinner, and I'm sorry."

He closed the distance between us and wrapped his arms tightly around me. "Hey, it's okay! It's okay. I'm sure you're tired, and you haven't been feeling well. This is great. Chinese sounds perfect."

Collin couldn't stop smiling, and it was scaring me so much that I was shaking. Collin only smiled like this on Saturday mornings before I took the test, when we were out with other people, or after he'd finished giving me a punishment and was trying to make up for it. He'd been extremely gentle and somewhat caring all week, but he hadn't been like this.

"H-how was work?"

"Fine," he responded offhandedly. "I decided I don't want to wait. What do you say?"

My eyebrows rose in confusion. "What? What aren't we waiting for?"

"Tomorrow morning!" He said the words like I should have already known what we were talking about. "This is all I think about at work, and it's driving me crazy to wait. I have to know."

My face and stomach fell. "Um, but—"

"What difference is a night going to make?"

"B-but it *is* evening, and . . . and . . . and you shouldn't take the tests in the evening. They say on the box to take them first thing in the morning, right? Didn't you tell me that? That's why I take them after I wake up." I was going to be sick. I hadn't eaten once today, but it felt like I was going to lose the imaginary contents of my stomach.

Collin's smile vanished just as suddenly as he stepped away from me. "Why are you trying to put this off, Harlow?" he asked darkly.

"I'm not!" I tried to assure him, but judging by the way his breaths were slowly getting rougher, I wasn't succeeding. I scrambled to think of anything to say, and thought back to what

I'd said to him while we were dancing at the fund-raiser for the firehouse. "I'm just scared! I've thought that this was it, but what if it's not? What if I've gotten both our hopes up? I told you that I was worried about that. This test has been looming over my head and terrifying me, because what if I let you down again? I *hate* letting you down, Collin!" I choked out.

I didn't have to fake the fear, the shaking, or the tears. All of it was very real. Letting Collin down was the last thing I wanted to do, just not for the reasons he thought.

The loving Collin was back as if a light switch had been thrown, and once again he wrapped me tightly in his arms. "Why didn't you tell me it was this bad? I would've done anything to let you know that no matter what, I love you, and we're going to get through this. No result on a test is going to change what I feel for you, baby. But that's even more of a reason to just do it now; then you won't have to lose sleep tonight worrying. Let's just do it."

"Collin, please don't—"

"Harlow," he snapped, then collected himself again. "We're doing the test. Now."

Gripping my wrist in his hand, he led me back to our bathroom and bent down to get a test. The tears began forming once the foil-wrapped stick was in my hand, but I kept my eyes away from him so he wouldn't see them. I'd thought I still had time. I was wrong. I suddenly wanted Knox's phone. I was wondering why I hadn't let him take me away, and why I knew even still that I wouldn't.

Collin took the stick like he always did and set it on the counter before pulling me into his arms to wait. A couple of minutes later his breathing stopped, and I squeezed my eyes shut and braced myself.

"Harlow!" he shouted, and my eyes shot open to look at the stick.

"What?" I choked out, and gripped the counter when it felt like I was going to faint. There were two lines instead of the normal one.

Collin turned me so I was facing him, and pulled me close to press his mouth to mine, and I cried through the kiss. I tried to play off the tears as something happy, but all I could think was that my world was crashing down around me, and I had already ruined this baby's life by letting it have Collin as a father.

Chapter 9

Knox
Present Day—Richland

AS SOON AS we got back to the firehouse and got our stuff ready for the next call, I headed back to my room to relax for as long as possible. I knew it was how the job went, but given the situation, I hated that I'd had to hang up on Harlow. She'd barely come back into my life, but I knew each time I spoke to her that it could be the last. Grabbing up my phone, I saw there was a message from her, and couldn't open it fast enough.

Harlow: To the stars . . .

My mouth twitched into a smile as I stared at her words, and for a few seconds it felt like I was nineteen again as I tapped out a response. But I wasn't. And the girl sending me that message was married to an abusive prick.

Knox: Always

As soon as I pushed SEND, I put my phone on the end table and fell onto my bed to try to relax until our next call. But relaxing didn't come easy these days, and soon my body was tense and I was crossing my arms over my chest to keep them from shaking. All I could see was the way Collin's fingers dug into her arm, and the marks that were already bruising. I kept seeing flashes of how thin Harlow was now. She looked sick, and after seeing the way her husband treated her in public—and hearing that her family was in danger—it wasn't hard to see why. I needed to help her; I needed to save her. But I couldn't do that if she wouldn't let me. I couldn't force my way into her marriage. And then all I could think about was the fact that she'd chosen him over me.

The only thing I'd ever done to her was ask her to wait.

Summer 2010—Seattle

"HOW BIG DO you think they are?"

I slowly cracked open my eyes, and glanced over to where Harlow was lying next to me on the blanket. She was leaving for college in a couple of days. This was my last chance to be with her until she finally turned eighteen. My last chance to remind her of what she had waiting for her back home. She might not understand why I was about to do what I'd promised to do over the next few months . . . but hopefully one day she would realize it was all for her. Everything always had been.

We'd been out at a secluded spot for hours, and when just kissing hadn't been enough, I'd rolled away from her and started counting the days until her birthday, over and over again to calm down. But her question about how big something was wasn't helping.

"Hmm?"

Harlow gestured toward the sky with her eyes, then moved her body so she could face it. "How big do you think the stars are? They're so far away, but they look so close. And if you said the closest star is the sun, then I want to know how big the others are."

"I don't know, Low."

She elbowed my side and rolled back over so she was leaning over me. "You said you got an A in astronomy."

I laughed and brushed away the hair hanging in front of her face. "I only paid attention in that class because it had to do with stars, which makes me think of you."

She didn't respond, just continued to look at me expectantly.

"I don't know how big they are, but I know they vary. Some are really small, and some are bigger than the sun."

Harlow's head jerked back, and she looked up at the sky again. "Seriously?"

"Seriously," I confirmed. "A lot bigger."

After looking at the night sky for a few more seconds, she brought her face back in front of mine. The serious look on her face caught me off guard, but before I could ask what was wrong, she said, "I can't begin to imagine how far away they are if they look that small in comparison to the sun, and some are bigger. And you love me to them."

It wasn't a question, but I nodded anyway. "I do."

"The years, my boyfriend and your girlfriend . . . how has it not all been too much?"

It blew my mind that after all this time she still didn't understand exactly what she meant to me. "I knew within days of meeting you that I wanted you for the rest of my life. Waiting a few years isn't a lot compared to what I'll have with you after. The others? They were distractions to help get us here, and you and I both know they were bad ones. Otherwise the calls would've stopped and we would've grown apart—and that never happened. You said some people aren't lucky enough to know our kind of love. For a lot of people, all that would've been too much. For us, it was just part of our story."

Harlow's blue eyes widened in awe, and for a few seconds, she just stared at me. "You . . .." She trailed off and shook her head. "You are such a charmer, Knox Alexander; always have been. Are you this romantic with every other girl?"

A short laugh burst from my chest. "Romantic," I said, deadpan.

"Yes."

I sucked in air through my teeth and shook my head. "Low, I've told you, I'm the opposite of romantic."

She lowered her body onto mine and leaned close enough that her lips brushed against mine when she spoke. "I want to love you to the stars? It was just part of our story?"

I caught her mouth for a lingering kiss before saying, "But that's all true."

"Romantic."

"Then it's only you," I promised. "No one gets this side of me; no one else ever has."

Just as she was leaning in for another kiss, she jolted and her eyes widened.

"What's wrong?" I asked when she didn't say anything or move.

"I think . . ."

"What?"

"Did a bird just poop on my head?" she asked in a horrified voice.

I laughed loudly, and looked at her like she'd lost it. "In the middle of the night? I doubt it." Still laughing, I rolled us over and pressed my body closer to hers. As I brought my mouth back down to hers, I felt the rain start falling against the back of my neck. I let out a sigh against her lips and said, "And that would be your bird."

"No, no!" Harlow scrambled out from under me and off the blanket, and tried to take off in the direction of my truck, but I was up and after her within seconds.

I hooked an arm around her waist before she could get far, and swung her body back against mine.

"Knox!" she screamed through her laughs as she tried to get away from me. "We need to get back to the truck!"

"What's a little rain when you're from Seattle?"

"Because I always look awful when I see you, and I actually tried to look nice this time!" She giggled and tried to pull away again, but stopped when I pressed her back to my chest.

"You wanted romantic," I whispered into her ear, and tightened my arm around her waist. I played with the sliver of skin exposed on her stomach, and smiled when she shivered against me. Taking the loose collar of her shirt in my other hand, I pulled until it fell down her arm, and moved my mouth in a line across her shoulder. "Dance with me."

Harlow turned her head slowly toward mine, and our eyes locked for heated seconds as I swayed us back and forth. An audible exhale blew past her lips when I traced the bridge of my nose along her jaw and trailed the tips of my fingers up her stomach, across her chest, and down her arms. Grabbing her hands in mine, I turned her around so we were facing each other, and pulled her close again as I resumed the slow dance.

I'd played this out differently in my head when I'd stopped her from running back to my truck. I'd thought of having fun with the dance and making her laugh in that way that always got to me. But this . . . with our slow movements in the pouring rain with the girl I'd waited years for . . . I wouldn't want it any other way.

Drops of rain raced down her face and dripped off her nose and lips, and I watched as her breathing grew heavier and her eyes moved over my face and down to my chest. I'd never seen her look more beautiful than she did in that moment.

I'd waited years for her, and that time of waiting was almost up, but somehow it still felt like I'd never been *waiting*. It felt like I'd had her all this time. Like I'd spent the past two years loving her and making her mine in a completely different way than what I knew we were both craving.

Harlow unwound her arms from me and moved her hands across my rain-soaked shirt while her eyes watched her fingers in fascination. With a slowness that both drove me crazy and gave me more time to remind myself that I should stop her, she moved her hands inside my shirt, and let one hand press against my stomach while the other gripped the top of my jeans.

I should stop this. I should grab the blanket, and walk her back to the truck right now. She needs to know that she affects me more than she realizes.

My will to stay away from her had already been weak when I first met her, and had only weakened every time I'd seen her— tonight and the night in her friend's apartment were proof. Now I wasn't sure if I had any left at all.

"Knox," Harlow began, her voice barely audible above the rain.

"We should go," I said, cutting her off.

Her wide eyes met mine, and her head shook faintly. And god- damn if that wasn't the exact response I did and didn't want.

I crushed my mouth to hers so fast she gasped in surprise, and I used the movement to slide my tongue against hers. She met my kiss greedily as her fingers curled against my abdomen; but suddenly they were gone, and before I could stop her, she pulled her shirt over her head and pressed her body and mouth back against mine.

I instinctively put my hands around her waist to push her back, but the feel of her slick skin beneath my fingers had a growl building in my chest, and soon I'd forgotten every reason why I'd needed us to stop.

Grabbing her up in my arms, I walked her back the few feet to the now-soaked blanket and laid her down. I wanted to study every inch of her exposed skin—*later*. I rested my body on top of hers, but propped myself back up to tear off my shirt when she began pulling at it. She captured my mouth with hers as soon as I was lying on top of her again, and I slid my hand up her leg until I got to her knee, and curled it around my hip as I began moving against her.

Harlow broke away from the kiss and dropped her head back on the blanket, and the sexiest noise I've ever heard escaped her lips when I rocked against her again. I would've done anything in that moment if she would make that sound again.

Releasing her knee, I slowly slid my hand up her thigh and pushed up the material of the skirt she was wearing until it was bunched around her hips. I pressed my mouth to the swell of her breasts, and gently bit down as I trailed my fingers to the inside of her thighs.

"Knox, please," she whimpered just before I touched her.

And that plea, those two words I'd fantasized about for years and were finally hearing, was what snapped me back.

"Fuck," I groaned against her skin, and righted her skirt. "Fuck. I can't," I said through harsh breaths. Everything in me was roaring with the need to taste of her, but I knew I couldn't. This night would end up meaning a lot more than it was ever supposed to if I let myself continue. "As much as I want you right here, and right now, I will hate myself later for it if I don't do this the right way."

"It's a few months, Knox, it doesn't matter to me!"

"It should, because nothing has ever been as important to me." Shaking my head, I pushed myself away from her and had to drop my head back so I wasn't looking at her anymore. After taking a minute to gather myself, I looked directly into her eyes. "I've waited for you, Harlow Evans, and I will *continue* to wait for you until you're eighteen."

A sharp breath burst from her, and I could see the hurt in her eyes, but she tried to cover it with a teasing smile on her face. "I can't try to change your mind when you say things like that." Cupping my face in her hands, she pulled me down to kiss me softly. "I will never love anyone the way I love you. But you better understand that in three months there's no more running away from me. You're mine after that."

I smirked. She had no idea.

Present Day—Richland

THE SHRILL SOUND of a bell jerked me awake. I didn't know how long I'd been asleep, but in the two seconds it took for me to realize what was happening and fly off my bed and out of the room, I'd already noticed it was dark outside, and I hadn't moved from the rigid position I'd fallen asleep in. My body ached as I ran to the bay, but soon the adrenaline that always pumped through my veins had me forgetting about the stiff muscles, and I was shaking for a different reason than I had been when I'd gone to sleep. There was a house fire that was quickly spreading to the dwelling next to it; these kinds of calls were what I lived for, were why I became a firefighter in the first place. Being there for EMS to help people who were hurt, yes, any day. Helping old women get their cats out of trees, yeah, it actually happened. Small fires, of course, were the majority of our calls, and were just as important as the freaking cats in the damn trees. But huge house and structure fires, judging by the excited energy that rolled through the truck as we sped through town, were why we were all here.

We'd barely pulled up and started jumping off the truck when a teenage girl in nothing but an oversize T-shirt came running up to us, screaming, "She's still in there! Please, you have to get her! I can't believe I did this," she murmured.

I didn't have time to ask about that last statement but knew we'd need to talk to her after. "Who?" I yelled over the noise of the roaring fire and other members of my crew.

"Shit, shit, shit. Natalie! The girl I'm babysitting, she's only three! I swear I didn't know anything would happen. We fell asleep. The candles!"

She was pulling at her hair and obviously panicking; her breathing was shallow when she wasn't swearing over and over again. I grabbed her arm and pushed her back a few steps toward my sergeant as I quickly asked, "Where was she when you last saw her?"

"Sleeping in her room. We tried to go to her window, but the fire was too big there!"

"Where is that?"

"Th-th-the very back of the house on the first floor! Last room on the hall!"

I was already running toward the house before she'd finished telling me. Our rapid conversation had barely lasted a minute, but that minute still could've been too long. The fire was too big—most of it near the back of the house where the girl's room supposedly was. The smoke alone had been doing damage the whole time.

"Natalie!" I yelled as I rushed into the house with another firefighter, Pete, right behind me, echoing her name.

"Natalie, call out to me if you can hear me!" I yelled again, even though I wasn't near the rear of the house. The front was covered with smoke and it was hard to see, but there was a possibility she'd gotten scared and tried to run from the fire.

We slowed as the smoke thickened and flames licked at the walls and doorways of the hall we were going down, but we never stopped calling out her name. With only a second to assess the flames coming into the hall from the room where I bet the fire had started, Pete and I barreled through and came to a closed door.

"Natalie! If you can hear me, back away from the door!" Pete roared only seconds before he forced the door open.

The back wall of the room was covered in flames, the rest of the room was filled with smoke, and there was no child on the unmade bed.

"Natalie?" I called out, and crouched low to the ground.

I'd only gone a few paces before my flashlight went across a pair of eyes looking back at me from under the bed.

"Natalie, I'm a firefighter, I'm here to help you!" I shouted as I crawled toward the bed. "Can you crawl out to me?"

Seconds passed before she started coming toward me, and by the time she was out from under the bed, I had made it over to her. I sat up, grabbed her up into my arms, and took off out of the room at the same time I put an oxygen mask over her face. Pete reached for my shoulder just as I slid to a stop in the hallway— I'd forgotten about the fire that separated us from the other side. There was still a sliver of space left that the fire wasn't touching, but I was now holding a little girl wearing only a nightgown and holding a small blanket.

I moved the mask away for a few seconds as she coughed, then gave it back when she was done. She tried to move away from the mask and cried out for her mom. "I've got you," I promised near the top of her head. "We're going to get you out of here, and then we're going to get you to your mom, I promise." Glancing at Pete as he spoke into his radio, I said, "Get the comforter off her bed."

Natalie turned her blackened, tear-streaked face on me, and though her bottom lip continued to tremble violently, it was obvious she was trying to put on a brave face. I held up the mask and she moved toward it, so I offered her a reassuring smile.

"You're brave, Natalie, huh?"

She nodded, but didn't try to speak.

"Can you trust us for a few minutes?"

Again, she nodded without any hesitation.

I set her down when Pete came back, and spoke as quickly as I could while trying to keep my tone calm for the girl's sake. "We're going to wrap this around you, and I want you to squeeze your eyes real tight when we do. When I pick you back up, I want you to pretend that you're flying, okay?"

Behind the mask, I got a hint of a smile, and I was going to take that as approval, because we didn't have any more time to waste. Wrapping the comforter so there wasn't a part of her showing, I yelled for Natalie to close her eyes and get ready to fly, then followed Pete through the fire. We didn't stop running, but Pete slowed to go behind us, and I knew he was making sure that the comforter had made it through without catching.

We passed the guys with the hose just as they were coming into the house, and as soon as we were a good distance outside, I set Natalie down and ripped the comforter off her. I brushed the hair off her blackened face, and smiled when I realized she was still squeezing her eyes shut.

I grabbed the oxygen mask again and said, "You can open your eyes, brave girl."

She cracked them open before letting them widen, and greedily took the mask from me with the hand that wasn't holding her blanket. "I flew," she said matter-of-factly before she put it to her face.

Pete came up behind me and held a hand up for her. "That was some great flying, little girl!"

Natalie slapped at his hand with her blanket-covered one.

"Natalie!" the babysitter screamed as she ran toward us. "Oh my God, Natalie!"

On some unknown instinct, I grabbed Natalie into my arms before the babysitter could get to her, and stood.

She looked at me with a frenzied expression. "Please, let me hold her."

"Have you spoken to anyone about how the fire started?"

"Y-yes, I just finished. *Please* let me hold her."

"She needs to be looked over by EMS," I responded, just so Natalie wouldn't have to go back to her, and began walking over to one of the trucks.

"Parents are on their way here," Sergeant murmured as we passed him, then followed us. He quickly became enamored with the brave three-year-old, and stood there talking with her as she told him about how she flew in the dark while the EMTs looked her over.

"Is she going to be okay?" the babysitter asked, and tried to get into the truck, but I shot an arm out in front of her. "W-we didn't mean to! I had no idea what would happen. I thought the candles were far enough from the curtains."

"We?" I asked in a dangerously low tone.

She looked at my sergeant, then back to me, and after her mouth opened and shut a few times, she stuttered, "M-m-my boyfriend came over. We used the guest room next to Natalie's room; I lit a bu— A few candles. Some were on the window seat, and there are long curtains there, but I thought they were far enough away, I swear, I thought they were!"

I nodded slowly and shrugged. "Well, accidents like this can happen if you're not careful." Relief started washing over her features at my reaction to what she'd been telling me, but quickly left when I leveled a glare at her and asked, "What I want to know is, why you didn't grab Natalie on your way out. You said you tried to go to her window from the *outside,* but if the fire started in the room next to Natalie's, then why wouldn't you have just grabbed her before you ran out?"

"Alexander," Sergeant warned, but I didn't stop glaring at the teenage girl in front of me, or waiting for a response.

"Because it got too big," she said too quickly, and her eyes darted everywhere except to look at me.

"No, you could've easily gotten her. Try again. Why didn't you grab her?"

She swallowed roughly a couple of times, and her body seemed to crumble. "We left the room to get ice cream, and then never went back in there because he wanted . . . because I—" She started sobbing and slapped a hand over her mouth. "I didn't know it would happen!"

"So you didn't fall asleep then?"

"What?" she asked with wide eyes.

"Earlier, you said you fell asleep. Are you saying that didn't happen?"

"N-no."

I watched as she looked all around, her shoulders jerking with silent sobs. "Are you going to arrest me?"

I huffed. "No, I'm not a cop. I'm just not letting you near that little girl, and I wanted the real story because the first one didn't make sense. Where's your boyfriend anyway?"

Her eyes got impossibly wider with fear, but before she could make up some other bullshit excuse, she shrugged like she was exhausted and said, "He was afraid he was going to get in trouble.

He ran as soon as your truck started coming down the street."

"Well, he sounds great. Some advice: dump him, and stay away from me for the rest of the night."

"Alexander," Sergeant said again in an annoyed tone.

"I'm done," I responded, and turned back to the truck to find the EMTs finishing up with Natalie; her smile widened when she saw me. "Superman!"

I barked out a laugh. "Superman? Is that who I am?"

"Yes, because you can fly," she responded, as if it were old news.

I sat down near where she was sitting on the stretcher and made a face. "But I don't have a cape," I said lamely. "Superman has a cape."

Natalie looked like I'd just given her the worst news in the world, but then gasped and held up the blanket I'd seen her gripping earlier—a blanket covered in stars. "Here!"

I gently took the blanket from her, and couldn't stop the smile in response to hers. "But this is your cape; it helped you fly."

"Only because you fly," she whispered, like we were sharing a deep secret.

Most of her face had been cleaned, and I couldn't stop smiling at the brave, dimpled girl who thought I was Superman and wanted to give me her starry blanket. "I think you should keep this." Natalie's face fell, so I quickly continued. "That way you can remember the night you got to fly with Superman. Besides, it looks like it's a special blanket."

"Cape!" she corrected with a stern look.

"Cape," I amended.

She took the blanket back and ran her tiny fingers across it a few times before admitting, "The stars kept me safe until you came to save me." She poked a few of the stars on the pattern as she spoke. Without waiting for me to ask what she meant, she gave me a shy look, slowly placed the blanket around her mouth and nose, and took a few exaggerated breaths.

"That was a very smart thing to do."

Natalie nodded and removed the blanket, then looked up toward the night sky, which was blocked by what little remained of the fire and the dark smoke. "Do you like stars, Superman?"

My lips twitched into a smile. "The stars and I are old friends."

She gasped excitedly and asked, "You're friends? What do they say to you?"

Without missing a beat I said, "That you're the bravest little girl."

"I am," she responded seriously, and patted my arm with her tiny hand; her head was still tilted back in a vain attempt to see the stars. "And you're my bravest Superman."

Chapter 10

Harlow
Summer 2010—Walla Walla

I STARED AT my phone for a few seconds once it stopped spinning, then put my fingers on the screen and gave it another spin.

"Just call him," I whispered to my empty dorm room for probably the twentieth time this afternoon. "He'll answer this time . . ." *He has to.* I thought the last words to myself, unable to voice them.

Slamming my hand down on the phone, I brought the screen to life and tapped on it a few times until it was dialing Knox. The small pieces of my heart that had been cracking over the past month broke off as the phone continued to ring.

When his voice mail began, I hung up without leaving a message.

I'd only been gone from Seattle for a month, and already it

felt as if I'd lost him. It had felt like that within the first two weeks. He hadn't answered any of my calls, and had only called me twice. They had been short conversations, of him asking if I was having fun, and pushing me to go have more fun. "Go experience everything you can," he'd said before the last call had ended.

For the first time in more than two years, he hadn't told me he was waiting for me. The only hope I'd clung to was his parting phrase of "To the stars, Low."

His few texts each week didn't seem like the guy who was always dying to talk to me. None of it was like Knox at all, and I'd cried myself to sleep every night since leaving Seattle—much to my roommate's frustration.

She just didn't understand—not that I'd attempted to explain it to her, since she wasn't what you would call friendly—that it felt like I was losing what I knew would be the greatest love of my life. It didn't matter if I wasn't even eighteen yet, and it didn't matter if I'd never been allowed to be with Knox.

It's impossible to find the other half of your soul and not recognize it for what it is. So how do you explain to someone that the other half of your soul is pulling away? How do I explain it to myself?

Knox's texts just kept prompting me to go have fun . . . to live it up. I didn't *want* to live it up without him. When he finally did text me I didn't want to only talk about what party I had been to. I wanted to tell him how much I missed him and to know that he was missing me.

Instead, I was now stuck between a place of knowing I had to get in touch with him and hoping I wouldn't hear from him, because I didn't know how to tell him what was going on in my life.

I'd been grabbing coffee on campus my first week here, and nearly every seat had been taken. Two guys who were starting their junior years walked in and asked if they could use the remaining chairs at my table. Somehow I'd ended up talking to them for a while, then only one of them, and then I'd found myself at an all-night diner with him for hours after. I'd seen him regularly over the past weeks, the first few times refusing to admit I was on a date with someone. And now . . . I looked at my phone for the time and released a nervous breath when I saw I only had a few minutes before he showed up to take me on another date.

It's just a date, I reminded myself. *It's just a date. You and Knox have both had dates. You've both been in relationships.* I tried to ignore the fact that it'd been well over a year for both of us as I kept chanting. *He'll be okay with some dates . . . if he ever decides to call again.*

When a text popped up from Knox I gasped and reached for my phone faster than should've been possible. My fingers fumbled to open up the message, and when I read it my body sagged.

Knox Alexander: Gonna be busy this weekend, Low. You should be too! Go have fun.

I felt another crack form in my heart as I read the words over and over again, searching for any kind of hidden meaning. I didn't find one, but I knew then that I was right. I was losing him.

I wanted to beg him to tell me what was going on. I wanted to plead with him to reassure me that nothing could ever come between us. I wanted him to stop breaking my heart.

I cleared my throat and blinked back tears when there was

a knock on my door. As much as I wanted to tell the guy waiting for me on the other side that tonight wasn't the best night, I
knew a night out with him was exactly what I needed. As soon
as I'd stopped comparing him to Knox, I'd started enjoying being
around him more and more. And though I'd never admit it to
him, I craved the way his perfect smile unintentionally healed
each crack Knox left in my heart.

"Collin, hey!" I said brightly when I opened the door, and
was taken aback—as I always was—by how overwhelmingly
gorgeous he was.

"You look beautiful," he murmured as he leaned in to kiss my
cheek.

My eyes widened, and I tried to suppress my smile at the unex-
pected act. I didn't know what to think about the fact that it also
wasn't unwelcome.

Collin took a step back. "Are you ready?"

"Uh, yes. I just need my purse," I mumbled as I grabbed it off
my bed. With one last look at my phone, I left it lying on the desk.
I knew if I had it on me, I would want to check it. "So where are
we going?"

"Dinner," he said with a nonchalant shrug. I would've worried about how quiet he was being, but the way his lips kept tilting up eased the awkwardness. "I already know you don't like
eggs . . . but is there anything else I should know about?"

I shook my head slowly as I thought about it. "No," I said,
drawing out the word. "I don't think so. Why, are we going somewhere with weird food? I've never had sushi, so I can't really tell
you if I'll like it."

He huffed. "We're not going to get sushi."

"Okay, well then, I'm sure whatever it is will be—oh how cute," I whispered as we exited the building, only to see a horse-drawn carriage out front. I turned to walk toward the parking lot, but stumbled awkwardly when Collin led me toward the carriage instead. "What are you doing?"

Collin glanced at the carriage, then back to me. Suddenly his sheepish smile from inside the building made sense. "I thought we'd go to dinner like this."

"In a carriage?" I asked in awe.

"Why not?" he asked with another shrug.

"Oh, right, because everyone does this," I mumbled to myself as he helped me into the carriage, and ignored his laughing. "Okay, this is actually pretty amazing," I admitted a couple of minutes into the ride.

"I'm glad you think so," he said distractedly as he reached under the bench for something. He stopped to give me a quick smile, but then went back to looking for whatever he must have dropped. "This is for you," he said when he found what he'd been looking for.

My eyes widened, and I blinked a few times when I looked at the deep red, rectangular box in his hand. There was a gold design around the edges of the box, and it looked beautiful—but I had a feeling the *box* wasn't what he was giving me.

"Uh," I breathed, and took the box from his hand. "Thank you?"

I opened the lid of the box, and my eyes widened further when I saw the beautiful bracelet inside. Small, double chains attached to a white gold circle pendant with the word LOVE engraved on the top and bottom. *Wait, is that a diamond as one of the O's?* My mouth popped open and a puff of air left my lungs when I looked up. On the black underside of the lid, etched in gold, read *Cartier.*

I snapped the lid shut and looked at Collin. "This better be a joke; please tell me this is a joke."

His brow furrowed, and he gave me a look like he thought I was being adorably stupid. "Why would it be a joke?"

"Is it real?"

"Of course it is. Do you like it?"

"Like it? Collin, it says 'Cartier' on the box." I half-whispered so the driver of the carriage wouldn't hear me. When Collin's expression showed his confusion, I continued: "We've only been dating for a few weeks—"

"Technically tonight's a month," he corrected, but I didn't stop talking.

"—you are *not* supposed to give me these things! What if I never go on another date with you after tonight?"

"Do you plan on this being our last date?" he asked, and raised an eyebrow.

"Well, no, I haven't really been thinking that far ahead. I've just been taking it one day at a time. It's not like I planned on marrying you tonight, though!"

He laughed, again like he thought I was being adorably stupid. "It's a bracelet, Harlow, not an engagement ring." Taking the box from my hand, he opened it up and took the bracelet from it. "A simple 'thank you' would've been fine," he teased. "Can I put it on you?"

I looked at him blankly, but still held out my wrist. "Whatever happened to flowers?"

"Do you like flowers?"

"What girl doesn't like flowers?"

"So that's a yes?" he asked, his voice bordering on a tease.

"Of course—well, no, I mean I do. I just don't like roses."

Collin nodded, and bit back a smile. "All right. No roses."

I held up my arm to look at the bracelet, then dropped it back to my lap and let my eyes close. After taking a deep breath, I opened them and looked at Collin. "Can you please just tell me it's fake so I'll feel better about taking this from you?"

"No."

"Who are you that you do this after only a month of dating? Are you secretly a prince or something?"

His next laugh was louder, freer, and I found myself smiling at the sound of it.

"As far as I know, my family just comes from old money."

I sat back in the carriage and slowly exhaled. I didn't know what to say or how to respond. "All of this—it's so much. Too much . . . it's crazy."

Collin looked at the horse and driver, then down to the red box in his hand. Again he shrugged. "Maybe one day it won't seem like that to you."

My eyebrows rose at his implication, but I didn't respond. Growing up, I'd had this fantasy of going away to college, and then meeting the person that I would marry sometime after. That's how it had been for my parents, so I'd thought that was just how people did it. I was also so sure that twenty-year-old guys were ready for a good time, not looking to start long-term relationships. I had thought of Knox as the exception, and I'd always considered us lucky to have found each other early. Now to have Collin— who often had girls falling over themselves to talk to him—hint that he planned for our casual dating to turn into something more was sending a flurry of emotions through me.

I was shocked and flattered, but guilt tore at me, and I felt another piece of my heart crumble as I wondered what had happened to the love I'd been so sure of.

"Collin," I said awhile later, "I've been dating you . . . I *want* to date you. You didn't have to do this, you know. You don't have to buy me."

"I'm not. I told you, maybe one day it won't seem crazy to you."

"So this is the norm for you then?"

He smirked and eyed me. "Only with girls I'm not willing to let go."

Present Day—Richland

I SAT QUIETLY in the corner of the office, away from watchful eyes since I couldn't seem to stop my uncontrollable shaking. It was Monday afternoon and I was waiting to see my OB, and somehow this appointment had turned into something more terrifying than my Saturday morning tests.

I couldn't stomach the thought of getting rid of a baby, but I also wouldn't be able to live with myself if I brought a life into that house. I kept thinking I could just run away, and then I was positive that's exactly what I was going to do . . . until I remembered the failed attempt before. I had no idea what I was going to do, but I was ready to scream, "I can't have a baby!" to the next person who spoke to me.

My purse vibrated, and my shaking paused for only a second before growing more intense . . . because I also had no idea what I was going to do about that. Seeing how I was holding my cell phone in my hand, I knew the cause of the vibration was Knox's phone. Just before I'd left, I'd run out to the back porch to grab it, telling myself "Just in case," but still hadn't responded to the few messages he'd sent since Friday because I didn't know what to say to him. I knew Knox was worrying and I didn't want him to, but I felt like I'd betrayed him. How was I supposed to tell him I was pregnant?

That thought made me roll my eyes for the hundredth time. It couldn't be any more backward. Not knowing how to tell an old love that I was pregnant with my husband's baby . . . but even before Knox fell back into my life, I'd felt like I still belonged to him, not Collin. So the guilt I felt over the current situation was making it so hard to let him know that I was fine . . . because I was the furthest thing from *fine*.

Reaching into my purse, I pulled out the phone and opened up the texts.

Friday

> *Knox: Always.*
> *Knox: I'm at work until Sunday afternoon. But if you need me, I'm here.*

Yesterday

> *Knox: I've never hated a weekend more. Keep yourself safe.*

Today

> *Knox: Low . . . I'm pretty sure that week you "bought" is up. I won't ask details, but I need to know that you're okay.*

Looking at the time on the phone, I thought about how long I would have after this appointment before I needed to get to the grocery store and get home to cook dinner. As long as I was pregnant, Collin wouldn't touch me, and Knox needed to know that I would be safe so he wasn't constantly worrying about me. But this wasn't something I could tell him through a text or over the phone. I'd already ruined him once with a phone call; I wasn't about to do it again.

Tapping out a message to him, I sent it and went back to shaking and trying to be invisible to the other women in the waiting room.

> Harlow: I'm fine. But I need to talk to you, it's important.
> Can you meet me today?

Less than a minute later, the secret phone was vibrating in my hand, but it wasn't a message like I'd been expecting. I tapped the screen and brought the phone to my ear.

"Hello?"

Fall 2010—Walla Walla

"ONE OF THESE days my roommate is going to come back when you're in here and I'm going to be in so much trouble."

Collin laughed huskily and made a slow trail up my stomach with his lips. "Because I'm in your bed? Doubtful."

I pushed at his chest when he moved over me, but pulled him back to kiss me. "Because you're naked in my bed," I corrected against his mouth. "There's a difference."

"Maybe she'll enjoy the view," he offered.

I scoffed and rolled my eyes.

"Kidding, Harlow." With another lingering kiss, he pushed away from me and jumped off my bed. "As much as I want to stay in bed with you all afternoon, I need to go take a test."

I grumbled, but followed him off the bed and started grabbing my clothes when he did.

Collin grabbed me from behind when I bent over to put my underwear back on, and pressed me against his chest. "Well, if you keep teasing me, maybe I'll just take the F."

I laughed and elbowed him gently in the stomach. "I'm just getting dressed. And you're too smart to fail a test! Get dressed so you can go." I laughed again when he nipped at my neck, but my laughter ended with a gasp when Collin's hand appeared in front of me. A deep red box with gold designs sat in the palm of his hand.

"Collin," I breathed, and shook my head.

"Aren't you going to open it?" he said laughing.

I was still shaking my head as I reached for the box; my unsteady hands fumbled to open it. I sucked in another quick gasp when I looked at the necklace inside. "Collin, no. I can't."

The necklace matched the bracelet currently hanging from my wrist. A thin chain led to a large, circle pendant with six diamonds lining the white gold. I'd looked up my bracelet on the Cartier website . . . it was more than two thousand dollars. This necklace had to be at least twice as much.

"I can't accept this."

"Yes, you can. Happy birthday."

"Collin, no." I turned my head to catch his eyes, and tried to figure out how to tell him that these gifts he gave me were beyond outrageous. They were the kinds of gifts wealthy couples gave each other for wedding anniversaries—not college students as *just because* gifts. Again, what ever happened to flowers? Or just buying me a coffee? "Thank you . . . thank you *so* much for everything you have given me, but I can't keep accepting these things. You're spending so much money on me, and we've only been dating a few months."

Collin nodded, and a slow smirk covered his face as he moved my hand away from where it was hovering over the necklace. I turned to look at what he was doing when his eyes focused on the action, and watched as he flipped over the necklace.

LOVE was engraved along the bottom, just as it was on my bracelet. On top, the engraving was something I knew didn't come standard with this necklace: C&H.

All the air in my lungs left in a rush as I understood what he was implying this time with this piece of the Cartier Love collection. Could I be in love with Collin?

"As always, Harlow, a simple 'thank you' would've been fine," he teased.

"Thank you," I said.

My skin tingled where his hands trailed over my neck as he placed the necklace on me, and a burst of fluttering wings took residence in my stomach when his lips brushed across my shoulder.

I might not be *in* love with Collin Doherty, but I was falling . . . fast.

Even though his gifts were too much, he was always quick to give them to me, as if I deserved them and more. Even though we hadn't been together long, he treated me like I was his everything—so much so that I'd never worried that one day I wouldn't be. On the night I'd offered him *me,* he hadn't stopped us . . . he hadn't turned me down. He'd taken me, worshipped me, and made me feel like I was something precious.

I looked up to watch him walk over to gather his clothes, and couldn't stop the smile that crossed my face. *Definitely falling,* I thought to myself, and went to grab my phone when it began ringing.

Without looking to see who was calling, I answered, "Hello?"

"Happy birthday, Low. I waited for you."

The instant his voice filtered through the phone, my body stilled and warmed at the same time. My breath came out in a soft, audible huff and my eyes shut as hundreds of welcome memories flooded my mind.

I didn't have to look at the screen to know it was Knox who was calling. I would know that voice anywhere, and I should have been expecting his call. Not just his call. *This* call. We'd been preparing for and talking about this call for two and a half years now.

My lips and fingers trembled, and I almost dropped the phone as I tried to make my throat work.

"I waited for you" played over and over again like a broken record. A broken record with the most beautiful music still coming from it.

Turning my head just enough to look over my shoulder, I eyed the guy shrugging into his shirt, and my chest ached when I faced forward again. Three months ago I would've been certain this phone call would go completely differently, but then I'd met Collin . . .

Now I needed to choose between the two.

The guy I'd waited years for and knew I would always love, or the guy I'd given myself to and was falling so in love with.

Part of me screamed that the answer was obvious . . . but Knox still only called once every other week, if that. They were always short calls, and nothing like what I'd grown used to. He was always distracted . . . *distant*, even. For the first time in more than two years, there'd been no monthly flowers. I was so sure that my leaving had started something that had been unavoidable—that maybe he'd even been waiting for. A time where I was gone so he could feel free of me. As my heart had slowly broken, Collin had been there, piecing together what he could. Something I would never forget and would always be grateful for.

No longer seeing the dorm room I was standing in, I let my memories with Knox consume me. All the good—and there were *so* many good—followed by the recent bad. "I—" I took a shaky breath in, and my voice came out as a strained whisper. "I didn't wait for you."

There was nothing. No sound, no response—only the most heartbreaking silence I've ever endured.

I wondered how many times my heart could break over a man I'd thought would have it forever.

"Knox, I'm so sorry. I didn't mean for this to happen," I whispered into the phone, and tried to mask the way my voice broke with emotion.

Then again, how did either of us expect it *not* to happen when lately he'd made me feel as though I was only an obligation? How could he have expected me to wait for him when I'd been so sure he'd stopped waiting for me?

"Say something," I begged when another half minute passed without a word.

Knox cleared his throat, and a few more seconds passed before he said, "I will always love you. Nothing can change that. Happy birthday, Harlow."

He ended the call abruptly after, and I stood there staring at the wall in my dark room, listening to the rain beat against the windows, and holding the phone against my chest. I didn't know how to feel when my heart felt like it had just shattered because of my own actions, but still seemed full because of the person just a few feet behind me.

"I gotta go, baby," Collin said into my ear, then pressed a kiss to my neck. "See you tonight." He took a few steps away, then stopped and asked, "Hey, are you okay?"

I turned to look at him, and forced a smile on my face. "Of course."

"Who was on the phone?"

I looked down at the phone and smiled sadly. "Uh, just someone I needed to say goodbye to."

He nodded slowly as he took a step back, but tilted his head as he stared just below my throat. "Didn't you mention liking stars?"

"What?" I asked breathlessly, sure I'd heard him wrong.

"Stars . . . didn't you say you liked them?"

Loved them, something inside of me whispered. "Yes."

"I didn't notice before, but now that you're wearing it, the diamonds on the necklace look like little stars."

My breath caught in my throat, and my hand reached up to touch the present as Collin called out a goodbye and left my dorm room. The tears in my eyes barely waited until the door shut before they began to fall. I prayed I hadn't just made the biggest mistake of my life.

Present Day—Richland

"WHAT DID HE do?" Knox asked, his voice dark.

"Nothing, I told you I'm fine."

His relieved breath filled the phone. "I've been going out of my mind thinking of everything he could've done to you this weekend."

"He's not going to do anything, Knox, but I need to talk to you, just not over the phone. Can you meet me in an hour at the Starbucks where we ran into each other? Or are you working?"

"No, I'm home, and yeah, I'll be there."

The door leading back to the rooms opened, and a woman called my name. I stood and whispered into the phone, "I have to go, but I'll see you in an hour."

I hung up and followed the nurse through the office, each step harder than the last. I wanted this to be only a nightmare, but each passing second made it more obvious it wasn't.

After I finished peeing in a cup, I was led back to a room where the doctor was already waiting for me.

"Harlow, take a seat up here for me." Once I was seated on the exam table, she continued. "I'll need to go back out to get the results and look over some things, but I wanted to talk to you for a minute first."

"Okay."

"I didn't know you were trying to get pregnant."

"I wasn't! I have that implant; I thought it lasted for three years!" I said quickly, and a little too urgently. I tried to calm myself, but my body was shaking again.

She nodded and sent me a sympathetic smile. "Well, like everything, it's not one hundred percent effective. Now, Harlow," she said in a softer voice as she pulled up a chair next to where I was sitting, "there are a couple of reasons why I wanted to see you right away when you called us this morning to let us know you had a positive test. You said you don't know when your last menstrual cycle was since yours have been very light and don't come as often with the implant, which is common, but it means we don't know how far along you are."

I nodded and waited for the rest of what she would say.

"The second is, when you were here getting the implant, you were very . . . well, you appeared to be very nervous about getting it done. You made sure it was something no one would be able to find out about, and that isn't a common request we get with married women. With that visit, the way you seem to drop weight you don't have to spare between each yearly exam, and what you just said about not trying to get pregnant . . ." She paused and leaned close. "Do you need me to get you help?"

"What?" I asked, horrified.

"We can get you help if you need it."

No, no you can't. No one can help me. Collin knows people everywhere! "No! No, I don't want help. I-I don't need it." I laughed uneasily and shrugged. "I just don't want a, uh, baby, you know? I don't think I'm one of those women cut out to be mothers, but my husband, he wants this baby, he really wants a baby. He's so excited."

She wore a fake smile, one I knew well because I wore it when I was out with Collin, and waited to see if I would change my mind. But I wouldn't, I couldn't. I knew I wasn't doing a good job of convincing anyone lately, but it was hard when my entire world had flipped within the span of a week and a half. Knox showing up, then me finding out I was pregnant after doing everything to prevent it for years.

"Okay then, well I—" She was cut off by a knock on the door, and a nurse came in.

"Hi, I'm sorry. Mrs. Doherty? Your husband is here, and he wants to come in. Is that okay with you?"

"Of course," I said faintly after a beat of silence. I couldn't stop the way my body noticeably locked up and my eyes widened, and from the look on the doctor's face when I turned back toward her, she'd seen it.

The first day Collin had ever left work early in his life, I was with a woman who was trying to see if I needed help getting away from him, knew about my birth control implant, and I'd made plans to meet Knox afterward. And that's when I realized: *Oh my God I have the secret phone in my purse.* I quickly reached into my purse and shut the secret phone off, just in case Knox called or texted again, and was waiting for Collin with a bright smile when he walked in.

"Hey, baby." He gave me a quick kiss, then shook the doctor's hand and gave her his million-dollar smile as he introduced himself. "Sorry to interrupt. I just wanted to be here for the first appointment."

Of course, I thought, and held back a defeated laugh when it all made sense. Collin wasn't here simply because he was excited. He was here because he didn't trust me to be with the doctor alone. It was the same reason he wouldn't force me into seeing a fertility specialist even though there was seemingly no reason that I never got pregnant. He was afraid they would find evidence of our home life—of the toll my body took as a result of my husband turning into a monster.

My doctor glanced at me before giving Collin her attention again. "Not a problem. I was just telling Harlow that we needed to get her in now since we had no way of knowing how far along she is."

My arms tightened around my body at where this conversation was already going, and if Collin noticed from where he was rubbing my back, he didn't make any indication.

"Harlow has very irregular menstrual cycles, but that is common with young women like her. Her metabolism is so high that she can't keep weight on, and then it starts messing with her cycle."

"Ah, of course!" Collin said, as if her explanation made complete sense.

Another knock sounded on the door. This time the nurse came in, handed something to the doctor, and walked back out.

Collin and I both stilled at her expression.

"Are you okay?" he finally asked her.

Her eyes flicked up to mine, and in the brief second that they met, I could've sworn that I saw worry, but didn't understand why. "Yes, I need to do an ultrasound, though. So if you could follow me down the hall." Halfway to the room, she said, "It will be internal, so it's up to you, Harlow, if you want your husband in there."

Collin's fingers dug into my elbow, so I quickly said, "Of course . . . I want him in there."

The doctor held her arm out to show us into the room, and again that fake smile was on her face. "Okay then. Undress from the waist down, and I'll be back in a minute."

"Weird woman," Collin said once we were in the room and I was undressing. He didn't seem happy, as he had the entire last week; he was just staring at the closed door with a confused look—like he was trying to figure the doctor out. When I was up on the exam table and covered with the sheet left there, he looked back at me and smiled. "Are you excited?"

"I am," I lied, trying to pass off my fear as the good kind of nervousness. "I was starting to worry we'd never get here."

"I'm back," the doctor said as she peeked in. "You ready?"

"We are," Collin answered, and stepped back so she could come in. With a cold glance in her direction, he came to my side and took my hand as he asked her, "Are you sure you're okay? You looked worried in the room back there."

The doctor quickly explained how the ultrasound was going to work, then looked at Collin as she began. "The results from Harlow's urine came back, and her levels looked low. What we would consider a negative pregnancy test, low. But I was planning on doing an ultrasound anyway to get a good idea of where we were at, so I didn't want to scare anyone since tests can always be weird."

My eyes shot over to Collin, and I watched as his chest stopped moving and his body quickly locked up. Long moments passed before he started breathing again, but he wasn't looking at me. He was looking at the screen on the wall, where he'd been expecting a baby . . . where there was nothing. Collin's hand started squeezing mine harder and harder, but he never moved to touch me anywhere else, and his eyes never left the screen.

After another few minutes, the doctor stopped the ultrasound and sighed sadly when I sat up.

"She lost the baby?" Collin asked softly, a hint of darkness in his tone.

"No, I'm sorry. It uh . . . it looks like Harlow was never pregnant. The test must have been a false positive. Not as common as a false negative, but it can happen. Old tests, defective tests, prescriptions you may be taking, that sort of thing."

A high-pitched ringing filled my ears, and I didn't hear anything else the doctor or Collin said after that. Collin continued to dig his fingers into spots along the inside of my wrist, forearm, and elbow, but I'm not sure I was even reacting to them. All I could think about was what was to come.

Maybe if I had been pregnant and lost the baby, Collin would have gone easy—well, easier—on me. But to not have been pregnant at all? To get his hopes up even more than I'd planned to with my original lie? It didn't matter that I didn't take prescriptions. It didn't matter that Collin bought all the tests, gave them to me, and watched me take them; I knew he would see this as my fault—as something I'd done.

I was suddenly slammed back onto the table, and Collin's finger was digging into a pressure point on the bottom of my abdomen. My mouth opened and a soft gasp escaped my throat before his face was directly above mine.

"Shut up, Harlow," he gritted out.

My eyes darted around the room, but I didn't see the doctor. I hadn't even realized she'd left.

"Where's the baby?" he asked in a soft, dark voice.

My head shook quickly, and I tried to repeat the words that the doctor had said, but all that was coming out were squeaks of pain.

"Do *not* show your pain." He emphasized his demand by digging in harder, and moved his other hand down my leg to press his fingers into the inside of my thigh. "Where is the baby?"

"C-Collin, p-please. I-I-I"

He removed his hands and paced away from me. "Get dressed," he ordered without looking at me. As I dressed, he spoke. "We're going to go home. You'll drive in front of me, and you will *stay* in front of me. I don't think I need to tell you what could happen if you tried to get away from me, do I?"

"No!"

"Good; dress faster." He continued pacing and clenched his hands into fists over and over again. "I will use that time to calm down, and you will use that time to come up with a damn good explanation for what happened Friday night and today, you understand me?"

"Collin, how can—"

He closed the distance between us so fast, I started falling back. "*Do* you understand me?" he seethed.

"Yes! Yes, of course I do!" I whispered frantically.

Collin nodded and gave me a once-over, then brushed back my hair, which must have gotten messed up when he slammed me down. "Good. Let's go." We walked quickly out of the office and the building, but just before we got to my car, he stopped me and held out his hand. "Give me your purse."

I knew better than to question him when he asked for something, and normally I wouldn't have thought twice, but now all I could think of was the secret phone. On shaky legs, I handed over the purse and tried not to gasp out loud when he reached inside.

"You won't need this. I don't need you making any calls, and you shouldn't be driving stupid enough to get pulled over." He handed over my keys and stalked away from me.

I blew out a ragged breath once I was in my car, but the fear only grew with each passing moment on the drive home. I was supposed to be meeting Knox in half an hour, and not only would that not be happening, but I wouldn't able to let him know that I wouldn't be there, or why.

By the time we got home I was doing everything not to throw up, but thank God Collin didn't seem to be any angrier than when we'd left, which hopefully meant he hadn't found the other phone.

Collin put his arm around me as we walked up to the house, but I knew it was all a ruse for anyone who might be watching us, as everything was. I wasn't foolish enough to think that the drive home had actually given him time to calm down. Collin only calmed down when he was done teaching me a lesson.

As soon as the front door was shut behind us, Collin grabbed my hair and flung me back against the door.

Putting a hand on either side of my head so he was caging me in, he leaned close. "Where is the baby?"

"You heard her, there was no—"

"Then how the fuck did you get that test to say positive? How have you been *magically* feeling like this may be our time, Harlow?" he screamed.

"I don't know why it said that. You heard her!"

Collin grabbed my shoulders and shook me once before slamming me back, making my head smash against the door. "Not good enough, Harlow!" When my head rolled forward, he grabbed the top of my hair and yanked my head back. "You are worthless," he spit out. "You mess up time and time again, I'm constantly having to correct you, and you can't give me what a wife should. After two and a half years, we should at the very least be past me having to correct you, don't you think? Shit, we should have been past that after the first month!"

"I try," I whimpered, and attempted to blink away the darkening in my vision. "I don't want to mess up, I—" My slurred words stopped, and my head rolled forward again.

"Jesus Christ," he scoffed, and yanked my head back up, but this time his other hand wrapped around my throat and began squeezing. "I've looked every time and I've never found any birth control pills, which means you hide things better than I thought, or there's something else going on. But I *know* there is something going on, Harlow."

I tried desperately to bring in air, but there was nothing, and he didn't seem too affected by the fact that I wasn't breathing or that I was gripping and scratching at his hand and arm, trying to get him to release me.

"So let's do this differently. Are you going to try to get pregnant now?"

Nothing but choking sounds left my mouth as I continued clawing at his arm.

Collin made an annoyed face and sighed. "Poor, poor Hadley. She'll never get married, or have children. All because her big sister didn't care enough to try to protect her."

My arms and body hung uselessly, and my vision was almost completely black by the time Collin let me slowly slide to the ground, but his grip on my throat never loosened.

The last thing I remembered was his voice saying, "I'll let you think this over."

I woke up to the sound of hoarse screaming, and soon realized it was mine. The realization came seconds before the pain did.

My head felt like someone was taking a jackhammer to the back of it, and my body felt like it was being pricked by thousands of needles. I automatically tried to move from where I was, but froze at the sound of Collin's menacing voice.

"Do not move."

Even though I'd thought my eyes were open, it took force to get them to, and then it was only halfway. I was on the ground in the shower, and Collin was sitting outside it with a gun aimed right at me.

He waved the gun at the rest of my body. "You took too long to wake up. So I thought I'd do it for you."

It was a few moments before I felt like I could look away from the weapon in his hand; I was worried what would happen the second I did. When I finally managed to tear my eyes from it, I sluggishly looked down, and my eyebrows pulled together. I was covered in ice cubes . . . so much so that I couldn't see my body, and water was coming down on me from every angle in the shower. After a few seconds I realized I couldn't feel the water coming down or the ice, and I didn't understand why I wasn't shaking.

"You know," Collin said laughing, "the guy at the gas station asked if I was having a party when I bought all the ice. For some reason that was hilarious to me, because I was planning on announcing your pregnancy at my parents' anniversary party this week had your appointment gone differently this afternoon. That won't be happening now. But I guess this is kind of a party, too, if you want to count it as one."

"H-h-h-h-h-h-h-how . . ." I didn't try to get anything out after that, and it was then that I realized that I *was* shaking. I was shaking so hard my teeth were actually rattling.

Collin studied me for a few seconds, but then it was too hard to keep my eyes open. "How long have you been out?" he asked, trying to guess my question. "About an hour. How long have you been in the ice shower? About ten minutes, and you're almost done."

What felt like seconds later, I was waking up much like I had before. Screaming. This time in agony. The water was hot. Scalding hot. There was still some ice on me, but Collin was pulling me up, and the water felt like it was burning me.

"Don't show your pain, Harlow," he reminded me with a gentle voice.

I tried to clench my teeth together, but soon I was screaming again. I didn't understand why the pain wasn't stopping. I thought Collin had been pulling me up; I thought I'd been getting out of the shower . . . where had he gone? The hoarse screams continued for a minute before they slowly started dying out, and soon they were gone. I gradually became aware of the fact that my face was pressed against the shower floor, which was now clear of ice, and that I was choking on water . . . but I didn't care anymore. I wanted to go back to sleep again.

Everything in me hurt. Everything in me ached. Everything in me screamed.

"Good girl, don't show your pain," he whispered. The water shut off, and Collin picked me up off the floor again, but I couldn't stand on my legs, so he pulled me up into his arms. "Let's get you in bed."

Collin laid me in the bed without a towel, and wrapped the sheets and comforter tightly around me until all that showed was my face and wet hair. He sat on the edge of the bed as he ran his hand over my hair a few times, and leaned down to kiss my forehead. Without leaning back, he whispered against my skin, "Before you woke up the last time, a friend of the family who works at your doctor's office called me back. I had her check your records. She backed up your story that you don't have a prescription for birth control, and that you've never had any procedures to prevent a pregnancy."

I was glad I didn't have the strength to show a reaction to what he'd said. If I would've known that there were family friends in the office, I would've never risked getting the implant done there, but I was so grateful for whoever had left it off my records.

"Hadley is safe, too."

My body relaxed and I felt myself drifting again. "Thank you," I mouthed before sleep claimed me.

Chapter 11

Knox

Present Day—Richland

I GLANCED AT my phone to check the time again, and finally broke down to call Harlow. She was an hour late. Normally I wouldn't have waited that long for anyone, and normally I would've called if the person I was meeting was a little late, but I already knew how much it scared Harlow to have the phone I'd bought for her. I didn't want to continuously scare her by reminding her of it every time I started worrying about her.

Tapping on her name, I brought the phone up to my ear and tried to calm the shaking in my arms and legs.

Fall 2010—Walla Walla

I COULDN'T STOP shaking as I waited for her to pick up her phone. The entire last three months had been more of the same: constant bouncing knees and shaking hands; but it was all about to be over soon. Within minutes, I was going to have the girl I'd been waiting for. As soon as I heard her answer the phone, I looked up at her dorm and couldn't hide the wide smile that spread across my face.

"KNOX, I'M SO sorry. I didn't mean for this to happen," Harlow whispered into the phone a couple of minutes later.

Didn't mean for this to happen? The girl I've waited for just told me she didn't wait for me. She apologized to me, this isn't a joke—this is actually happening. The girl I love doesn't love me anymore.

"Say something," she begged.

I worked my throat a few times to make sure I could actually speak before saying anything, but even then, I felt dead when I said, "I will always love you. Nothing can change that. Happy birthday, Harlow."

I couldn't end the call fast enough. I couldn't get away fast enough; but I also couldn't move.

I don't know how long I'd been standing there in the rain when someone said, "Whatever you did, that's a good start, man—but it's only a start."

It took a few seconds to comprehend the voice was talking to me. I looked up at the guy walking in my direction away from Harlow's dorm, and gave him a confused look.

He gestured to the flowers in my hand—red poppies. "You look like shit and you're holding flowers. It's a good start, but you're better off buying something she can show off. Know what I mean? Sure way to make them happy and forget whatever happened." He laughed and smacked my shoulder as he walked past me, but it was enough to get me to move.

I turned around and headed back toward the parking lot, only stopping to hand over the flowers to the first girl I passed. As soon as I was in my car, I sat there for what felt like hours playing with the ring I'd had in my pocket before finally putting it back in the box it had come in, and started the drive back to Seattle.

I'd known it was crazy, and probably a long shot, but I'd gone to Harlow's dad a week before she'd left for college to ask if I could marry her. It had been a long talk that had ultimately ended in me promising that we wouldn't get married until she graduated, among some other conditions, but he'd given me his blessing to ask her after she turned eighteen, and I'd gone to buy a ring that night.

Because I'd known that nothing would come between us. And now, all I wanted to do was blame her dad. The conversation I'd had with him months ago flashed through my mind, and I bit back a curse because I knew this was his fault . . . all of it was his fault.

"I can't believe I'm about to say this," Mr. Evans said after long minutes of staring blankly at the floor. "Knox, you may ask her to marry you, but there are conditions."

I straightened in the chair and tried to contain my smile. "Anything."

"She needs to graduate before you get married."

I wanted to remind him that that was another four years away, but still didn't care as long as it meant she was mine. "Done."

"And this one might be harder for you . . ."

"Harder than waiting another four years?" I teased, but Mr. Evans didn't seem to find it funny.

"When she leaves for school in a week, I want her to try to enjoy it."

"Of course," I immediately agreed.

Mr. Evans shook his head. "Knox, the wife and I like you. Not many young men would treat our daughter with the respect you have, and that quickly earned our *respect. However, we're worried that her mind is so focused on you that she will miss out on life, which is why we pushed her to go away to school instead of staying in Seattle. If all she thinks about is making it to her eighteenth birthday, then she won't try to enjoy her time when she is away from you—do you understand?"*

"I'm not sure," I said slowly, but I was worried I did.

"You've always given her space, but not the kind of space I think she should have when she leaves. You've let her be her own person, but she needs to decide who she is now, and she can't do that with you always there beside her. She sees her future as Harlow and Knox; I need her to see what it could be as just Harlow. Like I said, the wife and I like you, and I would be glad to have Harlow marry you . . . but I want her to be sure this is what she wants once she finally gets to be on her own and makes her own decisions. I don't want my daughter to ever look back on her life and regret it. You look confused," he grumbled, and searched for the words to explain himself.

I didn't need him to explain more. I got it . . . I just didn't like it.

"Now, I'm not asking you to push her into dating other guys. Just make sure she enjoys her time there, and lives a normal college student life. The constant phone calls, the flowers—they should be scaled back. Way back. I would ask you not to call her at all, but I don't think you'd respect that wish, and my daughter may never forgive me for it. And you may not have been dating my daughter the last couple of years, but to everyone else that is what it has looked like, and, son, I don't want her to go away to school with a boyfriend. Do you understand what I'm saying?"

My heart sank as I realized exactly how far he wanted me to take this. "I can't . . . I can't break up with her."

"I'm just asking you not to be the boyfriend you technically aren't yet, okay?"

I nodded hesitantly, and he tried to give me a reassuring smile.

"Even though those few months don't seem like much, those first few months away from home are everything, as I'm sure you remember. So, if you are what she wants once they're over . . . then you may ask my daughter to marry you. And, Knox, I have no doubt that you will be asking my daughter to marry you."

I nodded once and shook his hand. I also had no doubt that come Harlow's eighteenth birthday, I would be doing just that.

But now none of that mattered. Graham and Deacon had been right. All of the waiting, and all of the time spent getting ready for this day, had been a game for Harlow. And now the game was over.

Present Day—Richland

THE SHAKING IN my arms and legs abruptly stopped when the call to Harlow went straight to voice mail. Ending the call, I waited a couple of seconds before tapping on her name again, and held my breath until I got the same result.

"Shit," I hissed, and dropped my phone onto the table I was sitting at. *She's okay,* I chanted to myself over and over again. *Give her another thirty minutes.*

But after ten minutes and another phone call with the same result, I was running out of the coffee shop and to my truck. I knew I was risking a lot, but I had to know she was okay. After looking up her address, which I'd stored in my phone, and putting it in my GPS, I took off for her house, but slowed to a stop a couple of houses away when I saw two cars parked in the driveway.

My tense grip on the steering wheel loosened, and I blew out a ragged breath. "You've got to be kidding me," I groaned, and ran my hands over my face.

I was paranoid. I was turning into a psychotic ex who always thought the worst because of what had happened before. As much as I hated the situation she was in, and as much as I wanted to get her away from her husband, I knew I couldn't do this to Harlow. And as I gripped my chest, I realized I couldn't do it to myself. It felt like I was going to make myself have a heart attack with how bad I was stressing over all of this.

She told me she was fine, and would be fine. She probably couldn't meet me because her plans changed too fast for her to be able to even warn me. And I'd somehow turned that into her needing me to save her. I was beginning to worry about my sanity.

After another look at her house, I turned my car around and headed back to Thatch.

"WHY IS IT we always find you pacing when we've come home the last couple of weeks?" Deacon asked distractedly when he came home hours later.

Because Harlow's husband is home by now. Because she will have hidden the phone I bought her by now. Because now I don't know what she needed to tell me in person, and I'm back to worrying about her safety when I probably don't have a reason to. And because now I'm pissed-off that she never warned me she wouldn't make it to the coffee shop or turned the phone back on to at least let me know she was okay. A laugh that sounded more like a sneer burst from my chest when I remembered: *She's married; she doesn't have to tell me anything.*

I never once stopped pacing during my inner rant, or looked at Deacon, since he usually didn't stop on the way to his room to wait for an answer, but after a few seconds I realized he was standing there watching me with a worried expression, his phone now forgotten.

The door opened again to Graham, and I sighed in relief when Grey didn't follow him in. She seemed to only show up recently when I'd seen or talked to Harlow, like she knew I'd done something she'd warned me against, and it was impossible for me to hide things from her.

"Why are we staring at each other?" Graham asked, but before either of us could answer, his eyes narrowed. "Are you murdering the carpet again? Jesus, what is going on?"

I wanted to tell them. Despite how everything had gone down in college, neither of them had gloated or been happy when Harlow had ended things, or when I'd finally gotten on board with what our plan had been all along for college. They'd both been more worried about me than they had in the years leading up to that point, and had even asked if I'd heard from Harlow or if she'd changed her mind a few times before they'd understood not to ever bring her up again.

I knew they were trying to protect me back in college. I knew it now, hated it then, but it didn't stop me from feeling like one of them was going to unleash some seven-year, built-up wrath on me whenever I even thought about Harlow. And even though Jagger and Grey had warned me to stay away from Harlow, everything was different now that I knew the truth about her marriage.

But I was choking on the words, not sure how to make them come out.

"Christ. Tell me you didn't, Knox," Graham said. "Tell you didn't get some girl pregnant."

"Damn it," Deacon said in a grave tone. "Is it mine? I'm not ready to be a mom or grow a vagina."

Despite the frustration and worry that had been building, I barked out a laugh, and Graham cracked a smile, but I knew he was still waiting for an answer.

"No, no kids coming."

Deacon gave Graham an uneasy look, then they both walked over to sit on one of the couches. As soon as they were seated, Deacon said, "We've been talking about you and your drastic change the last couple of weeks. You haven't gone out with us even when you're not working, you haven't had anyone over or been anywhere since the one who walked out naked, and this is the fourth time we've caught you pacing. So I already texted . . ." He trailed off and looked at his phone to check. " . . . Melanie, and she's not expecting me anymore. And we're all going to sit in the living room until you tell us what's going on."

Throughout everything he'd said, Graham had sat there nodding, and now they were both looking at me expectantly.

"I don't know how to," I admitted, and Graham's brow rose in shock while Deacon looked hurt.

"You're serious right now?" Deacon asked. "You don't know how to tell us something? When have we ever not told each other anything, no matter how fucked-up, disgusting, or ridiculous it was?"

"You sound like a girl," Graham mumbled to Deacon, then cleared his throat and looked back to me. "But he's right. We've been best friends for over a dozen years; we don't know how to *not* tell each other things."

My head was shaking slowly. "You guys don't understand. It's not just telling you, it's what can happen because of telling you.

It's how I'm struggling with this just knowing about it," I said through clenched teeth, and realized my entire body was vibrating with the need to get Harlow away from her husband. "And it's also years of not talking about it, and then years before that of the two of you harassing me for it."

Both looked confused but didn't say anything, just waited for me to continue even though it took me a couple of minutes of pacing to figure out where to start.

"You know Flynn Doherty?" I asked.

"Nope," Deacon responded immediately.

"Yes, you do," Graham said in an annoyed tone.

"Yep," Deacon amended.

"He's the Benton County prosecutor," Graham explained, and Deacon made a face.

"Ah. The guy with the smile and the son."

I nodded. The prosecutor was known for his too-perfect smile, and his son—who was supposed to be running for something in the near future—had it, too. They were always all over the news together. "Yeah, him. His son's name is Collin."

"Cool?" Deacon offered when I didn't continue, but Graham's eyes had zeroed in on my hands fisting over and over again.

"Do you remember when I went to Walla Walla for Harlow's eighteenth birthday?"

Surprise covered both of their faces; they hadn't expected her name to ever be mentioned again.

"When I was there, this guy talked to me for a second, but I didn't really pay attention to him because I'd just gotten off the phone with Harlow. I didn't think much about him then, but I recognized him when he started showing up on TV with his dad." When I didn't get a response, I continued, but didn't look at the guys. "That was *Collin* Doherty. He lives in Richland."

"Again . . . cool?" Deacon said slowly, drawing the words.

After a few rough breaths, I sneered, "He lives there with Harlow . . . they're married. *He* is the reason I didn't end up with Harlow."

"How long have you known this?" Deacon asked.

"*How* do you know?" Graham interjected.

"Yeah, that's what I meant. How do you know?"

I finally stopped pacing and looked at them, and Graham's face morphed back into confusion when he saw the agony and rage I'd been trying to conceal the last couple of weeks. "I ran into her when I was on my way home two weeks ago."

"Shit," Deacon breathed.

"Then they were at the fund-raiser for the firehouse that weekend, and he—" I cut off and ground my teeth. After a few seconds I gritted out: "In front of everyone, he was using pressure points on her. He's threatened to kill her family, he abuses Harlow, and she's fucking terrified of him! *This* is the guy she left me for, and I can't help her!" I raked my hands over my face and groaned. "She looks sick. She's so thin; I thought she was dying. She's not who she was, and it's because of him."

"Knox, you can't go through this again with her," Deacon said.

I glared at him. "Go through what again? Her husband is beating her!"

"So she says," Graham said.

"No—what? Why do you guys do this every time Harlow is involved? It's like you *have* to make her seem as bad as you can!"

"Knox, she played you for over two years. Now it's been, what, shit, almost five? And all of a sudden, you run into her and she just happens to tell you that her husband—whose dad is the *prosecuting attorney,* as we already talked about—is beating her and threatening her family? Who just comes out and says that?"

"She didn't! And I told you, I saw him doing it in front of everyone. I saw the fucking bruises!"

Both stayed quiet for a moment, then Graham sighed. "If what you're saying is true . . . if she is in an abusive relationship, what exactly is it you think you can do? You've known for two weeks, and since you're just telling us, then I'm guessing you haven't gone to the police yet. Do you plan to?"

My mouth formed a tight line, and I shook my head. "She said I couldn't."

Graham nodded. "And you can't just go in there and rip her away from her marriage, no matter how much you want to."

"You say that like I don't already know that," I sneered.

"I'm just saying, Knox, you're already driving yourself crazy over something you can't change, no matter how much it may seem like it sucks."

My eyes narrowed. He still didn't believe me.

I looked at Deacon to find him shaking his head like he was annoyed. Finally, he said, "We already know she likes playing games, man. You never know, she's probably beating herself. She could be one of those women who are psychotic and fake the whole thing so they can ruin their husband's life, too."

I huffed, and Graham whispered, "That was too much."

I took a step back and sighed heavily as I said, "And this is another reason why I didn't know how to tell you. Fuck you both."

"You know just as well as we do that if you actually believed her, you would've gone to the cops as soon as you found out. Don't act like we're the bad guys in this."

I stopped on my way out of the room and stared ahead for a second, then looked over my shoulder. "I've thought about it at least a hundred times. Every time I did, I also thought about someone in her family being killed because of me, and how her father-in-law would get her husband cleared of any charges. How her husband would come after her again, and how this time, she might not be alive when he was done with her. I have been in physical pain thinking about what's been happening to her. But it doesn't compare to the thought of losing her, and for now, at least, I know exactly where she is. I *will* get her away from her husband, but it's not going to be as simple as showing up like some white fucking knight. You two made it hell for Harlow and me before, I'm letting you know now, that if you do it again, or if you keep pulling the shit you just did, I will walk away from thirteen years of friendship with both of you, and I won't look back."

Chapter 12

Harlow
Present Day—Richland

I WOKE UP gasping the next day, then quickly began choking. My mind whirled as I fought to open my heavy eyelids, and I wondered what Collin was doing to me. But there was no pain other than the dull ache in my throat and pounding in the back of my head. There were no harsh words or demands to hide my pain, and the sensation of being choked slowly faded, leaving me to gasp for air again. But I knew it was all in my mind. I knew if I could just open my eyes I would *know* Collin wasn't there, and I would *know* that I could breathe. Just as I finally wrenched my eyes open, I heard heavy and quick steps pounding down the hall.

I shot up in bed and looked around to the rumpled comforter and sheets covering me, and blinked against the harsh light coming through the open window as Collin came running into the bedroom with a wild look in his eyes that immediately calmed when he saw me sitting there.

Collin came around to the side of the bed and sat in front of me, but didn't touch me until my breathing was mostly under control, and then it was just to grasp my chin and tilt my head back to look at my throat for a few seconds.

After he released my chin, his fingers gently ran down my bruised throat, and he mumbled, "Look at me, Harlow."

I dropped my head but was having a hard time keeping eye contact with him. All I could see was how Collin had pointed the gun at me the day before, and everything else that had happened after that dreaded doctor appointment.

"I thought you had finally—" He broke off suddenly and looked away for a few seconds; his eyes were red and glassy when he looked back to me. Every muscle in my body tensed at the sight. "I thought you had finally decided you couldn't live like this anymore. When I heard you, I thought you were . . . I thought you were trying to . . . well I guess it doesn't matter, does it?"

Even with his indifferent words, it didn't change his tone, it didn't change his broken and unsure sentences, and it didn't change the look in his eyes or the slight tremble in his chin. He thought I'd been trying to kill myself, and he was trying not to cry. Some women might feel like their men were more human after seeing them get emotional for the first time. Some might even have the urge to comfort their strong husbands when they show this rare vulnerable side, but I couldn't move and I wasn't breathing. I was afraid the tears were a trick, and if I made a wrong move I was going to pay for it.

"Do you love me, Harlow?" he asked softly. For the first time, it sounded like a genuine question, and he looked like he didn't know what my answer would be. When I didn't respond, his eyebrows pinched together, the light in his eyes died, and a rage I knew all too well covered his face as one of his hands shot out and grabbed my wrist. But just as soon as I felt the pain of him digging his thumb into the pressure point there, it was gone as he snatched his hand back, as if he'd realized what he was doing. Collin closed his eyes, and after a deep breath in and out, he slowly opened them again with a calmer expression. "Do you love me?"

"You know I do," I said in a hoarse voice. The lie came easily, thanks to the years of practice with him.

"And do you know that I love you?" he asked warily.

Something in his voice made my chest ache. Not for his love, and not for the guy I'd fallen in love with before he became my monster. But for all the lies I'd said in the past five years, for the lie I'd been living, and for the pain this man had cost me—only for him to now act like this was hard for *him*.

Before I could respond, fear flooded my veins when tears started quickly slipping down my cheeks. I tried to stop them, tried to gather whatever strength I could find, but there was nothing as more tears continued to fall. A sob burst from my chest, and my body slumped forward when I decided that after what had happened the day before, I didn't have enough in me to care that he was seeing me break down. And once he'd seen the tears, there was no point in lying to him. But the tears also served as my answer, an answer Collin would have never accepted in the past, and an answer I didn't think he was going to accept then.

I waited for my monster; I waited for the pain. My body jerked when his fingers trailed over mine and then slowly up my arms; but instead of stopping at any of the number of pressure points on my arms, Collin gently pulled me onto his lap.

"I do love you," he whispered into my ear. "I swear to God I love you, Harlow."

All I could manage was a nod against his chest while I internally screamed, *You're a monster! You don't know what love is!*

"What I do, I do for us; to better our relationship, to better you as a woman and my wife."

There he was . . . my monster. Still hiding, but there in Collin's words. Always waiting, teasing me, lurking behind the perfect mask of my seemingly perfect husband.

"I'm sorry," he murmured before his mouth was on my skin.

It took all my strength not to recoil when his lips brushed against my neck, and then again when he tilted my head back to brush a deceptively soft kiss to the hand-shaped bruise on my throat. His lips slowly moved up my neck, but just before they reached my own, he paused. Seconds passed as his breath mixed with mine, and I slowly let my eyes open. His blue eyes were narrowed into slits, and the sight didn't match his broken words.

"You're shaking. You're scared of me," he said softly, the last statement sounding more like a question—as if he didn't understand why or how that was a possibility.

And if he hadn't been right, and if I hadn't been in his arms, I might have laughed. But I was scared of him; I was *terrified* of the man holding me. And I'd never been more terrified than I was in that moment. He didn't apologize to me like this, he didn't cry, and he didn't worry about me not loving him. No matter how much I wanted to believe that things could change, that I could have a future without living in fear of what would come next from Collin, I knew it would be stupid and dangerous to let myself believe that the past few minutes were signs of change for us. I also knew that not answering *this* question would be a mistake, but my throat wouldn't work as his blue eyes lost the life behind them.

Oh God.

My head shook slowly at first, then faster. "No, no," I swore, and ran my hands through his blond hair.

Collin swallowed roughly, then did it again, and even though there wasn't a change in his eyes, and his hands were starting to hold me tighter and tighter, I could tell in his expression that he was trying to remain calm.

"Yesterday?" he asked, and I hesitated in my reassuring brushes through his hair and against his neck while I waited for something more.

"Yesterday?" I repeated, and let my eyebrows slowly rise to hint that I didn't know what he wanted me to say.

"You're scared because of yesterday."

I forced my gaze not to leave his even though I desperately needed that small break from his intense stare to attempt to gather myself. "Of course not."

"Good girl," he murmured, and his tight grip eased up. With a soft kiss to the corner of my mouth, he whispered, "You know I would never hurt you."

I didn't respond because it sounded like he was saying it more for himself than for me.

"So, what do you do on Tuesdays? What do you have to do today?" he asked, and I suppressed a relieved breath when I saw his blue eyes light up again, since I knew that for now, my monster was gone.

"Uh . . ." I blinked quickly, and tried to remember what he'd asked rather than focus on his eyes. "Tuesdays?" I asked warily. Collin never asked about my routine. "I clean; I cook dinner. There isn't much else unless you give me your card on those mornings. I need to go to the grocery store. I was going to go yesterday after the, um . . ." I cleared my throat and this time my eyes did dart away from his for a moment. "After the appointment."

Collin was watching me intently while I spoke, so it was impossible to miss the slight hardening of his stare when I mentioned the store. "The store? Do you *need* to go to the store?"

"Yes, I . . ." My voice died and stomach dropped when it hit me. There was no food in the house at all. Usually if Collin felt bad for a punishment, then he would cook, but we didn't have food last night, and I'd slept through the afternoon and night. "L-last night. I'm so—I'm so sorry. There wasn't any food. I didn't—"

"I do know how to fend for myself, Harlow," he said with a sly grin. "Why do you have to go today?"

I didn't understand what he was trying to trick me into saying with these questions. I went every week; he *knew* I went. I had to go every week *because* of one of Collin's forms of teaching, as he liked to call it. He threw away every item of food in the pantry and fridge on Sunday nights—not including spices and what was needed for breakfast on Monday. "*You're the one wasting the food, Harlow, since you can't seem to figure out how to buy the right amount of groceries,*" he always said.

I swallowed and tried to push down my irritation with him for making me explain something that he so often used against me. "Because I only buy enough food for the week when I go, so we don't have any food."

Collin's eyes flickered to the side, like he'd just remembered that fact, then his eyes fell to my throat. "I guess if we have no food then you have no choice, but I'm going with you."

My hand shot up to the large bruise on my throat, and it was then that I *finally* understood the questions, and understood how he could forget about our foodless house. Collin didn't want me leaving the house at all because he'd left visible proof. He was going to the store with me to make sure I didn't do something stupid, like tell someone.

"Get ready and let's go."

I tried to hide my confusion as he got off the bed. How long had I slept if he was able to go to the store with me now? I glanced at the clock, and my head whipped around to look at Collin again when I saw it was only eleven in the morning. "Shouldn't you be at work?" My body tightened the second the question left my lips. It had been a simple question, and an honest one, but that wasn't something I could ask Collin. I wasn't allowed to question anything he did, and I couldn't believe I'd done it just then.

Collin's head slowly tilted to the side, and I wanted nothing more than to run from the dark, lifeless look he was giving me. A look of pain flashed across his face as he took the few steps back to the bed and knelt onto it. If it weren't for his eyes— which were focused just under my chin—I would think he was about to beg for forgiveness judging by the expression on his face. His fingers faintly traced over the bruise before his entire hand was wrapping around my neck and he was slamming me onto the bed. My shocked gasp was cut off when he covered my mouth with his and, one at a time, tightened his fingers on my throat. "Shouldn't you be getting ready?" he asked quietly against my lips.

As if my monster had never made an appearance, Collin's hand jerked away from me and he got off the bed. I watched as the hand that had been on me flexed and relaxed over and over again as he tried to keep himself in check; his eyes never once left me. "Get dressed, Harlow," he demanded so softly I barely caught the words. "Make sure you cover that—just cover yourself."

I waited until he walked out of the bedroom before I released a shaky breath that sounded more like a sob, and let the tremors take over my body. I'd thought it would be dangerous to let myself believe that we could change. I was wrong . . . that wasn't the danger. The danger was that for the first time, Collin was trying to control the monster inside of him, and was now more unpredictable than ever.

Chapter 13

Harlow

Present Day—Richland

I AUTOMATICALLY REACHED out and opened my mouth to stop Collin when he pulled a pack of eggs off the store shelf an hour and a half later, and realized a second too late what I was doing.

His arm froze with the eggs in the air. "What?" he sneered, soft enough that his voice wouldn't carry.

"Um, it's just, well that's a lot."

"You said you needed these."

"We do," I said quickly, and finally got the carton out of his hands. "But not three dozen. I'm lucky if you finish a dozen in a week."

Collin turned to smile at me, but from where I was standing I could see he was clenching his teeth. He leaned in and brushed his lips against my jaw. "Watch yourself, Harlow," he warned, then took the eggs back from me and placed them into the shopping cart. "Now what?"

I glanced at the list on my phone, but before I could say the next item we needed, a deep voice called out my husband's name.

"Collin Doherty. Playing hooky, are we?"

I looked up in time to see Collin's million-dollar smile as we both turned to see who had called him, and my skin crawled.

"Ah, Ren. I guess that makes two of us." Collin put his hand on the small of my back and brought me closer to his side when Ren stopped next to me. "Ren, you remember my wife, Harlow?"

"Of course." Ren barely spared me a glance as his meaty hand drifted from my elbow down to my wrist, and didn't seem to notice the way Collin pulled me back a step as Ren asked, "What has you away from work today? And who is taking care of the county's money if you are here, and old Alfred McKenzie is probably out getting a hip replaced?"

Collin laughed. "The money is fine. Besides, the wife and I have some personal things we need to take care of this week. I'll probably be working from home a lot."

That was news to me, and unwelcome news at that. *Personal things don't usually include ice showers, guns, and bruises, and don't need to be hidden behind a lot of makeup and scarves,* I thought to myself.

"I'm sure you do," Ren said with a chuckle. "I myself had some personal things to take care of, and now I'm here trying to get things to make dinner for the wife. She somehow seems to be catching on to these *personal* days." His eyes raked over my body with his last couple of words, and I forced myself to look at the shelves of refrigerated food, then to Collin. Even though Collin had never liked Ren, and the dislike had grown into something stronger since the night of the fund-raiser, I knew that if I showed a hint of disgust for the man in front of us, I would pay for it later.

Collin's smile never faltered, but I felt the way his body stiffened and noticed the slight change in his eyes. "I'm sure your wife will enjoy the dinner."

Ren made an annoyed face. "So, the sheriff threw a fit over the new chief yesterday; it didn't . . ." He trailed off and his hand shot out to rest on my hip. "Young girl, be a sweetheart and leave the men to talk about things that you don't need to be around for."

I tensed when Collin's fingers dug into my back but tried to relax my body. I knew it wasn't because of something I'd done, and I knew Collin was thinking of a hundred different things he could do to make Ren pay.

I didn't move, mostly because I couldn't with Collin's hold on me, and we both stayed silent as Ren opened his mouth to talk to Collin, only to shut it when he realized I wasn't leaving.

"Young girl," he began again, "that wasn't a suggestion."

A low rumble sounded in Collin's chest as he turned me toward him. Dread filled me when I noticed the dead look in his eyes, but he just pulled me close and kissed my cheek. "Keep shopping; I'll come find you when we're finished here."

"You need to teach that wife of yours how to listen," I heard Ren say as I escaped down the aisle, and a tiny smile pulled at my lips with Collin's response.

"She does listen . . . to me."

I grabbed the last two things on the list, then headed back to the produce section since Collin had been too frustrated to stay in it for more than a couple of minutes earlier, and I knew there would be hell to pay if I didn't get the rest of the vegetables. Using the face of my phone as a mirror, I glanced around to make sure no one was looking at me before holding it up for only a second to make sure the infinity scarf was still hiding what needed to stay hidden. Even though Collin had spent five minutes before we'd left making sure it wouldn't move, the light material had me second-guessing it every time I started walking. And now that Collin wasn't next to me to keep an eye on it, I was shaking just thinking that someone might see something they weren't supposed to.

My head instinctively snapped up when I heard a screech, only to find a small girl running across the produce section to launch herself at a man.

"Oh my God," I whispered.

Knox was standing with a few men in dark blue Richland Fire Department shirts and was holding up the smiling, dimpled girl.

A girl with dark brown hair nearly identical to Knox's. A girl who was talking a mile a minute and looking at Knox like he was her favorite person in the world. A girl whose mom had just joined them.

I took a few quick steps backward, not wanting to look at the mother, not wanting to see the woman Knox had a daughter with, and hit something.

"Excuse you!" a woman hissed.

"I'm so sorry!"

"You do realize you are in a crowded store; you can't just go flying around without looking where you're going."

"I know," I whispered, even though I hadn't been able to hear Knox and the girl, so I knew they couldn't hear me. "I'm sorry, I wasn't thinking."

She rolled her eyes and threw the can of food she'd been holding into her cart. Her already loud voice grew louder and raised an octave. "Well, don't you think that was a little obvious when you tried to run me over?"

"Yeah, prob—" The word cut off when I felt a presence behind me, and the woman's eyes snapped up and rounded.

"Low," Knox's deep voice rumbled. "Everything okay here?"

Knox
Present Day—Richland

"I'M TELLIN' YOU, this girl is the one. I'm gonna get a ring and put it on her finger, and get out of the bachelor life for good," Pete said as we walked into the grocery store to get food for the firehouse. The rest of the guys and I rolled our eyes.

Every couple of months or so Pete had a new girl he liked to claim was "the one," only to replace her with someone else not long after. So if he was talking about getting a ring, then I was sure this girl only had a few days to a week left with Pete before she found herself single.

"I saw that! I saw you roll your eyes, but none of you have met her. You haven't seen her . . ."

I turned to look at the guys, and mouthed the rest of what Pete said as he said it.

" . . . she's got wife material written all over her."

I laughed when Pete smacked my arm. It was what he said about all of them. "One day you'll actually find someone, Pete," I said. "And maybe then we'll stop making fun of you." I gave him a look and shrugged. "Maybe."

We all tensed at the high-pitched shriek, ready for whatever it could mean, but my body relaxed and a smile crossed my face the second I caught a dimpled three-year-old running full speed toward me.

I bent down and grabbed her up into my arms as she yelled, "My Superman!"

"Hey, little flyer!" Pete said, and held up a hand for a high-five.

After slapping his hand quickly, she looked back at me and began talking as fast as ever. "Superman, I miss you. Can you come back so we can fly? We aren't at my house, we're at my aunt's house, but you can find us at my aunt's house, right? Because the fire hurt mine? But we're going back to our house. Mommy said so, so we can. Where's your cape?"

"Where's yours?" I asked, and gave a disapproving look when I didn't see the starry blanket in her hands.

She leaned close to whisper, "It's in Mommy's car because I can't fly in here, she said."

Natalie's mom, whom I'd met later on the night of the fire, walked up to us and gave an awkward wave. "Hi, guys. Sorry about this; she saw you and was so excited."

"Not a problem," I murmured, and smiled when Natalie patted me excitedly and looked at her mom.

"Mommy, did you see? Superman is here!"

"I saw," she said with wide, apologetic eyes. "We should let him go though, sweetie; they have things to do."

Ignoring her mom, Natalie looked at me with the most excited expression and softly asked, "How are the stars?"

My smile widened and I whispered back, "Still saying you're the bravest little girl."

With a secretive smile, she again agreed. "I am."

"Natalie, honey," her mom said.

"I have to go," the little girl said with a sad sigh.

"See you around, Natalie," I said as I set her back down on the ground.

"Promise?"

"If the stars can see you, I can see you."

Natalie sent me the cheesiest grin and took off after her mom, but after a few seconds turned and ran back to smack into my legs. Hugging them tightly, Natalie said, "You're my favorite, Superman."

I couldn't respond as she released me, I just watched her go, my gaze only leaving her to automatically look over my shoulder when a woman yelled, "Excuse you!"

My body froze when I noticed Harlow trying to calm a woman down who kept yelling at her. Despite my instant irritation at someone yelling at my Harlow, relief surged through my body at seeing Harlow here. She was okay.

"You do realize you're in a crowded store; you can't just go flying around without looking where you're going," the woman continued, and by that point, I was already stalking toward them despite the confused calls from my crew.

The woman put her hands on her hips and gave Harlow a look that clearly said Harlow was beneath her. "Well, don't you think that was a little obvious when you tried to run me over?"

"Yeah, prob—" Harlow began, but stopped when the other woman's head tilted back to take me in, her eyes widening as she did.

"Low," I mumbled. "Everything okay here?"

Harlow's body sagged. "Yes," she said softly.

I didn't take my eyes off the other woman, and they narrowed when she opened her mouth and put a hand up like she was about to disagree with Harlow. Her mouth snapped shut.

"Again. Is everything okay here?"

Harlow swayed back toward me as we waited for the woman to respond, and I lifted an arm to grasp her thin waist in my hand. But the second I touched her, her body jolted and she moved away from me like I'd electrocuted her.

"Fine, fine. Just your everyday grocery store collision," the woman tried to joke, but when she saw the frustration on my face from Harlow jumping away from me, she nodded absentmindedly, grabbed her cart, and took off in the opposite direction.

"Low," I began, but Harlow whirled around and whispered, "You need to leave!"

My eyebrows slammed down and my shoulders went up as I threw a hand out. "Why are you always trying to make me leave?"

"He's here, Collin is in the store, and I don't know when he's going to come looking for me. You can't be here when he does."

I automatically looked behind me, then took the step back to get out of the aisle and look up and down the store. When I didn't see her husband, I walked back into the aisle and pushed her farther into it with me.

"No, no, no, no, Knox, no!" she said. "He cannot find me with you!"

I turned her so her back was against the shelf of bread and caged her in. "Tell me what the hell happened yesterday."

"He's going to find us," she whispered, and tried to look past where my arms were blocking her line of sight.

"I waited for you at the coffee shop. I was fucking *terrified* that something had happened to you. And then you didn't show . . ."

"Please, Knox. You *have* to leave," she tried to speak over me, but I kept talking.

" . . . there was no call; nothing. I went by your house, but—"

"You went by my house yesterday?" she asked, her tone matching the horror on her face.

"Yes, but there was another car there, so I thought you had company. Jesus, Low, I know most the time you won't be able to use that phone, but you can't pull the shit you did yesterday. You can't say you need to talk to me in person, then not show and not fucking let me know that you're okay," I said. "I needed something . . . *anything*."

She'd stopped trying to get me to leave and stopped looking for her husband, but I couldn't stop talking. I hated that after vowing to never waste another minute with her, I was doing exactly that, but I had to get everything out.

I cupped her cheek and leaned close enough that my nose brushed hers. Her mouth parted when she inhaled softly, and my eyes zeroed in on the action. I pressed my body closer to hers and had to remind myself repeatedly that we were in a store when she blinked slowly, then looked up at me under her thick lashes. My beautiful Harlow.

My tone was low and rough from having her so close but keeping myself from taking any more of her. "Do you know what it's like, living every day not knowing if you're okay?" I brushed my thumb across a single tear that had slipped down her cheek and whispered, "Everything about your situation scares me. I've never been more scared of anything in my life. Not while running into a house on fire, not while rescuing people; nothing. You, knowing he's hurting you, the possibility of losing you . . . Harlow, I spend every day on edge, ready to break at the littlest thing."

"I'm so sorry," she choked out. "I never wanted you to get caught up in this."

I looked at her in confusion. "Caught up in . . . Low, I love you. I would do anything for you; I want to take you away from this. I'll do anything to get you out of this. This isn't some hardship; it just kills me that you won't let me help."

"You think this isn't hard for me, too? Seeing you, knowing that you're there and willing to help me after what I did to you all those years ago. I've been worried I wouldn't see you again, but I can't do this to you. I can't let something happen to you or your family! When were you going to tell me that you have a daughter?"

My head jerked back. "What the hell? Daughter? What are you talking about?"

"That girl you were holding," she said as she gestured her head toward the end of the aisle, her tone now defeated. "Why didn't you tell—because you didn't have to," she mumbled to herself.

"Natalie?" I balked. "Harlow, I saved her from a fire last week; she's not my daughter." I shook my head, and my lips tilted into a smirk as I took in Harlow's crushed look. Leaning in so my mouth brushed against hers as I spoke, I said, "I love that something like that made you as crazy as the fact that you're married makes me."

One of her hands fisted in my shirt against my stomach and pulled me closer. "That's not funny." Her lips were barely touching mine, and even though her hand was still pulling me close, I could see the fear in her eyes.

"It isn't," I agreed, and pulled back. "But it was good to see nonetheless. You still haven't told me about yesterday. What were you going to say, and why didn't you ever text me again?"

Harlow blinked a few times, like she was trying to gather herself, then shrugged helplessly. "Collin took my purse right after I got off the phone with you. It had both my phones in—" She quickly stopped and gasped, her eyes widened as she looked around her. "Oh my God," she whispered. "Collin's here, I completely forgot. I can't be near you. He has to be done talking to Ren by now," she mumbled to herself.

If it weren't for the facts that the woman I loved was freaking out over her abusive husband finding us, and that he'd taken away all my communication to her, I would have smiled knowing that I could make her forget about everything else.

Though I'd already pushed our luck enough, I pulled her close once more. "Quickly, Harlow. Does he know about our phone?"

"No, I don't think so."

"Good, *please* if you can, let me know how you are when you get your purse back."

Her head was going back and forth to look all around us, but she nodded. "Of course, I—"

I gripped her chin and brought my mouth down to hers. The kiss was quick and hard, but she still stumbled toward me when I pulled away. I would've given anything right then to have more time with her. Relaxing my grip on her chin, I ran my thumb over her bottom lip and whispered, "I love you, Low."

"To the stars," she vowed.

Gritting my teeth, I forced myself to release her and walked away. It didn't take long to find my crew; they were still lingering in the produce section, not even trying to act like they hadn't been watching everything between us.

"Pete's over here talking about the fortieth girl he's fallen in love with, Knox finds random women to make out with in the store, and I can't get girls to stick around for the third date. I think I'm doing something wrong," Jake, one of the guys on my crew said. I laughed.

"Maybe because women want a man who is big enough to make them feel protected, not so big that they're afraid he'll suffocate them if he rolls over in his sleep," Pete suggested.

"They love this," Jake countered quickly, and slowly flexed, making every woman in the produce section stop to watch.

I rolled my eyes and turned to start grabbing what we needed, busying myself so I wouldn't search out Harlow again.

"If you're done putting on your show . . ." Pete trailed off in an annoyed tone as he gestured at Jake. "You're over six and a half feet tall and have muscles on top of muscles. You're a freak, dude. You look like you could kill someone just by thinking about it. *That* is why you can't get someone on a third date. You scare guys by looking at them, and you scare women when they think of getting into bed with you." There was a silence before Pete continued, "What the hell are you doing?"

"Making you think I'm going to kill you just by thinking about it."

I snorted and turned to see Pete roll his eyes while Jake continued to glare at him. Pete scoffed and said, "*I* know you're more scared of spiders than most of the women I know, so there's no way in hell that's going to work on me."

I opened my mouth to jump back into the conversation, but my words died in my throat when I looked up and watched Collin Doherty look down the aisle I'd just been in with Harlow, then turn and walk into it. We'd been too close.

Harlow
Present Day—Richland

AFTER TAKING A minute to collect myself, I turned my cart around to go to the produce section, and gasped when I found my husband standing right behind me.

"Collin!" I said breathlessly.

He put a possessive hand around my waist and growled softly into my ear, "People are not allowed to touch what is mine."

My heart pounded in my chest as I waited for whatever was to come. *How long has he been standing there? How much did he see and hear?* I wondered.

"Never take orders from someone else, especially someone like Ren."

I held in a sigh and thanked God that he couldn't see the relief on my face. "I didn't," I assured him, even though he had been standing with Ren and me the entire time.

"If he didn't work with my dad . . ." he began, but didn't continue. He took a deep breath in, then released it as he asked, "Did you get everything?"

My eyes drifted over the cart, and my face pinched with worry for a second before I could control it.

"What?"

"Well, we didn't finish getting the produce." Collin's face fell, so I quickly added, "But I know you didn't like being in there, so we don't have to if you don't want to. I can figure something out."

Collin pinched the bridge of his nose and grumbled, "I can handle five minutes in the produce."

Whether it was from feeling dizzy with relief that Collin

hadn't seen me with Knox, or if it was simply from seeing Collin so out of sorts just being at a grocery store, a laugh bubbled past my lips before I could stop it. I slapped a hand over my mouth and stared at Collin wide-eyed. The last time I'd laughed at him, we'd still been engaged. I'd learned quickly not to do that, and couldn't believe I'd done it just then.

He moved his fingers away from his nose, but didn't put his arm down, and I was shocked to see that the expression on his face was the exact opposite of what I'd been expecting. Collin's eyes were full of confusion and surprise, his lips were parted, and one corner of his mouth was pulled up like he was about to smile. He took a step toward me, but rocked back on his heel and looked around us at the empty aisle, like he'd forgotten we were in public.

When he was sure we were alone, he stepped close and said, "I didn't know how much I missed that sound until I heard it just then." Collin trailed his fingers along my waist. "Come on, let's finish this and go home."

I let Collin lead us out of the aisle, and although I kept my head down, I couldn't stop my eyes from peeking up to look around the front of the store for Knox. A faint sigh of relief escaped my lips when I only saw a few women in the brief glance I'd allowed myself, but soon died when I felt that familiar energy. It took all my strength not to turn around. No matter how much I wanted one more glimpse of him, I knew I couldn't while I was standing next to Collin. Not only would my husband notice, but it would kill me to see that same look of betrayal and pain that Knox had worn the night of the fund-raiser when he'd watched me with a man he hated.

Keeping my eyes trained to the floor, I held my body stiff

and once again forced myself to walk away from where I'd left my heart.

Knox
Present Day—Richland

MY BODY TENSED as I watched them walk out of the aisle a couple of minutes later. A growl came from low in my chest as her husband wrapped his arm around her waist, and without giving myself a second to think about what I was going to do, I took three steps in their direction before a strong hand came down on my shoulder to stop me.

I jerked to a stop and my head whipped to the side to glare at whoever had stopped me, and found Pete laughing so hard, no sound was coming out. I started to step away from him, but those few moments were what I'd needed in order to breathe and remember what *could* happen to Harlow if I were to try to approach her in front of her husband.

I forced my body to relax—a process that took longer than it should have—and plastered a smile as I turned to look at the other guys, who were laughing as hard as Pete was. I was just glad they hadn't seen Harlow with her husband; I didn't need that shit from them. "What did I miss?"

Everyone sobered up when distinct tones went off on our radios, followed by a dispatcher's voice calling out which engines, ladders, and battalions were needed to go out to a structure fire. Before the dispatcher had even finished, we were already hurrying to the front of the store. The rest of the guys ran toward the truck, but Pete and I went to leave the cart containing bags of the vegetables and fruits we had managed to grab in the short time we'd been in there with an employee.

As we turned to head out, I caught a glimpse of Harlow walking toward the checkout lanes. Her face was filled with pain— not the kind I would expect when she was near her husband, but a kind I knew and felt deep. Pain because we were so close, but there was still so much separating us. Pain because we'd lost years, and didn't know if we'd ever be able to make them up. Pain because I had always loved her, and knew she still loved me, and even after seven years, she was still *technically* untouchable.

Chapter 14

Harlow
Present Day—Richland

FLIP EGGS; DON'T burn the eggs. Flip eggs; don't burn the eggs—they have to be perfect. Flip eggs; then grab the toast. Coffee . . . coffee comes last, I chanted ceaselessly to myself two days later. It was the only way to keep myself composed at that moment.

I slid the spatula under the edge of one of Collin's eggs, and after checking the bottom of it, flipped it over, then did the same with the other. *Don't leave them long; they need to be perfect. Put away the bread. Grab the toast and butter it, then check the eggs again.* I took a step away from the stove and reached for the loaf of bread, but my hand stilled on it when I finally noticed the unpleasant feeling moving through my veins. He'd come in silently, but I knew he was there.

It wasn't at all like the feeling I had when I was in a room with Knox. That kind of energy left me feeling like I was floating—like his presence, or even just the sound of his voice, was giving me the greatest kind of high. This energy that filled the room whenever Collin was near had a pit forming in my stomach. It left me shaking, and I would often find myself holding my breath—as if somehow that inane act could help me get in control of my body again. Or maybe because I was secretly hoping that it could help me disappear from his radar.

Child . . . my husband had reduced me to a chanting, frightened child.

Forcing myself to continue making Collin's breakfast and not acknowledge his presence, I failed to stop my shaking even though my lungs were protesting the lack of oxygen.

Tie the bread off; put it up. Grab the knife; stop shaking. Stop shaking. Stop shaking. Damn it; stop shaking! Butter the toast; grab a plate. Check his eggs . . . they need to be perfect. You can't make him mad again.

I'd woken up to my monster this morning. No. Not my monster. My new monster . . . the unpredictable one—even more terrifying than the one I'd been living with for the past two and a half years. The rest of Tuesday and all day Wednesday, he'd been strange. He'd tried to be loving and attentive, but had moments where he'd lash out, only to rein it in just as fast. He'd also told me not to work so hard. *The house is already spotless, Harlow. Why are you cleaning? I can make lunch for us. Why don't I take you out to dinner tonight; you do too much for me. Just make sure to cover up that . . . thing,* he'd said as he gestured to my throat.

This morning, however, had been different:

I'd woken up with his hand covering my nose and mouth;

my arms and legs were flailing before I was even fully conscious.

"Two days of spoiling you, and suddenly you just sleep
through alarms?" he'd yelled.

A deep, warning growl soon followed when I'd finally connected with his stomach. It had been the wrong thing to do, but
it was instinct when he was making it impossible to breathe. He'd
released my face, and I'd immediately began dragging in air. But
before I could take in two breaths, the back of his hand had come
down across my right cheek.

A shocked cry escaped me a second before my air was cut off
again, and his face was directly in front of mine. "Do not show
your pain," he'd snarled, forcing each word out in short, staccato
bursts.

I'd clawed at his forearm, but he hadn't so much as flinched. It
wasn't until I'd stopped fighting and my vision started to darken
that I noticed a spark in his otherwise lifeless eyes. He'd snatched
his hand back and sat up on his knees, and his chest had moved
roughly up and down as I pulled in air as fast as I could—like
he was having as much trouble breathing as I was. The sound of
our joined ragged breathing had been uncomfortably loud in the
room.

"You are selfish," he said moments later, his lip curled up in
a sneer. "You are spoiled, and you don't deserve all that I do for
you when you can barely give me anything in return."

I'd pressed a hand to my aching chest and rolled to the side,
just wanting to get away from his crazed stare, but he had flipped
me back. His hand had been up, this time in a fist, but instead of
releasing it on me, he relaxed the fist and flexed his hand a few
times, then dropped it to his side.

"You have no idea how lucky you are that I love you, Harlow."

I had nodded, knowing at the time that even if I could speak, I would most likely say the wrong thing.

"I want my breakfast ready when I get out of the shower. Surely you can't screw that up, too." With that, he'd moved away from me and let me climb off the bed.

START KEURIG. SET the plate on the table. Grab silverware and mug; go back to the table. Don't spill his coffee.

"Now you don't look at me?" Collin asked in a dark tone, but there was no mistaking the humor in it.

After I set the mug and fork down, I turned to look up at him. A very small part of me was happy that there was some light in his blue eyes; the rest of me just hated him. Hated that he could be the way he was—hated that he could switch from Collin to the monster so quickly, and then back again like it was nothing at all.

His eyes drifted to the kitchen table, then back to me. "Eat it," he said simply.

I glanced at the food, just to confirm that there wasn't something else there that I might have missed. "I don't—you know I don't like eggs."

"Eat it."

"I'm not hungry, Collin."

"*Eat it!*" he snapped.

I jerked at the boom of his voice and hurried over to the table. After scooting everything over to my place, I went to sit in my chair, but Collin just moved the food back to where it had been. He held out his chair, and after watching him warily for a moment, I sat in it.

"Now eat it."

I was shaking so hard, I wasn't sure I could. Most meals I could hardly stomach, and that was when I was eating something I enjoyed. I held back a grimace and reached for the fork, but Collin's hand beat me to it.

He slammed the prongs onto one of the eggs to pick it up whole, and with his other hand, he squeezed my jaw so that my mouth popped open.

"Ah do eh!" I forced out, knowing he understood what I was trying to say, but he didn't stop.

I pushed toward his chest, trying to escape from his grasp, but he just gripped tighter and stood behind the chair so it wouldn't move. Collin shoved the entire egg into my mouth, flung the fork onto the plate, then used both hands to shut my mouth. And just like I'd found myself this morning, he was soon covering my mouth and pinching my nose so I couldn't breathe.

"Swallow it," he demanded. When all I did was scream against his hand and scratch at his arm, he took a step back, kicked the chair out from under me, and then followed me onto the floor. "Swallow it, Harlow!" Tipping my head back, he kept everything blocked off so not only was I still unable to breathe, but I was now choking on the food. "Chew!"

I thrashed against him, but it was only making things worse for me. Forcing myself to calm, I focused on trying to chew and swallow, even though those actions felt impossible when my body was screaming for air—screaming to get away from his hands. My eyes widened and I slapped furiously against the floor when I'd finally choked the egg down, and when Collin released me the first breath I took sounded like an inverted scream. But the scream didn't last long. Collin reached onto the table and shoved the next egg into my mouth before I could get a full breath in.

"Which one did you poison? This is really how you planned to kill me? You thought I wouldn't know?" he yelled while I continued to choke, but that egg I'd been somewhat prepared for.

Once the second egg was gone, Collin sat there with me on the floor until my breathing sounded somewhat normal, but his eyes never left my face.

"You're insane," I rasped. Saying those words out loud for the first time felt so good, like a sweet release. I wanted to say them over and over, but I let myself be content with once. "What poison?"

His dark blond eyebrows pinched together in confusion. Any other day, I would have been thrilled that he didn't look angry after what I'd just said to him, but after today, after what I'd endured on Monday, after the kind of monster he was turning into now . . . I no longer cared.

"Why aren't you dying? I watched you," he said angrily, and pointed up to the counter. "I watched you pour something into the salt shaker before you sprinkled it onto the eggs. And then you refused to look at me even though I know you *knew* I was there. You couldn't have been more obvious than a child who'd gotten caught with her hand in the cookie jar!"

My face fell and my heart pounded in my chest. I had rolled onto my side at some point after he'd released me and was curled into a ball now. I had to swallow back the forced food that was trying to make its reappearance now that I knew what all that had been for. I'd just been choked and nearly suffocated because I'd been trying to keep myself busy while waiting for his eggs to cook. "Salt," I whispered as heavy tears fell onto the hardwood. "I was refilling the salt shaker with salt."

There was a pause, then Collin sighed and reached out for

me. Before he could touch me, my stomach lurched again, and I scrambled up and took off for the guest bathroom to get rid of the eggs.

Collin was standing near the front door when I finally emerged from the hallway with an apologetic look on his face. "You don't have to make dinner tonight. My parents' anniversary party is this evening."

"I know."

"Try to be ready by the time I get home. I, uh . . . I need to get to work." When I nodded, he gestured to his throat and said, "Find something that will cover that for tonight. I can't have you going anywhere today, Harlow, and after—well, after this morning, I can't have you calling anyone. You understand?"

Of course I understood. My throat was still bruised an ugly shade of yellow and purple, and he thought I would call the police. He'd hidden my purse before I woke up on Tuesday morning, and I figured from his words that he was going to keep it for a while longer. I tried to keep my face blank, but I hated the fact that now he wouldn't be with me, and he would have Knox's phone.

"Your keys, phone, even the house phones. I can't risk it."

My eyebrows shot up, but I kept my mouth shut. He'd never taken the house phones with him.

Aggravation replaced the apologetic expression. "I need to—"

"I understand," I said before he could finish.

Collin took a step toward me, but then rocked back and sighed. "I love you," he whispered, turned, and left.

Tears filled my eyes, but I didn't let them fall until I heard his car start. Once he was gone, a strained sob burst from my chest, and I stood there staring at the front door like I didn't know what to do. I felt lost. This wasn't my monster; this wasn't my husband. My monster didn't leave visible marks on my throat. My monster didn't cut off my air until I passed out and point a gun at me. He didn't try to stop me from breathing multiple times in one day, or force me to eat food while choking on it.

I glanced to the left to the knocked-over chair, forgotten toast and coffee, and bits of egg on the floor, and a part of me wanted to finally give up. To say forget everything, warn my family, and just leave. But before I was able to understand the movements, I was walking into the kitchen and cleaning.

He's trained me well, I thought disdainfully, then pushed that thought out of my head. I wasn't cleaning this for him; nothing I did was for him. Everything I did was to hopefully spare me from more pain. I might have learned what to do and not to do to make *Collin* happy over the years, but that was simply because I'd slowly realized that it was my greatest form of self-defense from him.

AFTER CLEANING THE house and doing a load of laundry, I stood in the shower for forty-five minutes while sobbing and trying to figure out what to do, then finally pulled myself together and stepped out.

I grimaced when I looked at myself in the mirror. I'd been trying to avoid it lately, but now that I was looking, I couldn't stop. Large, fading bruises along my ribs and hips, little dots along my arms that looked like everyday bruises if you didn't know differently, and the monstrosity on my throat. If it were possible, I looked thinner. Looking at my reflection made me feel sick even though the bones that jutted out weren't anything new.

I ran my fingers over the bones, then the bruises. When I got to my throat, I leaned closer and noticed that the area around my mouth looked red from where his hand had smashed down, and it looked like I was blushing on only one side of my face where he'd backhanded me. I pressed the tips of my fingers against my cheek and winced. I'd wondered which was worse, the beatings I'd always endured, or how he'd been this week. But one look at myself, one painful reminder of how it had felt to not breathe, and I knew I had my answer. I would gladly go back to the beatings, because I knew in my gut that with this new monster, one day soon he was going to kill me.

"Over something as simple as salt," I whispered to my reflection.

Tearing my eyes from the mirror, I grabbed a towel and walked out of the bathroom so I wouldn't be tempted to look again.

Once I finished dressing, I walked over to my side of the bed to grab the towel where I'd left it after drying off, and paused. Peeking out of the bottom shelf of my nightstand was my mini iPad. I'd taken it out of my purse to charge last week sometime, and I knew that if Collin had known it was here, he would have taken it with him.

I must have spent half an hour holding it and weighing the options before pulling up the iMessage app and typing in Knox's number, only to let another fifteen minutes pass as I tried to figure out what to say—and if I should say anything at all.

Collin had my phone. If he checked it, he would see it. But as far as I knew, he left my purse in his trunk. Then again, right now, after everything, I didn't care. I'm sure in a couple of hours when I came to my senses I would, but at the moment I had so much excited adrenaline coursing through my veins, only one thing mattered.

Knox.

I could still feel his hands and lips on me—phantom touches from Tuesday that left me trembling. That left me needing more of him, more of us. But more than that, I needed his energy; I needed it to feel like I could make it another day with my new monster. So after typing out a message to him, I let my finger hover over the SEND button for only a second before tapping on the screen. Then I waited.

Chapter 15

Knox
Present Day—Richland

I WAS STOPPED at a light halfway home after my shift when my
phone buzzed in the cup holder. I'd barely glanced at the screen,
but did a double take and reached for the phone as fast as I could
when I saw the last word in the text.

> *(509) 555-8643: I need to see the stars.*

There were only two people who knew about stars and who
could have Richland area codes: Harlow and Natalie. It was a
statement that would fit the latter so much, but I doubted little
Natalie had somehow conned a way into finding out my number,
or could text at three years old. But I didn't understand why

Harlow would be texting me from a phone that wasn't the one I'd bought her.

Tapping on the number, I hit CALL and waited while it rang and rang until it picked up and Harlow's voice mail filled my ear.

"Shit," I murmured, and ended the call.

I drummed my free hand on the steering wheel quickly as I thought about what this could mean, and what I should do. And when the light turned green, I flipped an illegal U, earning me a couple of horns, and sped off toward Harlow's house.

Since she'd texted me, only to let an immediate call go unanswered, I was worried that her husband still had her phone. I was afraid he'd finally found the phone I'd given her—the only way he could know about the stars—but then it still didn't make sense why he'd used her other phone to text me. Regardless, I was afraid to respond to her text or call her again, and I was afraid of what he could be doing to her.

I parked a couple of houses away and tried to walk up casually, but practically stalked up to the front door. The only comfort I took was that only her car was in the driveway. With a heavy exhale, I braced for anything and knocked on the door. Less than a minute later, the door was flung open, and Harlow's eyes widened in surprise and relief.

"You're here!"

"Where is he?" I demanded in a low tone, but the vibration in my body from nervous energy started lessening when tears started falling down her face. "Low," I whispered, and reached out to touch her, but stopped and looked around.

"Come in, hurry," she said, and stepped back. Once I was inside, she shut and locked the door and flung herself into my arms.

I pulled back enough that I could tilt her head up using my thumb under her jaw. "Babe, I need you to tell me where he is."

Her eyes were still wet with tears, but they weren't falling anymore. "He's at work," she said in a confused tone.

"Who texted me?"

"I . . . did." She whispered the last word. She said my name, but I couldn't respond to her. I couldn't speak. I was shaking so hard I was afraid I was going to break her, and I knew I needed to let go of her before I hurt her—hurt her more than *he* already had.

"What . . . the fuck . . . is that?" I asked in a dark tone, my eyes stayed locked on her slim throat.

I didn't have to be watching her face to know when she realized what I was seeing. Her body beneath my arm locked up and she muttered, "Oh God."

"I will kill him. I'm going to kill him, I swear to God I will."

"No, I-I-I . . ." she stuttered, then flew away from me. I only let her go because I was terrified of hurting her more.

Harlow took off across the entryway and living room, and down a hall with me not far behind her. I followed her into her bedroom and slowed to a walk when I got in there. I hated seeing the bed where he'd touched her, I hated being in *their* space. I wanted to take away every memory of him and replace it with memories of us. I looked up when Harlow came out of a closet with a light scarf in her hands—the same scarf she'd been wearing on Tuesday—and the sight made me growl.

I closed the distance between us and grabbed the filmy material to stop her as she began putting it on. "I've already seen it."

"Please, let me put it on! You didn't respond to me, I didn't know you were going to show up. By the time you knocked on the door, I wasn't thinking, I just rushed to answer it."

My head jerked back. "Respond to you? Harlow, I called you as soon as you texted me; you didn't answer. And why didn't you use the phone I bought you?"

"I couldn't!" she yelled. "He still has both of my phones, my car keys; he even took the house phones. He has *everything*! I texted you from my iPad. I'm still terrified that Collin will see it on my phone, but I needed to see you—*please* give it back!" she begged as she reached for the scarf.

"Why? So you can try to pretend he didn't do this to you?" I seethed. "So you can hide that part of you away from me? You aren't supposed to hide yourself from me, Harlow!"

"Well, what do you expect me to do when you're looking at me like I'm broken?" she cried.

"I expect you to let me fix it!"

She flung an arm out in exasperation. "I've told you, you can't. I *can't* let you do anything!"

"You also can't stop me from trying," I said roughly. The words were a promise, not defiance, because I *would* fix this.

Taking the last step toward her, I grabbed her face in my hands as gently as possible and covered her mouth with mine. Her hands came up to cling to my shoulders, and soon she was giving me as much of her as I was giving. But it wasn't enough, it never had been enough with Harlow, and I knew it never *would* be.

As gently as I could, I lifted her into my arms, and my face pinched in agony. She was so light—too light. I felt her spine in a way that wasn't natural, and it killed me.

"Guest room," she said between kisses. "All the way down the hall."

I walked us out of their room and down the hall without ever breaking from our kiss again, and easily found the untouched guest room, which looked like it belonged in a magazine—as the rest of their house did. I gently laid Harlow on the bed and followed her down, but kept myself hovering over her. Not because I was worried about where this would lead or that we would go too fast . . . but because I was scared of crushing her.

As if she read my thoughts, she fisted my shirt like she had in the store and pulled my body closer to hers. "You aren't going to hurt me," she whispered against my lips.

I settled my hips against hers, only to lift back off to help her when she started tugging at my shirt. Instead of putting any weight back on her, I rested on my knees and planted my hands against the bed on either side of her head.

Slowly moving from her mouth, I trailed my lips along her jaw and down her throat in slow kisses. As much as I wanted to do the opposite, I forced my eyes to stay open and locked on her bruised throat as I did. I needed this; I needed to see what he'd done to her while I was trying to take it away.

I moved down her chest, and my fingers went to the buttons on her shirt—my mouth followed my hands down as the shirt opened a little wider. When the last button was undone, Harlow whimpered when I placed an openmouthed kiss just above her shorts, followed by a soft bite.

Sitting up on my knees, I pulled her up with me and shoved the shirt away from her chest and down her shoulders, but left it around her arms so they were locked behind her back as I bent to suck on her nipple through her bra.

"Knox," she whispered, and her legs shifted between mine.

She struggled to move her arms, and I finally released them as I moved to give the same attention to her other breast. Her hands went to my head and pulled at my hair to bring my face up to hers. She crushed our mouths together and leaned back until we were lying down again.

When my hands went behind her back to unfasten her bra, hers went to the button on her shorts, and I pulled back in time to watch her push them and her underwear off her hips. I got off the bed and slowly finished pulling them off for her, and tossed them onto the floor with everything else. Letting my eyes find hers, I started there and worked my way down her body as I rid myself of the rest of my clothes. When I finished and looked back into her eyes, I saw the worry there mixed with the need and passion.

"Cracked," I said, changing her earlier word. Her eyebrows pinched when she understood what I was saying, like she was in pain, but smoothed out when I continued: "But still *my* Harlow, and still so beautiful." And she was. She was bruised everywhere and she was too thin, but you couldn't take Harlow's beauty from her.

When I climbed on top of her again, I spent minutes kissing every single bruise on the front and sides of her body. My throat tightened, but I swallowed past the invisible lump there. I couldn't let this break me.

"What are you doing?" she asked in a gentle tone when she realized that everything had slowed down.

With my lips on her ribs and eyes on hers, I whispered, "Fixing it."

She didn't speak for the next couple of minutes as I focused on her torso and arms. After I was sure I'd gotten them all—and had silently vowed to get her back later—I kissed her throat and then her lips; then I noticed the wetness gathered in her eyes.

"Still cracked?" she asked, her voice broke on the last word.

I held my hand against her cheek and took comfort in the fact that she pressed her face closer to it. "You tell me."

Her blue eyes focused on me, and her lips spread into a shaky smile. "Not even a little bit."

One of her legs curled around my back, causing me to settle against her heat. A needy groan rose up my throat, but as much as I wanted to take what was right there, I never had taken anything from Harlow that I knew I couldn't have—and I wouldn't start now.

"Even though you didn't make it easy sometimes, I have waited for you for seven years, Harlow Evans." I used her maiden name on purpose, and she didn't try to correct me or seem to mind—judging by the way she lifted an eyebrow in amusement. "If you ask me to, I will leave this bed and gladly wait until I can have you . . . but, God, *please* tell me I can finally make you mine."

A smile so much like the one I'd fallen in love with lit up her face, and her fingers threaded through my hair. "You've wasted so much time waiting for me," she murmured, and a look of awe spread across her face.

"I'd gladly do it all over again if it meant ending up right here with you."

Her hand curled around the back of my head and pulled me down until we were a breath apart. "I have *always* been yours, Knox. I love you."

My lips spread into a slow smile. "To the stars?"

Harlow's head tilted back when I pushed into her, and she exhaled a breathy "Always."

I'd worried that I wouldn't remember to be gentle with her—when her body so obviously screamed that she needed gentle—but even though all coherent thoughts fled my mind the second I was finally inside her, I shouldn't have been nervous.

This was my Harlow. My soul knew her and knew what she needed.

Each movement was slow and sure, and I knew that this moment had been worth the wait. *She* had been worth the wait. What I hadn't expected was the way she pieced me back together with every pass of her lips against my skin. I'd thought of her as the broken one, but I'd forgotten how much losing Harlow had broken me.

Her nails trailed across my shoulders and down my back, each pass rougher than the previous—a silent plea to go harder. A plea I eagerly met as she tightened around me and her blue eyes fluttered shut.

"Oh—Knox, please," Harlow whispered, and her head fell back onto the bed as her labored breaths turned into soft moans.

I ground my teeth as I tried to hold off until she came, and pushed harder inside her—drawing out the most intoxicating sounds from her. I felt each hushed word and moan like a shock to my chest. These words, this overwhelming, addicting feeling of having her underneath me, was finally happening after years of dreaming about it—and I knew I would never forget a second of it.

Harlow's nails dug into my shoulders and her breaths stopped for a few seconds before her body began trembling beneath mine—and the force of her orgasm pushed me into my own. I gripped at the sheets to hold my shaking body above hers, and captured her mouth with mine, swallowing my name on her lips.

She was mine. I was going to take her from this place, and never look back.

"I NEED TO tell you about this week," she said sometime later. I'd lain down beside her to pull her close, and had been trying to figure out a way to bring up wanting her to leave this house again. The words sounded like they took all her strength, but she continued: "I don't want to do this, especially not now, after . . . but Collin's been so unpredictable this week that I feel like I don't have a choice. I'd planned on telling you as soon as you came over, and now I don't know how much time we'll have."

My eyes narrowed at her last worried words, but I didn't comment on it. As much as I wanted to put this off because this seemed like the worst time to finally do this, I wouldn't. I lazily traced shapes onto Harlow's bare stomach to keep myself calm, and said, "Right; you never told me what happened on Monday."

Her face pinched in worry and pain, and my body tensed in preparation for whatever she was about to tell me. "I thought I was pregnant," she said after a few silent moments.

I nodded slowly. "You bought yourself a week."

She shook her head. "On Friday he made me take a test. It was positive."

My face and arm fell, but I didn't try to move away from her. I just didn't know how to keep it up anymore. I hadn't missed the word *thought,* but it was hard to think about her having a positive pregnancy test at all with another man when I'd just finished making her mine.

"I didn't know how to tell you. I've always been careful so I wouldn't get pregnant with him. On Monday I was waiting at the doctor's office when you and I talked on the phone. I wanted to tell you in person after, but then Collin showed up at the appointment."

Harlow's body started shaking. It took all my strength to move my arm to pull her close again, but I didn't comment on the near-violent trembling.

"He's never missed work, or left early, a day that we've been married. But he went, and that's when we found out that there was no baby. There *hadn't* been a baby. Collin was . . . Collin was . . ." She trailed off, and her head shook slowly as one hand came up to rest on her throat. Her eyes weren't focused, and I knew she wasn't seeing me, or the room we were in. She choked out a sob and turned onto her side to press her forehead into my chest.

I ran my hand over her back and tried not to think of the way her shoulder blades and spine felt against my palm, or the way her hip felt digging into my stomach.

"He's changed," she murmured. "He's changed, and it's terrifying."

"Wasn't he terrifying before?"

I hardly breathed for minutes as Harlow whispered about things Collin had done to her; she described them in a way that suggested *she'd* done something wrong—dirty even. I'd seen every bruise by that point, but I hadn't imagined anything half as bad as what she'd described. "Oh my God," I finally said. "I'm taking you from here. I need to—"

"No, that was before," she said, and lifted her head to look into my eyes. Her eyes were round with understanding and worry. "He—he's not doing that now. Some ways it's better, I guess. But it really is so much worse."

My mouth opened, but no sound came out. All I could think

was, *How can anything be worse?* Then I looked down to her throat, and I thought I might understand.

It wasn't until she told me about the shower on Monday, and what had happened with the eggs that morning, that I realized I didn't.

"Now you know," she said with fresh tears in her eyes. "Now you know everything. I swore I would never tell anyone what was happening, or what had happened, but I know with this change, each day my monster comes out is only going to get worse and worse until there isn't another day for me."

A sob hitched in my throat, but I choked it back down. I knew that if she was saying those words, then she meant them. Harlow wouldn't say them for sympathy or dramatic effect. Not after she'd endured years of what she'd just explained to me, and had tried before to tell me she was fine and could handle it.

"Why?" I finally asked. "Why did you choose him? There had to have been some sign that he was this guy."

"None. I look back and still don't see it. But, Knox, I'd thought I'd lost you before my eighteenth birthday ever came." My brow furrowed, but she continued before I could ask. "I know what was going on back then because my dad told me, but when I left Seattle and you pulled away from me, I was so sure that you were pulling away for good—that you were done waiting for me. My heart broke every day until Collin had healed it enough that it finally stopped."

It felt like I was back at that day. It felt like my heart was being ripped out all over again. "You thought I was pulling away from you?" I asked, horror coating my words. "Harlow, no, I was pushing you to go have a life, and giving you time to know exactly what you wanted because your dad made me promise I would!"

"I know," she said. Tears fell from her eyes, and she brought a hand up to cover my cheek. "I was so confused when you called me on my birthday. Confused in my feelings and why you were calling at all. I was sure you only called for the same reason you sporadically called in the months before—out of obligation. But even though I thought *you* were done with me, I still was so worried that I'd made a mistake in choosing him. I'm so sorry," she choked out. "Not waiting for you was the biggest mistake of my life, Knox Alexander."

I shook my head, unable to grasp how badly everything had gotten fucked-up back then. I'd blamed Harlow . . . I'd blamed her dad . . . and now I knew I had to blame myself. I'd unintentionally broken her heart and sent her into Collin's arms while I wrecked myself just trying to give her a few months of freedom. "How long did it take you to realize that?"

Her face twisted with grief. "What difference will it make?" The words were so soft, even with her pressed this close to me I could barely hear them.

"I want to know," I assured her.

"It will only hurt you mo—"

"Harlow."

She sighed, and her eyes drifted to the side, like she was remembering things from those years apart. "I always *wondered*. I dream of you most nights, and it started right after that phone call on my eighteenth birthday. I'd wake up in the middle of the night from the dreams crying, and would cry until I fell asleep again. But I kept telling myself that I was in love with Collin—

well, I *was* in love with Collin. I think I told myself I wasn't in love with you anymore because I knew you weren't in love with me." Her head shook once. "The day he asked me to marry him was when I first *thought* I'd made the wrong choice.

"When he asked, I had this flashback to the night you told me you were going to marry me—that night we planned our whole future—and all I could see was you when I told him 'yes.' Collin started changing that night. Just subtle things, but I think I just loved him enough that I kept excusing what he did, or making myself believe that it hadn't really happened. Then somehow time kept passing. Right before the wedding, every time I woke from a dream of you, I had this deep sense of longing and loss. That's when I *knew* that I'd chosen the wrong man. But it didn't matter; it was too late for us. Too much time had passed, and I was getting married to a man I loved, even if I could never love him the way I loved you. I just kept telling myself that even if I had chosen you, so much had changed and there had been so much heartbreak in those months after I'd left that we never would've been able to go back to how we had been."

"It never would've been too late for us," I insisted.

Harlow looked at me sadly, and the hand on my cheek curled. "I know that now."

Harlow
Fall 2012—Richland

"OH, HARLOW."

I turned and caught sight of my dad in the doorway my mom and sisters had just walked out of.

"You look . . ." He trailed off and shook his head once. His chin quivered, and my eyes widened.

"No, no! Please don't cry, Daddy! If you cry I'm going to ruin my makeup because you know I won't be able to hold it in. Please don't cry."

"I'm not," he said gruffly, and cleared his throat. After taking a second to look around the room to gather himself, he faced me again with a proud smile. "You look beautiful."

"Thanks, Dad," I whispered, and ran my shaking hands over my wedding dress.

"It's about that time; are you ready?"

I let out a slow breath and smiled up at him. Even after swallowing past the tightness in my throat, I still couldn't voice a word, so I nodded instead and grabbed my bouquet.

"Now, if you're not, we can still call this whole thing off and I won't think less of you. But I asked Hayley the same question before she got married, and I will ask Hadley, too. Are you sure you're making the right choice?"

I felt his question like a punch to my stomach. It had to be a normal question, right? Yet it felt like it meant so much more, because I *wasn't* sure. I was sure I loved Collin, but I knew I could never love him as much as I was capable of loving someone. Because I had loved someone with all that I am. I still loved that person with everything in me, and while I knew firsthand that you could love two men at the same time, you couldn't love them equally. One might have your heart, but the other would have your soul—*Knox Alexander* would always have my soul.

So was I making the right choice? Maybe today, but I would always live with the knowledge that two years ago, I didn't.

Before I could respond, my dad laughed lightly, like he'd

amused himself. "What am I saying? Of course you're sure you're making the right choice; otherwise it would've been a different man waiting in the church for you."

My brow pinched in confusion. "What? Dad, what are you talking about?"

He waved off my question. "Nothing, nothing. Are you ready?"

"No, tell me. What were you talking about?" I asked, and smiled reassuringly, hoping it would encourage him to tell me.

Dad debated with himself for a second, then finally said, "Well, a couple years ago, we all thought you would've married that Alexander boy."

Knox, I thought . . . or maybe screamed. I just knew my knees were barely holding me anymore.

"When he came to me before you left for school asking if he could marry you, I didn't know what to say. I mean you weren't even eighteen yet, but I also didn't think I could keep the two of you apart."

I wasn't sure how I was still standing. My body felt weighed down, but at the same time I was sure I was having an out-of-body experience. *He'd asked for permission to marry me?*

"I told him he could ask you once you were of age, but there were conditions. I wanted you to graduate first, and I wanted him to give you some space before then. I wanted you to be able to experience life without Knox always in the background. I told him if he promised to do that and kept my wishes, and after those months if you decided he was still what you wanted, then he could ask you." Dad shrugged and a wide grin crossed his face, like he hadn't just thrown my entire world on its side. "Next thing we know, you're with Collin and never mention Knox again. I figure if anyone could take you from that Alexander boy, then you would have to be sure of him. And we really couldn't be happier with Collin; your mother and I just think the world of him. I wish you would've waited to marry him until you graduated, but I know I don't always get what I wish for, and you really did find a good one."

I tried to smile and nod in acknowledgment, but I don't know if I succeeded.

"It eases a father's worry to know his daughter is loved and will be well cared for. Now, what do you say we start this thing?" he asked, oblivious to the devastation I was feeling.

"Uh, yeah, I just need one minute, Dad. I'll meet you in the lobby."

His carefree smile suddenly slipped, and his brow furrowed.

"I just realized I forgot to put my garter on," I lied quickly. "Really, I'll be right out."

He made a face that suggested he would've preferred not knowing, and turned to leave the room I was in.

The second the door shut, the pained cry I'd been holding back burst from my chest. The room spun and my stomach churned as my dad's words replayed in my mind, as if they were taunting me.

Experience life without Knox always in the background.

If he promised to do that and kept my wishes . . . he could ask you.

Experience life without Knox always in the background.

If he promised to do that and kept my wishes . . . he could ask you.

Guilt flooded my veins, burning and choking me as it surged through me.

Knox *had* waited for me.

I hadn't waited for him . . . and now it was too late.

Knox
Present Day—Richland

HARLOW'S FINGERS MOVED down my cheek and traced over my lips when she finished telling me the story. "I've never hated myself more than I did in that moment. Guilt felt like a living thing inside me. Then Collin and I got married, and I met my monster for the first time that night. I quickly found out there was nothing left of Collin to love."

I grabbed her hand in mine and turned my head to kiss her palm. "I'm taking you away from him," I mumbled against her skin.

She sighed, like my words had just put a weight on her. "You can't."

"I can, and I am."

"Knox, you don't understand what he'll do."

"No, I do," I disagreed, and my eyes fell to her right cheek, which was still slightly red from where he'd hit her earlier. "You made a decision today when you texted me. You knew he might see it, and you did it anyway. Before today, you never would've let me in this house because you would've been too scared for him to find me here, or find out about it."

Her eyes fell away from mine, but I knew she couldn't deny it.

"You made a decision when you let me make you mine. After that, you can't expect me to ever let you go." I tilted her head up until she was looking at me, then continued talking. "You also told me before that you wouldn't tell me what happened between you two, unless you were ready to leave."

"But, Knox—"

"You told me yourself that he's changing, and if he's getting careless enough to do what he's done this week, then not only am I not letting you go, but there's no way I'm leaving you with him for another day."

Harlow's head was shaking before I finished speaking. "After running into you that day in the coffee shop," she said, "I would've done anything to have you take me away right then. I *still* would give and do anything to have you take me away." Her next smile looked pained, but her eyes were distant. "Collin had me found just inside Oregon and arrested on a false charge when I tried to run from him. That's why I'm trying to tell you that you can't take me. He *will* find me, and he *will* bring me back. But that's the least of my worries. I told you; he threatens my family. He had someone set fire to a house they were in the night I tried to leave. He went after Hadley with his gun one night when she was here, but I got her out before she noticed, and he killed my dog because I *did* get her out."

My eyes were wide with shock and disgust, but before I could comment on everything, it hit me. "Where does he keep his gun?"

"You think I haven't tried to find it? I'm here all day, almost every day. I clean the house from top to bottom. I look for hidden places, too; I have yet to find anything." She rolled her eyes as she said, "I mean, Collin thought I was trying to poison him with salt today. I don't think he'd leave a gun somewhere where I could find it."

"*That* is not funny," I said with a growl.

Her face softened. "I'm sorry."

Seconds passed before I once again vowed, "I'm getting you away from him. Today, Harlow. We'll call your family; we'll figure something out. I'll keep you safe, I'll figure out a way to keep them all safe." I didn't try to hide the urgency in my tone.

She needed to know how serious I was; she needed to know that I meant right now, not sometime in the future. "Go and pack whatever you need; whatever you don't get I'll take care of—"

Her hands went back to cradle my face, and her thumbs brushed across my lips in a way to stop me from talking—and somehow it worked. I knew she wasn't going to agree. I knew, and it was frustrating me as much as it was making me panic. "I love you," she said simply.

"Harlow . . ."

"I've always loved you, Knox, and I will always love you; but I can't lea—"

"Yes, you can!"

"I can't!"

"Then tell me what this was," I demanded as I pulled away from her and got off the bed. My voice rose as I took a few steps away, then turned to look at her again. "Tell me why you just gave yourself to me after seven goddamn years, Harlow!"

She pushed herself up with one arm, and her face showed how much all this hurt her—but it was hurting me more.

I continued when she opened her mouth to respond. "Was it some goodbye? Did you want to see what we would be like together since I wouldn't touch you before? To see what you'd given up?" I sneered, and she exhaled heavily, like I'd punched her.

"Knox." My name was barely audible, but her tone told me everything.

I already knew that had been low; I'd known it the second it had left my mouth—but I hadn't been able to stop it. "I told you, you made a decision today," I began again, though this time the anger was fading from each word. "I know you, Harlow, and you know me. You know I would never be okay with only having a portion of you, and I know you would never ask me to do that. What we did before, we did because I *knew* I would have all of you one day. What we did today, we did because I know I *have* all of you. And now that I do, you can't try to take part of you away again."

Tears had been steadily falling down her cheeks since I'd gotten off the bed, but at my last words a muffled sob left her, and she dropped her head so I couldn't see her face anymore. "I did make a decision today," she whispered when I knelt onto the bed and pulled her into my arms. "But it's not the one you think I did, and it's not the one I wish I could have."

My body tensed, but I remained quiet.

"I made a decision to love you—completely—for the rest of my life."

In any other situation, those words would have made me happier than I could begin to describe . . . but not now. The way her voice broke on the last few words told me exactly what she meant, and told me exactly what I didn't want to hear.

She'd already hinted that with Collin's unpredictable behavior, she didn't think she had long to live. So Harlow was giving herself to me the only way she could until the day came where Collin didn't stop himself.

And I wasn't going to accept that.

"You just said that you would do anything to have me take you away." I tried to hold some type of accusation in my tone, but my words were shaky and sounded defeated.

"I would, Knox. If my fam—" She broke off and inhaled audibly. "Collin."

"What?"

"He's home!" she hissed, and looked around wildly.

"How do you know?" I asked as I jumped off the bed and began grabbing clothes off the floor. I tossed Harlow's in her direction as I came across them.

"His car is in the driveway."

I stood quickly from where I was pulling on my boxer briefs and looked toward the window—the curtains were closed.

Before I could ask, she answered: "It's like he's trained me to be terrified of the sound of his car on our driveway; I couldn't miss the sound of it even if I tried." She pulled her shirt over her head and immediately began tidying the bed. "Oh God, oh God, oh God! Why is he coming home early?" she whispered to herself. "He never does this, why does he keep doing this?"

As soon as I was dressed, I pulled her away from the bed and into my arms. I cut off her harried whispering with my mouth, and even though her body was tense at first, it quickly melted against mine until we heard the key in the lock.

"You have to go!" she said, but I knew in her hopeless expression that there was no way I was getting out of there without her husband knowing about it.

"I'm a firefighter, Low. I can just climb out the window," I suggested.

"No!" she said too loudly, and began pushing me toward the closet in the room. "All the windows have alarms on them. If you open one, it'll chime throughout the house. Just—"

"Harlow!" Collin yelled, and her body seemed to crumple while remaining upright.

"We have his parents' anniversary dinner tonight, it's hours away, but you'll be—"

"Harlow?" Collin called out again, his voice sounding farther away, but more aggravated.

My eyes narrowed and my body prepared to fight.

"Please," Harlow whispered. "Don't."

With that she turned and walked calmly out of the room, and I strained to hear every sound, and every word.

Chapter 16

Harlow
Present Day—Richland

COLLIN WALKED INTO the living room at the same time I walked out of the hallway. Thankfully he'd missed what room I'd come from.

"Where the hell have you been?" he snapped, and my head jerked back.

I blinked slowly, and prayed to whoever was listening that my shaking wasn't as bad as I feared it was. I needed to make this look convincing. Forcing my body to move slowly, I looked behind me, then back to Collin. "I—what time? I fell asleep after my shower . . ." I let my eyes widen and my breathing deepen, and hoped that my fear of my husband finding Knox in the house showed well enough like the way my fear of Collin usually did. "Oh—I'm so sorry; I can't believe I slept so long. I-I-I'll be ready so soon, I—"

"It's only one P.M., Harlow."

I knew I still had a part to play, I knew I needed to make him think something . . . but at that moment I couldn't remember what, because I'd just noticed his eyes. Lifeless. He was now coming home early because of my monster.

"Collin," I whispered as he inched closer.

"You know, I was at work and there was just something about this morning that I couldn't stop thinking about." He moved a couple of steps closer, and I finally figured out how to move back, but he quickened his pace as he continued speaking. "Do you know what it was?"

I shook my head hastily and my body jerked when I backed into the wall.

"Guess, Harlow."

"Um, you . . . I don't—um. You didn't eat. I didn't make you anything else that you could to take with you and you didn't eat breakfast?" I sputtered out quickly.

"No, but close." He waited until his body was pressed against mine and he was looking down at me before he spoke again. "You threw up."

If I wasn't so worried about what he was about to do—not only for me, but because I knew Knox would try to interfere—I would have given him a questioning look. As it was, I stood there breathing shallowly, trying to figure out where this was going. "Y-yes," I said, but it sounded more like a question.

"I know you don't like eggs, but you didn't have a reason to throw them up, unless you *did* in fact poison them. Why else would you need them out of your body so quickly?"

No. No, no, not this again. My voice was barely above a whisper when I said, "Collin, no."

"What did you put in the salt shaker?"

"Salt, Collin, I told you. I will go make something else and eat it all if it will convince you!"

A wicked smile pulled at his lips; the look on his face said it was too little, too late.

I shook uncontrollably as I waited for something . . . *anything*. But instead of what I was used to, or any of the new things, he tilted his head to the side and all the blood drained from my head when he asked, "How's Hadley?"

My body instantly swayed, but he was standing close enough that I didn't go far. "No. No," I whimpered. "Please, no. It was salt; I swear to you it was salt. Don't touch my sister!" I begged.

"Touch her?" he scoffed. "*I* would never do that, *wife*."

With the way he was looking at me, and the way he called me "wife," I was so sure he knew about Knox. But as I stood there holding my breath, he didn't mention him or the secret phone.

Collin reached into his back pocket, and a second later he was pushing my cell phone against my stomach. Once I had it in my hands, he stepped back and dipped his head in the phone's direction. "I had to come home because I have no doubt someone is going to be calling you soon." He turned and walked toward the couch, and the humor in his tone was unmistakable. "It's convenient that your sister decided to stay in Richland over the summer, isn't it?"

My stomach churned, and the dread that filled me over the next few minutes was enough to make me almost forget that Knox was hiding out in the guest room.

I jumped when my phone rang, and my chin began trembling when I saw "Mom" on the screen.

I looked over to where Collin sat on the couch with a sly grin and asked, "What did you do?"

His smile fell. "Me? That's a bold accusation, especially considering neither of us actually has any idea what you're even talking about. You should probably answer your phone."

After tapping on the screen and bringing the phone to my ear, the tears began falling when I heard my mom sobbing on the other end. "Mom?"

"Oh, Harlow," she whimpered, and her sobs increased. "Harlow, it's Hadley, she—she drove her car into a-a-a—" She broke off, and I heard the phone being shuffled.

My dad's voice didn't sound much better, but he was able to get the words out. "Honey? We're on our way, but can you get to the hospital? Hadley drove her car into a house. She's alive, she's going to be fine, but they said they think she was under the influence of something," he said. "Did you know she was into this? How did we not know?" he asked himself before I could answer.

Not that I could or would anyway. I couldn't even speak. My sister drank at parties, but never even to the point where she had to make up for it the day after. She definitely didn't drink in the afternoon, and I could only assume "something" meant something other than alcohol. And that wasn't Hadley. My eyes found Collin's. No life, but they were still smiling.

I wanted to scream that it was Collin's fault; that whatever Hadley had done was because of him. But then I would pay, Knox would try to save me, who knew what would happen to him, and then the rest of my family would pay even more than they already were.

"Harlow?" Dad asked. "Can you get there? She needs one of us there, and we're still three hours away."

"Of course, I'll be there as soon as I can," I said.

Dad choked out a sob. "It'll be okay, Harlow. She'll be okay. She will. She'll be okay."

I nodded, though he couldn't see me. Because Hadley *would* be okay, as long as I kept my mouth shut and tried to make Collin happy. "See you soon. Love you," I whispered, then ended the call.

"Go make yourself presentable. Try to cover your cheek, and make sure your neck is covered. I'll take you," Collin said in a businesslike tone. "We can't have you around them by yourself, now can we?"

I'd been staring at the floor, but when he finished talking, I slowly looked up at him. Inside I was screaming how much I hated him. I was taking all my anger from the last two and a half years out on him. I was making him regret ever touching me. On the outside I was still as stone as tears silently fell from my cheeks onto the floor.

WHEN WE GOT home hours later, I understood just how much planning had gone into that punishment—and in only a matter of hours that morning. Once my parents had arrived at the hospital, we'd only been able to stay for another twenty minutes before Collin had told them about his parents' anniversary dinner, which we "weren't allowed to miss." But only after swearing we would be back, and promising he would get Hadley moved to a suite in the hospital. Just enough time for my parents to see that I was alive and mostly well, and well loved and spoiled by my husband, and to remember why Collin was their favorite.

But not long enough for them to notice my hatred toward him, why I would tense whenever he went near Hadley, or why he would give me a look that promised so many horrible things when I left his side for more than a second. And of course, with everyone so focused on Hadley, no one noticed my shaking, my too-thin body, or the red mark on my cheek I hadn't attempted to cover.

Hadley had had a nearly lethal dose of PCP in her system when she'd driven her car into the side of a house. In her state, she'd climbed out of the car—even with a broken arm—and had fought police officers when they'd attempted to restrain her. Police officers who had just *happened* to be following her.

She was heavily sedated and handcuffed to the hospital bed with those same officers stationed outside her room when we'd arrived. But then Collin had *saved the day* when he announced he'd make sure all the charges against her were dropped, and would take care of the damage costs. Of course, he'd waited to do all this when my parents had shown.

In their hysterical state, my parents had only been thankful for my husband and what he was doing. While I was thankful this wouldn't go on Hadley's record, I couldn't stop from study-ing the officers as they'd taken the cuffs off my sister, and then left. Because there was no way something like that could just go away the way Collin had made it—especially with this new chief Collin hated so much—I knew they were receiving money from my husband. Just as the officer who had arrested me had.

"Get ready," Collin said without a glance in my direction as he took off for the bedroom.

I waited until he was in there before going into the guest room to check the closet. I'd known—well, hoped—Knox would know to leave when we did, but was still disappointed when I found the closet empty and bed made. The windows in there were still closed and locked, and the front door had been locked when we'd come home, so I wasn't sure how he'd left, and knew I didn't have time to go around trying to find out.

I walked into the bedroom just as Collin came out of the closet—already in a different dress shirt with a tie in his hand. His face showed that he'd been wondering where I was.

"I told you to get ready," he growled.

"How did Hadley have PCP in her system?" I asked shakily. I knew I shouldn't, I knew I wasn't supposed to question him, but he could've killed her.

Collin's eyes narrowed. "Ask her yourself when she's back to normal. It's probably from all those clubs she goes—"

"She doesn't go to clubs. What did you do, Collin?" I whispered, pain for my sister evident in my voice. "It was *salt*. I threw up because I'd been so scared and unable to breathe while trying to eat the eggs, that my stomach kept churning until they came back up. I would *never* poison you, and you almost killed Had—"

"Don't finish that assumption," he warned.

"Where did you even see her? Why can't you just leave my family out of this?" I knew what I was about to say could have the opposite reaction I was going for, but I had to try. "If I wasn't always so afraid of you hurting them, I probably wouldn't mess up so often!"

His lips twitched, and he turned to look into a mirror so he could knot his tie. "Don't act like this was anyone's fault other than your own. It was just a coincidence that I decided to have lunch at the same place Hadley was at with a friend. We talked for a few minutes when her friend went to the bathroom, and I made sure Hadley had . . ." His hands stopped fidgeting with his tie, and his eyes found mine in the mirror. " . . . salt."

I inhaled audibly and my head started shaking, like I could make the words go away. I'd known, but hearing his pseudo-admission still shocked me. I don't know why—nothing should have shocked me about Collin anymore. "I hate you."

A few things happened at the exact moment I realized I'd said those words out loud instead of just thinking them. I stopped breathing, Collin froze and his lifeless eyes turned murderous, and I knew—I *knew*—I'd made a mistake. Not just in finally saying those fated three words, but with Knox. In not letting him take me away . . . in not trying to get away from Collin.

I knew right then that if I had my whole life to do over again, I would've waited for Knox. That if I only had the past two and a half years to do over again, I would've fought harder to get away from Collin until I'd succeeded. That if I only had the past two weeks to do over again, I would've begged Knox to help me get away from Collin, and would've spent my life running from my monster, as long as I got to spend it with the man who had always held my heart.

Funny the things you realize, the things you wish you'd done differently, and the things you just wish you'd *done* when you know your life is about to end. And I had no doubt my life was minutes from being over.

With a slowness that sent a chill through my veins, Collin dropped his head and turned to face me. When his body was facing mine, his head stayed down but his eyes lifted. "Do you want to repeat that?"

I didn't move, and I didn't respond. I knew he didn't want me to.

He took one slow step toward me, and my body tightened in preparation for what was to come. He took another, and my eyes met his. He took another, and I turned and ran from the room.

I'd only made it two steps into the hallway before he grabbed on to my hair and slammed me into the hallway wall—the force sent a couple of pictures and a painting crashing onto the hardwood floor. My head bounced off the wall, and I tripped over one of the pictures as I tried to keep going, but he still had my hair fisted in his hand.

Collin pulled me back roughly until my back was to his chest, and he whispered into my ear, "Again. Do you want to repeat that?"

I blinked away the dark spots in my vision, and then realized I had blood dripping from my forehead. I swiped at it and whimpered when he jerked my head back. "Collin, please."

"Please, what?"

"Don't do this."

He laughed, but it sounded more like a sneer. "Not a question this time. Repeat what you said," he demanded.

I shook my head and a cry bubbled up my throat.

"Tell me what you said!" His entire body jerked with the force of his command.

"I hate you." The words were a whisper, and I barely had them out before he moved from behind me and flung me onto the floor. I hadn't had time to brace for the impact, and now it felt like my entire head was ready to explode.

Collin's weight fell onto me quickly, his knees pinned my

hands to the hard ground, and like he had done so many times this week, his hand went around my throat and squeezed. His hand forced a cry out of me, and I immediately began bucking underneath him.

"You hate me now? After everything I've done for you? After everything I've *given* you?" he roared, and squeezed tighter.

I'd stopped fighting against him by the time he'd finished yelling. Hitting my head twice, losing so much blood from my forehead, and him cutting off my air made the fight go out of me faster than it ever had before.

When I was on the edge of losing consciousness, his fingers loosened one at a time, and I began choking as I tried to suck in air. My eyes were wide open as I looked around wildly, but when I caught the briefest glimpse of Collin's, I'd wished I'd kept them closed.

Not lifeless. Still murderous. Not my monster. Something new, something terrifying, something I knew I would never see again because he was finally finished with me. Collin's lips twitched into a quick smile, and he grabbed my hair in his hand as he stood up and began dragging me over frames and broken glass.

I think some type of cry was forced from my chest, but it sounded weak. My whole body felt weak. The left side of my face was wet and warm, and even though I could breathe freely now, I wasn't sure how long I had before I could no longer keep my eyes open.

The hardwood below me changed to carpet, and something like horror spiked through my body when I realized he was dragging me through the guest room. In between trying to keep myself conscious, I once again thought that Collin must know about Knox, must have somehow known that he'd been in the house this afternoon—but then Collin kept dragging me until I was on tile.

I heard the bathwater turn on and whimpered in protest. We didn't have a tub in our bathroom, mostly because Collin hated them, and whenever he cleaned me up or had some kind of water punishment, it was done in the shower—never the bath. Regardless, I hated those punishments, and didn't want to have to fight this. But instead of undressing me like he normally would, Collin lifted me just to drop me into the large tub, which had hardly any water in it yet. I cried out when my body smacked down on the hard acrylic, and even though I didn't try to get up, Collin pressed his hands against my chest to keep me in place after he put the stopper in to let the water start collecting.

I looked up at him in panic. His face was perfectly composed—he almost looked bored, as if he was watching grass grow. The murderous look had left, but in its place was an emptiness I'd never seen. I'd thought his eyes had been lifeless before— but this was like he was really dead.

"Collin. Collin!" I tried to yell, but my voice was hoarse and soft. "Collin, please!" I started breathing too roughly—but the movements made breathing harder from how much weight he was putting on my chest—and as the water rose higher and higher, I began hyperventilating. My thrashing in the tub wasn't helping me. "Collin!"

He sighed, and his eyes drifted to where the water was splashing over the edge of the tub, and then down to his arms. "Now I'm going to have to change again." He sounded annoyed by that, but he didn't move his arms as the water rose higher up them and over his tie. "Which shirt should I wear tonight, Harlow? I think

I'd like to wear my green tie. Do you know which one? Not the one with the design on it. The solid green one."

"Collin!" I screamed over the water, and tried to raise my head higher when it started drifting over my lips.

"Well, do you know which tie, or not?"

"Forest green," I spit out, and he nodded absentmindedly.

"Now, which shirt do I wear with that, Harlow, and don't say black. I need to know."

I blinked quickly and tried to calm my mind. The sooner I thought of a shirt, the sooner he'd let me up. "Um. Gray. Light gray." My panic went into overdrive when I saw the slightest twitch at the corner of his lips, and knew he didn't like my answer. "P-pale green! Gray vest!" I shouted around more water. "Collin, *please*!"

Collin dipped his head in a slight nod, as if he was happy with what I'd suggested, and then his dead eyes finally met mine again. "You claimed you didn't feel well after visiting your sister, so I decided to let you stay home. How horrible will it be for your parents when they find out *you* are the reason their youngest daughter has gotten into the drug scene? That your guilt over her near-death experience drove you to . . ." He smirked and clicked his tongue. "Well."

"Collin! Collin, no!" I screamed, and my thrashing increased.

He leaned over the tub to kiss my forehead. All of his weight on my chest caused me to sink deeper and the air to rush out of me. I tried to grab at him, but I couldn't get a good hold on him, and my panic was making me clumsy in my movements.

"Collin! I'll do whatever you want, *be* whatever you need," I promised as water filled my mouth and slid down my throat. "*Please* don't do this!"

He used my chest as support to stand up, and shook his head once. "I love you," he said in a detached voice before he released my chest.

The last thing I remember was using what little energy I had left to push out of the water before he grabbed the side of my head and slammed it down onto the edge of the tub. I was sliding into the water when darkness pulled me into its arms.

Chapter 17

Knox
Present Day—Thatch

"STOP MURDERING THE damn carpet, Christ!" Graham yelled when he stepped inside the house a few hours after I'd snuck out Harlow's back door.

I turned and halted when I saw Grey and Jagger standing there with confused looks. Of *course* she would be here today.

"Murdering the . . . what?" Grey finally asked before coming up to give me a hug. She must have noticed how tense I was, because she gave me a strange look when she backed away from me to go into her husband's arms.

"He's always pacing when we come home. *Always,*" Graham answered as he walked into the living room. The look he gave me as he shouldered past me to sit on the couch let me know he knew exactly why I was pacing, and he wasn't happy about it.

He began divvying up the food that he'd carried in. "I brought you food, too," he said to me.

"Not hungry."

"Guilt eating at you?" he mumbled, and his eyes flashed up to me.

My eyebrows pulled down low over my eyes, and I had to take a calming breath so I wouldn't lash out at him in front of his sister and brother-in-law. "I'm not doing this today," I said in a clipped tone, then turned and stalked to my room.

Unfortunately, my pacing in that space consisted of two steps before turning to go back the opposite way, and within just a couple of minutes I felt like I needed to get out of there. I needed to get to Harlow, but I didn't know where she was. I just knew they left, and I knew they had that dinner tonight, so there was no chance of me being able to get in touch with her in any way. But knowing she was with him, after I had found out how bad it had been all this time and how much worse it was getting, I hated every minute that passed without her by my side.

It felt like each passing hour was taunting me, choking me. I had to find her. I had to save her. I had to get her away from that house and keep her from that bastard for the rest of her life. And I would do everything in my power to make sure that life was long.

"Oh, Knox," Grey said in a musical lilt as she walked into my room. Her eyes studied me as she leaned against a wall and absentmindedly played with her large stomach. "I'm actually on my way to work. Graham wanted to spend time with Jagger, and I wanted to see you and Deacon before I had to go in. But why do I have a feeling that Graham wanted Jagger here for a reason?"

I lifted an eyebrow and tried to mask the fear and adrenaline pumping through my body. "What do you mean?"

"Usually Jagger just sees you guys if I'm here. But Graham was adamant that Jagger be here, and tonight you're not working, and there was a lot of tension between you and my brother out there. So it's not really hard for us to figure out that Graham wanted a buffer. I want to know why one was even needed."

"Your guess is as good as mine." I shrugged, and her eyes narrowed, but I didn't offer any other explanation. With how Graham and Deacon had reacted, and how pissed-off Grey had been when she'd found out Harlow was married, I knew that telling her any portion of the truth right now would be pointless.

"Fine," Grey eventually said. "I have to go." She pushed from the wall and walked to the door, but before she left she looked at me and said, "If you ever decide you need to tell someone what's happening, I *will* listen. I may not agree with you, but I'll listen."

I didn't respond, just watched until she left, then I resumed my compact pacing. Graham could bring in a buffer all he wanted; I didn't plan on going out there anyway.

Harlow
Present Day—Richland

I CHOKED ON water, and my heavy eyelids slowly blinked open. Each felt like it weighed fifty pounds, and lifting them like one of the hardest things I'd ever done. But I was still choking, and I knew I had to keep them open.

I was in the tub, mostly floating. My top half was twisted so only one of my eyes was out of the water, and I gasped when I remembered Collin—causing me to inhale the water that was tinted red with my blood, making me choke harder. I struggled to sit upright as I forced water out of my lungs, and looked around the guest bathroom for any signs of my monster, but he wasn't in there with me. I heard the sound of running water, but it still took me a few moments to realize that it was coming from the tub faucet, and that water was covering the bathroom floor.

I hurried to shut it off then sat still as stone as I waited for sounds other than my wheezing breaths. He would have heard me, and he would come for me soon if he was still here.

I'm not sure how long I waited, but I had two coughing fits that I wasn't able to stop in that time. I was worried with each one that Collin would come rushing in to finish what he'd started. I tried to stand but couldn't force the lower half of my body to cooperate yet, and ended up pulling myself out of the tub instead.

My sharp gasp filled the bathroom when I landed hard on the wet floor, and long minutes passed before I felt like I was able to make myself move again. But by that time, my legs were working again. They were shaky, but working. Although I knew it was a vulnerable position, I crawled as far as the hallway before I was able to push myself onto my feet, and then had to use the wall to help me walk.

I didn't know how long I'd been unconscious, and even though I would've bet my life that Collin would come running in at the first sign of me waking up, I was now second-guessing everything because I didn't know my monster at all anymore. He could have been waiting, for all I knew. Watching with those dead eyes from somewhere in the house as I slowly dragged one foot in front of the other toward the front door, the whole time a sick smile played on his face. I was soaked head to toe, but I didn't care. I didn't have time or the strength to go into my bedroom to change. I needed to get out. I needed to run.

Just before I made it to the front door, I caught sight of myself in the large mirror in the entryway, and what I saw made my already-trembling body start jerking from the force of my silent sobs. I looked like someone coming back from the dead to get their revenge. I was so terrifying I was only able to look at myself for a split second before I looked away. I didn't have time to change the wet clothes or shoes, but I also couldn't afford to have anyone call the police if they saw me and my blood-tinted shirt.

Turning around, I pulled open the entry closet and grabbed one of Collin's dark hoodies. It swallowed me whole, but none of my coats in that closet had hoods, and I needed something to hide the gash on my forehead, which was pumping out blood again.

My shoulders dropped in relief when I finally made it outside and didn't see Collin's car, but I knew better than to let my guard down now.

He can still be playing a game with you. He may have just moved his car to make you think he left. You need to get out of here, Harlow. You need to run. You need to go faster than this. You need to run! I chanted to myself, and was glad to see that each step was a little easier, and a little faster than the last.

There was something freeing in running—well, shuffling—from that house. From him. There was also something close to panic that was threatening to cripple me. Something that kept screaming at me to go back so I wouldn't make Collin mad; that screamed he would find me. I tried to push those thoughts aside. He'd changed things tonight.

I'd thought at the hospital that I'd have to be good in order to keep Hadley and my family safe, but then I hadn't been able to keep my mouth shut. And then it had happened, what I'd been afraid of all day, but had still thought could be weeks, even months, away. Collin had snapped. No, Collin's *monster* had snapped, and he'd decided he was done. He had tried to kill me.

I stopped walking when that thought floated through my mind, and couldn't stop the sharp cry that burst from my chest before I was able to slap my hands over my mouth. Through everything over the last two and a half years, I'd known I could get through it. And it had escalated to this all within a few short days. I'd hated my life, I'd hated him, but I'd never thought we'd get to this day. Knowing we had, remembering the look in his eyes and on his face, remembering the panic that had consumed me before the dark had welcomed me, was making it hard to breathe now.

Move, Harlow. Move.

I forced myself forward and didn't stop until I found myself at the front of the neighborhood. I hadn't thought this far ahead; I'd just known I needed to leave the house. Now I was turning in circles trying to figure out where to go from here. I was worried that if I started knocking on doors asking to use a phone, people would call the police either on me or for me.

I jumped when I heard a voice call out, "You lost, kid?"

I turned and found a man not much older than myself looking at me from across the street. He was holding a leash attached to a fierce-looking dog, but the dog was too excited about the car directly next to him to notice me. The man's eyes squinted and he bent in an effort see inside the hood I had pulled down low. My hands twisted nervously as I stuttered out in a hoarse voice, "N-no, I'm trying to get to Thatch. But I don't have a ride or a phone."

He laughed, and I found myself relaxing at the sound. It was calm and amused, not a hint of the evil I'd lived with and had come to know so well. "What teenager doesn't have a phone these days?"

I didn't correct him on the *teenager* part.

He pointed at me as he continued. "I'd be damn lucky to have you in one of my classes. I feel like I spend more time taking phones away than I do teaching."

I nodded and glanced away for a second to gather myself. I needed to ask him to use his phone, but that meant I'd get closer to him . . . and that's where this all got tricky. "Can I—"

"What are you headed to Thatch for?" he asked, and his tone held a hint of something other than curiosity. It sounded like worry, but that didn't make sense; he didn't know me in order to worry about me. When I looked at him again, he'd let the dog into his car and had his door open, but he continued to stand there watching me.

It took me a few seconds to think of the best response, and from his face it was a few seconds too long. "I'm going *back* to Thatch. I'm not supposed to be here."

The man thought for a minute, then sighed. "Look, kid, if you were one of my students, I would call your parents and wait with you until they showed. But you're not, and I'm already running late to get to my fiancée's house—which is just on the other side of Thatch."

I wanted to tell him he couldn't be more than a few years older than me, but decided to keep my mouth shut and waited.

"If you can promise me, and I mean *really* promise me, that you'll maybe reconsider whatever it is you've been doing that you would need to find a ride back to Thatch, I'll give you a ride there."

As long as it got me out of this neighborhood and as far away from Collin as I could get right now, I would promise him anything. "I promise."

He gestured toward his car, and when I walked toward it, he held his hands up. "I mean, I know grown-ups aren't cool, and parents are the least cool of them all, but they usually know what they're talking about."

I nodded, not knowing what else to do or say, and paused outside the passenger door. "Um, I'm wet. I was . . . thrown into a pool with my clothes on."

"The seats will be fine," he said after only a second to consider. I could tell by his body language that he was anxious to start driving.

Once we were driving out of the neighborhood, he began talking again. "This is Spartacus," he said, gesturing toward the Rottweiler who was sniffing and licking the jacket I was wearing. "I'm Max, but I guess that's weird since everyone your age calls me Mr. Farro."

"Low," I responded, my voice still too hoarse to sound normal. When it looked like he was waiting for me to finish speaking, I clarified, "My name is Low."

He made a noise in the back of his throat. "Interesting name."

"Thank you so much for doing this."

Max waved off my thanks. "Just consider what I said. Things seem fun at the time, and it can be fun and exciting to rebel, but you can end up regretting it. Trust me, I've been there before—and I have to see it all the time with my students."

Again, I didn't know how to respond to that. "I'm sorry, but may I use your phone?" I didn't know how to tell him I didn't know where I was going; I also didn't know how I was going to explain it once we got into Thatch, but I needed to let Knox know I was coming.

After debating for a few seconds, he reached into his pocket and pulled a phone out. "Don't go calling your boyfriend or anything. Call your parents, or someone who can help you out tonight."

Despite the afternoon and evening that had been weighing me down, I smiled to myself. He talked like a grandpa who thought he needed to make sure I went down the right path in life. If I weren't covered in blood and bruises, I would've given anything to see his reaction if I pulled off my hood. "Of course," I murmured.

After dialing Knox's number, I held my breath while it rang and rang, and my stomach sank when his voice mail eventually picked up. *No. No, I need to get to you, I don't know how to find you!* I hung up and tried again, but got the same result. This time I left a short, direct message.

"It's Low, I'll be in Thatch soon."

I hung up and reluctantly handed Max's phone back to him. I hoped his phone would ring sometime on the drive, but it didn't. So I sat there worrying over how I was going to find Knox, and what was going to happen with my family and Collin, while letting Spartacus lick my borrowed jacket and listening to Max talk about the history class he taught at Hanford High School.

"Where to?" Max asked when we entered Thatch.

"Uh . . ." I looked around, not knowing what to do. Thatch was a small town—incredibly small—but I still couldn't go door-to-door. That would take forever, and again, would probably result in police. "You can just drop me off here," I suggested as we came up on a few shops.

"Are you sure?" Max asked, his tone disapproving. He was in grandpa mode again. Mid-twenties going on sixty.

"Yes, I'd prefer it, if you don't mind."

With a heavy sigh, Max pulled his car over. He sent me a wary glance and once again tried to look in my hood. "You keep yourself safe, get yourself home, and thank your parents for being so awesome."

I cracked another smile I knew he couldn't see. "Of course. Thank you, Max."

"That's Mr. Farro to you," he said, his voice teasing.

I stumbled out of his car, and tried to gain my footing as quickly as possible without showing any more signs of how dizzy or uncomfortable I was. I couldn't tell if my head was bleeding anymore, but it had bled enough, and now that I was standing again, everything was tilting to the side—making me feel like I was drunk.

Concentrating on each step, I put one foot in front of the other and walked into a little shop directly in front of me. And only then did Max drive off.

"Can I help you?" a man asked from behind the counter. "Before you demand it, I don't have more than thirty bucks in the register."

"Oh, I don't want—no, I—" I huffed, and only regretted my wardrobe choice for a second before remembering it was necessary. "I just need to find Knox Alexander."

Like Max had done, the man squinted as he tried to see in the hood. "Know him, don't know how to get in touch with him. Sorry, little lady."

I nodded and thanked the man, then went to the next shop, only to get similar results—that time complete with a death glare from a girl standing in the store. The next place over, which was half coffee shop, half bookstore, had at least a dozen people in it and made me feel a little more hopeful. But I was now swaying again from how long I'd been standing. I wasn't sure how I'd been able to make it all the way to the front of my neighborhood earlier when I could barely stay standing for a few minutes now.

I was breathing heavily by the time I forced myself over to the counter. There was a pregnant girl probably around my age standing behind it, and her eyebrows rose when she saw me.

"Hi," she said awkwardly. And while she didn't try to look into my hood, she kept giving me close looks, like she was worried about what I was going to do. "What can I make you?"

"Nothing. I need—"

Her eyes widened with dread, and her hands instinctively covered her swollen stomach.

"No, no I don't want to hurt you," I said. The hoarseness of my voice made my words sound weak and whiny, but that also could have had something to do with the fact that I knew I didn't have long before I couldn't keep myself upright, and I wasn't getting any closer to finding Knox. "I just need to find Knox Alexander. I *have* to talk to him. Do you know him?"

The pregnant girl relaxed and shook her head. "You and every other girl in this town as well as the surrounding cities. Sorry, but you're going to have to get in line with all the other women trying to find him again."

Her words hurt, but what did I expect? I'd known he'd tried to forget me. I'd made him do that; I hadn't waited for him.

"Do you know where he is? Or how to get in touch with someone who does? Or can I just use your phone?" I was desperate, and I knew I'd already tried that, but I was hoping enough time had passed that he'd answer now. "I was with him today. He will come get me, and I *need* to see him."

She huffed, but she didn't sound annoyed; there was pity behind it. "Well, now I know you're lying. And, no, I'm not letting you use the phone, and I'm not giving you his number."

Tears slid down my cheeks, and I wanted to scream. She knew him; she knew where he was. I was so close, and she wasn't going to let me get any closer. "I have his number, I just need a phone. *Please!*"

The pregnant girl now looked at me closely, just like everyone else had—eyebrows pinched and eyes narrowed. "If you have his number, why don't you use your own phone?" she asked, but her question sounded genuine.

"I don't have it."

"And why not?"

"I-I . . . I just don't," I whimpered, and swayed. "Please, it's so important for me to find him as soon as possible."

The girl tried to lean closer to me, but her swelling stomach wouldn't allow it. After a few silent seconds, she quietly asked, "What's your name?"

I wasn't sure why it mattered, but I found myself answering her anyway. "My name is Harlow."

I'd barely gotten my entire name out before her eyes widened and she rocked back on her heels. "Oh my God. Oh my God. Oh my . . . shit. Anne!" she yelled. "Anne! I need to go home! Right now, I'm leaving right now. I'm sorry, I'll make it up to you tomorrow!" She'd been taking off her dark apron as she talked, and she gave it to a woman—Anne, I presumed—without stopping. She rounded the counter and grabbed my hand to tow me outside with her. "Come with me," she said when I stumbled after her.

"Look, I don't know how you know Knox, but I don't have time for this." *Or the strength,* I thought lamely. "I *really—*"

The girl whirled on me and wrapped her arms around me. I stilled and bit back a cry of pain. "I always knew you'd come for him." When she pulled back, her eyes were glistening. "Stupid hormones. Get in the car; I'll explain."

Knowing I didn't have another option, I followed her to her car and slid into the passenger side. My face twisted in pain, but I knew my hood hid it.

Once we were driving, she started talking. "I just realized you might not know me. But I know everything about you, and everything about you and Knox. I have for *years.*" She glanced at me quickly and flashed a smile. "My brother is one of his best friends and roommates; my name is Grey."

Oh no. She was going to drive me as far away as she possibly could. "Grey, as in Graham's sister?"

Her eyes widened. "You do know me?"

"Yes, but . . . look, I know you all hate me, but it's an emergency. I *need* to see Knox."

"Hate you?" she asked incredulously. "I don't hate you . . ." She trailed off and looked sheepish for a moment. "There have been times I hated you for what you did to Knox. But he loves you, always has." She paused again, and this time when she spoke she didn't have the same excitement in her tone. "I didn't agree with you seeing each other while you were married. But if you're coming to him, then that must mean you made a decision, right?"

Decision. There was that word again. Yes, so many decisions had been made today. So many different ones I'd never expected to make.

When I didn't respond, Grey swore and slowly pulled off to the side of the road. After putting her car in park, she drummed her fingers quickly on the steering wheel for a few seconds and said, "I won't help you cheat on your husband."

My head whipped to the side to look at her, and I sucked in a sharp breath at the movement. "No, ah . . ." I sucked in another breath and waited until I was composed before I spoke again. "What exactly did Knox tell you?"

Grey gave me a quick once-over; her face was pinched in confusion like she was trying to figure out why I'd just hissed in pain. "I was the first one he told when he ran into you. He told me that he thought you weren't happy with your husband. That you cried when you saw him . . . that kind of stuff. When you told me who you were, I was excited because I want you for Knox, but not this way."

I was surprised he hadn't told her more, but thankful at the same time. I didn't need that. "There is so much that you don't know, so much I can't tell you. But I promise you that if it were as simple as me not being happy with my husband, I would not be in Thatch trying to find Knox. I told you, this is an emergency. One I can't call the police for."

Something in my tone must have convinced her, or at least prompted her to continue driving. But she didn't speak to me the rest of the way there, and she kept sending me worried glances—and I knew it wasn't me she was worried for.

We pulled up to the house and parked behind a few cars in the driveway. When I started opening the door to get out, Grey's soft voice stopped me. "I love Knox. He's like a brother. He means a lot to me, just like Deacon does. If all you want from him is to have fun, or to have someone besides your husband to make you feel loved, then I want you to know that he deserves more than that." She nodded in the direction of the house. "My husband is in there. If you have an emergency and need help, he can help you and we'll make sure Knox never knows. But you being here like this, Knox is going to think he can have you. If he can't . . . I can't let you go in there."

I opened the car door the rest of the way, and my voice broke when I said, "Then I guess I'm going in there."

A smile briefly covered her face before she could stop it, and then she followed me out of the car and up to the front door. She didn't knock; she just walked in. I heard a bunch of guys talking and laughing before they noticed Grey and started yelling her name.

"The love of my life!" Deacon called out.

Graham threw something at him and shouted back, "Dude, shut up! She's married; she doesn't want you!"

A guy walked quickly over to Grey and gave me a suspicious look as he pulled her into his arms and kissed her. "Why are you already off work, and who is this?"

The two other guys noticed me at the same time, but they couldn't see me with my hood up, and I wasn't taking it off for them.

Without answering them, Grey asked, "Where's Knox?"

"Here," he called out from somewhere in the house. His voice sounded distracted, and I turned to watch him walk down the hall, only to come to a halt when he saw me. Knox's head jerked back as his eyes narrowed, and then his entire body sagged. "Low?"

I took a tentative step toward him, still worried about what everyone else was about to do, but Knox quickly closed the distance and pulled me into his arms. One of his hands went up to the back of my head to cradle me close, and a sharp cry burst from my chest. Knox released me as quickly as possible but didn't move back. In a move just as fast, but still gentle, he unzipped the hoodie and pushed the hood off my head.

His eyes widened and he bent slightly at his waist, like the air had been knocked from his body, but rage quickly covered his face and he began shaking. "I'm going to kill—"

"You can't," I whispered urgently. My reminder sounded like a mix of warning and begging.

"Harlow," he seethed as his hand ran over the dried blood on my face. "Nothing's stopping me this time."

"You've got to be kidding me," a deep voice raged behind us.

Chapter 18

Harlow

Present Day—Thatch

I TURNED TO see Deacon and Graham standing there watching us. Graham looked shocked to see me there . . . but the blood and bruises could've had something to do with that. Deacon's lip was curled, but it quickly fell along with the rest of his face when he whispered, "Holy shit."

Grey was crying and mumbling something about hormones to the guy I assumed was her husband, and Knox was pulling me away from all of them.

"Knox!" One of the guys called out after I'd turned to allow him to pull me down the hall, but he didn't stop moving until we were in a bathroom.

"What happened?" he asked, and his tone was a deadly calm . . . detached even. But not detached in the same way Collin got. Knox was trying to help me, and he couldn't help me when all he wanted to do was kill my husband.

"He tried to kill Hadley," I murmured as he pulled the hoodie and my wet shirt off my body. "He gave her a lethal dose of PCP, she wrecked her car into—" My words broke off when my legs finally decided they'd had enough and gave out beneath me, but Knox caught me in his arms and held me despite the pained whimper that bubbled up my throat.

He walked me back a few steps, put the toilet lid down, and sat me on it. His hands brushed over my face and down my arms, making sure I was able to support my head and upper body before he released me and started searching through the cabinets under the sink. "We'll get into Hadley later, but I meant you. What did he do to *you*?"

"I have to tell you about Hadley so you'll know why I made him snap."

His dark eyebrows slammed down. "*You* didn't cause this," he sneered. Knox took another deep breath to continue but shut his mouth instead, and nodded for me to go on.

"Knox," Graham said as he opened the door, and I scrambled to pull the hoodie over my mostly bare chest. Deacon was right behind him.

"Get out," Knox growled. His eyes never left the cabinet in front of him as he searched through it.

They didn't move. Their eyes just stayed on me—their expressions going back and forth between worried and shocked. It was so unlike anything I'd ever seen from them.

Knox was suddenly in front of me again. He pushed the hair away from my face and ground his jaw when I flinched as he gently pressed all over my head. "Is there anywhere on your head you're not hurt?"

"It's just three spots." I showed him where, and tried to take steadying breaths when he began cleaning the cut on my forehead.

"Tell me what happened." When my eyes drifted to the side, he said, "Don't look at them. Keep your eyes on me, Low, and tell me what happened."

"He gave Hadley PCP, and when we got home from the hospital I started questioning him. He admitted to it, kind of—in so many words."

"What did he say?" Graham asked. His tone and expression showed he was invested in the short part of the story he'd already heard, but I didn't trust it. After everything over the years, I couldn't trust he would suddenly care about what happened to me.

I stared at him, waiting for it to happen—for the yelling to start—but Knox's annoyed huff was the only sound that came from any of the guys as he continued working on me. "I'm sorry. My bathroom is too small for this, otherwise I would've taken you in there. Keep talking."

I blinked slowly and looked back at him. "Um, could you hear what he said this afternoon before we left? What he couldn't stop thinking—"

"You were with her this afternoon?" Deacon's voice boomed in the small bathroom, making me jump.

This was it, what I'd been waiting for.

Graham smacked Deacon's head, and Deacon stumbled over his quick words, "Shit, wait no. Sorry! Habit . . . it's a habit. What happened this afternoon?"

"What is happening?" I whispered as I looked at the two men watching me.

"I don't know," Knox said; his voice showed he was just as confused. "Whatever you two are up to, now is obviously not the fucking time. Get out," he demanded, and waited until they reluctantly left. When Knox looked back at me he said, "The eggs. Throwing up."

I took a few deep breaths, and nodded as I pushed Deacon and Graham's weirdness from my mind. I quickly went over the conversation with Collin in my head, and then thought about what followed. Now that I didn't have the two men taking my focus and confusing me, my body was trembling again. I just didn't know if it was from talking about Hadley, remembering what she looked like on that bed, or feeling so weak.

"What happened with the eggs . . . that's why he did that to Hadley," I continued. "He still thinks the salt was poison, so he tried to kill her. So after he admitted to it—saying he made sure she had *salt,* I accidentally said that I hated him." I was quick to continue. "I didn't mean to, I didn't realize I said it out loud! I would've never said that to him, and he snapped. I didn't mean to!" I promised, and only when Knox dropped what he'd been using to clean my head and brought his face close to mine, did I realize my voice had gotten louder and louder until I'd been yelling as I tried to make him believe me.

He tried to quiet me and waited until my eyes were locked on his before whispering, "You're okay. You're here with me. I don't care what you said to him, Low; nothing would make you deserve this. Calm down, breathe, and tell me the rest." When he was sure I was calm, he released me and went back to work.

My voice was soft when I continued, afraid of repeating what had happened too loudly. "He wasn't my monster, Knox. He was different. I knew . . . I knew the second I realized I'd said it out loud that he was going to kill me. He came after me and I ran. He slammed my head into the wall"—Knox's hand paused from where it was still cleaning the wound on my forehead, and a muscle in his jaw ticked—"he threw me down, and he sat on me and started choking me. He dragged me into the guest bathroom and dropped me into the tub right after he turned on the water. He held me down as it filled, and it was like he was dead the entire time he watched what he was doing. When the water started covering my face, he told me how he would explain my *suicide* to people. Then he released me and I tried to get out, but he slammed my head onto the side of the tub. I woke up later choking on water."

"Oh my God," one of the guys whispered in horror, and I turned my head quickly to find them both standing in the door-way again.

"Jesus Christ," Deacon said. "We need to call the cops. We need to do something. Holy shit! Where's my phone?"

"No!" I yelled, and tried to stand. Knox didn't stop me, but he also didn't move, so I wasn't able to make it far. I reached out even though I could not have stopped Deacon from dialing from where I was. "No! Please don't! He has dirty cops working for him; please don't! If you do, he'll get me, and then he *will* finish killing me. He'll kill my sister, the rest of my family. *Please* don't!" I was yelling again by the time I finished, and both guys were staring at me like they didn't know what to do with me. "He's going to come after me because I left, and I'm already wor-ried that he might know about Knox—and Collin *will* kill him if he does—but if you call the cops . . . then there's no chance of us ever getting away."

"This needs to be stop—" Graham began, but Knox cut him off.

"Guys," he said with a sharp tone. "Leave, and please trust me when I say Harlow knows what she's talking about. Calling the cops is the last thing we want to do." Knox didn't wait to see if his friends left, which, after more worried looks, they did; he just went back to finishing up the cut on my forehead. "Grey brought you here," he said as he placed butterfly bandages on the cut.

It hadn't been a question, but I quickly explained all about finding Max, and then Grey. Despite everything, Knox smiled a few times, and even laughed at Max's attempts to parent me.

"That could've been dangerous, Low. You didn't know him, what kind of person he was . . ."

"It was all I had. I called you, but you didn't answer."

Knox's brow furrowed as he thought, and then relaxed. "My phone is in the living room. I wouldn't go back in there once Graham came home. I only came out because I heard the guys yelling for Grey, and knew she'd just left for work only an hour before. I thought maybe she was going into labor early, or something."

I nodded, and even though his fingers were moving gently as he began removing the rest of my clothes—as if he was afraid to touch me—my breathing deepened as I remembered his touches from earlier.

"I want to kill him," Knox admitted; his eyes were on his hands as he helped me out of my wet jeans.

That had been the first time he'd said *want*.

"You can't," I said again.

"I know," he whispered, then finally looked into my eyes. "I vowed I would never waste another moment with you, and I still have—too many to count. I've let you get hurt too many times since then, and I le—" His voice broke, and he stopped talking for a few seconds. After he cleared his throat, he continued: "I let tonight happen."

"No."

"If I'd stayed—"

"Don't do this," I pleaded. "You didn't know . . . *I* didn't know!"

His dark eyes dropped again. "You did," he argued gently.

"Not tonight. I didn't think it would happen tonight."

"Regardless . . . if I killed him, I would lose too many moments with you, maybe the rest of them. And I'm not willing to do that." He kept his gaze away from me as silence filled the bathroom, then finally asked, "Why isn't this scaring you?"

"What?"

"Our conversation."

"Why would—"

"Because I mean every word," Knox said darkly.

Meaning if he could do it and not go to prison, he *would* kill Collin. When the weight of his words settled over me, all I could do was nod. Finally, I admitted, "I'm more scared of losing you than your darkest thoughts. Besides, they aren't far off from my own. I've spent years thinking of what I would do to him if I knew I could get away with it—granted, I never thought of . . . I don't think I could . . ." I drifted off, unable to say the words myself.

"I know," Knox murmured, and placed his hand over my cheek as he had so many times. The touch was comforting and relaxed my tense and aching body. "I need to rinse your hair. You have a lot of blood in it, and more on your neck and shoulders. I can either have you bend over the sink, or stand in the shower, but I think the sink would be hard with how much you're already hurting."

I glanced over to it. "Probably."

He moved my face back so I was watching him. "He tried to drown you, so I'm not letting you get in that shower alone in case anything happens—you break down, freak out . . . anything. All I'm going to do is rinse the blood off, okay?"

"Okay," I answered as he turned on the water, but with my confusion, it sounded like a question. It wasn't until he reached behind me to unclasp my bra, then gently gripped the top of my underwear to push them down, that I realized why he was trying to get me to understand *all* that would be happening in the shower.

I watched as he removed his clothes, and had to resist the urge to touch him. I knew I couldn't handle it right now anyway. He was holding me up, and my knees were still shaking despite it. But he was there in front of me, and there was nothing stopping us. Once again, what we'd done today kept replaying in my mind. From the look in his eyes, I wasn't the only one who was feeling the phantom touches and kisses, but he was keeping himself in control.

After testing the water, he helped me into the shower and kept me far enough away that I wasn't directly under the spray. He used his hands to bring the water where he needed it, and had me tilt my head back so he could try to keep the cut dry that he'd been working on earlier while getting the blood out of the front of my hair.

When he was sure all the blood was off me, he helped me back out and turned off the water before following. He grabbed a large towel off the rack, and with a gentleness a guy like Knox shouldn't be able to have, he dried my hair—making sure to be even more careful around the spots where I'd hit my head. Once he was done, he opened up the towel and stepped close to me to wrap it around us both. He kept it closed tightly at my back, and just held me in his arms for long minutes, like he was afraid to let me go.

"Come on," he eventually whispered against my bare shoulder, then pulled away, but maneuvered out of the towel so I could cover back up in it.

"Where are we going?" I asked as he wrapped another towel low on his hips and then bent to pick up all of our clothes.

He passed his lips softly across mine as he walked over to open the door. "I'm taking you to bed. To sleep," he clarified when he noticed the way my eyes widened. "You need to rest."

Knox led me down the hall and into a bedroom, and I stood there awkwardly as I watched him move around the room. I didn't want to think about how many girls he'd had in here, but it was impossible not to. I was beginning to understand the glare directed at my bed that afternoon.

"Put these on; I'll be right back."

I glanced down to the clothes he'd placed in my hand, and couldn't stop the smile. I'd never worn his clothes, but I remembered begging him for shirts of his I could wear to bed when I was in high school. He'd promised me all of his shirts once I was eighteen. I'd never understood why he'd made me wait, but there I was, standing in his room, twenty-two years old and holding a shirt and pair of boxers in my hands.

Because I'd finally decided to get away from my husband . . .

My smile fell, and I quickly pulled the clothes on when I heard

Knox coming down the hall. My face morphed into confusion when he held out his cell phone to me. "Wha—"

"Call your parents. Warn them, do whatever you have to do."

My stomach dropped. How could I have forgotten? "Hadley's still in the hospital," I whispered. "Collin had her moved to a suite."

"Then they need to get her out."

I nodded as I tapped out my mom's number as fast as my fingers would let me. My dad answered instead.

"Hello," he said sternly.

"Dad, it's Harlow."

There was a brief pause. "Harlow, whose number is this?"

"Uh . . . that doesn't matter right now. I need to talk to you, and I need you to listen to every word I say, and ask as little as possible," I begged in a shaky voice. "Just know that I'm doing this to save all of us. It's an emergency."

"What in the hell are you going on about, Harlow?"

"Harlow?" my mom's distant voice sounded on the other end. "What's happening, is she okay?"

"She's talking about saving—"

"Dad, have you seen Collin since we left this afternoon?"

"Well, no."

The relief I felt was minimal, but it was still something. "And no police officers came back?"

"No. Are they going to? Is Hadley still in trouble?"

"Not like that. This is where I need you to listen to me, and just trust me, okay, Dad?"

"Harlow," he began.

"Dad, *please.*"

"Okay. Okay, I'm listening."

I took in a shaky breath and looked up at Knox, who nodded in encouragement as he stood there with his arms folded across his bare chest. My mouth opened, but no words came out. My throat had stopped working. I'd spent years avoiding this exact conversation, years *fearing* this conversation.

Seeing the panic that must have settled over my features, Knox let one hand go out to cradle my cheek while the other stayed tucked under his arm, and I let his presence calm my trembling body.

"Honey, you still there?" my dad asked.

I squeezed my eyes shut and tried to remember the way I'd felt when I'd first realized Collin was going to kill me. *I need to save them. I need to warn them,* I said to myself, and before I could psych myself out again, blurted, "Dad, I need you to get Hadley out of the hospital, and I need you to get to Connecticut to Hayley tonight. If not tonight, then first thing tomorrow. Don't tell anyone; don't even tell Hayley."

When I opened my eyes Knox was nodding, and I knew he agreed with my decision to get them as far from here as possible.

"Dad . . . Collin is bad," I choked out.

"What?" he asked in disbelief, and I knew this would be hard on him—on my whole family. Collin walked on water, as far as they were concerned.

"He's abusive," I started, but he cut me off.

"Harlow," he said in a disapproving voice.

"I'm telling you the truth!" I said a silent prayer as tears welled in my eyes—I needed him to believe me. My voice continued to waver and crack as I tried to make him understand. "He tried to drown me in the tub after we got home from the hospital. He was going to blame me for Hadley. He admitted to giving her the drugs this afternoon."

"What?" he repeated, but this time it sounded like he was in shock.

"He's been beating me since we got married, I haven't left because he always threatens to kill one of you. He thought I tried to poison him this morning; that's why Hadley is in the hospital." I was sobbing now. "I promise I didn't—but it's my fault she's in there. Dad, you *need* to get her out, and get all of you out of the state. He thinks I'm dead, but soon he's going to know I'm not."

My dad cursed and started mumbling something to my mom.

"Don't tell anyone," I reminded him. "Just leave."

"You'll meet us in Connecticut," he said flat out.

I started to agree, but stopped. "He'll be looking for me soon. He has police that work for him on the side . . . that's how he got Hadley's charges dropped. That's why they got to her so fast today in the first place; they'd been following her. If I go to the airport, he'll probably have airport police detain me. I can't risk it."

"Well, I'm not just leaving you here to deal with—"

"I have you," Knox said, having heard everything.

Dad stopped. "Who was that?"

I swallowed thickly. I didn't want to have to explain this over the phone, but I also would never be ashamed of the man standing in front of me. "It's Knox, Dad. Knox Alexander."

"Why would—is this his phone you called from?"

"Yes."

"You're going to explain yourself," he said suddenly. "You're going to have a lot to explain."

"I understand, but right now I just need you to believe me, and do what I said."

"Your mom is already on it. How do we get ahold of you if we need you?"

"My phone," Knox answered.

Another pause, then my dad said, "I'm going to have a talk with that man. For now, tell him to keep you safe."

"He will, Dad. I love you, and I'm so sorry."

"If what you're saying is true . . . well, I think we're the ones who have to apologize for not seeing it. Love you, too, baby girl."

A sharp sob burst from my chest when I ended the call, and I fell into Knox's waiting arms.

"They're going to be fine," he assured me, but he couldn't know.

Collin might not have been in the hospital room, but none of us knew where he was right now. I just nodded and let Knox lead me over to the bed. I crawled in when he pulled back the covers, and let my eyes follow him as he walked around the room to put on a pair of boxer briefs and toss our old clothes into a hamper. Once he was done, he flipped off the light and climbed in beside me. As gently as possible, he wrapped me in his arms, and I rested my head on his bicep when he pressed his body against mine.

"I've got you, Low. I'm not going anywhere. I love you."

"To the stars," I vowed, and let my heavy eyelids close.

Chapter 19

Knox
Present Day—Thatch

"SEATTLE?" I ASKED, and suppressed a groan as I glanced over my shoulder to where Harlow had been sleeping for the last few hours. Seattle was more than three hours from Richland. "Couldn't you go to the airport in Walla Walla? It's barely an hour from the hospital."

Harlow's dad sighed, and the sound let me know exactly how much this day had been weighing on him. I knew how he felt. "We couldn't get out on a flight until six tomorrow morning. There are flights that leave Seattle tonight just after ten P.M., and another just before eleven P.M. if we don't make that one." He paused for a moment, then said, "If what Harlow told us is true—"

"It is," I growled, my anger with their whole family apparent in those two words. I'd known within seconds of seeing Harlow that something was gravely wrong with her. I'd noticed Collin's fascination with pressure points within minutes of seeing them together . . . and her family had been blind to all of it. If they hadn't, Harlow wouldn't have always been worried about their safety, and she could've worried about her own long before it had gotten to this point. "I've seen it happen," I added, and heard him choke back a cry.

"Then . . . then Seattle was the right move. I need to get my family out of here tonight. I couldn't risk waiting until tomorrow."

"You're right," I murmured, but didn't add that Seattle might be the place Collin expected them to go back to. I didn't need to add any more fear. "What time will you be landing?"

"If we make the first flight, just after nine A.M. If we don't, then not until sometime after noon."

"All right. Call me as soon as you land, or if anything happens before."

He didn't respond, but I knew he was still there. Just when I was about to ask if he'd heard me, he whispered, "Why is my daughter with you?"

"Should I assume you mean physically, right now?"

Harlow's dad cleared his throat. "Right this moment, that is what I mean. After you answer that, we might get into the rest."

"She's here because it's where she should be—where she always should have been—and because I'm the one who's going to make sure Collin never touches her again."

When her dad spoke again, I instantly recognized the *I'm-the-father-she's-my-baby-girl* tone he was giving me—it was the same one I'd gotten when I'd asked him if I could marry Harlow years ago—but there was a hint of respect in his voice as well. "Now just how long has this been going on between the two of you?"

"Seven years," I said immediately, and without hesitation.

"Seven years?" he yelled, the respect now gone. "Young man, you have a *hell* of a lot to—"

"Mr. Evans," I began, cutting him off. "I ran into Harlow just over two weeks ago. That was the first I'd seen or heard from her in over four and a half years. But I never once stopped loving her or thinking about her in all that time. These past two weeks have consisted of her trying to hide what her husband has been doing to her, and me doing everything to help her—even though the idea of anyone helping her has terrified her. Please understand that I say this with as much respect as I still hold for you—which right now isn't much because I hate that you never noticed what was happening to your own daughter," I seethed. "Not that I will ever talk to you about our romantic relationship, but neither Harlow nor I have anything to answer for when it comes to us. Having said that, we've always meant something to each other throughout the past seven years."

Silence stretched on for long minutes, but given how I'd just laid everything out, I expected him to be even more upset with me than he already was, so I let him have his time with his thoughts. He sounded worn out again when he finally spoke. "If you weren't right, I wouldn't let you speak to me that way." He exhaled heavily and began speaking before he was done. "I always wondered what happened to you. My wife and I—well, we always thought it would be you."

"*Me?*" I asked incredulously. "You were the one who made me promise to push her into enjoying a life away from me when she left for college. If you hadn't, we probably wouldn't have spent years without each other. She wouldn't—" I cut myself off before I could say any more, but it was clear where I'd been going with that. If I hadn't agreed to his conditions, Harlow probably would have never had to feel the pain Collin had inflicted.

"Yes, you," he answered after a second. "We respected you, and the way *you* respected our daughter. If we hadn't, we never would have let you fill her head with ideas of being together later in life. I never would've given you permission to . . . I guess it ended up not mattering. None of us had expected it when that day came and went, and suddenly Collin was there instead, but it was even more surprising when you never came back."

My jaw clenched tight. I didn't need to be reminded that I hadn't fought for her.

"That, however," her dad continued, his voice stern again, "does *not* mean that we would be okay with you two together now. Despite what is going on, my daughter is a married woman, and you would be wise to let her have her own space until all of this is worked out. She will need plenty of time to deal with what has happened, and then more to decide what she wants with you—*if* anything. Do you understand that, Mr. Alexander?"

His words were so similar to ones I'd heard before. Back then I'd smirked the entire way to the jeweler, because I'd known there was nothing keeping me from making Harlow mine in every way once she turned eighteen. I wasn't smirking now.

I'd had a lot of women since losing Harlow—too many to count or even remember. All had been single, that was my only rule, until this afternoon with Harlow. Marriage, to me, was sacred. I knew that when I married I would marry for life;

which is why I had only ever mentioned it to one girl—unless you counted joking with Grey to make Graham mad. And not only was Harlow married to a man who wasn't me, but I wasn't stopping us from being together, and I knew I wouldn't continue to.

In my mind, she was mine. Collin had made a decision to break their vows the first time he'd hurt her, and Harlow had left him and their marriage emotionally at the same time since she couldn't leave physically. But others wouldn't see it that way.

"As I said, I will never talk to you about my romantic relationship with your daughter," I responded, my voice assertive, but not defiant. I didn't want to be in a position with Harlow that people questioned, but I also wouldn't *let* them question us.

I could tell he was disappointed, but the slightest hint of respect was back in his voice. "Well then, I guess I'll be speaking with you in the morning. Please watch over my daughter, and if anything . . ."

"I will let you know." I finished for him when he couldn't. "Safe travels, Mr. Evans."

"Thank you, Knox," he said softly before he hung up, and I knew it wasn't for my parting well wishes.

I released a heavy breath, dropped my elbows onto my knees, and let my head hang. A million thoughts were rushing through my mind. Some about my past with Harlow . . . some about our future. A lot about Collin and what he was doing now—or if he even knew Harlow was alive yet. And the rest about Harlow's family and if we did the right thing in having them fly out of the state.

A knock sounded on my bedroom door, and my head snapped

up, but I didn't move from my spot on the edge of the bed. I'd told Harlow I wasn't going anywhere, and the edge of the bed already felt too far for me.

After a few seconds, the door slowly opened, and Graham popped his head in. When he saw me sitting there, he took a few careful steps in.

"Asleep?" he whispered, and I nodded. "She okay?"

"Don't ask stupid questions, and don't act like you give a shit."

He seemed to deflate on himself, and crossed his arms over his chest to try to recover his original stance. "I do—we do," he amended, then looked behind him and called for Deacon.

A second later, Deacon rounded the corner into my room, and I rolled my eyes at his wounded expression.

"Can we talk in the living room?" Graham asked, but I didn't bother responding in any way. He took my silence and stillness as my answer, and sighed. "We do care," he said, still speaking soft enough that he wouldn't wake Harlow. "But it's hard when we're worried about what the consequences could be, when we've *always* worried about that."

"Try to see it from our perspective," Deacon cut in. "We were in college, and you only cared about a girl who was too young for you—who was considered illegal. And, I mean, for shit's sake—" He cut off when Graham gave him a look for talking too loud. When he started again, his voice was so soft I could barely hear him. "You told us everything. We were already sort of worried, but when you first told Harlow you would wait for her, and she told you that you would be wasting your time, that was it for us. We *knew* she was playing you. And then every time the two of you talked, she told you the same thing.

We didn't know why you were the only one who didn't see that you *were*."

"It was—that's not what she meant." I groaned and rubbed at my jaw. I scrambled for a way to explain it, but didn't know how to. "It was . . . our thing, I guess."

"That's a weird fucking thing," Deacon mumbled, then waved off my warning glare. "Were we dicks during those first few years? Yeah, we took it too far. We'll admit that now. But then she turned eighteen, and she did exactly what we'd always worried she would, and did we rub it in your face?"

I didn't answer.

"And now this. You haven't seen her in years, but it's like no time has passed for you. You're ready to take up where you left off. Once again, we're worried. Even more so, because not only is she married, but we had to watch the kind of person you turned into for those first couple of years after what she did to you the first time."

Graham was nodding, and before I could ask what Deacon meant, Graham explained, "You never showed us that you were upset, but you were suddenly . . ." He trailed off and searched for the right word. "Uncontrollable. In everything. It wasn't until Grey's fiancé died three years ago that you finally snapped out of it and calmed down. Well, calmed down into the Knox we'd always known growing up."

"I-I didn't know," I whispered, but swallowed roughly, because now that I was thinking about it, I did. They drank and hooked up with girls, but I pushed for the nights to go longer, and the girls to multiply.

"It's okay," Deacon said when he noticed what I'd just realized. "Like I said, we know we took things too far back then. We know we made it hard for you two then, but can you understand our side at all?"

I didn't have to think about that answer. "Yes and no. I understand why you were scared for me, but I will never understand why you did what you did—and what you've been doing before tonight."

Graham raised an eyebrow. "Again, you couldn't see it from our side. All we knew was that she never once tried to find you or even contact you for years, and all of a sudden in the last two and a half weeks, she had you caught up in all this bullshit, and threatening to walk away from your best friends. There are red flags when a girl does that; there are *major* red flags when she's married and using you." He was quick to continue: "We get it; she wasn't. We know now that she wasn't lying, and that all this shit is real. That doesn't mean it was easy to believe *then*." His head dropped so he could look at the floor, and he shook it once. "Speaking of, what are you going to do about the husband? You really think he'll come after Harlow?"

"I know he will, but I don't know what we're going to do about him yet. I don't know how many officers he has on the take, but I know from what Harlow told me this afternoon that it stretches farther than Benton County, or even the state of Washington."

"Shit," they said at the same time.

Even though the only light in the room was coming in from the hallway, I could tell Graham's eyes were fixated behind me. After a moment he said, "You can tell that it's not just today, or even just this week, or this month. It's like you said: she looks sick. Even if she didn't show up covered in blood tonight, it would've been obvious."

"She looks haunted," Deacon finished for him. "Knox, man,

we know what she means to you. During all this time, that has never been something we've questioned. But, if you ever get past all this with her husband, what are you going to do? With what she's been through, she might not be the girl you fell in love with."

I twisted to look at her, and something in my chest tightened painfully. My eyes never left her face as I admitted, "She's not. The Harlow I knew was full of life, and never stopped laughing or smiling. But she had to build hundreds of walls to protect herself from him because he's been trying to break her for years." *Cracked,* my earlier assessment floated through my mind, and my lips twitched. "She's there, though. Somewhere. I'll find her, no matter how long it takes."

"Well, we've decided that from now on, we won't try to stand between you two," Graham said. Deacon snorted.

"Yeah, because there's already enough doing that for us." When Graham shot him another look, Deacon rolled his eyes. "Best-friend code, dude. We'll stop. Promise. We know it won't make up for everything before, but we can be supportive now. And whatever you need with Psycho, just let us know."

A genuine smile crossed my face, and I nodded once in thanks.

"On that note," Deacon mumbled, then walked out of the room.

Graham just stood there with a withdrawn smile when I gave him a questioning look.

When Deacon came back, he was carrying two takeout boxes and a plastic bag. "We got you both dinner, and we made Grey take us shopping to get Harlow a new outfit. But no one knew what sizes to get her, because your girl is fucking skin and bones.

So if it doesn't fit . . . we'll just blame Grey. And should you be letting her sleep? She bled out in our entryway earlier."

My grateful expression fell, and I glared at Deacon. "She didn't bleed out in the entryway, and are you really questioning me about whether she should sleep? I'm the firefighter." When they continued to look at me expectantly, I sighed. "Her pupils were fine, she didn't throw up, and she was walking fine at the end. Besides, I was planning on waking her up every few hours."

Neither spoke; they just continued to stare.

"This is where you leave," I hinted.

"Well, have you done it yet?" Deacon asked.

I'd planned on waking her up once I got off the phone with her dad, but I figured telling them that would make them want to stay, so I avoided answering the question directly. "I'm thankful you've both had a change of heart, or whatever, but it was weirding her out in the bathroom earlier, so I know if she wakes up and finds you here, you're going to scare the shit out of her."

They looked like they were about to argue to stay, but after a hard glare in their direction, they looked dejectedly at the floor.

"Well, we brought food," Deacon said lamely. "I guess we'll just go."

"Thank you," I murmured when they turned. From the nods they gave in return, they knew I wasn't thanking them for leaving.

Once the door was shut and I was sure they weren't going to walk back in, I rolled onto the bed and rested my hand lightly on Harlow's cheek. Even in sleep, her full lips moved into a pout before falling open again, and her face tried to move closer to my palm.

I gently brushed my thumb over her cheekbone and leaned close to whisper against her forehead, "Wake up, Low. I need you to wake up."

Though I wasn't looking at her, I knew the second she woke. Her entire body stilled and her soft breaths halted for long seconds before they started up again as her rigid frame slowly relaxed.

Moving down so I was directly in front of her face, her eyes widened minimally, and she stopped breathing again.

"Low?" I asked uneasily, and my stomach dropped when her eyes filled with tears. "Harlow, what's wrong?" I said louder, as something close to panic gripped at my chest.

"Is this a dream?" she asked softly, and the panicked feeling immediately subsided.

"Dream? No, why?"

One of her hands moved from where mine was still resting on her cheek. She slid it up my arm and then clung to my shoulder. "Knox?" she mouthed.

"Yeah," I responded, clueless as to what was happening.

Her breathing hitched and her eyes shut, but I didn't have to wait to know what was happening. She started rambling soft words before I could ask. "You're here, you're not a dream. I'm with you. I left. I left Collin—oh God. It was all real. You're here. I always dream of you, I thought I still was—but you're here. Oh, Hadley."

I gently wrapped her body in my arms, and held her as she tried to come to terms with the fact that everything from that day *had* happened. When her words stopped, I said, "Your family is on their way to Seattle; they're catching a flight tonight. They'll keep us updated. They haven't seen or heard from Collin, and your dad said he'd been watching for cars following them, he thought they were fine."

Harlow nodded against my chest, and her body relaxed a little more.

When a couple more minutes passed, I pulled away and sat up, then waited while she did the same—but I studied her every move. "How do you feel?"

"Sore," she murmured, but her eyes flashed away. I knew she was holding back.

"So how do you really feel?"

Harlow chewed on her lower lip and shrugged—even that movement seemed hard to do—but she wouldn't hold my eyes. "My head is throbbing all over. The back of my body hurts from where I fell and was dropped, but I don't feel as weak as I did earlier."

"Good." I pressed two fingers to her chin and turned her head until she was looking at me. "Don't hold back with me. I need to know, or I can't help you. Okay?"

Instead of answering, her eyes went to something past me and widened.

"Can we help you?" I asked before I turned to find the guys in the room again. One was holding a bottle of water; one was holding a bottle of Tylenol. I leaned over and held an arm out so they could put both bottles in my hand; my glare never left them. "You're acting like a bunch of old fussing women," I grumbled, and then sat back up.

"You okay?"

"Deacon," I hissed, and shook my head.

Harlow didn't answer him, but I don't think she knew how to. She was still staring at them like she didn't understand why they were being so nice.

"Thank you, Graham," I grumbled when he unnecessarily took the to-go boxes and bag of clothes from my nightstand, and then put them on the bed near Harlow's legs. "Goodbye, Graham and Deacon," I hinted, and waited until they were gone to say, "They've had a change of heart when it comes to you, and I don't think they know what to do with themselves now that they know what you went through tonight. They bought you a new outfit, and brought us dinner."

"Oh," Harlow whispered, still in shock.

"Are you hungry?"

Her eyes darted down to the boxes, and her face twisted. "Not really. Um, I don't—I don't eat . . . much."

"Low, that's not hard to figure," I said, and looked pointedly at her.

"It's hard to with him . . ." She trailed off.

"You don't have to explain that right now, or ever, if you don't want. But I need you to eat if you can. You need to put weight back on. You need to have energy, especially after what happened today. So if you think you can eat, then it's here for you. Okay?"

She nodded, and slowly picked at the food in her box while I ate mine. I only counted five bites small enough for a toddler before she stopped tearing her food into pieces and pretending to eat it.

After I was done, I pulled her into my arms and leaned back against the headboard. The relieved sigh and way her body seemed to melt into me made me smile, but I didn't comment on it. Mostly because we hadn't talked since we'd started eating. I knew if we talked, we'd have to talk about what to do with Collin, and it was obvious she wasn't ready to figure that out yet. So I would give her the night if that was what she needed.

Not long after, her mouth parted and her breathing evened out, and minutes later, I followed her into sleep.

Chapter 20

Harlow
Present Day—Thatch

I WOKE SLOWLY. Something about the action felt foreign; normally when I woke, I woke with a start. Though warning bells were going off in my head, my body knew differently. Knew whose arms I was in. Knew I wasn't in any danger from him. Knew that I didn't need to be on the defensive from the moment I woke to the moment I fell into a fitful sleep.

Even though it was still dark in Knox's room, my body was reveling from the best sleep I'd gotten in more than two years. I hadn't felt this alert or energized in . . . I couldn't remember how long it had been. I hadn't felt this relaxed since before I'd married Collin—and that was including the tension in my shoulders and back from worrying over my family and deranged husband.

Sometime in the unknown hours we'd been sleeping, I'd

twisted in Knox's arms so I was partially on my side, partially chest to chest with him. And despite the fear that was slowly moving through my body at what we were up against, I felt myself smile. For years I'd wondered what it would be like to wake up next to this man, and though I knew it could be a thousand times better than it was in this moment, this moment still felt something like bliss.

Hoping not to wake him, I traced the line of his jaw with the tips of my fingers and let my eyes follow the movement. I faintly brushed over his cheekbones then back down his jaw, and finally over his lips. When my fingers got there, I glanced up to find his dark eyes piercing mine.

Without a word, and without releasing me from his intense stare, he unwrapped one of his arms from my body and grabbed my hand in his. Before he pulled it away from his mouth, he pressed the tips of my fingers closer to kiss them and then intertwined our fingers.

"I didn't mean to wake you," I whispered. My throat hurt worse than it had last night, but even so, lying like this with Knox, in his bed in the dark, anything above a whisper would have felt wrong.

His head shook once, the movement nearly unnoticeable. "I've been checking on you throughout the night. Every move and every noise had me worried something was happening."

"I'm sorry."

Knox smirked, and I watched as his eyes drifted to the door. "Your new mother hens woke me a lot more than you did."

"Oh." I didn't understand. There had to be a hidden agenda . . . they had to be playing at something. That possibility had me more wary of them than I ever had been before.

When Knox saw the confusion on my face, his lips curved up in the faintest of smiles. "Let me worry about them. You don't need that added on top of everything." He sighed, and gave me a worried look as he said cautiously, "We need to talk about Collin."

"I know. There's no way he doesn't know by now." I let out a laugh, but there was no humor behind it. "I still don't know how he didn't know before . . ." I let the words trail off.

"How did you get away?"

"He must have gone to his parents' anniversary party. It doesn't make sense—*none* of it makes sense. I kept waiting for him to be there, watching me, but he was gone. Collin's never been so careless in what he's done. The only way I can make sense of it is that he snapped last night, he wasn't himself at all; I told you, he wasn't my monster. He had to have thought he'd actually killed me." My voice dropped low on the last two words, and Knox's eyes tightened in pain.

He nodded absentmindedly for a few seconds, then mumbled, "I don't know who to go to. I don't know who is on his side, I don't know who will believe you—or even if they do, if he's paying to keep them quiet. But I swear to you, we will find something."

"I know," I replied, and then softer, "I didn't want you brought into this."

"I didn't exactly give you a choice, Low," he reminded me, but that didn't change anything. Knox was still in danger; he was already risking his life to save me. "Harlow," he said, and waited until he had my attention again. "You told me yesterday that you couldn't leave Collin, but you came here last night."

I nodded. He hadn't asked a question, but I didn't need him to in order to answer. "Yesterday I was sure I was going to die *soon*. Last night I knew I was going to die *then*. When that knowledge hit me I realized how many mistakes I'd made by not letting you take me away. So when I woke up in the bathtub with somehow another chance in life, I left."

"You left *him*?" he asked, trying to clarify what I was saying by putting the slightest emphasis on his last word.

I pulled myself up until I was on my knees, straddling his hips. Bringing my hands together, I grabbed my engagement ring and wedding band. "If I never see him again it will still be too soon."

My eyes filled with tears as I slowly slid the rings off my finger. It wasn't physically hard to remove them, they were too large for my bony finger, but emotionally, it was one of the hardest things I've done. I was letting go of a life filled with hate and fear. I was saying goodbye to a man who had ruined me. And I was leaving behind a part of myself I felt like I didn't even know—a part I wish I'd never had to embrace.

With each centimeter my rings slid on my finger, I felt more weight lifting off my body. My shoulders, my chest, my back . . . my heart. "Yesterday wasn't fair to you," I mumbled when I was finally holding the rings in my palm. Glancing up at Knox's intense eyes, I said, "I should've never given myself to you when he still had his sick hold on me—when I was so sure I would never be able to get away from him. I will never regret any time that is with you, Knox Alexander, but after how long we waited, you deserved all of me the way I got all of you."

His dark eyes remained on my face, his features unreadable even when he asked in a low voice, "And now?"

Cupping my hand holding the rings, I tossed them over the side of the bed. "As much as your kisses healed me, after last night I feel like I'm still broken," I confessed, and my cheeks heated from embarrassment.

"Cracked," he corrected.

"I don't know if I'll ever be able to find myself again," I admitted, and hated that it was the truth.

But Knox's lips twitched in amusement, like there was something I didn't know. "I'll find you."

I smiled shakily and cradled his face in my hands. "Then if you want me, you can have me. *All* of me."

Knox sat up and crushed his mouth to mine in a kiss unlike anything I'd ever experienced before. We'd shared a kiss that had been a deliberate claim on each other, but this . . . this kiss was his soul claiming my own.

He moved his legs so he could roll onto his knees, and slowly lowered me onto the bed without ever breaking the kiss. Once I was lying down, he moved his mouth down my throat and pressed the tips of his fingers to my hips, just underneath the shirt I was wearing. With a soft dragging motion, he lifted the shirt higher and higher up my body as his fingers trailed along my skin. Then he broke away from where he was kissing behind my ear to pull the shirt off me and toss it away.

My hands moved over the tightening muscles in his back when he covered my body again, and I shivered when his teeth grazed my throat. His hips rocked against mine, eliciting a moan from me. With one last searing kiss, he moved down my body, and pressed openmouthed kisses all the way down, causing me to tremble when he slowly—*so* slowly—pulled the boxers down my legs while his mouth followed the cloth.

I felt the faint brush of his lips as they raced back up my leg, and stopped near my hip long enough for a soft kiss, then continued until his face was directly above mine again. His dark eyes captured mine and conveyed all of his need, all the words that he wasn't saying, when his fingers began gently teasing me.

I was his, and he was never letting me go.

My back arched away from the bed, and my eyes fluttered shut as he brought me closer to an orgasm—but his touches were just light enough that it felt like I wouldn't get there. It was driving me crazy in the most amazing way. From the soft laugh in my ear when Knox bent over me again, he knew it. I had been so focused on trying to get closer to his touch that I hadn't noticed when he'd pulled down his boxer briefs, and Knox had to cover my mouth with his own when I cried out in surprise and pleasure when he quickly filled me—forcing me over the edge I'd been barely hanging on to.

Every inch of my body felt like it was buzzing, tingling, floating as my orgasm surged through me. A deep growl rumbled through Knox's chest and passed from his mouth to mine when my fingernails dug into his back as he moved inside me and my second one started before I could even be sure that my first one had ended.

Just like the day before, our bodies moved in a way I'd never known they could—like they knew they'd been made for each other. Every move from him was met with one of my own. It was perfect, harmonized . . . beautiful. But I should've known it would've been perfect with Knox, whereas everything with Collin had been tainted, even from the beginning.

I tilted my head away from him, exposing more of my neck as his lips ghosted down it and his movements quickened. It was all I could do at that point just to hold on to him—my body was spent and still trembling, but I wrapped my legs around his back and held on to his shoulders as tight as I could. The soft lips on my neck were replaced with his teeth, and my eyes rolled back at the erotic combination of the bite, the vibration and sound of his groan, and the way his fingers dug into the bed—just barely gripping my arms—as his body stilled above mine.

His. Everything about his position then screamed that, just as the way I clung to him showed he was mine.

"I love you," I whispered into the dark room as he continued to hold me—not willing to let this moment end, while I wasn't willing to let him go.

Knox placed a soft kiss where he'd bitten down, then moved his head to whisper in my ear. "To the stars, Low."

I exhaled slowly and smiled as I ran my fingers through his hair. To some, it might not mean much. But to us, those words meant more than just "I love you."

When Knox did pull away, he kept his body touching mine as long as he could by sliding down and kissing my lower stomach and the top of one of my thighs before reluctantly moving away from me and off the bed. He ducked into what I assumed was his bathroom, and after a minute, came back with a warm, damp washcloth, then proceeded to kiss me slowly, tenderly, as he helped me clean up.

The look on his face before he left again was clear, and I'm sure mirrored my own. He didn't want to leave this bed for the rest of the day, but we had a lot we had to figure out and deal with. So when he walked back to the bathroom, I climbed off the bed and grabbed the bag of clothes Deacon and Graham had bought last night.

I'd half-expected the clothes to be for someone five sizes bigger than me, just because it was something they would've done in the past—but I was surprised when they ended up fitting me better than most of my clothes did now. They'd even bought a new scarf to cover the bruises on my throat.

Knox was walking back into the room by the time I was dressed and headed toward the bathroom—since the guys had been gracious enough to also grab toiletries for me—and hooked an arm around my waist to kiss me softly.

"No matter what happens when we walk out of this room, we're going to spend the next fifty years waking up next to each other. Just remember that. All right?"

I smiled and nodded. "Why not sixty?"

Knox's dark eyes danced. "For you, I'll make sure it's sixty."

I hurried into the bathroom when he released me; when I came back out I found him dressed and waiting for me on the edge of the bed, with a guarded look on his face.

He nodded toward the door. "Your mother hens came to check on you." Knox looked like he didn't know what to say, and shrugged. "They're good guys, Harlow, the best . . . but I know they've never shown you that side of them. I don't expect you to ever forgive them; they already know I don't. Even though they are acting weird and taking this new thing to an extreme level of protecting you and taking care of you, I can promise you it's genuine. You don't have to be worried about them. I think they've always *only* thought of you as a liar, and now that they know you aren't, and know a sliver of what you've been through, they will protect you as much as I would."

He must have noticed the skeptical look in my eyes.

"Do you remember my sister, Sara?" When I nodded, he continued. "I don't know if I ever talked to you about how often she was bullied in school."

"Because she's gay?"

Knox grunted in confirmation and said, "Deacon and Graham were always right there with me, defending her like she was their sister. Then Grey . . . she's been through a lot of bad shit since you turned eighteen. A lot. But you know none of us see her as just Graham's sister; she's *our* sister. And through all those times, Deacon and Graham were the most loyal and protective brothers those girls could have."

My eyes moved to the closed bedroom door. In a way, I could see it. Not just because of last night, but because they'd seen me as a threat to Knox . . . their "brother," and they'd done everything they could to make sure that threat went away.

"Graham and Deacon know that I would walk away from our friendship for you, and—"

"I don't want that," I said quickly, and looked back at him. "I've never wanted that."

"I know. But they didn't give me a lot of other options with the way they'd treated you, and our relationship." When I started to speak again, Knox stood from the bed and lifted his hand to stop me. "Let me finish. They know I would walk, so if it ever got to that point again, I would leave with you and never once regret my decision. But with how they are, I don't see that happening. They know you're mine, but being mine means you get them, too. They will treat you how they treat Grey and Sara. They will be protective and loyal to a fault, and right now you're in danger, so they're going to be a little overwhelming. But—and I'm not trying to ask you to forget what they've done in the past—if you can be open to starting over, they will be the greatest guys to have in your life. And I know that if anything hap—" Knox cut off and looked away for a minute. When he spoke again, he still wouldn't hold my gaze. "If something happens so that I can't be the one to take care of you, they'll do it for me."

"Knox," I whispered, and shook my head. "What are you— you said you weren't going to do anything!"

"I don't plan to," he said carefully, and finally looked back at me. "But if it comes down to it, I will do whatever I have to in order to keep you safe, and away from him. No matter what that means."

"You just promised me sixty years," I said when he pulled me into his chest.

He didn't respond right away, and when he did, his voice was tight. "I plan to keep that promise."

But I knew what he wasn't saying. That it might not be possible. And with Collin waiting for us somewhere outside this house . . . I knew Knox was right.

Chapter 21

Harlow
Present Day—Thatch

GRAHAM AND DEACON were sitting at the kitchen table when we finally left the room and went to search for them, and both of them shot up out of their chairs when they saw us walking toward them.

"Hey, right," Graham said, and his eyes dropped to the table where there were more to-go boxes.

"Clothes fit," Deacon observed, then cleared his throat. "I mean, do the clothes fit?"

"We bought breakfast," Graham said before I could answer Deacon's question, and my eyes widened when he continued. "Are you hungry? You should probably eat, we got a lot of food, take whatever you want."

"Yeah, but we didn't get eggs!" Deacon blurted. "No eggs,

so you don't have to—" Graham shoved his arm, and Deacon looked worried, like I might break down right there in their kitchen. "Um, so how's your head? We should probably look at the cut," Deacon mumbled as his eyes locked on my forehead.

"*We* don't need to do anything. I cleaned it again before we came out here," Knox said, his tone annoyed, but clearly amused.

Knox had given them a perfect description. Mother hens.

I stopped playing with my hands and gestured to the food. "Thank you, and thank you for the clothes, and everything. Just . . . thank . . . you," I ended lamely. Because before I'd finished with my thanks, Deacon and Graham were already moving into action.

Deacon was grabbing a plate and cup out of cupboards, and after handing off the plate to Graham, went over to the fridge to fill up the cup with orange juice while Graham piled food onto the plate. Graham was still filling the plate when Deacon set the drink down, so he turned right back around to grab silverware, and placed it in front of me at the same time Graham slid the beyond-full plate toward me.

"I can't . . ." I began, but didn't finish. Both guys were staring at me like they were proud of what they'd done, and eager to have me eat.

"I'll eat what you can't," Knox promised softly in my ear, but the guys still heard.

"Get your own, that's hers!" Deacon huffed.

Knox looked at me, the hint of a smile playing on his lips. His eyes dragged over to where the guys were now getting more plates for themselves and mouthed, "Mother hens."

Knox held out a chair for me, then walked into the kitchen once I was seated. When he slid into the chair next to me, all he had was a fork. My eyes were still wide as I alternated staring at the plate and eyeing the other two guys in the kitchen. I hated eating in front of people. They always noticed too much, things I didn't want them to—not that these three didn't already know enough. And from what Graham had placed in front of me, he and Deacon planned on me eating a lot.

There were two biscuits—each one bigger than one of my fists—smothered in gravy, four sausage patties, four strips of bacon, a mountain of hash browns, and the largest cinnamon roll I'd ever seen.

Knox's lips went to my ear. "They aren't expecting anything, they're just giving you a choice. They won't judge you, Low." With a kiss to my jaw, he pulled away, only to bring my chair closer to his as he dug into the food.

I looked over the table as the other two guys followed his lead, and tried to sort through the twisting in my stomach and warming in my chest. Everything felt so conflicted, and I couldn't make sense of it. This morning felt good, right even. Waking up in Knox's arms, spending unhurried time learning each other's bodies, and now eating breakfast with him and his friends—that was the warming in my chest. Sitting there, I could see this happening for years to come. But then my stomach twisted tighter.

No matter how right it all felt, no matter how much I wanted it, it felt like a lie in that moment. We were pretending that my monster wasn't somewhere waiting for me, probably already making plans to hurt those I loved—if he wasn't already trying to carry them out.

I don't know how long I sat there, staring at the table but seeing nothing, before Knox tilted my head to the side so I was facing him.

"What is it?" he asked, his voice low and tone dark. His body was on alert suddenly, and the guys felt the anxious energy rolling off Knox, judging by the way they both dropped their forks.

I held Knox's stare for a few seconds as I debated telling him. I didn't want to ruin the morning, but we couldn't avoid it forever. "I need to do something about Collin. Soon."

Knox was nodding before I finished talking. "We know. We're going to talk about our plans when we're done eating."

I glanced to Deacon and Graham, and took in their worried but determined expressions, and wondered just how much the three of them had done while I'd slept last night. While looking at them, I noticed it was still somewhat dark behind the closed blinds in the kitchen, and looked around the kitchen until I found a clock.

"Six fifteen? Why are you guys awake—how long have you *been* awake? And how did you get all this food?"

Deacon shrugged. "We had things to do, and Mama's Café opens at six, but we have connections."

"*He* has connections," Graham corrected.

Once again, Deacon shrugged. "My grandma is 'Mama.' "

"Oh." I felt my cheeks burn. I hadn't had anyone go through this much trouble for me ever, and didn't know how to respond to it. "Thank you."

"Just eat," Graham prompted. "Like Knox said, we'll talk after."

From his tone, I knew they had plenty to talk about.

I was able to finish part of a sausage patty, two bites of biscuit and gravy, one bite of hash browns, and the entire center of the cinnamon roll. I smiled to myself and placed a hand on my stomach as I wondered when the last time was that I'd been full, but my smile fell when I looked up to see Graham and Deacon with twin looks of sympathy.

They were *trying* to look understanding, but it was obvious they wished I'd eaten more. And since the three of them were able to polish the rest of the food off, I was willing to bet it wasn't because they were worried about any of it being wasted.

Graham's eyes drifted over to Knox and quickly hit the table, then Deacon did the same. I didn't know what Knox's expression looked like, but I figured I didn't want to and was glad for the interruption from Graham and Deacon.

The forks hadn't hit the plates before they'd all started talking at the same time.

"So what'd you see?" Knox asked.

"There's a weird car on our street," Graham whispered in a rush.

"Here's what I think you should do," Deacon said as he dropped his elbows onto the table.

They all sat back and looked at each other. Knox was the first to speak again. "What do you mean weird car. What kind of car?"

"Like, a car that doesn't belong here," Graham answered. "I can't be sure, but I'm almost positive it was there last night when we left to get Harlow the outfit, but I hadn't been looking then. But it was definitely there when I left to check the house, it was there when I came back, and it was there this morning when Deacon left to get the food."

"What kind of car?" Knox asked again.

"Dark, some BMW," Graham said immediately, and I felt Knox stop breathing at the same time my body began shaking.

"Wait, you think this is Collin?"

All the guys looked at me for a few seconds before Deacon asked slowly, "Yeah, what'd you think we were talking about?"

"Not Collin! I thought this was normal, nosy neighborhood talk. Why would you think he'd know where to find me? I'm not even sure if he does know about Knox, and he doesn't know about either of you. I've never even mentioned knowing anyone in Thatch."

"Because he has cops working for him, and if he's found you running away before, he can find you now," Knox explained.

"But I was driving my car that time. This time I walked, and took different cars, and . . ." I trailed off as dread spread through my stomach. "And it was too easy." My head snapped up and I held Knox's worried stare. "I told you it didn't make sense that he'd just not be there, or that I'd be able to leave. It didn't make sense; he could've followed me. Oh my God. I can't stay here, I can't put you in danger like this."

Knox squeezed my hand reassuringly and glanced at Graham for a second. "Do you have any idea what kind of BM—"

"One of the X's," Graham said with a snap. "The SUV ones."

I exhaled so quickly, it sounded like I was in pain.

"Is it his?"

"No," Knox answered Graham so I wouldn't have to. "But he does have a dark BMW." Knox bent close to me. "What kind of cars do his parents have?"

"The exact same, just different colors."

Knox rolled his eyes, because I also had the same car in another color as well. "Isn't that cute," he sneered.

I took a calming breath and asked, "How would you know a car doesn't belong here?"

This time Deacon answered. "Thatch is small. Everyone here

knows everyone and their business. During the summer we have visitors out by the lake, or the center of town, but it's rare when you don't know a car in one of the neighborhoods—especially your own neighborhood. We know everyone who lives around us, know their cars, and know the cars that are usually there visiting. It's hard not to when we've all grown up together. So when there's a different car on a street, people start talking." He shrugged and grinned widely. "People don't think twice about random cars here, because too many girls come in and out of—" He broke off quickly when Knox and Graham shot him a look, and my stomach fell. "Regardless, we don't know that car, and it caught enough attention that a woman down the street asked if it I knew whose it was when I saw her walking her dog this morning."

"Where is it?" Knox asked.

"Three houses that way," Deacon said, and pointed in the direction behind Knox and me.

"Back to your earlier question," Graham said, and his eyes darted to me. "There were two cars in the driveway when I drove past at one this morning. Two BMWs."

It took me a second to understand what he was saying, and then all the blood drained from my face. "You went—you went. Why!"

Knox squeezed my hand as Graham continued. "I already knew what those two cars looked like, but I didn't know if maybe the car on our street was some other—anyway, you already answered about that. But all the lights were on in the house, and I mean *all* of the lights. It was lit up bright and the blinds were open. It was weird for how late it was."

"I never opened the curtains or blinds yesterday," I mumbled. "That was dangerous going there."

"I didn't even slow down as I passed your house," he assured me.

"Deacon?" Knox murmured.

"Is Collin's dad like this, too? I don't just mean with the abuse, but with the money and paying people off."

"No," I responded, at first surprised he would ask, but then I understood and continued. "No, he's just a very rich man who thinks his son can do no wrong. He thinks he and Collin can rule the world, and that's his only downfall. Everything Flynn does is by the book, other than pulling a few strings to get Collin into the treasury office. Collin's parents are the nicest people, but they both came from money, grew into even more of it after they married, and I think it's intoxicating to them and they might be insecure without it. They want the best because they want people to think they are the best, so they made sure Collin grew up that way, too. And it shows; we have everything he wants and thinks I could ever want. But I don't know how my monster came from those people. Still, I think Flynn would do anything to keep Collin out of trouble, no matter what Collin did."

The guys accepted that answer.

Deacon took a deep breath and looked to Knox, his expression somber. "Okay. You need to take Harlow somewhere safe while you do this. There's no way around it. With who Collin is . . . who his dad is—even if he is an okay guy—and knowing that Collin has police receiving kickbacks from him, that means they could have people pretty much anywhere. Once you get her somewhere we're all positive is safe, then we'll start working on a way to expose Collin and get him arrested," he said, gesturing to the guys.

I shot up from my chair, but Knox quickly pulled me into his lap. "No," I said sternly. "No, absolutely not."

"Low," Knox growled.

I twisted in his lap to look at him. "I'm not letting you put all of your lives on the line because of this!"

"Babe, what do you think we were planning on doing? Nothing?"

"No, of course not. I know you'd be there—but just to keep me safe, not to be the ones who put *everything* they have in danger." I leaned closer to him so it felt like it was a conversation between only us, though I was sure the others could still hear. "Do you remember how hard I tried to push you away? How I constantly told you not to help me? I knew that coming to you last night was me giving that up and letting you help, but that's all it is, Knox. *Help.* Not do everything for me while *I* hide away."

His dark eyes glistened with unshed tears. "I can't let you near him."

"Do you think I can stomach the thought of *you* near him?"

"I have spent the past two weeks dying every day thinking of what you could be going through while I paced around here doing nothing," he said. "Only to find out my fears didn't skim the surface of what you'd actually been enduring. And then last night? I wouldn't be able to live with myself if he ever got close enough to touch you again."

I placed both hands against his cheeks and kissed him softly. When I pulled back, it was all over his face that he knew what I was about to say. "I did not spend the last two and a half years living with him, and living with what he was doing to me, just to let someone else finish things for me. He's *my* problem. I need you, Knox. But I need you to help me stay strong in this, okay?"

He wouldn't respond to me, because he and I both knew he didn't plan on letting me do this my way.

After a minute passed, Knox's eyes went past me, and Deacon cleared his throat before he started talking. "Right, so. I have nothing then." When Knox's eyes narrowed, Deacon said, "I was *going* to say we needed to start thinking of safe places. Maybe the fire department, unless you think Collin has people there, too."

"It's doubtful," Knox said.

"Not that it matters, but the treasury is in control of the fire department's money," I added, but Knox shook his head.

"I still don't think—"

"But we can't know," Graham interjected.

"Well, she can't stay with friends or family. He'll know to look there first," Deacon said with a sigh, and sank into his chair.

"But if he does find out that she's with me, he would quickly find out that I'm a firefighter," Knox argued.

"Yeah, but I doubt he'd think you'd hide her with a bunch of them."

"It still wouldn't matter. I'm not hiding," I said defiantly, and hoped only Knox noticed my shaking since he was holding me. "You don't understand, I *can't*. He'll go after everyone I love if I do. My family won't have that much time. I need to figure out what I'm going to do, and do it today."

We all sat there in silence for a while until Graham eventually asked me, "What was your plan? You can't go back to him."

I laughed uneasily. "I would never go back to him. I just don't have a—" I straightened and gasped. "The new chief of police in Richland! I-I don't know who he is, but I've heard Collin talk about him in the last few weeks. They're all mad because he's not from here, and they wanted the Benton County sheriff's cousin, or something like that, to get the promotion. They were livid over it—still are. Collin and one of his dad's coworkers were just talking about it this week. If they hate him so much, then he's our best bet."

"Done," Graham and Deacon said together, then Graham asked, "Knox?"

When I looked back at Knox, I saw the muscle in his jaw twitch. He refused to meet my gaze. "One of you, find out a way for us to meet with him. Don't bother us until it's set up." Without another word, he slid me off his lap, stood up, and pulled me down the hall with him.

He was furious.

Knox didn't stop walking until we got to his bed, and then it was only to pause to sit me down on it before he began pacing in tight circles. A few minutes passed before he finally stopped and turned to look at me, and my heart sank at the rage and pain I saw in his eyes.

"Why won't you let me take care of this for you?"

"I told you."

"Harlow—"

"I'm here, Knox. I left him. I'm letting you help me, but I can't let you do this *for* me. Please understand that."

"I can't!" he yelled, and my body jerked from the sudden boom of his voice. He groaned and ran a hand over his face. "I'm sorry. I'm sorry, I just—Harlow, I can't," he choked out and shut his eyes. A single tear ran down his cheek when he did.

I stood from the bed and pressed close to his body—his arms

immediately wrapped around me. "We're both going to be okay."

Knox's dark eyes opened, and I knew he didn't believe me. Then again, I wasn't sure I did, either. "He has police, Low. I know what you said about Collin not liking this guy, but we can't know. It feels like a trap that *we're* setting up."

"And *that's* exactly why you'll be there."

"What?" Knox whispered when there was a knock on his door—like the sound alone was too much for him right now, because it meant there was some news.

"Some lady said the chief will be in at eight and you can just show up. I didn't say names, just said I wanted a meeting with him."

Knox shut his eyes and inhaled deeply, but didn't respond. So I gave my thanks to Deacon and waited for him to leave. Once the door shut, I pulled Knox back onto the bed and situated us in the middle, pressed close to each other.

We didn't speak over the next forty-five minutes, just lay there watching each other. Every now and then, Knox would cradle my cheek in his large hand, and I tried to memorize the feeling.

My body started trembling, and Knox looked sick when Graham and Deacon came in later.

When we didn't move, Deacon murmured, "The sooner we get this done, the sooner we can all stop worrying."

"*We* get this done?" I asked. "No. You're not coming."

"Yes, we are," Graham said, and left no room for argument. At least the guys weren't acting like mother hens anymore. They'd stopped after breakfast.

"Look, I appreciate what—"

"Harlow," Graham said, and looked directly at me. "I under-

stand what you want. I understand it and respect that you want
to be the one to finish this. But it's stupid for us not to go with
you. Even if you're worried about us, you have to admit how
stupid it is for you to go alone—"

"I'm letting Knox come," I interjected, but he kept talking.

"—and how stupid it is for only him to go with you. He's so
in love with you that he won't be able to think clearly. Which
is where we come in. Besides, do you think with the unknown
amount of dirty cops, that you would just be able to walk into
the police department alone without one of them telling Collin
where to find you? Or taking you to him? You need us there."

"Oh," I whispered. That hadn't been something I'd thought of,
and I felt stupid for not thinking that far ahead. That didn't mean
I wanted these three guys to put themselves in even more immediate danger. I turned to look at Knox's guarded expression.
"You knew they were going to do this?"

"I told you," he mumbled. "Being mine means you get them,
too. We didn't discuss it, but I know what I would do if the roles
were reversed. I figured they would come."

I looked back to Deacon and Graham and shook my head. "I
really wish you—"

"Well, I guess it's a good thing we've never listened to you
before," Deacon said. "We already discussed it; we'll go in a separate truck just in case anything comes up where we would need
to put you in a different one." When I just continued to shake my
head, he turned around and marched from the room as he said,
"Get over it, Harlow: we're coming with you."

Graham raised an eyebrow in challenge, but I didn't say anything; just let my shoulders sag. After a few seconds he said,
"You're the bravest person I've ever met, and, in a way, the

strongest. But even the bravest warriors needed armies with them."

"I'm not a warrior," I said softly.

"You sure about that?" His eyes darted to Knox. "Time to go."

I was still staring at the spot where Graham had been standing when Knox pulled me off the bed. He slowly walked us to the front of the house with my hand clasped tightly in his.

"Stay a few car lengths behind us, and let me know if you see any dark BMWs following us," Knox ordered, but he sounded exhausted. "When we get there, whoever is driving, stay in the truck; the other can follow us into the station a couple of minutes later. Try to stay somewhere where you can look out for—shit. Do you even know what he looks like?"

"Think so," Graham mumbled.

"I do," Deacon said. "The guy with the smile's son. I told you before. He has the smile, too."

"But how do you know that, and what if he isn't smiling?" Knox asked.

"I watch the news."

"Since when?" Knox and Graham asked at the same time, but before he could respond, Knox continued. "Never mind. Let's just get this over with."

None of us moved. But after a minute Knox clenched his teeth and turned to leave with me tucked close to his side. Once we were outside, I stopped breathing and felt Knox's body grow tense. It was obvious that even though his head was still, he was looking everywhere for someone who shouldn't be there.

He opened the passenger door to his truck, but before he let me get in, pulled me close and captured my mouth with his.

The kiss was slow and unhurried, and completely didn't fit the anxious and worried mood that had just filled his entryway, but I needed it all the same. I traced the line of his jaw with one hand while clinging to him with the other, and a soft cry fell past my lips when he reluctantly pulled away.

"We're going to be fine," he whispered against my forehead, careful not to touch the huge cut on the side.

I simply nodded, and didn't bother to acknowledge out loud the fact that he'd sounded like he was trying to convince both of us.

It felt like we were both shaking from how tight we were holding our bodies once we were in the truck and driving away from his house. Each house we passed felt like it took an eternity, and I wondered how we were going to survive this drive, just from our fear alone.

We'd just passed the center of Thatch when Knox's phone rang. We both jumped, and I wanted to laugh at us, but couldn't find it in me to.

Knox cursed, then answered the call. "What, Deacon?" he growled, his tone laced with worry as he put the call on speaker.

"That car from our street is behind you. The BMW we talked about at breakfast. It could be a coincidence; we don't know how long it's been there. We waited a minute after you left before even leaving the house to get into Graham's truck."

Knox and I were both looking in the side- and rearview mirrors, and the mumbled curses continued. "Okay, I see the car. Can't see the driver; they're too far back. I didn't even look for it when we left; I just focused on driving."

"Like I said, it *could* be a coincidence. Do you want to turn somewhere? See if the car follows?"

"Where, Deacon? I just passed the last damn street. I'm about to hit the bridge before the freeway."

Deacon and Graham shouted curses, and I turned to look behind us just in time to see the BMW smash into the back of Knox's truck.

"Fuck!" Knox yelled, and tried to correct the truck when it slid. "Face forward!" he yelled, but I couldn't move. My eyes were frozen on the man driving the SUV pushing ours across a bridge.

"Collin," I whispered.

Chapter 22

Knox
Present Day—Thatch

I THREW MY truck in reverse and slammed my foot down on the gas. "Low, forward, baby!"

"It's Collin!" she whispered in horror.

I didn't need to be able to see him to know that. I couldn't think of anyone else who would try to push us off a bridge. After gaining a few feet back, and then feeling the resistance coming from the SUV, I glanced at Harlow to make sure she was facing straight ahead.

Without giving Collin a chance to let off the brake, I slammed my truck back into drive and took off in the direction of Richland. I pushed my truck as hard as she would go, but Collin was in a BMW; it didn't take long before I saw him eating up the distance in my rearview mirror.

"Hold on, Low," I gritted as he closed in, and braced for the impact. We jerked and swerved, but I corrected it quickly. "You okay?" I shouted as I floored it again.

"Yes! Go!"

I was already going 115 mph on a 55 mph road, and Collin was still right behind me. My truck was shaking; I couldn't push it much more.

"Harlow, I'm going to hit the brakes, okay?"

"What?"

"On the count of three, be ready for the brakes!"

She didn't respond, but I saw her bracing herself out of the corner of my eye. I waited until Collin was within a car length from me, and watched as he slowly began moving to the side as he prepared to come up beside me for the next hit.

"One . . . two . . ." I watched the SUV closely, then shouted, "Shit!" as I slammed on the brakes.

We hadn't even come to a full stop when I saw Collin's airbag deploy, and I took off again.

"That wasn't three," Harlow choked out, and I glanced over to see her entire body shaking and tears streaming down her face.

"I'm sorry." I brushed her hair back from her face and looked her over quickly before paying attention to the road again. I tapped on my phone when it rang, and put it on speaker. "Yeah?"

"Whatever the fuck that was, it hurt like a bitch!" Deacon yelled. "But he's already driving."

"Are you okay?" I asked, and glanced into the mirror. My stomach fell and fear flooded my veins when I saw the misshapen front of the BMW coming up not far in the distance. "Shit."

"Yeah, we were getting ready to try a pit on him whenever that last thing just happened. We're coming, but he's fuckin' fast, man."

"I know," I groaned as Collin got closer. "I'm almost to the city. If I can get there, he'll back off. He won't do anything in public."

I could see Harlow nodding as she sobbed.

"It's gonna be okay, Harlow. We've got this." Deacon tried to sound encouraging for her, but I could tell through the phone that he was in pain.

I tried to coax my truck to go a little faster, but it wasn't happening, and Collin was almost to us. "Come on, come on, come on," I mumbled, and only felt the tiniest bit of relief when we started getting into civilization. Deacon was still trying to calm Harlow, and Collin was going faster than ever—despite having smashed into the back of my truck.

He knew he was about to lose his opportunity.

I glanced down to my speedometer, 118 mph, and we were finally seeing cars now. Collin and I wove in and out of them. Horns were honked and cars swerved out of the way, but I didn't slow down. When I got on another stretch where there were no cars, I allowed myself to feel some small bit of hope.

"We're almost there, Low."

We had three, maybe four minutes before we got to a place where the traffic would be too heavy to continue at high speed. And while I was betting Collin would stop then, I had also thought earlier that he would've stopped as soon as we got around other cars, and he hadn't.

Collin pulled up directly behind us again, but this time he drifted to the right, and I did a double take when I saw him leaning out of the driver's window.

"What in the fuck," I whispered as my eyes darted between the road and my rearview mirror. "What is—" I broke off suddenly, and felt sick when I saw why he was risking leaning out. "Shit," I hissed, and started using the entire road to drive, hoping it would make it harder for him. "Don't look back!" I yelled when I saw Harlow turn. "Just keep talking to Deacon, Low. Close your eyes and talk to Deacon," I begged.

Harlow was right. He'd snapped.

Harlow screamed when Collin shot his gun, and I shouted another curse but didn't stop driving. Another shot rang out, and Harlow started whimpering incoherent words. I'd barely registered the third shot before my truck swerved from where he'd hit the rear right tire. I didn't stop, but it gave Collin the perfect amount of time to line up for another shot—and hit the front right tire. My truck swerved across the entire road as the first tire Collin had hit shredded from how fast I'd been going. I clipped the front of the car Collin was driving as we swerved, and shot my arm out in front of Harlow's chest when I felt my truck start to defy gravity.

She grabbed on to me, and it somehow felt like I had all the time in the world to turn my head to look at her—and yet, no time at all—as my truck started flipping.

The last thing I remember was looking into her panicked blue eyes before the airbags went off.

Harlow

Present Day—Richland

MY EYES SLOWLY cracked open, and at first all I saw was white and started to panic. But then slowly I heard noises—like people shouting—smelled something acrid, and realized the white thing in front of me was squishy.

I looked to the left and a sob burst from my chest when I saw Knox sitting there, unresponsive. I hurried to unbuckle my seat belt so I could try to climb over the center console to get to him, and had just gotten it undone when the passenger door was ripped open.

Someone grabbed at me, and at first I thought it must've been someone coming to check on us, but I should've known who it was by the way his hands gripped at me possessively—should've known he wouldn't stop.

"No!" I shouted, and tried to get away from him, not that there was anywhere else I could go in the truck. But if he was trying to pull me out of it, I wanted to stay in there, and I wanted to stay with Knox. "No! Knox! Knox, wake up!" I screamed, and kicked at Collin as he pulled me from the cab of the truck.

"I have a feeling this belongs to you." Collin tossed my secret cell phone into the truck, then turned us both away. "Walk," Collin demanded. His voice was the same as it was last night. Soft, bored, detached, but still held power.

"Let me go!" I yelled, and thrashed against him.

Cars had stopped on the freeway; people were out of their cars and watching us—some had their phones pointed at us, and some were talking on them. But Collin didn't care, because he wasn't Collin anymore, and he wasn't my monster.

"People are not allowed to touch what is mine," he said simply, as if reminding me.

"I am not *yours*," I spat out, accentuating each word. "You left me to die!"

He laughed, and the humorless sound sent a chill up my spine. "Well, I'd hoped, but you're stronger than I give you credit for," he continued on with that same nonchalant voice. "But if I hadn't stuck around to find out, I wouldn't have known to follow you all the way to Thatch, now would I?"

We were nearing the smashed SUV he'd been driving, and I was putting up more and more of a fight—but I had always been weaker than Collin, and he hadn't just been in a truck that had rolled.

"Now, get in the—"

"Collin!" a deep, fluid voice rang out about everything else, and it sounded so beautiful in that moment that I cried out in relief when Collin turned us around to face where Knox was standing at the back of his truck. He was swaying; but still standing. "Let her go!"

Without hesitation, Collin raised his free arm, gun in hand, and aimed right at Knox. I screamed and lunged for it as he pulled the trigger.

I'd knocked Collin's arm to the side, but out of the corner of my eye still saw Knox stumble back. A sharp sob burst from my chest, and everything grew to a deafening level then. It was piercing, but I didn't know what the sound was. I only knew that I needed to get to Knox, but Collin was aiming again.

Gripping Collin's hand that was holding the gun, I pulled it close to my body and placed myself between Collin and Knox, and held tight when Collin tried to throw me down with his free hand. My foot got caught between his, causing him to stumble, and soon the force from him throwing me aside had us both falling—with him above me and the gun now sandwiched between us, our fingers both on the trigger.

In those last few seconds, a sense of peace washed over me. I saw Deacon and Graham in a dead sprint in our direction and knew they would help Knox. I knew this was how it was

supposed to end, and wondered how I thought it would ever
end any other way. I'd prayed for God to show me some kind of
mercy and to take me from Collin, and now I was finally getting my prayers answered. And with such a public act, I knew
Collin wouldn't get away with this.

A smile crossed my face and I let my eyes close.

It wasn't all for nothing, I told myself as we crashed down, and
the force of our fall caused us to squeeze off one final round.

Knox
Present Day—Richland

"HARLOW!" I SHOUTED as I ran with what little energy I had in
my body toward where she and Collin were falling to the pavement. "Harlow!"

The sound of the sixth gunshot tore through me, causing me
to stumble until I was on my knees, unable to move. I needed
to get up, I needed to get to her, to make sure she was alive—
because surely she was still alive—but instead, I bent toward
the pavement, and a sob was forced from my chest when countless seconds passed without movement from either of them. The
bullet that was embedded in my right arm hadn't hurt as much as
the sound of that last gunshot was destroying me.

I looked up when I felt hands on my shoulders and shoved
Deacon away from me. He fell backward and came toward me
again, but didn't try to touch me. He was saying something—
shouting, but I couldn't hear anything. I forced myself up and
stumbled a few times as I headed toward Collin and Harlow.

Graham was already there, carefully stepping up behind where Collin was still lying on top of her.

Deacon hurried over to them and helped Graham heave Collin's body off of Harlow—but I couldn't focus on them. All I could see was my world lying still on the ground as Graham ran back and hovered over her.

I approached her slowly, like each step was trying to get through quicksand, and didn't understand Graham's smile or what he was trying to say to me. I glanced at Harlow once more before looking over at him again, and my legs began shaking when Graham moved away from Harlow's bloodied body and slowly disentangled the gun from her thin hands to lay it on the ground beside them.

"Fucking warrior," he said; pride coated each word.

I dropped down next to her, and cried out when I saw her chest faintly moving. "Low," I said, and cradled her cheeks in my hands. "Babe, open your eyes," I whispered against her lips, and kissed her softly.

"He's gone," I heard Deacon say behind me, and I nodded, even though he had probably been telling Graham.

"Low, it's over. I need you to open your eyes."

I held her for a few more minutes, and didn't care that tears were falling relentlessly down my face as I waited for anything from her. Ambulances pulled up then, and just when I was about to beg her to open her eyes again, her blue eyes shot open and she gasped.

"YES, MR. EVANS," I said a few hours later, and held back a sigh as he and his wife asked the same questions I'd just answered. "You all know everything I do at this point, and I promise I'll keep you updated, but I'm going to go back in to check on her now."

"Well, what did the doctor say? Why won't you tell us?" Harlow's mom asked over the speaker.

"I'm not sure; he wouldn't talk with me in there. I'll let you know if there was anything wrong, but I'm sure she was fine." I tried to keep my tone even because I knew they were worried, but I'd already spoken with them half a dozen times since entering the hospital, and I had other things I was worrying about.

I smiled politely at the doctor when he walked out of Harlow's room, and said, "I have to go now; I'll keep you updated." As soon as I was able to hang up, I walked into the room and took my seat next to Harlow's bed.

My truck had flipped twice, but the impact had been mostly on my side—and the worst of my injuries had only given me problems directly after. I'd had trouble getting my legs to move but was fine for the most part now. Even still, my captain had informed me over the phone that I was looking at at least a month off because of getting shot. They'd removed the bullet and sewn me up, and had barely been able to keep me there long enough to bandage me before I'd tried to leave to find Harlow's room.

Deacon and Graham were fine, just a little bruised from when they'd smashed into the back of the SUV Collin had been driving. And Collin was gone. That final bullet could have gone anywhere, from the way Harlow had explained the gun had been pinned between them. But somehow it'd gone between both their bodies, through Collin's throat, and up into his brainstem. He'd died immediately.

Harlow was malnourished—not a surprise. She had bruises

all over her body and cracked ribs—almost all of which were from Collin prior to today. The reason the doctor had been in there just then had been to talk to her about the X-ray and scans they'd done on her skull. But the doctor had refused to talk with me in the room since I wasn't family, so I'd stepped out to give her parents another update.

"What'd he say?" I asked gently.

"I've hit my head a lot." Harlow shrugged. "Really, he didn't tell me anything I don't already know. Just that I need to avoid hitting my head from now on, that I was lucky there wasn't permanent damage, and that it was likely if I do hit my head again—if it's hard enough—each time I will probably go unconscious for some period of time. But I'd kind of started figuring that out on my own. It's happened every time lately."

I clenched my jaw, but tried to relax by repeating over and over that Collin couldn't touch her again. "It won't happen again," I reminded her, and she just nodded.

Harlow had been different since she woke up and realized there was no danger; reserved, almost. I'd mentioned it in the ambulance, and she'd shaken her head. I'd brought it up again after we'd gotten to the hospital and things had calmed down, and she'd just looked away from me. And she hadn't once looked at me since.

"Your family is already trying to get tickets back here. Hayley and her family are coming, too. They'll call me when they have something."

And that time, it looked like she hadn't even heard me. Instead of pushing it, I just sat back and waited.

When another thirty minutes went by without her saying

anything or looking in my direction, I slowly stood from my chair. My chest ached, but I didn't know what to do.

I stared at the back wall and swallowed a few times before I trusted myself to speak. "I guess I'll, uh, I'll let you rest."

Harlow didn't respond, but when I turned to leave, I saw the tears falling down her cheeks.

"What's wrong?" I asked softly, and tried to rein in my frustration when she still didn't answer. I sat on the edge of her bed, gripped her chin gently in my fingers, and turned her head so she was looking at me. "Come back to me," I begged, and the ache in my chest grew when her chin began quivering and a sob forced its way up her throat.

"I killed him," she said between muted sobs. "I killed him, Knox."

I gripped her hand in mine, and exhaled in relief when I felt her squeeze back. "He was going to kill you," I reminded her. "He *tried* to kill you."

"But I don't want to have this on me," she cried out, and lifted her hands up, as if Collin's blood would be there. "I don't want to know that I took someone's life—no matter what the reason! And I—" She broke off, and sobbed as she shook her head.

"You what?"

Long moments passed as she continued to cry and shake her head while murmuring, "I was ready to die." Harlow eventually looked up at me and shrugged, like she didn't know how to explain it. "I knew it was happening, and I knew it was how it was supposed to happen. I was okay with it. I knew you were going to be okay, and I was okay. I hate that I was okay! What does that mean for me?"

"Nothing," I assured her, and pulled her close.

"You don't understand," she whispered, like she was ashamed. "I smiled. I smiled because I knew it was all as it should've been. What's wrong with me?"

"Nothing," I repeated, and held her as she cried everything away. During that time she started relaxing into me and clinging to me, now that she'd finally let her worries out.

It felt like hours had passed when she said, "I don't know how to feel about it all. I feel wrong . . . broken."

I smiled and corrected her. "Cracked." Pulling back enough so I could tilt her head up, I searched her eyes and promised, "But I'm going to fix it. I love you, Harlow."

She smiled shakily, and one hand lifted to frame my mouth as she leaned in to kiss me. But just before her mouth met mine, she vowed, "To the stars."

Chapter 23

Harlow
Present Day—Richland

"Who said we were leaving?"

"Family only? Don't we look like family? We're her brothers, we're practically triplets," Deacon said, and imitated Graham's intimidating stance.

"This is no longer about family; visiting hours are about to be over," the older nurse said sternly.

She was met with twin looks of indifference. "And?" Graham finally said.

The nurse's eyes bounced back and forth between the two, then over to Knox, and then to me.

I had to fight back a smile. "I'm sorry, but the other nurse said she was getting my discharge papers?"

"Right, because we're leaving and taking our *sister* with us," Deacon said arrogantly.

"Deac," Knox murmured, then shook his head once when he had Deacon's attention.

When she left with an exaggerated huff, Deacon turned and asked, "Where's the nurse from earlier? The hot one," he clarified. "She needs to come back; she didn't question us being in here." He snorted, then mumbled to himself, "Like we're just gonna leave without you."

I shook my head as Graham studied the monitors even though I was no longer hooked up to them, and Deacon started on his definition of "family." I looked at Knox and we both mouthed, "Mother hens."

There was a quick knock on the door a couple of minutes later, and Knox cursed. "If you got security called on us, I will never forgive you," he said as Deacon went to answer the door.

"We're not leaving," Deacon said as he swung the door open. "Have a nice night!"

The door was halfway shut on my parents' confused faces before I could yell, "Wait!"

"Harlow!" my mom cried out, and pushed past the door. My dad and Hadley followed, and a sharp cry burst from my chest seeing my sister so much better than she'd been just the day before.

Knox mumbled something, and he and my mother hens all stepped closer to my bed in unison—as if to protect me from my family—but I just looked at the doorway expectantly.

"Where's Hayley?"

"She and the family are getting a hotel for all of us so we don't have to worry about it when you can get out," Mom explained as she hurried to my side. She grabbed my hand and sat on the side of the bed as her eyes roamed all over my body. "Oh, sweetie, how could you not tell us?"

Graham scoffed, and Knox sneered, "How could you not *notice*?"

"Knox," I whispered, hoping he would get the hint.

"I knew within seconds of—"

"Knox," I said harder, and held his stare for a moment. "I had a role I had to play in front of them. I couldn't let them see what he was doing to me."

My mom held my hand up, and gently ran the fingers from her other hand over my arm and across my knuckles. She sobbed freely as she studied me. "You're so thin, Harlow. So thin," she whispered. "You look so sick," she continued, but it sounded like the words were meant for her. Her eyes fell over my face, and her next words were so soft they were nearly inaudible. "Your cheeks . . . your collarbones. Your eyes looks so—oh, honey!"

The need to defend my family was suddenly gone. I knew that other than the bandages on my forehead and the fact that I was lying in a hospital bed, I couldn't look much different from when I'd seen them yesterday, or even a few months ago. But she wasn't mentioning the bandages. My mom was mentioning things that had been noticeable for years. Physical parts of me I'd worried endlessly over every time I'd been near any member of my family, because I'd known they could give something away. Physical parts of me that I'd made myself sick over with the worry that they would see something they weren't supposed to.

And now . . . now a part of me *was* angry. Angry that they could see it all that time and had just refused to; but I knew I couldn't think that way. Because like I'd just told Knox, I'd played a part. And like I'd known every time, if they would've seen, it would've been so bad for them.

"You need to come back to Seattle, where we can take care of you, where we can help you get better. We'll make sure that you recover from this the way you need to."

"No."

My mom straightened her back, and looked over to Knox for the first time at his response. The room filled with tension as everyone looked at each other, and my parents no doubt were wondering who Graham and Deacon were as the two glared at my family. I hadn't mentioned them to my parents all those years ago, since things had always been so tense between Knox's friends and me—that had been reserved for rants to my sisters. And as the boys looked at my family like they were ready to fight to keep me with them and Knox, I couldn't help but be taken aback again at how things had drastically changed with them.

"Knox, honey, it's so very good to see you," Mom began again. "But Harlow *needs* her father and me to get through this time."

Knox's mouth opened, probably to tell her no again, but snapped shut. After a deep breath, his eyes slid over to me. His voice was gruff when he said, "I think it's time Harlow gets to decide what happens in her life—no matter what that means." Despite the ache in those last words, I knew he meant them.

An uneasy minute passed without a word from anyone as all of our eyes went from one person to the next.

Finally, I asked, "Knox, guys, can I have time with my parents?"

Knox moved immediately, but my mother hens didn't move

until Knox uttered a low "Out." With one last glance in my direction, Knox shut the door behind them. I released the breath
I'd been holding as I looked at my family.

"Hadley, how are you?" I asked, barely able to choke out the
question.

She shrugged and smiled weakly. "Fine; a little sore. Mostly
I feel sick because I was the closest one to you, and I feel like if
anyone should have seen what was happening, it should have
been me."

"No," I said before she'd finished speaking. "No, you shouldn't
have. You saw me the most often, so the changes weren't as drastic to you. But, Hadley, you have no idea how glad I am that you
never saw them," I said, my voice wavering as I thought about
every threat to my family—but Hadley specifically. "He threatened Hadley the most because she was the closest, physically.
Hadley, if you had noticed something—if *any* of you would have
noticed something—he would have done whatever it took to shut
you up. I don't know if Dad told you, but what happened to you
yesterday was because Collin thought I tried to poison him when
all I'd done was refill the salt shaker."

My mom gasped, but from their expressions, I knew it wasn't
the first time they'd heard this.

I held my mom's stare and tried to steady my quivering jaw,
but failed. "As much as I hate that you *can* see a difference and
just didn't over the years, you know just a fraction of what he was
like—so you will never know how thankful I am that you *didn't*
see what was happening."

Mom's tears fell faster, and she covered her face as sobs tore
through her body. My dad went to comfort her, but it looked like
he needed the comfort just as much.

"Couldn't you have left him before yesterday?" Hadley asked.

I stared at her blankly, unsure what part of Collin's psychotic tendencies she didn't understand. "No, Hadley. Do you not remember what just happened to you yesterday?"

"Of course I do, but why didn't you just leave him before? You left last night; why did you wait so long?"

"I tried leaving him at the beginning of our marriage. Do you remember the night that beach house you guys vacationed in caught fire? I made it to Oregon before I was pulled over and arrested for DWI without even having a sobriety test done. Collin picked me up soon after and made me wait with my phone for hours when we got home until I got the call from you."

Hadley's eyes widened in disbelief, and my mom's cries got louder.

"Leaving him meant losing you. I couldn't risk that. Staying with him, no matter what it meant for me . . ." I said through my tears, and had to stop when it got too hard to speak. "Staying meant you were supposed to be safe."

"But at what cost?" Dad asked; his tone was hard, but his face was filled with grief. "You haven't told us most of what happened, and I can't begin to imagine because I don't *want* to. Seeing what happened that led to you being in a hospital tells me more than I need to know; I can see now that those years with him aren't something that you should've gone through—no matter what it meant for us. We could've figured something out, Harlow!"

I shook my head, because none of them could understand that it wouldn't have been that simple, but stilled and reached toward my dad when he stopped fighting it and finally burst into tears. "Dad," I whispered. "I'm sorry, I know you don't understand, but I couldn't tell you. Collin was my burden, and I never would have forgiven myself if I'd let his evil slip into your lives more than it was already able to."

"Oh, honey," Mom whispered, but then the room quieted except for their soft sobs. "We'll make this up to you somehow. We'll take care of you, I promise. We'll find a doctor you can talk to in Seattle, and—"

"Mom." I cut her off quietly. "I love you, but what you're doing . . . there's no point for it. You don't have to make up for anything."

"That's not it," she assured me.

"That's a lot of it," I argued gently. "I know you want me close after everything that's happened, too, but most of this is just guilt that you don't need to feel. And Seattle? Mom, I don't want to be there." My throat tightened again and tears filled my eyes, but I smiled through them. "After years without him, I just found Knox again. I never stopped loving him, and I never stopped regretting the mistake I made in choosing Collin over him. Now that he's here, I can't go back to a life where he isn't."

My parents shared a look, and Hadley turned to look at the door as if expecting Knox to walk through it again. When she turned back around, she nodded and gave me a reassuring smile—but I'd had no doubts she would take my side. Of course Hadley would side with love.

"Harlow, we've respected Knox for a long time, and we're thankful he was here for you," Dad finally said. "However, after the events of the last couple days now might not be the best time to make this kind of decision. Starting a relationship with Knox would also probably not be the wisest decision. You need time."

"I plan on taking things one day at a time, Dad. I won't rush into anything with him just because he's back in my life. But staying *here* with him . . . I know that's what is right for me. *He* has always been right for me. I just lost my way for a little while."

Before anyone could respond, there was a knock on the door, and one of the earlier nurses came in with some papers in her hands.

"Are you ready to go home?" she asked brightly.

"I'm ready to leave," I responded, and wondered at the word *home*. At the moment, it felt like I didn't have one. The house I'd lived in with Collin could never be considered a home.

My eyes flitted up to the person now filling the doorway, and my tensed body eased seeing Knox's warm smile.

I might not have a home now, but I knew in that smile that someday, with that man, I would.

Knox
Present Day—Richland

"WE'LL CALL A company to come pick it up. All of it can be donated," Harlow said dismissively a week later.

"Donate—what about—wait, don't you want to go through any of it?" Mrs. Evans asked, stumbling over her words as she looked around the piles of things in Harlow's old living room.

Harlow looked at her mom, then the piles with a confused expression. "We've spent most of this week going through all of it. Everything else went to the dump; this all gets donated."

Her mom waved off Harlow's words. "No, I meant don't you want to go through any of it to see if you want to keep it."

Even Harlow's sisters looked shocked.

Hadley sifted through a pile closest to her. "The jewelry in here alone has to be worth close to a million," she said in awe. "You can't tell me you don't want it."

"What about the furniture?" Harlow's dad asked. "It'll help with that apartment you're getting."

"You can't just give all this away!"

"Mom's right," Harlow's older sister, Hayley, said. "At least sell it if you don't want to keep it."

The only people in the house not trying to persuade Harlow to do something with everything she and Collin had bought together, or that he'd forced her to buy, were Graham, Deacon, and me.

I knew she didn't want to keep anything from their fucked-up life together—who would? And whether Graham and Deacon understood that or not, they just wanted whatever Harlow wanted.

"No," Harlow said with a shake of her head. "Donate."

"Har—" Her mom began again, but was cut off.

"Everything in this house is a memory in the form of a nightmare. I don't want it, and I don't want the money from it," Harlow whispered harshly, each word holding a pain none of us could imagine. But from the looks on her family's faces, they weren't going to try to push her anymore.

"I'll look up a company and arrange a pickup," Hayley's husband said, and immediately began tapping on his phone.

"Thank you," Harlow said, and her body relaxed as she closed the distance between us. "I just want to be out of here and done with this place."

When she got close, I pulled her into my arms and pressed my lips to the top of her head. "Soon," I promised.

We'd all stayed in the hotel, with the exception of Graham

and Deacon, for three nights before Harlow's entire family had
piled into our house. No one had wanted to stay in Harlow's old
house. I couldn't blame them, and my roommates didn't complain as long as they got to put an endless amount of food in front
of Harlow.

When we hadn't been clearing out the old house, we'd been
apartment hunting for Harlow. She'd wanted, and found, a place
in Richland so it was close to me, but still far enough away that
she felt like she could have her space to figure things out. Her
family didn't understand why she was renting and continued to
remind her it was a waste of money when she had enough to
buy a new house with cash. Deacon and Graham had moped for
nearly an hour when they'd found out the location. I'd gone with
her to sign the papers and had smiled through it, because I knew
it was what she needed.

I wanted her next to me every second of every day, but this
apartment was what was best for her now—and for us later.

Harlow had picked up the keys this morning, but wanted to
wait until her family left for their homes tomorrow—Hadley
with her parents—to go shopping for the furniture and everything needed to move in.

She shifted in my arms when her phone chimed, and pulled
it out of her pocket. With a slow exhale, Harlow showed me the
screen, which held a text from Collin's mom, asking if she would
come over to talk.

"You gonna go?"

Harlow nodded once, then shook her head. "I've hardly talked
to them since everything happened. They're good people, Knox,"
she whispered. Words she'd said before. "They're good, but when
I *did* talk to them, they sounded so mad."

"They aren't mad at you. They're just having a hard time, too," I reminded her. "It's different than what you're going through. They probably didn't know this was happening."

"They couldn't have."

"Then they're probably in shock and didn't know how to react to the situation, or how to talk to you. But it looks like they're ready now . . . if you are."

Even though Harlow had reached out to them a few times, Collin's parents had been distant all week. They'd come by the house yesterday while everyone was gone to make sure there wasn't anything they wanted after we'd already piled up everything that was to be donated, and bagged what was to go to the dumpsters. As far as we could tell, however, they'd only taken a few of Collin's things from high school and college, and hadn't responded to most of Harlow's attempts to talk to them. Something that had been hard on her all week.

"I want to go, I know I need to. Will you go with me?"

I made a face and glanced back at the text, like it would give me the answer to whether or not I should go. "Do you think having me there the first time you see them would be best?"

"Probably not," she said laughing, but there was no real humor behind her tone. "But I'd thought they would have contacted me first. I had thought they would have come to see me. The fact that it's been the complete opposite is terrifying me for how it will be when I do see them."

My first reaction was to tell her that I would do anything she asked me to, but I was worried that if she was scared how they would react, then my presence might make it worse even though they wouldn't have any clue who I was.

One look into Harlow's eyes and I knew what my answer was then, and would always be. "Of course I'll go."

"I'M SORRY . . . what did you just say?" Harlow asked a couple of hours later once we were at the Dohertys' house. We'd barely gotten our introductions finished before they'd dropped a bomb on us.

Mrs. Doherty just continued on: "And we want to get you help for those things, dear. There's a place we can have you admitted to today; we know the director there. It's a great facility, the care is said to be some of the best."

"I don't need *help*. I'm not depressed, and I'm not on drugs!"

"We'll pay for the treatments and for your stay there," Mr. Doherty added. "With everything you put our son through, and now that he's gone, this is *very* generous of us."

I scoffed, but bit back the comments running through my head.

The prosecutor pinned a glare on me. "I'm still not sure why you're here." Looking back to Harlow, he said, "As for the drugs, we just have to make a call to the hospital to find out what was in your system last week. The depression won't be hard to prove, and it's not a bad thing to admit to."

The Dohertys sighed and gave each other a sad look. "Collin told us everything," Mrs. Doherty said. "He's been telling us for nearly a year about your depression with being unable to get pregnant, and for months about your substance abuse because of the depression. We've stayed quiet about it because he was worried it would only get worse if you knew that we were aware of what was going on. But now that he's gone, we feel we have no other option."

"Wha—no!" Harlow yelled, clearly in shock. "No, none of that is true! I haven't been getting pregnant, because I refused to have a child with your son!"

"Harlow," Mrs. Doherty said disapprovingly.

"I had an implant put in so I wouldn't get pregnant, and so Collin wouldn't find out about it! Your son was abusive; there is no way I would've let a child enter into that house wi—"

"Young lady, hold your tongue! Our son has given you the world," Mrs. Doherty seethed. "Every single thing you have ever asked for he has given you, and more. To speak of him this way—"

"Asked for?" Harlow asked, cutting her mother-in-law off, and laughed humorlessly. "Asked for? I never wanted any of it, which is why *all* of it is being donated and I'm not keeping any of it. He *forced* me to buy things for myself, and if I didn't I had to pay for it in ways you couldn't begin to imagine! He threatened my family to keep me with him, and tried to kill my sister the morning of your anniversary party. That night he tried to drown me in our guest bathroom!"

"Drown you?" Mr. Doherty asked loudly. "Collin called us before the party started, panicking because you'd overdosed and were in the hospital. He was so worried that he was going to lose you that night!"

My eyebrows rose, and a shocked laugh ripped from my chest at how ridiculous each thing they said sounded.

"He said he was going to tell you that I was upset over Hadley and drowned myself . . ." Harlow whispered. Then, as if something had just clicked for her, she said, "You would've known that wasn't true if you'd tried to come see me when I was supposedly in the hospital."

"Collin didn't want us to miss our party."

This time Harlow laughed. "Miss your party?" She stood from the poolside chairs we were sitting at and took a few steps away before stomping back. "Miss your party?" she asked louder. "I know you're both all about image, but I've *always* said that the two of you are good people. I would've thought that if *you* thought your daughter-in-law was in the hospital, supposedly about to die, you would rather come see her than make it to your anniversary party!"

The Dohertys had the decency to look ashamed, at least, but didn't say anything.

"And how does *any* of it make sense in your minds? That Collin would be *so* worried about me, but make sure to keep you away from where I was? That the car chase between Collin and us began early the next morning in *Thatch*, and ended in Richland where we were on our way to go to the new chief of police— but I was supposedly in the hospital the night before *with* Collin from a drug overdose? And I know you've heard every detail of the chase because it's been all over the news."

"Us? Was that your truck?" the prosecutor asked me, and I nodded once. "Were you injured?"

I glanced at Harlow for guidance, but she was still looking at her in-laws with frustration and hurt. "I was shot," I finally responded, but didn't expand on the details.

From the way Mr. Doherty's face fell, I didn't need to. He was piecing it together on his own. "Collin has said for so long that you were depressed, and you looked it. With the weight loss, it wasn't hard to believe that everything else was true—it still isn't. We want to get you help."

When Harlow spoke again, the anger was gone. "I don't do drugs, but, honestly, I don't have to prove that to you. I'm sorry you lost your son—I'm *so* sorry. But I'm not sorry that I'm finally away from that nightmare. *Depressed* doesn't even come close to what I felt. It felt like I was dead, and I remember praying to be taken away from him. I'm sorry if that's hard to hear," she said when Mrs. Doherty began crying. "But even though I understand that you loved your son and want to believe he couldn't do this, you have to understand that I lived it and it hurts that you can't believe me when the evidence is right in front of you.

"I know you went by the house yesterday and took whatever you wanted to keep, but I want to know if you want what money is left in Collin's bank account, or our cars. I don't want them—I don't want anything. I don't want the house, you can have it."

Shock swept through me. I'd known she wanted to rid herself of everything that had to do with Collin, but I hadn't known about all of this. Other than paying her first and last month's rent, as she already had, she wouldn't be able to afford her apartment . . . or anything. And with the fight she'd already had with her family about wanting to do all of this herself, I doubted she would let me help.

I looked over to the Dohertys, and saw my shock multiplied on both of their faces.

Shock slowly morphed into confusion, and it was Mrs. Doherty's turn to ask, "I'm sorry, what did you say?"

"I don't want any of it," Harlow said, exhaustion laced through every word. "I just want to know if you do, before I find something else to do with all of it, like I did the things in the house."

"But that house, that house is paid for," Mr. Doherty said. "The cars are only a year—the money—Collin said . . ."

"From some of the things he's said, we were sure you'd take the money and valuables, and run," Mrs. Doherty finished. With a quick look at her husband, she said, "We don't want those things. They're yours. If—if he really was that kind of—no. Uh, those things belong to you, Harlow. Just . . ." She trailed off with a quiet sob.

A moment passed, and it looked like Harlow was trying to figure out if she should go comfort them or not. Eventually, she said, "I'm sorry you lost your son."

With a look at me, she nodded to the side of the house, and we quietly walked away from the Dohertys as their guilt for missing so much settled, and confusion with what they'd thought they'd known of their son mixed with their grief of losing him.

Chapter 24

Harlow
Present Day—Richland

I'D BEEN SITTING in my car in front of the house for nearly forty minutes. I didn't know what was so hard about what I was trying to do, because when I'd made the decision to do it, I hadn't had any hesitations. But now . . . now I was shaking and wringing my hands and considering just leaving instead.

It's not him, and it's not what you came to do . . . it's where you just came from, I reminded myself.

It'd been three weeks since I was released from the hospital, and I felt like I hadn't stopped running the whole time—which was probably a good thing. It kept my mind off of things for too long.

I'd moved into my apartment after selling both BMWs, buying a brand-new Camry in their place, and using some of the leftover money to furnish my new apartment. Since Collin's parents hadn't wanted any of the money, I'd tried to help the guys, but had been met with rejection after rejection. Graham had refused to let me pay for his truck repairs, and Knox had laughed before giving me a firm "No" when I'd tried to pay for his new truck, even though I knew insurance hadn't covered the entire cost. So after fighting with Knox on what I could do with the money since I didn't want it, we'd figured out how to go about dispersing it the way I wanted to. We were putting the two-part plan into action today now that the house was finally up for sale—which was where I'd just come from.

I'd taken my last walk through it to make sure we'd gotten everything. It was the first time I'd been in the house alone since the night Collin had tried to drown me. Every beating, every mental game, and every fear had flashed through my mind as I'd slowly walked through. And an odd mix of relief, exhaustion, and grief for the person I'd been while with him had filled me as I'd locked the door and left for the last time.

Which led to now, as I waited at my first of two stops.

My eyes darted to the clock, and I sighed. I'd been sitting there for fifty minutes now.

Movement in front of the house caught my eye, and I knew if I didn't do it now, I might not ever, as I saw the man walking his dog toward the car sitting in the driveway.

Taking a deep breath, I stepped out of my car and called out as I crossed the street. "Mr. Farro?"

His head jerked up as he brought the dog to a halt, but Spartacus had noticed me and was now trying to get to me. He made a command to the dog and eyed me warily. "May I help you?"

I kept walking but stopped at the edge of his driveway when I noticed his cautious stance. I held my hands up to try to convey I wasn't there to bother him. Funny how at night in an oversize hoodie he hadn't batted an eye, but in normal clothing in the middle of the day, he was leery of me. "I'm sorry, I didn't mean to scare you. I came to talk with you. I'm Harlow—Low. I'm Low. You helped me get to Thatch a few weeks ago."

His eyes widened, and he gave me a once-over, clearly surprised that I was older than he'd originally guessed. "Uh—you. I—"

"I need to thank you," I choked out.

"You're not in high school," he said awkwardly.

Despite the tightness in my throat, I laughed. "No, not even close." I cleared my throat and began fidgeting with the envelope in my hand, but forced my hands to my side and looked directly into his eyes. "Thank you, Max."

He was shaking his head, like he couldn't understand why he would need this kind of thanks for a ride.

"Helping me that night, and getting me to Thatch, saved my life."

Max's mouth lifted, like he was about to laugh, but something in my expression stopped him. "What do you—"

I waved off his question, because I knew I wouldn't answer it, and took a step forward. I held out the envelope toward him and waited for him to take it.

His brow pinched as he looked at the front, it was addressed to Max, the future Mrs. Farro, and Spartacus. Inside was a check for a portion of what had been left in our bank account, with a note that, again, thanked Max and asked them to use the money for their wedding or honeymoon.

"Open it the next time you're with your fiancée," I requested as I took quick steps back toward the street. "Thank you, Max," I whispered, and turned to hurry to my car.

"Wait, what happened? Are you okay?" he called out. "Do

you need me to get you help?" he asked, this time quieter, and I
knew he and Spartacus had followed me to my car.

I turned just before I got in, and smiled. "No. What you did
that night was more help than I could've ever asked for."

Max nodded after a few seconds, then slowly backed up to
let me get in my car. He and Spartacus stood at the end of their
driveway and watched until I left a neighborhood I had no intention of ever setting foot in again.

I drove to the address Knox had given me that morning, and
found his brand-new truck parked a few houses away, out of sight
from the house that was my second stop. He opened the back
door to my car as soon as I stopped, and a crooked smile crossed
his handsome face when he pulled the boxes out of my backseat.

His smile fell, and he looked at me earnestly. "You're sure you
want to do this?"

I tried not to roll my eyes; he'd asked the same question for
almost two weeks now. "Knox. You already know what I decided.
I'm keeping the leftover money from the cars, and that's it."

"You could still keep whatever you get for the house," he offered.

I bit my lip. *That* was the only thing I couldn't decide on. "I
know, I'm thinking about it." As much as it would help to start a
new life in a new house, it still felt like dirty money. Just like the
money did that I was using now, but I was forcing myself not to
think of it that way. "Anyway, yes, I'm sure I want to do this. Are
you sure they're here?"

"Positive." Knox's lips spread into another crooked smile, and
he dipped his head to kiss me thoroughly. When he pulled back,
pride shone through his eyes, but it didn't match the mischievous
grin now on his face. "Be right back," he whispered, then took off

running across the street with the boxes in hand to leave them on the porch of the house.

The larger box held a pink Superman cape and a large blanket covered in thousands upon thousands of stars for little Natalie—the girl I'd mistaken as Knox's daughter. Once he told me about the night of the fire and saving her, and seeing her again in the grocery store, I knew we had to do something for their family. And seeing the ruined side of their house from the fire now under construction as I'd driven up, I was happy with what the smaller box held for them.

It'd taken time to get the bank to get all of the cash, but it was the other half of what had been left in our bank account. The note on top of the money said: "Hope this helps—Richland FD."

I smiled as Knox came running back toward me, and braced myself when he barely stopped in time to pull me into his arms and press his mouth to mine. He tilted me back so I was against my car, and I fell into that kiss.

"You're incredible," he whispered against my mouth. And with one more lingering kiss, he straightened us just in time to see Natalie's mom walk outside and look down at the boxes, then around the street. After another moment passed, she picked up the boxes and carried them into the house. With another smile, Knox opened the door to my car and whispered, "Let's go."

Knox
Present Day—Thatch

AFTER SWINGING BY Harlow's apartment to drop off her car, we'd driven to Thatch to have dinner with everyone at Grey and Jagger's place, and had spent so long there that we'd decided to stay at my house instead of going back to Richland that night.

Everyone had welcomed Harlow into our little family in a way they never had before, and even after three weeks, there were still times I would catch Harlow staring at one of them with a wide-eyed look—like she didn't know how to handle them being so nice to her.

Graham and Deacon were now normal around her, if you didn't count how often they were shoving food in front of her. Grey and Harlow had quickly become close, and while it felt like she was trying to take Harlow from me, I hadn't mentioned anything, just enjoyed watching Harlow slowly piece bits of herself back together.

Harlow's smile had slowly become a normal sight, and watching it go from polite and reserved, to genuine and free had been a beautiful thing. Her blue eyes were something in itself to look at. They were haunted, and it was hard to stare into them and wonder what she was thinking, seeing, or feeling at that moment. But at the same time, there was a piece of them that showed the bits of the Harlow I'd fallen in love with all those years ago. It was like both sides of her were fighting each other, and neither was winning yet.

The most noticeable change to everyone else was her weight— which Graham and Deacon were taking credit for. Her face had filled out enough that she almost looked healthy, and while she said she was still two sizes smaller than what she'd been before she'd married Collin, it was a huge difference. She looked more beautiful each day.

For me, it was everything else. It was the way she always found a reason to touch me, the way she no longer had to hold herself together—like she might shatter if she didn't—and the way it was becoming less often that I had to beg her to come back to me after she woke up screaming in fear. More often than not over the last week, she reached out for me, and brought herself back.

I tilted her head back and passed a brief kiss across her lips as she grabbed a shirt out of one of my drawers to put on, then I walked into the bathroom to take a quick shower so she could have a few minutes to herself. I heard her come in at one point to brush her teeth, but she didn't say anything, so I didn't, either.

I knew whenever she got done seeing anyone now, whether it was her family or my friends, she needed time to just breathe and unwind since she was still getting used to people talking so freely about how Collin had been. But I'd also learned not to offer to give her the entire night to herself. She said she wanted me near her, and I didn't want to be anywhere else.

My heart pounded faster when I walked out of the bathroom and saw her sitting on my bed. I didn't know if I would ever get used to seeing her there, waiting for me, but I knew I didn't want to. I wanted to always be overwhelmed by how beautiful she was, and always wonder how she could still want me after all the bullshit we'd endured.

Harlow's head dropped, and she stared at where her hands were twisting together. "You don't call me *yours* anymore."

My lips twitched in amusement, since I'd just been thinking something close to that, but there was no humor in my voice when I declared, "You *are* mine."

She lifted her head to look at me thoughtfully. "You said it a lot when I was married. It took me a while to realize it, but you haven't said it since Collin died."

"Because it's not what you need." I walked over to the bed and sat in front of her, and wrapped an arm around her waist to pull her body closer to mine. "Right now you're still working through things, and you're trying to do things your own way for the first time . . . and I need to let you. You don't need me claiming that you're mine every day while you're doing that. And that's one of the reasons why I haven't given you my opinion on anything: because I want all these decisions to be only *yours*. I don't want you to make them for me or because of me. I know I'll be in your life, and I'll fit into whatever you've decided to have for yourself, and it will be perfect for us. If I was selfless, I would give you time alone—without me in your life—"

"No!" she whispered, horrified.

"—but I can't do that. Besides, I think we learned from the first time around that giving you that much space isn't good for us." I winked, and she rolled her eyes. "The space I'm giving you is as much as I'm willing to give up after having lost almost five years, but it *is* only because I think you need it."

Harlow sighed in relief. After taking a second to gather her thoughts, she argued, "You had an opinion on the money."

"That's because you were trying to pay for things for Graham and me, and we didn't need that. I only fought you when you tried to basically give it, or gift it, to us. And then I only questioned you when you wanted to give it to everyone else because I wanted to make sure you'd thought about it—that's all."

She nodded once, silently asking me to continue.

Letting the hand that was wrapped around her waist slowly trail up her side, I leaned closer and whispered, "If I thought you were ready, and I had my way, I wouldn't let you out of my sight. I would keep you in bed all day, and I would remind you constantly that you *are* mine." I placed a soft kiss just below her ear. My lips spread into a smile when Harlow quietly moaned. "I would hold you close every night and would spend every morning worshipping you—just to remind you that we still have sixty years together."

I leaned over her and gently pushed her back onto the bed, and groaned when I saw she didn't have anything on underneath my shirt she was wearing. My hand slid between her thighs, parting her, and I captured her mouth when she whimpered as I pressed two fingers inside her.

Her back arched away from the bed, and I swallowed her pleasured moan when she came minutes later. Even through the trembling in her body, she frantically grasped for the towel still hanging on my hips. Once she had it off, I reached over and began digging around in my nightstand without ever breaking from the kiss, and grabbed a condom. Harlow helped me roll it on as I pulled off her shirt, and before I even let her body hit the bed again, I was pushing into her.

"Knox!" she gasped, and gripped at my shoulders as I silently, and physically, claimed what had always been mine. I'd wanted to take this slow, but her moans earlier and the way her nails were digging into my back now were making it impossible.

I gripped her hips as she wrapped her long legs around my back, and a growl rumbled in my chest at her breathy plea for more. I moved quickly but thoroughly inside her as she matched each movement with one of her own, and dropped my head in the crook of her neck as I got closer to my release and felt her tightening around me. My hands moved to grip the comforter, and I bit down at the soft spot at the base of her throat as I tried to hold off my release for her, and the start of her second orgasm sent me into my own.

Harlow held me against her trembling body for minutes after, and I only moved away from her long enough to get rid of the condom in my bathroom before I returned to her side and pulled her into my arms.

We hadn't used condoms our first two times together, neither of us having thought about it at the time, or even after. Harlow still hadn't asked me to use one in the handful of times that we'd been together since then, but it was something I knew she needed—just like she needed the time of doing things on her own. While she said she trusted me, I'd still gotten tested again for both our peace of mind. But even though I was clean, it hadn't gone over well. Harlow's parents had come back into town and were at her new apartment, and her dad had found my results—which led to him asking why I'd needed to get tested anyway.

I'd had to have another talk with Harlow's dad because of that. Safe to say I was trying to figure out ways to get back on his good side.

"Knox?" Harlow murmured a few minutes later, and tilted her head back to look into my eyes.

I raised an eyebrow in question, but didn't speak, just tightened my grip on her and reveled in the fact that there was more of her to grip.

"Thank you . . . for everything. Not just tonight, not for the last month and a half, but for the last seven years. For always being there, for being what I needed at every point in my life, and for knowing what I needed even when I didn't." Her eyes filled with tears, and she smiled shakily. "There were times before, when my eighteenth birthday was so close, and it frustrated me that you wouldn't just let us be what we both wanted. Then with Collin, I was always so scared that he was going to find out about

you, and that you were going to get hurt—well, more hurt . . ."
She trailed off, and ran her fingers gently over where I'd been
shot. "It terrified me that you wouldn't listen to me, that you
kept saying you were going to get me away from him. I thought I
knew what was best, that we needed to just act like it wasn't happening so I could keep everyone safe. Then lately, even though
you were usually with me, I could feel that you were holding
back. I didn't know why you were, or what had come between
us, and it worried me."

"Low," I whispered. My forehead pinched and I pressed my
palm to her cheek. If I'd known it had been bothering her, we
would've talked about it before tonight.

"But at the same time it felt like nothing *was* between us, and
there has never been one moment where I couldn't see how much
you love me. So now that I know what you're doing, and why
you're doing it, it just makes me appreciate and love you more—
like everything else did." She pressed her hand against where
mine was and held my stare for a few seconds before continuing:
"I don't always understand why you do what you do; but I know
you always have a reason, and that reason is usually for my best
interest. So—just, thank you. I love you, Knox Alexander, and I
am *so* lucky to be loved by you."

My mouth was on hers before she could finish getting the last
word out, and a high-pitched sound of surprise turned into a
giggle as she wrapped her arms around me.

"When you say things like that, it makes me want to forget
why I'm giving you this time," I informed her, and she laughed
again as she pulled away from me.

"You say that, but I know you. I know you wouldn't follow
through with that." Her blue eyes searched mine, and I found

myself caught in them when I noticed that a part of Harlow was finally winning—*my* Harlow. "I want to ask you when you think we'll be ready to move on from all this, but I have no doubt you'll let me know."

I smiled knowingly. "As I said, Low, you won't be allowed out of bed—that will be your first clue."

She rolled her eyes, but her smile offset the action. Her eyelids slowly grew heavy, and just before she let them shut, she murmured, "Knox?"

My lips twitched. "Yeah, Low."

"I'm sorry for wasting time."

My face twisted and my chest ached. I swallowed past the tightness in my throat, and whispered honestly, "Never."

Epilogue

Knox
Six months later—Thatch

"WHERE ARE YOU?" I asked, and shifted my weight nervously from foot to foot.

"I just pulled up to the house," Harlow said excitedly, and tried, but failed, to suppress a giggle. "I love this house!"

I smiled to myself. I knew she did. Harlow had decided a few months ago that she wanted to be in Thatch so she could be closer to Grey and the baby, and since I'd moved into her apartment a month before, Graham and Deacon were glad that I was coming back to town. They'd acted like Harlow and I had betrayed them by living in Richland, since I'd lived with them for almost seven years, even though I was there half the time anyway for work.

And even though I no longer needed to give Harlow space now, I'd let her pick out our house. She'd hated her last house.

I knew this one needed to be perfect for her—and it ended up being perfect for us.

We'd finished moving in over the weekend, and I was still supposed to be at work until tomorrow morning, but I'd taken off the entire shift. After spending the day with her parents in Seattle yesterday, I'd made sure Harlow would be busy out of the house today while I transformed the entire entryway to look like a meadow of red poppies.

I heard Harlow's car door shut as she told me about her day, and my eyes snapped up to the front door as I listened to her voice get closer and closer.

"Harlow?"

"Yeah?" she asked when she put the key in the lock.

"Why would anyone waste their time only loving someone to the moon when they could love them to the stars?"

She'd finished the last few words with me as she opened the door, then said in confusion, "You're not at—" Harlow's eyes widened and her gasp filled the entryway as she dropped her arm holding the phone up to her ear. "Knox," she whispered in awe. "You remembered."

Like I could've forgotten.

I fingered the ring in my pocket, and swallowed roughly as I waited for her to look back at me. "I thought of buying you a new one, but I knew it belonged to you the instant I saw it five years ago, and every time I see it now, I know that's still true."

Harlow covered her mouth when it fell open, and her blue eyes brightened with unshed tears when I pulled the ring out and closed the distance between us. It had a white gold band that looked like twisted rope, with a round diamond solitaire resting on top.

Once I was in front of her, I took her left hand in mine and dropped down to one knee. "When I met you seven and a half years ago, I knew one day I would make you mine. It's taken us a little longer to get there than I'd originally planned, but I can't complain when I get you for the next fifty-nine and a half years."

She laughed behind her hand, and her left hand squeezed mine.

"No matter what happens in our lives, I will love you with everything that I am for the rest of mine, and I will make sure you know every day what it's like to be loved to the stars," I vowed. "Harlow Evans, will you marry me?"

"Yes!" she choked out, and barely gave me long enough to slide the ring on her finger before she launched herself into my arms and crushed her mouth to mine. She pulled back enough to look into my eyes and whispered, "Thank you for waiting for me."

"Always."

Acknowledgments

CORY. THANK YOU, thank you, *thank you*! Honestly, I could not have done this book without you. I know I always say that, but oh wow, we've never had a baby girl in our lives before this! Thank you for being so incredible! I love you!

Tessa Woodward. You're amazing. Thank you for letting me endlessly bother you with random questions—even when it took us to the Cartier and Harry Winston websites for far too long! Thank you for understanding my need to tell this story as it is. Creepy husband, and all!

Kevan Lyon. Thank you for finally letting me *tell* this story! Ha! You are, by far, the best agent ever.

A. L. Jackson. I don't know what I would do with every book if I didn't have you to bounce ideas off of. I love you, BB!

Kelly Simmon. I love you! Thank you! So many thank-yous and exclamation marks! I love that you just got the creep factor, and embraced it.

About the Author

Molly McAdams grew up in California but now lives in the oh-so-amazing state of Texas with her husband, daughter, and fur babies. Her hobbies include hiking, snowboarding, traveling and long walks on the beach . . . which roughly translates to being a homebody with her hubby and dishing out movie quotes.